"DEAR ONCE"

Books by ZELDA POPKIN

"DEAR ONCE"

A DEATH OF INNOCENCE

HERMAN HAD TWO DAUGHTERS

QUIET STREET

"DEAR ONCE"

A novel by
ZELDA POPKIN

J. B. LIPPINCOTT COMPANY
Philadelphia and New York

The characters and incidents in this novel are fictitious, and any similarity to actual persons and events is entirely coincidental.

U.S. Library of Congress Cataloging in Publication Data

Popkin, Zelda, birth date
    "Dear once".

    I. Title.
PZ3.P816Dau   [PS3531.0634]   813'.5'2   75–11870
ISBN–0–397–01053–2

"DEAR ONCE"

1 ❋

WHEN REUBEN MET the Springer girls at Ellis Island on an August afternoon in the last year of the last century, they didn't recognize their brother, he had changed so much. He'd been a chubby stripling, apple-cheeked, when they had seen him last, but this, coming toward them, was a man, stout and stocky, with a smudge of mustache on his lip—an American, a sport, wearing a flashy checked suit, a straw hat angle-tilted on his head, and a glittering stickpin in his four-in-hand.

People on the ship had warned them: beware; men of a certain character hang around the port to lure female immigrants into white slavery. And so they shrank away, trembling, until he called their names—their Yiddish names, with the affectionate diminutives: "Chay*ele*," "Chan*ele*," "Dvor*ele*"—and then they flung themselves upon him, embracing, snuggling, jabbering, vying with each other to let him know how sick they'd been—or how not sick—during the ocean voyage. Chaya, the eldest, who is my mother, Ada Samuelson, née Springer, boasted she hadn't had one moment's queasiness; *she* hadn't *dared* get sick—who would have looked after the others if she'd had to keep to her bunk? But Dvora, whom hereafter I shall refer to as Daisy, admitted she had been so sick that for three days she couldn't keep down a drop of food.

"Food! That was food? Back home the moujiks wouldn't throw it to the pigs. I told the waiter to his face." This was Chana, my Aunt Hannah.

"The waiter laughed in her face," Ada told Reuben.

He tskd. He patted their shoulders and their hands, comforting: I-am-here, you-are-safe-now, all-will-be-well.

"The One Above was taking care of us. He was watching over," Ada said.

"We suffered! Terrible we suffered!" Hannah added. "But Papa said to come, we came."

"Where is Papa?" Daisy asked it with a quaver, a sudden dread that Papa, too, had died and they were double orphans as well as strangers in New York.

Four years before, their father, my grandfather, Yankel Springer, had left the Russian-Lithuanian village (whose name I never learned to spell) with Reuben, his only son, aged sixteen. Reuben was in robust health, hence a certain prospect for conscription into the armies of the Czar. How shall we save Reuben? Dose him with vinegar to make him anemic? Chop off his index finger? Take him to that specialist who dislocates the shoulders or grows an eczema that he claims he can cure after the inspector has moved on? Or shall we send Reuben, clandestinely, to America?

Herschel Goldmark weighted the decision out of the kindness of his heart, just as, through the decades following, he accomplished other miracles for the Springer family. Herschel's attachment to Grandpa Springer was absolute, and its basis was unique. They had been *cheder* chums, sitting side by side on one bench. Yankel was a bright boy, Herschel a dullard; he got the knuckle rappings from the *rebbe*'s cane. Herschel's Bar Mitzvah was drawing near, and his parents were frantic. The stupid boy surely would disgrace them when he was called to read the *Maftir*, the Biblical Portion of the Week. Yankel Springer saved that family from disgrace. He drilled his friend, rehearsed him morning, noon, and evening, until Herschel learned to read the *Maftir* passably. And then and there a friendship was cemented, a bond so strong it lasted Grandpa's entire life and reached into his children's lives, for ill as well as benefit.

For although the reading of the Scriptures baffled Herschel, he was not a fool. His talents lay in commerce; he was a business genius, with the Midas touch. With his wife he emigrated in the early eighteen-nineties to verify a rumor that New York's streets were paved with gold. For him they were. And, loyal across the ocean, he wrote to Yankel Springer: "I'll send you a ship's ticket. Come. You'll get rich with me."

At home, Grandpa had led a double life, part-time prayer and study of the Talmud, part-time businessman, on the fringe of commerce—going along, by request, with the driver when a load of timber had to be delivered or sacks of grain purchased. He oversaw the handing over of the rubles—no cheating, no theft—and received a small commission for his honesty, his accuracy in arithmetic, and his unshakable dignity. Once he went as far as Vilna to help the village tailor consummate the purchase of a Singer sewing machine. From what my mother admits—and this reluctantly—Grandpa was no more than a pious mediocrity, yet he carried himself with such refined respectability that even Russian Christians were polite to him.

A personable young student, with mild pretensions to become a scholar, he had accepted, without doubt or question, the bride his parents chose for him. Malka (I am the name-after-her, Malka, anglicized to Mildred) was virtuous and energetic. They made a home; they raised a family; they lived a quiet, decent life. If they had experienced religious persecution, racial hatred, fear and struggle, doubts of one another, quarrels and distrusts, Grandpa never mentioned this. The ocean voyage had scoured his memory clean. What he'd retained of his past was the Yiddish language, the rituals of Orthodox Judaism, and the tradition that the wisdom of the father of a family has no limitations (though his love, presumably, is also boundless) and his authority is absolute. Not unlike the divine right of kings.

Ada was his first-born, accepted without grumbling: we are young; Malka will bear sons. Two years later, Reuben came, a plump and healthy boy. Rejoice! The Springer name will be perpetuated, and when the parents have been summoned to their eternal rest, a son is here, to say the Kaddish, the daily prayer for their souls. Two years after Reuben, another girl was born. Hannah was a disappointment, but let us not despair; Malka will produce another son. A full-term boy was delivered, stillborn,

9

strangled by the cord. All of Malka's deliveries had been difficult; her pelvis was narrow and her infants large. This one left her so weakened that three years passed before she bore another child: Daisy, a babe, as my mother puts it, so sweet you could spread her, like raspberry jelly, on your bread. Nevertheless, a girl. And time is passing; Malka grows no younger. Don't delay. Try again. A good wife does not refuse her husband. There were two miscarriages. Malka's womb was tired.

In a gentler world she might have enjoyed the luxury of rest in bed in pregnancy, of being waited on, kept off her feet. However, my grandmother, like many women of her time and place, rose at dawn, retired late, and in between worked like a horse. She had married a religious scholar; don't expect him to put aside his holy books and toil to feed a family. Malka had a shop—not a market stall like the peasant women, my mother has assured me, but a store with shelves and a glass window. She sold cloth by the yard, as well as the skirts and millinery her clever fingers put together after the children were in bed. In addition, she kept her house immaculate and baked and cooked. A tiny, wiry, bright-eyed woman, perpetually in motion, my mother describes her. Somewhat like a chipmunk, I imagine her.

The girls helped with the housework: Ada was strong and competent; Hannah was willing but a *klutz* (she'd spill half the water in the pail she carried from the well); Daisy was born with golden hands, quick and apt at every household task. Reuben lived like a prince, three sisters catering to him—a slab of fresh-baked *kuchen*, or cornbread, spread with chicken fat, waiting on the kitchen table to refresh him when he came from *cheder*. He was the treasure, wasn't he, the solitary guarantor of his parents' restful afterlife? Yankel Springer had lost hope of wresting another son from Malka's exhausted womb.

How timely Herschel Goldmark's invitation! Yankel will go to America and take his son along. The boy is out of peril; Malka, too. The width of the Atlantic Ocean is as reliable a means of contraception as any yet devised.

Herschel met the man and boy; he took them to the dwelling he had rented on one of the better blocks of New York's East Side.

Mrs. Goldmark fed them, made their beds, washed their socks and underwear. Herschel directed Reuben to a night school; Herschel found him a job. He led Yankel to a *shul*, and he engaged his honest friend to be the rent collector in tenements he owned.

"Goldmark did everything for them," my mother has made clear. "This, you unnistand, is what a *landsman* did those days— he gave the helping hand. You think only for your grandfather Goldmark did a lot? No. For nephews, nieces, cousins, his side and the wife's: 'I'll send the ticket, come. Pay back when you can.' No interest charge to anyone. Always some greenhorn sleeping on their parlor floor, always food on the table for whoever came to eat. And Lily Goldmark, may she rest in peace, nothing too hard, too much, for her to do for them. God paid attention. He rewarded Goldmark. Made him a rich millionaire."

Yankel's letters were infrequent, two or three a year, all vague. "If the Almighty is willing, soon I will be able to send for you. . . . We are well, the Goldmarks send regards." Soon. Maybe next year before Pesach; maybe this year after Succoth. The four years passed this way. Possibly Malka missed her husband, though my mother looked puzzled whenever she recalled that, during all this time, her mother seemed extraordinarily well. She hummed folk tunes in the evenings while she sewed; she snatched a moment here and there to gossip with a neighbor; she began to make inquiries, discreetly, about a suitable matrimonial prospect for her eldest daughter. Certainly she missed Reuben; they all did: he was the treasure, the light of their lives. Yet in all this time, Malka seemed so relaxed that when it happened it was unbelievable.

She had locked her shop early and walked home; picked like a bird at the supper Ada had prepared; complained mildly that the weather was unseasonably warm, she'd lost her appetite, she'd lie down, take a nap, eat after she had rested. You girls go ahead and eat your supper. Be good girls. *Be good girls.*

She stretched out on her bed, in her clothes, her shoes, her earth-brown wig. Daisy tiptoed in before she herself prepared for bed. Her mother lay on her side, one hand tucked beneath a cheek, her breathing all but imperceptible. Daisy started to remove her mother's shoes. Hannah saw her there and whispered, "Let her be.

11

Let her sleep. Don't wake Mama up." And so they tiptoed out, and in the morning they were racked as much with self-reproach as grief because Malka Springer lay cold in eternal sleep. They should have paid attention to her mention of fatigue; they should have taken off her shoes and, fumbling, awakened her. She might have mentioned she felt ill; they could have run for help. Should have, could have . . . the futile ifs of guilt. Now, she was gone, and without farewell. "Be good girls." What else?

All through the week of mourning, they were zombies, fed and comforted by neighbors and peripheral kin. A fortnight passed before they brought themselves to have a letter written to their father in New York. Ocean mail was slow; two months were gone before they heard from him: two letters, one to his daughters and one to a cousin, instructing him to sell the contents of Malka's shop as advantageously as possible, sell the household furnishings as well, and with the proceeds purchase steamship tickets for the girls. It was hoped there would be enough. If not, send a letter to New York; he, Yankel, would take a loan from Herschel Goldmark (who sends his regards). The letter to his daughters advised them he had given instructions to their cousin, and when all was arranged he would expect them in New York. The Holy One, blessed be His Name, would guard them on their journey. Meanwhile, he and Reuben were saying the Kaddish for Malka, whom the One Above who was All-wise and All-just had gathered to Himself, may she rest in peace.

Though she realized her father considered her helpless and a nincompoop, Ada told the cousin she could do without his help. Practical and competent, she haggled and she sold (at good prices, too); she gave away to the poor; she chose essentials, packed them for a journey, purchased tickets, found a scribe to let Yankel know what ship and date. The cousin gaped at her efficiency. Hannah did a lot of arguing about what needed to be done, but how much she accomplished—"Hannah is my own sister; we two are like one person; better I should not run her down. And Daisy? Daisy was a child. What could I expect from her? Besides, her eyes were sore from crying. All I needed was she could get blind." That's my mother's version.

12

Aunt Hannah told it somewhat differently. "Ada wants the credit, let her have the credit. But you should know what she did best—gave the orders: run here, go there, carry this, bring me that. . . . Like horses me and Daisy worked for her." Nevertheless, both my aunts agreed that Ada got them ready for the journey, admirably costumed in traveling dresses, black and pavement-sweeping, and proper millinery. Put on the record that the women of my family emerged from steerage wearing hats, not shawls or *babushkas*. Though they couldn't read or write, they did look upper-class.

Certain generalizations can be made about the physical appearance of the Springer girls; each of these has its exceptions. They were short, tending to be plump, except for Daisy, who was like her mother, slim-petite. They had pinkish-porcelain complexions, though Hannah's cheeks were lightly pitted, whether from a pox or just bad luck, no one's absolutely sure. Their eyes were large and lovely, a brown-amber color, but Ada's were myopic; until she started wearing glasses, she was a leaner forward, a peerer at. (Some people, including my father, Sammy Samuelson, were flattered by her close attentiveness.) All the girls had earth-brown hair, almost the shade of their mother's wig. They wore it plaited, smooth and shining, pinned up into snoods, except for Daisy, who, being just fifteen when they reached New York, still wore hanging braids.

And here they were: three attractive, wholesome-looking young ladies, in the Ellis Island waiting room, with their brother, who answered Daisy's "Where is Papa?" with "Papa is home. He is making the house ready." He marked their disbelief—the father they remembered had never raised a hand, not even to fix himself a glass of tea. Reuben went on to explain. "Papa bought a house for all of us. A fine, big house. You'll see. The Goldmarks—you remember Herschel?—he helped to buy the house. Him and his wife. And Fanny Kuper. They are helping Papa make everything ready." He eased their hands off his checked suit. "So! Pick up the valises. Follow me. Forward march!"

Ada had her wits about her. She remembered the trunk, and it was fortunate she did, since the trunk was crammed with treasures —the quilts and pillows stuffed with goose feathers and down, plucked and cleaned by the Springer girls themselves; the hand-woven heavy linen tablecloths they themselves had embroidered; the coarse linen sheets; the copper pots in which Malka had simmered chicken soup and *gefülte* fish; the silver serving spoons that had been her dowry; the satin cover for the Pesach *matzoh* plate; a threadbare purple-velvet bag for Yankel's phylacteries that Malka had embroidered as a bride's gift to her groom; and the brasses: the samovar, the candlesticks whose lights she had blessed each Friday at sundown, and the mortar and pestle in which peppercorns, cinnamon sticks, and nuts were pulverized—the peculiar treasures that had adorned a home, the tangibles of a family's past, the heirlooms future generations would disperse.

Reuben kept them standing while he went to find the trunk. Then he waved a lordly arm, crooked an index finger, summoning a porter; he gave the man instructions—masterful, impressive, my mother liked to recall—and after that, like a sultan with his harem, he marched his womenfolk, luggage-laden, behind him, to a ferryboat. He led them to an open doorway labeled "Women," told them how to sit: all three in one row, luggage at their feet—keep a good eye on it and do not answer if a stranger speaks to you; sit like dummies, staring at rope-tied valises and straw baskets, while you cross the harbor of New York.

"But, Mama," I once asked, "didn't you want to see the Statue of Liberty?"

"What liberty statue? All we saw was Reuben. He was standing like a statue, outside from the door. Come inside he couldn't; the place was marked for ladies only, unnistand? Watch us, keep a good eye, we shouldn't be in trouble, my brother had to do."

Yes, that was Reuben, the essence of my Uncle Reuben, then and evermore: looking after and directing, though within the rules.

The ferry docked; Reuben wagged that index finger for the girls to rise and pick their baggage up, emerge, and follow him— through the ferry's middle passageway (the porter and his barrow followed *them*) into a bilge-reeking building, through it to a cobbled street where horse-drawn trolleys rumbled and hackmen bawled for passengers. There, again, Reuben left them standing, with their luggage and his admonitions, while he disappeared to find a proper vehicle; and across a shifting swarm of people, horses, carriages, and drays, they stared at a jagged line of low brick buildings, baking underneath the August sun.

"Did New York excite you, Mama?" I had to know. "Were you thrilled?"

"What's to be excited? It was a lots of noise, a lots of people, more and bigger buildings. Different from over there."

"It was the same thing as over there," Aunt Hannah contradicted. "Dust and stink of horse manure. No gold in the streets."

Reuben returned, riding beside the driver of a two-seat carriage that had an open back. Reuben gave instructions: porter, pile the trunk and the valises in the back; girls, climb up, arrange yourselves upon the second seat. He dipped into a pocket, removed a purse, spread coins on his palm, selected his largesse, and like a *Graf* dropped his coin into the porter's palm, paled at the man's curses, and quickly added a half-dime. "That porter was an anti-Semite," my mother assured me. "Mind, that time I didn't unni-stand one word English. But by how he hollered, how he looked, I could tell he would kill a Jew. Believe me, I was frightened." But Reuben merely tamped his hat down to his ears and tweaked the coachman's sleeve. "Brooklyn," he told the man. "Hold fast," he told the girls.

The carriage bumped on cobbles, swayed around corners, and clopped onto a bridge. Through an iron web, they saw gray water far below; they heard trains roaring overhead, trolleys rattling, brewery wagons clomping alongside; and they clung to one another, pale and speechless, terrified.

Beyond the bridge, the noise abated; the drab streets grew monotonous. Dizzy-drunk with the jolting and the summer heat, with the exhaustion of arrival and excesses of emotion, swaying against each other, they fell asleep. Reuben woke them, shouting, "We are home!"

Home! Brownstone dwellings, each like every other one:

stone staircases rising to glass double doors, iron steps descending to a hidden basement door. Eyeless houses, dark shades drawn behind the window glass. Whatever—one brownstone, of all this similarity, was their home, the walls to embrace their feasts and funerals, the three stories and basement that Reuben eventually would refer to as the "family shrine." This day, however, he merely sprang down from his seat and told his sisters, "Climb down; be careful with the skirts."

A woman, buxom, yellow-haired, prim in a starched summer dress, came along the street, up to the basement entrance of the house next door. She veered around to gawk. Reuben touched his straw hat's brim. "Good afternoon, Missus Fitztsimmes, I am Mister Reuben Springer, your new neighbor. In this house. And these"—his arm swung back to trace an arc around his sisters—"these are my dear once."

And of all the surprises of the day of her arrival in the United States, this moment—this gesture and this little speech—was what, my mother says, impressed her most: Reuben tipping his hat to a strange woman, like a gentleman, an equal, not obsequiously bowing with bared head. "And speaking English." Mama giggled when she described the moment. "But with such a funny hacksen. My dear *once*."

By the time my mother told me this, she was also speaking English with a funny hacksen of her own.

What Mrs. Fitzsimmons answered, if she answered, remains in dispute. Aunt Hannah remembers that she grunted disagreeably; my mother insists she said, "How do you do?" which, depending on inflection, might have been a question, not a civility. All Aunt Daisy recalls is embarrassment—the horse had chosen that very moment to relieve himself.

Reuben shooed his sisters down a flight of iron steps into a dark and musty basement hall. They heard the clack of voices somewhere in the rear. "Ha-lo! Ha-lo!" Reuben shouted. Again, he wigwagged: follow me—into a long, narrow gaslighted room, where Mrs. Goldmark rushed at them; behind her, Herschel, beaming, arms upraised, in blessing; behind these two, their father,

16

thin and slightly stooped, black spade beard gray-threaded, looking from one to the other, as if unsure of who was who, at last stretching out his arms, reaching, not yet touching, and, low-voiced, saying "*kinder*," before they, swooping together, enfolded him, and all of them began to weep. "We remembered the mother," Mama told me. "It is a Jewish custom, Millie, first to remember the dead before the living can enjoy new happiness."

"Enough crying, everybody," Mrs. Goldmark said. "Now be happy, all."

Not yet. Yankel Springer needed to perform his ritual of greeting: he clasped each daughter's hands in turn, the two hands squeezed together, their backs patted twice, exactly twice, for each. And then, again, the girls were weeping, because, in all the past, their father had never been demonstrative.

Fanny Kuper ended this. She swooped in from the kitchen crying, "Ha-lo! Ha-lo! Ha-lo!" and Mrs. Goldmark introduced her. "My niece, Fanny. She is helping fix the supper."

"A little something cold. No meat. Hot weather, meat could make you sick," Fanny Kuper said.

That seems a sensible remark, yet I heard my mother declare, "Right away I didn't like that Fanny. Bossy. A trouble maker. I could tell it from the first minute. She knew better than anybody what everybody needs to eat."

However, it's my assumption that on the afternoon when she first met the Springer girls, Fanny Kuper was trying to be helpful, and her intentions were the best—though her motives may have been ulterior, since there is solid ground for suspicion that, from the moment she'd laid eyes on Reuben Springer, she had made up her mind to marry him. Eventually, that is, after he had finished his apprenticeship, under her watchful eyes and skillful tutelage. He was a salesman in a men's clothing store where she was the cashier-bookkeeper. The proprietor was her Uncle Herschel's friend. Herschel had recommended Reuben for the job, an honest chap, a quick learner, and Fanny, in the cashier's cage, would give him useful pointers. If it turned out they liked one another, who'd object? The young woman is respectable; she has a little money saved; the families are acquainted; everything is equal on both sides. Equal? Not precisely. There's a difference of ages, as my mother frequently brought up.

I've seen a photograph of young Fanny Kuper. She's stylishly dressed and wearing a small bustle—a superfluous protuberance, since nature had given her a big behind. She stands tall, which she was, taller by half a head than Reuben, who like all the Springers never topped five-foot-six. The eyes in her photograph are small and dark and sharp, the mouth and chin decisive, the straight nose rather delicate. By the time I got to know her, that nose was all but smothered by the balloons of her cheeks. "That's me when your uncle started courting me," she said when she showed me the picture. "A young girl. Only eighteen years."

My mother scoffs. "She was eighteen years like I was five years old when we landed in Ellis Island! Fanny is older than me, maybe ten years older than Reuben—of this I am sure and positive. She was an old maid already. Fat. But with money in the bank." All of which may be true or may be malice; there's no way to prove it one way or the other. Those days, immigrants from Eastern Europe rarely had proper birth certificates. You told people you were born on the second candle of Chanukah the winter it was so cold the water froze in the wells; let them figure out the date.

Nevertheless, what's fair is fair; give Fanny what is due her: she came into my mother's life in the euphoria of having rendered valuable service. It was she who had located the Brooklyn house —accidentally, but quick to grasp its possibilities. And it was her Uncle Herschel who had made the acquisition possible. The way I heard the story, a customer, a bachelor, middle-aged and Scandinavian, was paying Miss Kuper, the cashier, for a blue-serge two-pants suit. He happened to mention that though he liked this store and the quality of its merchandise, he might not be shopping there much longer; he planned to move from the neighborhood. He had been living with his widowed mother in a three-story brownstone —the old lady had run it as a rooming house, furnished rooms, no meals. She had died during the winter; he'd tried to keep the building going, but it wasn't a job for a bachelor, keeping the place clean and pacifying roomers. If he could get a reasonable offer, he'd clear out of Brooklyn, maybe locate in the country.

Reuben and Fanny went to see the house; Herschel Goldmark went to see it. (Grandpa Springer wasn't in on the inspection trips since he had a beard, and there was a suspicion a Jewish beard might not be welcome in an Irish-Scandinavian neighborhood.)

I've never quite approved of the process by which Yankel Springer became the owner of a Brooklyn brownstone dwelling. An exchange, my mother said it was. Herschel Goldmark had two "country" properties. One was woodland acreage in western Pennsylvania, adjacent to a locality where some oil had been found; the other was on the Long Island shore. At low tide this was a fine stretch of dunes; at high tide, wet sand. The bachelor saw it at low tide and was impressed—he could build a bungalow and for sure he wouldn't be plagued by cranky roomers there. He turned down the Pennsylvania oil prospect, though Herschel had had the foresight to sprinkle kerosene around, and he traded his substantial dwelling for a now-you-see-it-now-you-don't Long Island shore-front property. Herschel assumed the mortgage on the house and made a personal loan to Grandpa for modest renovations. This was—most people will agree—a handsome reward for teaching a Bar Mitzvah boy to read the Portion of the Week.

The building was ugly but solid, constructed by bricklayers and carpenters more concerned with honest workmanship than with aesthetics. The basement dining-living room was pitch dark, though the big kitchen back of it was bright and opened on a rectangle of grassy yard. There was a coal stove in the kitchen and a wooden box that held a cake of ice. (Who in the old country ever saw a piece of ice, except in winter when there was too much of it?) Water ran from taps into the kitchen sink—you'd never need to haul it from a well. Upstairs, there was a parlor and rooms in which to sleep—two rooms, starkly equipped with iron double beds. And a special room with a zinc bath tub, a marble washstand, and a pull-chain water closet.

The Springer girls were amazed and rapturous. Such luxuries! Even though it wasn't Friday, the girls all bathed before they went to sleep, three in one double bed.

In the morning, they scrubbed the floors, washed the windows, soaked and boiled their travel-sweaty underwear, and hung it out in the back yard. "We were ashamed," my mother recalls, "neighbors should see our underdrawers."

The neighbors kept their distance. Within the family's hearing, no one made invidious remarks. Not even the roomers on the upper floors, who trekked downstairs to pay the new landlord.

Getting provisions was an immediate problem—it would be till they located close-by kosher stores. And so it was decided that for the present Yankel Springer would carry two empty black oilcloth sacks to Manhattan every Thursday. Mrs. Goldmark would fill one with fresh-killed chickens, beef *flanken*, brisket, and *kalb-fleish*; the other with fish (yellow pike, whitefish, buffle), *matjes* herring, dill pickles, white radishes, pumpernickel, *chalah*, sweet butter, and farmer cheese—the essentials and the goodies that would provide a *shabbos* feast and a reasonably well-fed week.

The Americanization of the Springer girls began at once. Reuben managed this. He taught them the currency (a dollar can be silver but a paper one is just as good). He told them how much to pay for ice: swathe the cake in last week's *Tageblatt* to make it last longer and don't forget before you go to bed to empty the drip pan. He explained the transportation: take the elevated trains to Manhattan but use the trolley cars to get around Brooklyn; and some afternoons, when your housework is done, take the streetcar over to Fulton Street where the big stores are; look in the windows, see what kind of clothes American women wear; you shouldn't dress like greenhorns any more. Look also at furniture, see what kind is for American houses. Look. Don't buy. Goldmark can get everything wholesale.

Reuben also took them to night school. There they were given American names. What they would be called for the remainder of their lives was determined by the whim of the night-school registrar.

Ada, Hannah, Daisy, take these pencils, open up these books, learn to read and write English. It is the unvarnished truth that my mother and my aunts, when they arrived, were totally illiterate. They had never read a newspaper, magazine, or book in Yiddish,

Hebrew, or Russian, let alone English. And well they might have continued to believe that illiteracy was a Jewish woman's normal state had not Reuben decided they would have to go to work and thus would need to speak—and, possibly, to read and write—English.

He found jobs for them—for Ada and Hannah, that is—in a shirt factory in Manhattan, stitching buttonholes. Daisy needed to be sheltered from the crudities of the New World. Hence, she would stay at home, wash and iron, sweep and scrub, bake and cook, can peaches, pears, and cherries, make jams and jellies and chow-chow, be wife to the house, the mother substitute.

The female neighbors, curious about the exotic new family on the block, made friends with her and traded recipes. Mrs. Fitzsimmons (Fitztsimmes in Reuben's hacksen) used to spend a lot of time in Daisy's kitchen, drinking coffee and gossiping. Mrs. Fitzsimmons had an only son who'd gone to sea. Frequently she mentioned she'd be happier if he would settle down with a homebody like Daisy. "Now, mind, we are Catholics, and you are of the Hebrew faith, but there's good breeding and commen sense in you people, I can see." Daisy didn't argue; Daisy seldom did.

The parlor had acquired an upholstered "suit," a carpet on the floor, and lace curtains on the bay window by the time Sammy Samuelson came down from Canada looking for a wife. Montreal had candidates enough, but Sammy Samuelson was sensitive: too many people there still thought of him as the poor immigrant tailor he had been, not as the ladies' clothing manufacturer he was planning to become. I do not know who told him that Yankel Springer had three daughters, any one of whom would make an excellent wife—it may have been a marriage broker or the ubiquitous Herschel Goldmark. Herschel, my mother remembers, was present when Sammy Samuelson came on a Sunday to have dinner in the Brooklyn house. Daisy had prepared the meal; her sisters helped to serve it. (Hannah spilled the soup, Hannah did not spill the soup—this depends on who's remembering.) All the girls were nicely dressed; they were respectful to their father, cordial to the guests, and frankly curious about why this stranger—whose Yid-

21

dish inflection was like their own, whose origins were Litvak, too —had fled from one monarchy to pledge allegiance to another one. "My ship's ticket was for Halifax," he told them with a chortle and a shrug. "My *landsman* already was in business in Montreal. So I became a Canadian. King Edward doesn't bother me, I don't bother him."

He was a Mister Five-by-Five; a gold watch chain spanned his bulging middle; he had gingerish curly hair and blue eyes that sparkled when he laughed, which was frequently.

After dinner Herschel passed around cigars, and Reuben led the men up to the parlor to smoke while the girls washed and dried the dishes and jabbered about anything and everything except Sammy Samuelson, since pointed interest might have seemed indelicate. Then Reuben came down to announce that the men were going over to Manhattan to spend the night in a Turkish bath—that was Herschel's treat.

I also do not know whether a decision was sweated out of Sammy Samuelson or whether he'd decided on his own, but obviously, during the night, it was made clear to him that the eldest of the Springer girls was the only one currently available. Possibly, certain practical aspects of this match were stressed—he himself, joking, used to say he married Ada because it was cheaper than hiring her. He was going into ladies' clothing manufacturing; she had dressmaking experience.

And I am not certain, since my mother ducks the question, whether he actually proposed to her. Rather, it appears, the marriage was proposed to each of them and neither one resisted it.

"But, Mama, did you love him?"

"Who talked about love? I was the oldest; it was time for me to be married. Mr. Samuelson was a gentleman; he could make a living."

They were married in the parlor of the Brooklyn house, a small, private wedding. Ada sewed her wedding gown; Daisy and Hannah cooked the wedding feast. Mrs. Goldmark escorted Ada to a *mikvah* in Manhattan for the prenuptial ritual bath and backed her up when she maintained she didn't want her head to be shaved.

"The *sheitel* was for the old country." Those are Mrs. Goldmark's reported words. "We are modren people." Mr. Samuelson, the groom, was Orthodox but not fanatical; he didn't insist on the wig. Sammy Samuelson's personal "Herschel Goldmark" came down from Montreal—Sammy had no near kin on this continent. Grandpa Springer produced a handful of bearded *landsmen* from his *shul* to add up to the ten males for the essential *minyan*.

The couple took the midnight train to Montreal, sitting up in the day coach with Sammy Samuelson's sponsor across the aisle, keeping one eye open to make sure that the groom took no immodest liberties, in public, with his bride.

My mother had no freedom of choice, no courtship, no honeymoon, not even a side trip to Niagara Falls. That marriage lasted half a century, and with felicity.

The sisters weren't jealous. Hannah, the rebel, by this time had made plans. At night school, she had met David Hitzig, who taught English there, and though Davy called himself a freethinker who didn't believe in conventional marriage, Hannah was convinced that with patient and persistent argument, plus her physical appeal, she'd induce him to forget his principles.

As for Daisy, she was young; her turn would come. Meanwhile, her father needed her to look after him. There was never, as far as I could learn, any thought that Yankel Springer might marry again. He had a home; his meals were cooked and served, his personal laundry done; the cronies in his *shul* provided companionship; his sex drive had diminished with advancing age. And in any case, its purpose was fulfilled. He had a son. Reuben guaranteed the Kaddish for his father's eternal repose.

Reuben's was the second marriage. Fanny Kuper had grown bored with his inexpensive courtship: nickel rides on summer evenings on the Staten Island ferry, decorous Sunday strolls in Prospect Park or on Second Avenue and East Broadway in Manhattan, and visits with her relatives and his. Her Uncle Herschel paid for a catered wedding in a hall.

In the bridal photograph, Fanny wears a high-necked white gown, tight against her ample bust, a froth of veil descending to the drapery on her hips. She stands alongside the wicker chair in which her groom is seated. Reuben wears a tuxedo and a high silk hat. His mustache, which in time was to resemble Kaiser Wilhelm's, was then a pair of thin, inverted arcs. Fanny has her hand proprietarily on his shoulder. On the other side of his chair there is a rubber plant as tall as the bride. The picture was mailed to Montreal, because my mother couldn't travel to the wedding, being eight months pregnant with me.

On their wedding night, the couple moved into the Brooklyn house. A tenant on the second floor had been requested to give up a room that adjoined the bath. Reuben moved a double brass bed into it; Fanny brought her own quilts and pillows. They took their meals downstairs—Daisy cooked and washed and ironed for them. They lived in the house for a year, paying nothing for their board, going to work each morning, and saving passionately toward a home and business of their own.

Fanny's generous uncle helped them toward that goal. He lent them—without interest—whatever they required to equip a clothing store in an upstate New York town called Grady's Mills and to furnish a flat above the store. Reuben joined the *shul* and the Knights of Pythias there. He closed his store on Rosh Hashanah, Yom Kippur, and the first two days of Passover, when he and Fanny came to Brooklyn for Seder.

Within two years the Reuben Springers were sufficiently well off to buy a steamship ticket for Fanny's young brother, Benjamin. Ben lived with them and was apprenticed to the retail clothing trade, beginning early in the morning with sweeping out the store, ending in the evening with straightening the clothing racks. Ben came to Brooklyn with them for the holidays.

Exactly when Hannah married and with what nuptials, I'm not certain, though I gather there may have been harsh words and high dudgeon, since whenever I broached that bit of family history my mother put me off with, "That was a long time ago. Who remembers every little thing?" In any event, she married Davy Hitzig and promptly embarked on a career of raising geniuses. Her boys were named Karl Marx Hitzig, Eugene Debs Hitzig, Walt Whitman Hitzig, and Clarence Darrow Hitzig. That did shock the family,

24

since those individuals were not related and only one of them was Jewish.

Daisy remained in the Brooklyn house, seeing to her father's comfort, dutifully waiting for him to order her future, uncomplaining, trusting, and hopeful.

This was all before my blabber mouth and I came across the border and messed things up for her.

2 ❊

A STIFF BREEZE was ruffling my curls and wafting a fishy smell. I sat between Aunt Daisy and Ben Kuper in an open trolley car, bouncing past some reedy marshes and weather-grizzled shanties. Aunt Daisy and Ben looked happy because they were, I guess. I was happy because I was going to see the sea. The Atlantic Ocean was my birthday present. I had nagged until my parents had given in to me.

Children build their cravings on something heard about yet never seen. My obsession was the ocean. My brother, Bram, and the St. Lawrence River were to blame for this.

When Bram was little and obnoxious and Mama wanted peace and quiet in the house, she'd make me take him out for walks. Because his usual dress-up outfit was a serge or linen sailor suit, Bram considered himself a member of the Royal Navy. What he wanted was to view the fleet. We'd trudge down to the river, crawl out on a pier, and sit and watch the ships—the grain boats and the ore boats, Europe-bound, the freighters with foreign flags, steaming in.

"Where they going, Millie?"

"To the ocean, Bram."

"Where they coming from?"

"From the ocean, Bram."

"What's an ocean, Millie? What's it like?"

"Water, lots of water. Deep."

"Did you ever see an ocean, Millie?"

"No, I never did."

"Don't you want to see one?"

"Yes, I do." The invisible Atlantic was a pervasive presence in the inland port of Montreal, and growing more so as traffic to and from the Mother Country increased at the beginning of the war. "I want to see the ocean," I pleaded with my parents. "I must know what it's like."

"*Meshugah*," my father said, with his spread-hands shrug. "What kind of nonsense is this for a Jewish child?"

"An ocean is *feh;* it makes you sick," my mother said.

My parents had seen the ocean, each of them, for weeks. Dizzied by its swells, frightened by its turbulence, they'd had enough of it to last out their lives.

"I just want to see it, just see what it's like, not go on a ship. On a ship, I'd be afraid. Please, *please.*"

"Millie wants it, let her have the pleasure," my father finally agreed. "We'll send her to New York. Daisy could take her to Coney Island; she could have a look."

"It's time Millie made acquaintance with my family," Mama said.

I knew them, yet I didn't. I had met them only twice. They lived in that other country, just across the border, to be sure, so near and yet so far, as the cliché goes. Yet you had to travel on the train a full day or night, which made it an endurance test as well as an expense.

When my brother, Bram (Abraham, the name-after Papa's long-dead father), was born, Aunt Fanny, Uncle Reuben, Grandpa, and Aunt Daisy made the long trip up—the daylight journey because Aunt Fanny said she was too nervous to try to sleep in a berth. They came for Bram's circumcision. Uncle Reuben carried the infant on a pillow to the *mohel* and held the cushion while a sharp knife sliced Bram's tiny foreskin off. Grandpa stuffed a rag soaked with sweet wine into Bram's mouth to smother his outraged yell, and he led the prayers to welcome my brother into the Covenant of the children of Israel.

When the ceremony was finished, Uncle Reuben handed Papa

a ten-dollar bill (American) to start a bank account for Bram. Then he had to hurry to the train. Fanny's brother, Ben, had been left in charge of the clothing store in Grady's Mills. Ben was a greenhorn; his English wasn't yet reliable. The others all remained.

Being three years old, I remember little about that visit except the hollering. Aunt Fanny and Yvonne, our char, kept yelling at each other—one in French, one in English, neither understanding the other's language, each convinced that louder makes clearer. And Bram kept crying, whining, fussing, day and night. Mama was sure it was colic; she fretted about her milk—it was too rich or she had been eating what she shouldn't have—until she saw the rash. Aunt Fanny was responsible for it. (This I do not personally remember, but it has been repeated so often that I grew up knowing it as fact.) Aunt Fanny had insisted on taking care of Bram; she'd swaddled him in so many blankets he'd developed prickly heat. There's not another case on record for that January in the city of Montreal.

But I do have a personal recollection of taking a stroll with Aunt Daisy and Grandpa just around the block to get away from the noisy house. That morning the pavements were ice-packed and the air as sharp as the *mohel*'s knife. Our nose tips froze, and when we tried to turn the corner against the wind, Grandpa slipped on the ice. Daisy caught him before he touched the ground and held him up, which was fortunate because he might have broken his neck. She held his hand and mine and led us both back to the house. Mama was relieved when Grandpa left. With a fretful, newborn baby, she was in no position, she said, to nurse an old man's broken bones.

I, too, was relieved when Grandpa left; his smell had bothered me. He smoked cigars, and the odor of stale tobacco mingled with the camphor, lingering in his heavy winter clothes, was repellent to me. I kept hoping he wouldn't try to kiss me, which he didn't try to do. All he did was hold my hand an instant, on arrival and departure, press it, murmur, "Meelie," before he let me go.

A thin, small man, with a salt-and-pepper beard, wrapped up in himself, he seemed indifferent to other people, especially to

28

little ones. Yet he must have had affection for my brother Bram and me, since that very year he started a custom that lasted as long as he lived. Each Purim Bram and I received from him an American silver dollar, each Chanukah a tiny, shiny golden coin, worth two dollars fifty. The coins were always boxed and wrapped in layers of paper, sealed, square-tied with string. Grandpa was a peerless package maker.

The other family visit was a summer one when I was eight years old. Papa had rented a cottage for us up in the Laurentians. The cottage had an extra bedroom and a living room big enough to set up cots, and so Mama, who missed her family more than she was willing to admit, wrote her sisters and her brother: "Come. Enjoy with us." Fanny answered no, she and Reuben had just bought a house, they were busy trying to fix it up, but the Hitzigs thought it might be fine to have a summer holiday in Canada. They came early in July: Aunt Hannah, Uncle Davy, Karl, Eugene, and Walt, with Clarence still a watermelon, underneath his mother's skirt.

Uncle Davy had become a journalist, on a Socialist newspaper. They lived in a flat in a part of New York called the Bronx. Since Uncle Davy's salary was small, my father insisted on sending them railroad tickets for the trip. "If I invite company, it is for my pleasure," he explained to Mama. "Why should I put them to expense to visit me?" Mama was of two minds about his gesture, I could tell, because she frowned before she smiled and kissed her husband's forehead. She was finding it difficult to get used to the fact that Papa was making money.

I liked Aunt Hannah—she had a lusty liveliness. I liked Uncle Davy, too. He was rather dashing-looking, with crisp, coal-black hair and an impertinent beaked nose. They were easygoing, didn't fuss about what there was to eat or where they had to sleep, and they were quick in the bathroom in the mornings. Uncle Davy liked to lie in the hammock between the trees all day, reading a book he'd brought along and waiting to be called to meals. In the evenings he played dominoes and checkers with me and his boys. Aunt Hannah did the dishes with my mother, and Mama, when she wasn't busy frying, baking, roasting, sewed up Aunt Hannah's skirt hems that were forever dragging loose. They had fine times, gossiping in the kitchen, the sort of "Hannah, you remember?" "Ada, you remember?" chatter that a child, passing through, listens to with half an ear.

"Ada, you remember the bananas?"

My mother blushed. "That was a little nonsense."

"On purpose, for spite," Aunt Hannah persisted. "Fanny has to show the greenhorns up, she gives bananas; they never ate bananas in the old country."

"Hokay, so I took the first bite with the skin," my mother admitted.

Aunt Hannah chose to dribble salt on the old wound. "So how did Daisy know? Like every day in her life she ate bananas, she knew first you peel off skin."

"It was something more, not just how you eat bananas," Mama said. "Right away, we just come off the ship, she tries to make us fools, nothings, nobodies."

"So she's smart," Hannah retorted. "She catched Reuben. A bargain Reuben has. You have children; I have children. What does Reuben have?"

Mama tapped her forehead. "Woman trouble." She caught sight of me, lounging against the edge of the sink. "Millie, go outside, play with the cousins," she commanded me.

Little pitchers have big ears, though what they take in often baffles them.

I went out wondering what kind of trouble with women Uncle Reuben had and what that had to do with eating bananas with the skin. Just one thing seemed evident to me: my mother and my aunt endured but did not love this sister-in-law of theirs.

Papa came up Friday evenings for the weekends. He played pinochle with Uncle Davy and sometimes they had arguments. Uncle Davy was the one who started them. Once he called Papa a "capitalist exploiter." Mama got red-faced and started a sarcastic retort, but Papa laughed and laughed, his fat stomach jiggled, and tears rolled down his cheeks.

It was the boys who made the visit hell for me. Skinny little snot-noses, smart alecks, each and every one, younger than I but acting superior.

In the beginning Aunt Hannah had said she wanted them to run around naked. "A shame for the neighbors," Mama said, looking sidewise at me.

"There is no shame in the naked human body," Aunt Hannah countered. "This is just your bourgeois attitude."

Fortunately, we were having typical Laurentian weather. Summer, we used to say in the province of Quebec, was that day in July when you happened to be out of town. Nudity simply wasn't practical. And so the boys ran wild in ragged overalls and made friends with the French farmers in the neighborhood, slurped their pea soup, and tried to incite them to overthrow the King and Parliament. In a short while they were spouting patois, which was more than I could do. I resented their know-it-all airs and fought back tears whenever they badgered me.

"You're a slave," Karl would say.

"Slaf, slaf, slaf," Eugene would echo, wagging a dirty index finger.

"I'm not. I set the table for my mother because I like to help. That doesn't make me a slave."

"You're a subject of a king," Karl lectured me with an earnest tone and a lofty manner, incongruous for his age and size. "A subject is a slave because he bows down and kneels."

"I don't. I only kneel when I tie my shoes. I never bowed down in my life."

"You will, you will, Karl knows," Eugene chanted, warning me.

"You'll live a slave and die in chains unless my father makes his revolution," Karl guaranteed. "Get wise to yourself."

I was eight, and he was seven, neither of us ripe for the barricades, yet the warnings depressed me. Suppose he knew things I had not been taught in school? Suppose they were more advanced down in the States? Walt merely pulled my curls and left a clammy, ugly hoptoad in my bed.

31

My brother, Bram, was smart; he used to open his eyes very wide and nod, yes, yes, yes, when his cousins badgered him. Occasionally, they invited him to play catch, for which he seemed to have an aptitude.

Aunt Hannah said, before she left, that it would be nice if I could come down some time and visit them, I got along so well with the boys; they had found me a little naïve, of course, which stood to reason since I'd not had Karl and Eugene's educational opportunities.

The second week of August Aunt Daisy brought Grandpa up for a fortnight. He got the spare bedroom, and Mama put a cot into Bram's room for me so that Aunt Daisy could have my bed. I didn't mind because Aunt Daisy was so sweet, by far the prettiest of the Springer sisters, a beautiful complexion and lovely eyes and gentle in her ways. With her helping in the kitchen, Mama could get out more to enjoy the fresh air and mountain scenery. Grandpa got up practically at sunrise, put his *tallith* and *tfillim* on, stood on the porch, facing east (toward the Atlantic Ocean), and recited prayers. No matter how early, Daisy had his cup of coffee and his buttered roll on the kitchen table as soon as he had taken off his *tallith* and had washed his hands.

The rest of the day Grandpa prowled. He wouldn't lie in the hammock, couldn't find a thing to do in or out of the house, wouldn't walk in the woods, and once asked anxiously whether there were wolves around. He missed his cronies and his *shul*, and he muttered about needing to get back to look after business matters. At first, he did try to make friends with Bram by quizzing him about whether he had started *cheder*, which was rather silly since Bram was five and a half and barely out of kindergarten. But Bram must have been impressed with the attention, because one afternoon when Mama, Aunt Daisy, and I strolled down to the village with him, Bram said he wanted to buy Grandpa a present; it had occurred to him, Grandpa would look happier if someone gave him a present. What Bram chose was hideous: a thermometer and a bear's paw glued to a slab of varnished wood that was lettered *Souvenir de Québec*. Grandpa shuddered when it was

32

unwrapped for him, though he composed himself, shook Bram's hand, and said, "It will come to use."

Mama nudged me to give Grandpa some attention, too, and so I took out the candy box I had lined with Bram's old diaper flannel to make a soft bed for the silver dollars and gold pieces he had sent. "It's my secret treasure," I told him.

"You shouldn't use it for a play toy," he rebuked me. "You should save it in a bank." Then he picked up Papa's Yiddish paper—done with conversation, done with me.

I began to put the money back. "Millie's *nadan*," Papa jested. Millie's dowry.

"Millie is a beautiful girl," Aunt Daisy said. "She will never need a dowry."

"Do you?" Mama asked.

Aunt Daisy lowered her eyes, saying nothing.

"You are not getting younger," Mama persisted. "How long will you sit, waiting, in the house?"

"Who will look after . . . ?" Daisy glanced sidewise at Grandpa, buried behind the paper, speaking low so that he should not hear.

My father put his arm around her slender shoulders. "Stay with us, Daisy. We will find you a good husband. We will look after Grandpa Springer, too. Maybe"—he winked in Grandpa's direction—"a somebody for him, also. A kosher widow with a *knippel. . . .*"

Daisy shook her head. "The house is his home. He has a good life there. He can travel alone on the El to his *shul* and his friends in New York. The work he does for Goldmark keeps him a little busy. The winters are not too hard for him. And in the summer, on the hot days, I take him on the trolley car to Coney Island, to bathe in the ocean."

The ocean. That Atlantic Ocean I'd been yearning for. Grandpa saw it; Daisy saw it; I did not. Daisy must have read my thoughts, because before she left she said to Mama, "Why don't you send Millie to us for vacation? We could take her to Coney Island, and she could get better acquainted with our family. Your children should not grow up strangers, Ada, to their nearest and their dearest ones."

Two years later, as I approached my tenth birthday, that important one which is the middle age of childhood, letters were exchanged and a visit planned for me. Some friends of Papa's were traveling to the States to spend two weeks with *their* relations in Long Branch, New Jersey. They'd take me with them to New York. Aunt Daisy would meet the train; I'd stay with her and Grandpa for one week; then Aunt Fanny's brother, Ben Kuper, would call for me and take me on another train to Grady's Mills to visit with Uncle Reuben and Aunt Fanny. I was to see my Hitzig cousins, too, though not as a house guest. Aunt Hannah's place was too crowded with all those genius-revolutionaries, and Clarence Darrow, the new one, hadn't learned to use a potty. However, Aunt Hannah would bring the boys to Brooklyn for the birthday party Aunt Daisy was going to make for me. I couldn't object to that, though without knowing I was echoing a Queen of France I told Mama, "Let them eat my cake." Mama bought me a new bathing dress.

The long train trip was hot and sooty. Papa's friends, munching chicken sandwiches, sucking oranges and lemons, kept oohing and aahing at the scenery. I remained indifferent. Lake Champlain was an old acquaintance, a next-door neighbor so to speak, and the Hudson one more river, hurrying toward the ocean. Just like me.

Aunt Daisy darted from the huddle at the depot gate; she recognized me, I recognized her. Papa's friends didn't need to worry about getting rid of me. Daisy gave me a tight squeeze and kisses on both cheeks; she insisted on carrying my valise and took me on more trains, one underground, one overground. After we reached the house, she sponged my face and hands and neck, at her kitchen sink, and combed my hair. She twined the strands around her forefinger, to make fat sausage curls, bunched and tied them with a blue taffeta ribbon, a present, hers to me. "I wanted to match the color of your eyes, darlin'," she said. "This is a wee bit lighter. We don't have the blue eyes in our family. Only brown."

"My father has," I said. "I take after him."

"But the hair. Brown, darlin', like all the Springer girls." She touched her own, a shining crown of braids atop her head, plucked a bone hairpin from that crown, and pinned up my bunch of curls, to keep my neck cooler. She did it all so eagerly and tenderly, I realized it must be a treat to her to have me in her house. The way she kept calling me "darlin' " was caressing, too.

She brought out ice-cold lemonade and cookies, and we sat together at the kitchen table, being pleased with one another. "Now, Millie, I must get the supper ready. You can keep me company in the kitchen. Or better yet, go take a look around the house."

I've never been one for looking around houses, I guess because I've always lived in one, and ours was not particularly different from the houses of our friends: kitchen, dining room, and parlor downstairs; bedrooms up; a *mezzuza* on the front door; bone-china cups and saucers on a show-off shelf in the dining room. To me a house was merely where you eat and sleep and play after school—comfortable, clean, what more do you need? I started to say so and saw a flicker of disappointment on Aunt Daisy's face. "But, darlin', this is *your* house, too. It is the Springer family home. Don't you want to see what's here?"

She wants me to, I will.

"Go in there, dear, the dining room. You'll see some precious things we brought from our old home." She struck a match and lighted the gas in the dining room. The chandelier was a glass bowl, a patchwork of red and green and gold, fringed with green glass beads. The gaslight dropped a gleaming pool on a round oak table, so highly polished I could see myself in it. The oak sideboard was high-polished, too. On it, glistening, was a row of brass things set out on a cross-stitch embroidered cloth. All I recognized were candlesticks. "My mother's," Aunt Daisy said. "I light them every Friday, like she did. And that's the samovar we used to make our tea. And the other is the *shtasel*—a mortar

35

and pestle is what they call it here—Mama used to grind her pepper, cinnamon, and nuts." She smiled. "I do sometimes, too. Many things I do the way my mother did."

I dingdonged the pestle against the mortar. It made a pleasant sound. "You could use it for a bell." I hefted the pestle. "Or fight off enemies with it."

"We don't have enemies," she said.

"We do," I said. "The Kaiser is our enemy."

"Go upstairs, darlin'," she said. "See all our pretty things."

Dutifully, I climbed the stairs. The parlor's shades were partway drawn; the furniture wore linen shrouds; the floor was covered with straw matting instead of carpeting. Yet there was a kind of elegance in the gilt-framed mirror above the oak mantelpiece, in the gilt-trimmed black clock on the mantel shelf, in the porcelain shepherd and shepherdess, posed for dancing in the center of a mahogany table in the middle of the room, in the spindly golden side chairs and the whatnot cabinet's china vases and figurines. I raised the sofa's linen cover. The wooden frame was carved, the seat golden plush. The Springer family must be very rich, I thought. But if all this is really mine—mine, too—as Aunt Daisy says it is, all I'd want of it is one little golden chair, so I could make believe I was a princess on a throne. I sat on one, gingerly. I mustn't get too fat, I thought, or my golden chair will break.

Portieres of colored beads hung in the doorway; they jangled pleasantly as I passed through, into a spooky, cupboard-lined corridor, back toward the sleeping rooms, Aunt Daisy's and Grandpa's.

Aunt Daisy's door was ajar. Her bedroom looked lovely: bird's-eye maple furniture, streamers of pink rosebuds on the wallpaper, a cretonne spread with cabbage roses on her bed, pink embroidered pillow shams, and fine net curtains at the open windows, swaying in the modest breeze. Her dresser had an embroidered runner, a long pincushion to match, and a china pin tray and hair receiver with pink-painted rosebuds. Airy, dainty, pretty-pretty. Roses and rosebuds. It's peculiar that she doesn't have one flower of her name.

I opened Grandpa's bedroom door a crack. The room was dark, and it had Grandpa's cigar smell. I shut the door quickly. Then there was just the bathroom to look at, the old-fashioned tub and the colored window through which the sun pushed fading light, dappling the ceiling with red and yellow blobs. Another staircase going, up, up, up to a dim hall, and doors that were locked. I came down wondering where I was going to sleep.

Aunt Daisy was setting the table in the kitchen. "You saw everything, darlin'? You liked the house?"

"Where will I sleep, Aunt Daisy?"

"With me. In my bed. It's big. You'll sleep on feather pillows your mother and me, we made them in the old country. Now" —she brushed a hair strand from her forehead—"we'll go outside. To the yard. We'll sit and cool ourselves till Grandpa comes. The kitchen is a little warm. I had to make a fire in the stove to cook."

Bram's gift thermometer, with the bear paw, hung just inside the kitchen door. It registered eighty-two degrees.

We carried two kitchen chairs way back to the lengthening shadows of a tall and scraggly ailanthus tree. Aunt Daisy had a palm-leaf fan. We took turns flapping it. We watched the sky turn rosy red, then gray. A star emerged. The evening star, diamond bright. "I'll make a wish," I said. " 'Star light, star bright, first star I see tonight, I wish I may, I wish I might have this wish I wish tonight.' "

"What did you wish, Millie?"

I shook my head. "Secret. Tell your star wish, you won't get it." I was ashamed to tell her I had wished for the little golden chair. You visit people, you should not go greedy for their things.

"You don't need to tell me, darlin', and I will wish you get it. I myself, I also wish, many times, star, no star." She sighed and dropped the fan onto her lap. "I sit here by myself resting, waiting for my father to come home. And I wish my wish. Always it is the same wish, and I know I will not get it. I wish for the family. Our family. How it was in the old country. Our house. A wooden house, a small house. But nice. Because a whole family was there. My sisters and my brother, running in and out. My father, my mother, coming home to us. Such a wonderful thing to have a family! Such a hard thing to lose a family. First we lose our mother. She was a darlin' woman, Millie; you are the name-after-her. That is one reason—but only one—why you are special dear to me. She was such a sweet woman, Millie, so good, never complaining; whatever Papa needed, whatever he decided—"

She was getting too sad for me. I had to interrupt. "When do we go to the ocean?"

It took a couple of silent seconds for her to put away her memories. "Sunday, Millie. Ben cannot come till Sunday. Ben Kuper, your Aunt Fanny's brother. He is going with us." By the way she said it, I realized Ben Kuper's presence would make it a special treat. "Be patient, Millie. Wait."

Wait for Grandpa Springer. Wait for Ben Kuper. Waiting. The story of Aunt Daisy's life.

All the stars were out by the time Grandpa Springer came. He took off his alpaca jacket, hung it on a chair back; removed his bow tie, his celluloid collar, the collar button; laid them on a cupboard ledge and hitched his shirt sleeves up; put on his black *yarmulke* before he took my hands in his; pressed them, murmuring, "Meelie"; and dropped my hands to wash his at the sink and dry them on the roller, return to join us at the table, mumble a prayer, break off, and eat a morsel of bread. He looked pale, I thought, and uncomfortably warm.

Aunt Daisy asked, while she served him, "Papa, were you running around, climbing the stairs in this heat?"

"I was all afternoon in Goldmark's office."

"He has a fan?"

"He has a fan."

"You weren't sitting in a draft?" He didn't answer her. "Don't get sick, Papa." More like a mother than a daughter was the way she looked at him and spoke. "After supper, you go straight to bed."

His appetite was good. He ate steadily till he had cleaned his plate. Then he mopped the lip fringes of his beard and looked up to inquire about my parents' health. I said they were well and they sent regards. He asked whether Bram was studying hard in *cheder*. I said he was. He asked had I had a comfortable trip. I said I had. The conversation lapsed. Daisy served us tea and cake. He finished his, took his jacket from the chair, gathered up his collar, tie, and collar button, nodded wordlessly, and went upstairs.

I helped Aunt Daisy clear away and dried the dishes for her. She washed dishes frugally, stingy with hot water, since she had decided that after the train trip I would need a bath.

I bathed in the zinc tub, put on my nightgown in the bathroom. Aunt Daisy sponged herself after I was done and came out in her nightgown. We brushed each other's hair. Hers, when she took it down, was almost to her waist. It felt like silk when I braided it for her. And in her bed we weren't cramped, because both of us were small. I didn't snuggle, as I might have with some other older person whom I loved, because I felt Aunt Daisy was not an older person but more like a girl friend.

In the morning Grandpa prayed in his room, came down in his black alpaca suit, with a clean collar and the bow tie on. He had his breakfast and got up to depart for New York. Aunt Daisy followed him to the door. "Papa, don't walk in the sun. Don't sit in a draft."

I helped her with the breakfast dishes. Then we went shopping. We bought a wooden embroidery hoop, a white linen dresser runner, stamped for cross-stitching, and some skeins of red and blue silk floss. "You'll make a present for Aunt Fanny," she told me. "I'll teach you cross-stitch. It is easy."

She looked so happy teaching me, there wasn't any point in telling her Mama had taught me cross-stitch several years ago.

I sat in a shady corner of the yard and sewed while she polished up her house. But the house wasn't really hers—she'd said as much to me. It was the Springer family's house, an all-the-family's house, and if that was so, I ought to be polishing along with her. It wasn't fair for her to be the caretaker of what belonged to all of us. But if it was an everybody's house, then where was Daisy's own real home? Every person has to have one place that is absolutely hers or his.

Another thing that puzzled me about Aunt Daisy was the way she was different with different people. She was like a mother or a wife with Grandpa, like a best girl friend with me. And a third thing that puzzled me was her calling me darling without the *g*. That sounded Irish, and she was Jewish, the same as my mother was.

Where she picked that Irish accent up I realized when Mrs. Fitzsimmons, the next-door neighbor, stopped by and came out to the yard to be introduced to me. "Daisy, she's a darlin' little girl. The blue eyes and the dark hair, she could be a colleen on the Irish coast. Now, darlin', what will you be doin' here?"

"I came to see the family and the Atlantic Ocean." I glanced at Aunt Daisy.

"Sunday," she said firmly.

"On Sunday," I had to agree, "when Ben Kuper comes."

"Must she wait? Jimmy, he's my son, he's a sailor—the Merchant Marine—his ship come in the other night. I could ask him; he could take you. He'd be pleased to take the both of you."

"Sunday," Aunt Daisy said. "Mr. Kuper will take us." The way she looked when she said it, I realized that there was a third Aunt Daisy, different from the two I was acquainted with.

I finished the dresser runner. Aunt Daisy praised my work. She said now we'd buy a bib, stamped out for French knots (she would teach me); I'd have a present for Clarence Darrow Hitzig. I didn't tell her I'd been doing French knots for a year. That was sneaky, yet she did enjoy teaching me, and I enjoyed her praise.

Sitting in the yard and sewing was agreeable, but I was growing bored. I'd put the hoop aside, go upstairs, sit on a little golden chair, and imagine myself a princess or a fairy queen. Then I'd climb farther up, stare at the closed doors, and imagine the people who had rooms up there. I never met them, though sometimes, early in the mornings or at night, I'd hear their footsteps on the stairs. Strangers, living in our house. A peculiar house, full of mysteries.

Aunt Daisy must have sensed my boredom, for on the afternoon when I finished the bib, she wondered whether I'd like to take a trip to the Bronx to visit Aunt Hannah and the boys. It would be a long ride on the subway—I didn't get carsick, did I?

I hadn't been carsick on the train, I reminded her, and since a subway was a train, she needn't worry about me. She found some tissue paper and blue baby ribbon, and we wrapped the bib. Grandpa watched us wrapping, asked what, where, and when, then announced he'd go along; he hadn't seen his daughter Hannah and her boys for months. "We can bring cookies for the boys," he said.

"Hannah's house is not kosher," Aunt Daisy whispered to me. "So Grandpa brings his own refreshments. Presents for the family, he says."

The only good thing I can say about the junket to Aunt Hannah's is that it broke the monotony of sitting, sewing, and waiting for Sunday. The ride was long, smothering, and jolty—I didn't get carsick, but almost. Aunt Hannah's cluttered flat was steamy, the boys were rude to me, and fat Clarence (nicknamed Snooky), stark naked in his crib, smelled absolutely awful. Aunt Hannah said my bib was beautiful; Eugene Debs Hitzig said, "Too good for Snooky, Snooky is a slob." True, all too.

Aunt Hannah took a blue bottle from her icebox, spritzed seltzer into strawberry jam to make sweet, cool drinks for us, but Grandpa asked for hot tea in a glass. He removed his jacket, hung it on a chair, hitched his shirt sleeves clear of his wrists, and seated himself at the head of Aunt Hannah's dining table. There was something regal about him as he sat behind his glass of tea, now nibbling a cooky, now sipping tea, not saying a word to us, yet by his very presence dominating us: the head of his family, cloaked in natural authority.

The Hitzig boys kept skittering past, snatching cookies, eying Grandpa sidewise but making no obeisance. I sat between Aunt Hannah and Aunt Daisy, drinking strawberry seltzer, trying to answer Aunt Hannah's questions about my parents' health and welfare, while fat, naked Snooky, on his mother's lap, kept lunging for my curls. Aunt Hannah asked whether I wouldn't prefer to

41

go into the parlor and converse with the boys. The boys didn't leap at the suggestion either. One by one, they edged toward the apartment door. Aunt Hannah said she'd bring them to Brooklyn for my birthday. They wanted to get me a book for a birthday present; what would I like? Karl Marx Hitzig answered for me from the doorway: "*Rebecca of Sunnybrook Farm.*" It sounded like a sneer.

I'd begun to be afraid Sunday would never come when it finally arrived. And brought Ben Kuper to us. He came very early in the morning while my aunt and I were packing a picnic lunch into shoeboxes: cream-cheese and grape-jelly sandwiches on *chalah;* Swiss cheese on pumpernickel, hard-boiled eggs, yellow plum tomatoes (salt in a paper cornucopia), peaches, plums, and pears, and Aunt Daisy's delicious cookies—things that wouldn't be spoiled by the sun's heat on the beach. Our towels and bathing outfits were already packed into a straw basket that Aunt Daisy had brought from the old country.

Ben strode like a lance of sunlight into the dusky basement hall. "Ha-lo! Everybody ready?"

Prince Charming! Tall and shapely slender, light brown curly hair, cleft chin, pink cheeks, dark, soft, sparkling eyes. He saw me first—"The little foreigner!"—hugged me, kissed my forehead. "A *scheine maidele.*" A pretty little girl. "A good little girl," Aunt Daisy added as she came to greet him. He took her hands in his, held them tightly. She blushed, the crimson flooding her cheeks and throat, and I didn't blame her one single bit, because Ben Kuper was the Prince, come to wake the Sleeping Beauty with his kiss. Yet he hadn't kissed Aunt Daisy. His hands, his voice, his smile alone had made her glow.

"I've been waiting for you," I announced, to draw attention to myself. "I need to see the ocean."

He turned to me, grinning—"And ride the chute-de-chutes" —and turned again to Daisy. "The grandpa coming, too?"

"I don't think so," I replied for her. Grandpa Springer, in his shirt sleeves, was reading his paper in the yard and smoking a vile cigar.

42

"Go talk to him," Aunt Daisy told Ben.

"Good morning, Mr. Springer." Ben's voice, his manner, had changed; it seemed less self-assured.

Grandpa lowered his paper an inch, a brief nod, barely acknowledging the greeting.

"How do you feel, Mr. Springer?"

The paper descended another inch. "How should an old man feel?"

"You are coming with us, Mr. Springer?"

"No, Mr. Kuper." The paper descended to Grandpa's lap. "Today is for the young people. Meelie, my granddaughter, has come from Canada to go to Cooneyilan."

I shifted foot to foot, impatient. I knew that; Ben Kuper knew it; why waste our time discussing it?

"My daughter said I should come with. But maybe not. Yesterday I had some little *swindles* in my head." Grandpa rubbed his forehead. "So I decided better not. Today I will rest myself."

"There is cold *schav* in the icebox," Daisy said. "And pot cheese. And compote. Eat light today, Papa."

"My daughter takes good care of me," Grandpa said.

"Better you shouldn't smoke cigars today," Daisy said. "That could be what makes you dizzy, gives you the little *swindles* in the head."

He shrugged, ignoring her. "Mr. Kuper, how is my son, Reuben? He doesn't work too hard?"

"Aren't we going to the ocean?" I nagged.

Aunt Daisy touched my shoulder. "In a minute, in a minute. Grandpa wants to have a little *shmoos* with Mr. Kuper." Her eyes had an anxious expression I'd not seen there before. I gnawed a fingernail and scowled. I didn't know—how could I know?—how important this encounter was to her.

"My son Reuben goes to *mincha* every morning?" The morning prayers in the synagogue that my father sometimes mentioned but invariably ignored.

Ben glanced at Daisy, as if waiting for a cue to the correct answer. "Sometimes he *davens* home. The *shul* there does not always have a *minyan* in the morning."

"And you, Mr. Kuper?"

Again, a hesitation, a slight rise of color. "I have to go to open up the store."

Grandpa tugged his beard. "That is not good. You and my son Reuben could help to make a *minyan*." He cocked his head, considering something. "But Reuben keeps closed his store on *shabbos?*"

"He goes to *shul* in the morning," Ben Kuper hedged. "Before he goes to the store."

"And you?" Grandpa's expression had turned hard, demanding.

"I have to open up the store." Ben shrugged. "Somebody has to open up the store."

Grandpa raised a forefinger. "Half a *goy*. Bad. Bad."

Aunt Daisy's anxious frown deepened. I grumped portentously. At last Grandpa noticed me.

"Meelie has no patience. She has many years for pleasure. I have few. In my life I have had little pleasure."

"Except from your children," Ben Kuper said.

Grandpa sighed. "Daisy is a good daughter. She takes care of me. Your sister, Fanny, takes good care of Reuben?"

I coughed hard, demandingly.

"Go, go," Grandpa said. "The child has many years, so she is in a hurry."

At last we were off. Ben carried the straw basket, I the shoe boxes; Aunt Daisy had her rose-colored parasol and her satchel-sized pocketbook. Ben apologized for not relieving me of the shoe boxes. "If I carry in both hands, how can I help my ladies on the trolley?" *My ladies!* He was so much taller than the two of us that when we walked to the street car we looked like schoolgirls on each side of him. I skipped a step or two, now and then, but Aunt Daisy walked sedately, though perhaps her heart was skipping, too.

I heard the sea before I saw the sea—heard the rhythmic hoarseness of the surf, mingled with the sound of music, a hurdy-gurdy's tintinnabulation. Ben helped me off the trolley car, and Coney Island made its gross attack upon my senses—all of them—the sight of garish stalls and shops and painted signs, of moving contraptions, up high and down low, and of a mass of people, milling, jostling me with sweating arms, a human swarm, engulfing; the sounds, confusing, deafening, of the roller coaster's roar and rattle, the merry-go-round's tinny tinkle, the oompah-oompah of drums, the raucous hawkers shilling games of chance; and the smells that drove your taste buds crazy: meat and onions frying, corn and sweet potatoes boiling, the taffy-pull machine exuding the molasses sweetness, popcorn, redolent of rancid butter, the pungent heaviness of beer, and, mixed with all of it, the ocean's saltiness and the stench of its dead fish. I believe I felt sea spray on my cheeks, but maybe I imagined that. Surf Avenue, where the people and the noises and the odors came together, was still a distance from the waves.

Aunt Daisy said, "We'll change; then we'll have lunch on the beach."

There is a moment in every life, I do believe, when a window opens and, uncontrived, lets your future in. Within the sweltering cubbyhole they called a ladies' locker, that window opened for me when I saw Aunt Daisy naked. We had shared a bed, but each of us had put our nightgowns on in privacy. She was trying to be modest here, undressing beneath her chemise as I had done. But the place was very small, no bigger than a closet; it cramped her movements, made her clumsy. The bathing bloomers she was pulling on slipped from her hand, and when she bent to pick them up, I saw all of her: the rounded buttocks, the pink-tipped breasts like little pears, and the tuft of brown hair beneath her belly button, above the entrance to her private parts. It was the first time I had ever seen how a grown-up woman looked underneath her clothes. That make-believe I'd conjured up when we were brushing one another's hair, when we were sitting side by side in the yard, that we were girls together, playmates, best friends, vanished all at once and altogether. The sight of a woman's body, ripe and exquisite, startled and discomfited me.

She saw me staring, and a blush swept her face and throat. "Millie, better wait outside." She stammered a little. "It's too crowded here."

I stood on the stove-hot boards outside the locker, ashamed

45

for Daisy and for me, and peculiarly disturbed because something new was happening to me. I had, at Coney Island, one week before my tenth birthday, become aware of sexuality, the human female body's beauty and its equipment for the acts of love. Ten is very young to start to be aware of this. In 1915, when that awareness dawned on me, ten was much younger than it is these days.

When she emerged, Aunt Daisy was entirely covered up, a black bathing dress to below her knees, long black stockings, high-laced bathing shoes, and a kind of bonnet tied beneath her chin; nothing bare except her face and her lightly freckled arms. She wound around my wrist the elastic band that held the tag with the number of the locker where I had seen her nakedness— 37B. I still remember it.

She handed me the towels to carry; she had our lunch boxes and her rose-colored parasol. Ben was waiting for us at the head of the steps to the beach. He'd had to rent a bathing suit, a striped wool sack that came to below his knees. He took the parasol and opened it and held it over Daisy while we went down to the beach.

I saw the sand—a stretch of gray, with people sprawling, crawling, over it. Beyond them was a shimmering greenness, rising and descending and spewing foam upon the shore. It kept advancing, nearer, ever nearer to the lolling people; it growled as it advanced. I began to shiver because it frightened me.

Ben and Aunt Daisy didn't notice; they were busy hunting for a place to spread our towels and set our boxes down. "We could have a little dip before we have our lunch. You have to wait one hour after eating, or else you might get cramps."

So there were rules for challenging this wild green monster. Yet people were prancing in the ocean, plunging into its peaks. They didn't seem afraid. Why should I be? Because I am my parents' child. They'd been frightened by this monster before I was conceived.

"Come, Millie." Ben Kuper took my hand. "Don't be afraid. I'll take care of you." He reached his other hand to Daisy. "Of the both of you." He led us to the cold, wet rim of the sand. Foam

46

swirled around our feet and fled, sucked back. A breaker, mountainous from the distance, losing height but gaining speed, crashed in front of us. Water hit my knees; it drenched my bathing dress.

"Cold! Too cold!" I screeched. "I want to go back!"

My aunt and her friend laughed. Ben Kuper put his arms around me, held me, lifted me, and carried me directly in. "Don't be afraid," he repeated. "I'll hold on to you." He set me on my feet on shifting, slippery sand. "I'll show you how to jump the waves. Now watch, watch that wave, coming in. It gets close to us, we jump up, up, high up; we jump on top of it." Shuddering, I watched. "Jump!"

I jumped. Salt water filled my mouth and nose. I choked. Cold water slapped my ribs. I screamed, "Take me back, take me back!" At that moment I hated the ocean as much as my parents did.

Ben snuggled me against his side. "Poor Millie, she was scared. Don't worry, little Millie, you will get over it."

Never, not as long as I live.

He led me back to the dry sand. "Stay here, Millie, watch your aunt and me, watch us swim; you'll see it's nothing to be scared."

I watched him lead Aunt Daisy in, the two of them, hand in hand, to where the swirling water reached their chests and chins, blithely unconcerned, as if this was no mortally dangerous thing. I saw Aunt Daisy prone, in that awesome surf, her arms lifting rhythmically; I watched Ben leap into a giant wave and disappear. He's being drowned—oh, no, please no! Save him, somebody! Do not let him drown. And then I saw him standing up, shaking water from his ears, pulling Aunt Daisy to her feet, both of them laughing at the surf. How wonderful they are, those two! How brave!

We opened the shoe boxes and took out the lunch. Ben slapped his chest. "A pleasure. Gives you appetite." He smiled at me. "Next time, little Millie, next time you'll enjoy."

I smiled back weakly and began to peel an egg. Aunt Daisy said prosaically, "Here is salt for your egg."

"I've swallowed salt enough for a dozen eggs," I said.

We rested after lunch. Aunt Daisy unbraided her hair, to dry it in the sun. Ben stretched on a towel at her side. I sat upright, digging with my fingers, morosely sifting sand.

I saw Ben Kuper raise his arm to reach Aunt Daisy's streaming hair and twist and twirl the ends. I watched his hand slide up and down her freckled arm, inside the arm, brushing gently on her breast. I saw her throat and face flush scarlet, one arm rise, not to move his hand away but to touch her fingertips to his.

Oh, be careful, Ben and Daisy—I'd never heard that verse of Robert Burns, yet my mind was framing something similar—there's a child among you taking notes. She sees what she sees: those two spooning on this beach. As in the fairy tales, he loves her and she loves him. Write that on the sand.

They went in again. I didn't budge. They came out, dripping. Aunt Daisy said, "Let's finish up the fruit; then we will get dressed." Welcome words. The grit in my behind's creases was making me cranky. I ate a pear and a peach; Aunt Daisy had a peach; Ben took a pear. It was overripe; juice ran down his chin. I leaned across to mop it with my towel, and he thanked me with a smile and little hug. Aunt Daisy was busy clearing up. I guess she didn't see us; she might have been jealous.

Finally we got up to leave. Mildred Samuelson had seen the Atlantic Ocean, she had tasted it, and she was glad to turn her back on it.

Aunt Daisy made me shower under ice-cold water and remove my bathing stockings to get sand out from between my toes. Then she sent me scooting to show our number tag to a white-aproned woman who unlocked our cubicle. I dried myself and dressed in solitary while Aunt Daisy had her shower, and I stood on the burning boards outside until she emerged, dressed, to comb my hair. While she was shaping my curls around her finger, I remarked, to pierce her thoughtful silence, in which I sensed some disapproval of me, who'd screamed and sulked out there on the beach, "Ben is very nice." I said, "I think he's a darling!" I wasn't saying "Mr. Kuper," I was saying "Ben." My mind had moved him from the grownups' world to that of my peers. A playmate. A best friend. Aunt Daisy didn't answer me.

He was waiting, suit, collar, bow tie on, damp hair combed back in a curly pompadour, nose and forehead reddened by the sun. Prince Charming, bowing, taking our towel basket, linking his free hand into my arm. "Now we will give Millie her good time. What would the little lady like? Roller coaster? Chute-de-chutes, merry-go-round? Maybe Steeplechase? Or Luna Park?" He ticked them off as if he was selling each and all to me.

"I'll look, I'll see."

We drifted with the crowd along Surf Avenue, drinking in the sights and sounds and smells. "The merry-go-round, Millie? A horsie that goes up and down?"

"I don't know." Wanting to, yet drawing back, dreading another fiasco like that one in the sea.

"I'll get on with you. I'll take care of you." He turned to Aunt Daisy, questioning, "You, too?"

"I will watch." A trifle patronizing, it struck me: this is just for kids.

He boosted me up to the moving platform, chose a white horse, with a saddle of gold and crimson, helped me on, while the plaster animal moved up and down. He put reins into my hands, then leaped atop a pale blue tiger that had orange stripes. I rode gaily, waving at Aunt Daisy as I passed, until I noticed Ben was leaning out and up. Oh, Ben Kuper, dear, dear Ben, why are you so reckless? Must you risk your life?

The platform slowed. "Another ride, Millie?"

"No, thank you, it was nice."

He helped me down. "I almost got the brass ring," he told Aunt Daisy, with a kind of pride. A ring means getting married. He was, I decided, planning to marry Aunt Daisy with the merry-go-round's brass ring. My mistake. "If you catch the brass ring," he explained to me, "you get a free ride. . . . Now, Millie, how about the chute-de-chutes?"

"No," Aunt Daisy answered for me. "That is dangerous."

"The Ferris wheel? The roller coaster?"

My aunt shuddered for me. Ben looked disappointed. Probably he enjoyed these things himself as much as he enjoyed treating me. "But a frankfurter?"

"Not kosher." Aunt Daisy was beginning to be difficult.

"Then an ice-cream sandwich? Or popcorn?"

"She can have one. Only one," Daisy said. "We don't want Millie to get sick."

I decided on the ice-cream sandwich. Ben paid for it, then sidled over to another booth to buy a bag of popcorn. He stuffed it into his jacket pocket. For afterward, I guessed.

We meandered with the throng, my ice cream oozing at the edges of the crackers, running down my chin. Ben whipped out his handkerchief, mopped me, murmured, "Tit-for-tat," reminding me I'd tidied up his chin. "Hurry. Finish," he whispered. When I was done with ice cream, he pulled out the popcorn bag.

"You will spoil her," Daisy said, to be saying something, though she didn't seem displeased.

We passed another booth. It was displaying kewpie dolls, that were prizes for a sort of game played by rolling balls. Ben saw me eying it and sensed my greed. "I will win one for you." Aunt Daisy tugged his sleeve, halfheartedly. Smiling, he shook her off and strode ahead, laid down a dime, received some wooden balls, took aim, and rolled a ball. The ball rolled wide, scoring nothing. He rolled the other balls; he didn't score enough to win a doll. He fished out another dime, shook Aunt Daisy's fingers off his arm, glanced at me, munching popcorn, said, "Millie, you will have a kewpie doll." He removed his coat, handed it to me, gritted his teeth, took a stance, and with determination worthy of a nobler cause he kept spending dimes and rolling wooden balls. A crowd gathered, watching him. Aunt Daisy frowned.

How many dimes he spent, how many balls he rolled, I don't recall; all I remember clearly was the grin of triumph and the bow with which he handed me a kewpie doll. And I know I stood on tiptoe to put my arms around his neck and kiss him on the mouth.

"Now let us sit down and have a cold drink." He chose the place—a sort of restaurant, your food or theirs. "Basket Parties

Welcome," the sign outside announced. Heavy canvas draped the front of it, and inside it was dark, because moving pictures flickered at one end of the room. While we drank sarsaparilla, Aunt Daisy and I, we watched the jiggling figures on the distant screen. But Ben, a schooner of beer in front of him, was paying no attention to the screen. He was looking at Aunt Daisy all the time. Once, when I turned to sip my sarsaparilla, I saw his hand moving up her arm, up, up, to the top of it. This time she drew her arm away, to press his palm down on the table top and cover it with her own hand. I know they were talking, low-voiced, but what they said I couldn't hear, because up front a piano was thumping. And what they were saying to each other was not my business anyway.

Boys were hawking papers, yelling "Wuxtree" and something about the Europe war, when we left the place. Aunt Daisy said, "We must hurry; Papa will be waiting for supper." Ben sat next to Daisy on the trolley. He let me have the end of the bench and hand the nickels to the conductor, as if I were grown up.

Grandpa Springer wasn't home when we arrived. Exactly when he came, I do not know. In the morning he informed us at breakfast he had gone over to Manhattan to his friends the Goldmarks, he had had supper with them, and their chauffeur had driven him home in an automobile. He was polite to Ben at breakfast, a nod of greeting, though to me before he departed for Manhattan, he said, at parting, "Give a regards to my son, Reuben, and his wife," because Ben and I were leaving after breakfast to go to Grady's Mills.

Where Ben had been bedded for the night, I do not know—probably on the parlor sofa, since when I was going down for breakfast, I saw his jacket lying on the golden chair that I had wished for on an evening star. I'd fallen asleep the instant my head touched the goose-down pillows in Aunt Daisy's bed. What time she retired I also do not know, and whether she and Ben spooned in the parlor before Grandpa Springer came I have no way of knowing. Of only one thing was I sure: Ben Kuper was in love with Daisy and she was in love with him. And I with both of them. I expected confidently that all three of us would live happily ever afterward.

Ben took me, my kewpie doll, and my small valise on a ferry and a train. While we waited to board the train, he bought himself a Moxie and let me have a sip. When I said I liked the taste, he bought me a small glass. He also bought me a box of Crackerjack to eat on the train.

"Aunt Daisy is pretty," I said to Ben when we were in our seat.

"Daisy is pretty," he echoed.

"She is kind and good," I said.

"Kind and good," he said.

"I love her very much," I said.

He squeezed my hand and said, "The Crackerjack box has a prize in it. Look for it."

I found the prize, a tiny metal lantern with a window of red celluloid, supposed to imitate a real lantern's red-hot isinglass. It was a boy's prize, not a girl's, yet I pretended I was pleased. "I'll take it home to Bram. My brother will love it." My hands got sticky from the Crackerjack. Ben wiped them with the soiled handkerchief he'd used yesterday to wipe my chin.

We walked from the depot to First Street, where Uncle Reuben had his store. "Springer's Broadway Men's Apparel," the lettering on the awning read. Uncle Reuben's mustache tickled when he kissed me, and the heavy gold watch chain across his vest scratched my sunburn-tender skin. "Aunt Fanneh has the dinner ready. She is waiting," Uncle Reuben said.

Uncle Reuben walked me up a hill—Ben had stayed downtown to look after the store. He carried my valise; I carried my kewpie doll. On the way, when people greeted him, he stopped to introduce me: "My niece from Canada." I collected stares that seemed surprised I wasn't Eskimo or Indian, just an ordinary little Jewish girl. "They never met somebody from Canada," Uncle Reuben said.

Their wooden house was painted mustard color. We climbed steps to the porch. Aunt Fanny swung the front door open and smothered me in her embrace. "Such a traveler! Not even ten years! You're tired from the traveling? Come in, come in. . . . What is it on the nose? Aha, sunburn! Peeling. Your auntie didn't make you use a parasol?"

"Dinner, Fanneh. Talk later." Uncle Reuben hung his jacket on the hall hat rack. He kept his vest on.

"Go wash the hands, Millie." Aunt Fanny took my doll. "Aha, a kewpie! You brought it from Canada? They have kewpies there?"

"Ben won it for me at Coney Island yesterday."

"Soooo." Her eyes narrowed. She held it to the light, examining it minutely. "A hunk of junk," she decided. "How much did the *shmate* cost?"

"Where is the bathroom, Aunt Fanny?" A rudimentary instinct warned me the terrain was treacherous; stay clear.

"Upstairs. To the back. Use the roller—clean, I just put it on. Wash good with the soap."

"Bring the dinner, Fanneh," Uncle Reuben said. "I have to get back to the store."

He was halfway through his meal by the time I came downstairs. She was bustling between the gloomy dining room and the kitchen, serving him. She didn't tell me where to sit, or whether to. In fact, as far as I could see, no place had been set for me. I stood watching Uncle Reuben till he burped, wiped his mustache with his napkin, rolled the napkin into a celluloid ring, took out his watch, snapped up its golden lid, muttered, "Late, too late," snapped down the lid, and got up saying, "Bye-bye, Millie. Be a good girl. Mind your Auntie Fanneh." She cleared away his dishes and his cutlery and set a single place, and I sat down to thick, hot soup, roast meat and potatoes, pickles, stewed fruit, sponge cake, and hot tea. Being stuffed with Crackerjack, I wasn't very hungry.

"Aha!" Aunt Fanny observed. "I betcha Daisy spoiled your stomach with Cooneyilan *chaserei*."

The rudimentary instinct warned me not to mention Crackerjack.

While she was clearing away after me and setting another

53

place, Aunt Fanny commanded, "Now tell me, tell me everything. How did you enjoy?"

"Some things I liked, some things I didn't like."

She shook a finger at me. "A child must like everything her dear ones do for her."

"I liked the merry-go-round," I said.

"You didn't like the ocean bathing? That was healthy for you."

"I liked staying in Aunt Daisy's house. Her things are so pretty."

"*Her* house? The Springer family house. I, myself, I found the house for them." She paused, rolling her tongue around her lips while she considered something else I had to be informed about. "Any person can have good furniture when they have rich friends, like my Uncle Herschel Goldmark. (She told you about him?) My aunt, Lily Goldmark, they were moving to a bigger apartment, she offered me her old parlor suit. I said, 'Expensive or not expensive, I don't like secondhand. And what is more, I have a good taste of my own.'"

Her taste, I'd noticed in the parlor, ran to black mission furniture and tall rubber plants. I remarked that I'd never seen such plants.

"Your mama doesn't have rubber plants?" She sounded flabbergasted. I said no. She tskd. "Rubber plants are stylish. Maybe it's too cold for them up there." Her brow furrowed. "Daisy has a rubber plant? I don't remember. . . . No, she has the ferns. How are the ferns?"

I said I'd not seen ferns.

"She let them die! Daisy let them die!" There was anguish in her voice. "I betcha she gave them too much water. With plants you have to know exact how much to give. Like feeding little children. Too much is worse than too little. My rubber plants, I take care of them like children. You know what I give them every week? Castor oil. With castor oil I polish the leaves."

I let the good news settle while I rolled my napkin into a celluloid ring and rose. "I sewed a bureau scarf for you. It's in my suitcase. I'll go up and get it."

54

She made an effort to admire my handiwork, though she criticized. "Your Aunt Daisy told you I like red and blue? She didn't remember I told her myself the bedroom spread is green?"

I heard someone at the door. "Is that Ben? Is Ben coming?"

"A girl your age should say, 'Mr. Kuper.' From a young child 'Ben' is fresh."

Thus a dreadful week commenced. I prefer not to bore people with details, though sometimes they enjoy knowing how other people live, for instance what they eat. For breakfast I had a choice —Grape Nuts or Shredded Wheat—dished up with boiled milk that had the icky skin left on. Aunt Fanny said she'd read that the summer diarrhea that killed so many infants was due to unboiled milk. Ergo, though Millie is no infant, she must be treated as if. ("Your mother, Ada Samuelson, my sister-in-law, should never say I made her daughter sick.") Aunt Fanny breakfasted on stewed prunes and hot water. "For the bowels, not for me," she said.

Dinner at noon was the soup-meat-and-potatoes combination, regardless of the weather, but supper was light: egg salad, canned-salmon salad, or pot cheese and vegetables in sour cream; a sequence, in rotation.

However, the weirdest thing was that no one ate with anybody else. Ben had the first breakfast; he made his own coffee, with a roll and butter, early, because he had to open up the store. Then Aunt Fanny, uncorseted, in a wrapper, hair uncombed, beneath a net, came down with Uncle Reuben and served him Grape Nuts and Postum. My turn came after his; her prunes and hot water were the last. The same thing happened at dinnertime, except that Ben was last to eat, and at supper, for whatever reason —possibly a lingering misconception that I was still an infant, needing to be fed and sent to bed—I got the first serving of egg salad or salmon salad or pot cheese.

The downstairs of the house was fusty; the parlor windows were kept shut, and that room was dark, because of a big tree that shaded the front porch. The tree had enormous roots that pushed up the sidewalk slates, so that hopscotch wasn't feasible. Out back, there was a yard. Aunt Fanny urged me to go out there to play but hedged it with her don'ts: don't slide on the cellar door, you'll tear your underpants; don't sit on the grass, grass stains don't wash out.

The store was really what that family cared the most about: going to it, coming from it, discussing what was sold today and for what price, Aunt Fanny deploring she had so much to do at home this week (on account of me, it was implied) she couldn't get down to do the bookkeeping. Even Ben, who'd been my playmate Sunday, seemed wrapped up in the store—first there in the morning, last one home at night. After supper, he'd take off his shoes and collar, sit in the parlor, skimming the sports pages and the funnies in the evening paper, or go out to the porch to rock and watch for automobiles passing on the road. A different Ben Kuper from the one I had met in Brooklyn—subdued, chastised, I could almost say. I wondered, though I didn't dare to ask, whether Aunt Fanny had bawled him out for winning the kewpie doll for me.

Aunt Fanny. Honestly, she didn't know beans about entertaining an almost-ten-year-old. Although she moaned about how much work she had to do, she wouldn't let me help her with dishes or dusting. "In my house you are a guest. A guest does not work. A guest enjoys herself."

With what? The Victrola in the parlor? "Don't touch it, Millie, you could break the needle." Or crack a record. Or over-wind the mechanism. "Some evening, your Uncle Reuben will have time, he will give you a concert from grand opera."

The books behind glass in the three-shelf sectional bookcase? Encyclopedias. Top shelf, the International; second shelf, the Jewish. Heavy tomes, small print, long words. Now, wait! On the bottom shelf there is a storybook. A big, fat storybook! Two volumes, black-bound with gilt-lettered spines. *Hid from the World: The Story of a Clouded Life*. With pictures. Beautiful ladies in dresses of the olden days—bustles and leg-of-mutton sleeves—and handsome men in swallowtails. Ella. Marietta. Rudolph. Under one picture I read: "Rudolph told the young girl of his great love in passionate and burning words, and she sank in his arms weeping tears of pure joy." Was that Ella or Marietta, weeping with pure joy? Marietta, probably, because later on, underneath a picture, a caption said, "Ella behind the leafy screen"—watching a lovey-dovey couple. The way I'd watched my aunt and Ben? Yes, it had to be Ella, because here she was again, and under the picture they had printed, " 'Oh, all-powerful God, save me,' " she murmured, wringing her hands and gazing upward to the starry heaven! 'Why must I live deserted and forsaken?' "

Aunt Fanny caught me with the book and snatched it from my hands. "You will make the pages dirty! Your Uncle Reuben would be mad; he had those books from before he married me. Here." She plucked another volume from the bottom shelf. "This you will find more interesting. It has pictures, too." And so I sat on the mission sofa in the parlor and studied photographs of "The San Francisco Horror and Carnage." Interesting but not too, and strange to find this in my uncle's house, even stranger than his *Hid from the World.*

Most mornings, I sat on the top step of the porch and played jacks. I got to be so expert that I never missed, not even on the sprawled-out tensies. Sometimes, when I played, girls about my age walked past, looked in my direction, but didn't stop to talk. Sometimes, in the afternoons, after she had had her after-dinner nap, Aunt Fanny joined me on the porch, rocked, and watched me playing jacks. When younger people passed, she'd crook a finger, call them to the steps. "This is my niece from Canada." As if they cared. Not even a "How do you like it here?"

Give credit where credit is due. Aunt Fanny kept trying. She took out her family album and showed me her photographs, mostly of her wealthy relatives, the Goldmark family. "If not for them, Millie, your grandpa and your auntie would not have a roof for their heads." I'd never seen a Goldmark; I never expected to see one.

She must have told my Uncle Reuben about the boredom of my days, for one evening he decided to play the Victrola for me, and we sat in the parlor—all of us, including Ben—as still as mice, listening to grand opera. The singing was so loud we could not have conversed even had we had things to talk about. Another evening, Uncle Reuben came early—Aunt Fanny made a point of telling me what a sacrifice this was—and after supper he said he'd take me for a walk, show me Grady's Mills. He showed me the outside of his *shul* and the building where his Knights of Pythias met, after which he led me to the ice-cream parlor and asked me would I like a strawberry sundae. Or plain vanilla, maybe. I said I'd like a Moxie. His mustache bristled. "Moxie is too strong for you."

"Ben bought me some," I boasted, and he scowled.

"My brother-in-law is a little wild," he said.

On Friday, just as the dreadful week was ending, I made two mistakes: I took a walk alone, and after it I talked too much. Aunt Fanny was upstairs napping, and I was tired of playing jacks. I walked uphill, past the *shul,* past the houses, way up to where there was an open field, dotted with red clover, Queen Anne's lace, buttercups, and daisies. I waded in, weeds to my hips, and picked a bunch of daisies.

Aunt Fanny was upstairs when I returned, finished with her nap—I could hear her moving about—and I called up the staircase, "Aunt Fanny, I picked some flowers in the field."

"What field?"

"On top the hill."

"You went there by yourself?"

That didn't deserve an answer. "I need a jar to put them in."

She came to the head of the stairs, her corset strings trailing. "A milk bottle is on the back steps. Be careful you don't break it." She saw the bouquet in my hand. "Daisies, *feh!*" she said. "Throw away the weeds. Wash your hands. Come up and help me dressing."

Whenever Aunt Fanny put her corset on, she asked me to pull the strings, my spine braced against a bedpost, yanking, tighter, ever tighter, till she could barely breathe. Then, after she'd concealed the humps of her breasts beneath an embroidered corset cover and drawn on a petticoat, she handed me her buttonhook, to do her shoes. It was the only service she permitted me to do for her; Reuben, she did tell me, helped her ordinarily, though he was clumsy at it.

While I was kneeling with the buttonhook, she began a quiz. "Daisies you picked. You couldn't find some nicer flowers?"

"I love them. They remind me of my aunt."

"Your aunt is white and yellow?"

"No, but she is dainty, pretty, like the flower."

"Passable, passable."

"And she's kind and good."

"She's good to the father. She is lucky to have the father. If not for him, she would not have a home."

I stood up, finished, brandishing the buttonhook. "Oh, she'll always have a home. Ben will make a home for her when they're happily married."

Her face turned red as borscht. That wasn't just the tightness of the corset, because her eyes were glittering angry. "What kind of talk is this?"

I sensed I had blundered, and so I blundered on. "Oh, they're in love, I know they are."

"You know! What could you know?"

The tone was so bellicose I had to defend myself. "I saw them spooning, so I know."

I heard the hiss of indrawn breath. "The *nafke!*" (I didn't know the word meant "whore"; her inflection alone told me it must be disparaging.)

"I hope they'll get married soon and live happily ever after."

"Over my dead body," Aunt Fanny said.

Afterward, rocking on the porch, she said, intending to inform and impress me, "Your aunt is not a bad person. But she is an uneducated person. Night school she didn't even finish. You saw in this house, my house, the finest books, the encyclopedias, everything and anything you would want to know is there. Did you see in her house one single book? No. Not even a Victrola."

That was true. I couldn't argue, or explain to her that there'd been something in that house you couldn't find in books, the sweetness of an unspoiled personality.

"Ben Kuper, my brother, when it is time for him to get married, he could pick and choose from"—she spread her arms—"from the finest, rich, educated American girls."

I don't know what was said to Ben after I had gone to bed, but when I ran into him at noon on Saturday he scowled at me as if I had turned into an enemy. The wind had shifted. No one in that household was even pretending to be friends with me.

Yet on Sunday, when I was ready to leave, my aunt handed me a birthday present: a doll, twenty inches tall, yellow hair, a china face, a stuffed-cloth body. The doll wore a white frilly dress and fake patent-leather Mary Janes. Her eyelids moved and clicked when you laid her down. "I bet they don't have anything like this in Canada," Uncle Reuben said.

"Keep it in the box," Aunt Fanny said. "The dress should not get dirty." She also handed me a clipping from the local paper to take back to my family.

> Mr. and Mrs. Reuben Springer are entertaining their niece, Miss Mildred Samuelson of Montreal, Canada. Miss Samuelson is impressed with our lively city. Mr. Springer is the proprietor of Springer's Broadway Men's Apparel Store, a leading First Street business establishment.

Though she tried to induce me to abandon my kewpie, I packed it into my valise and apologized to it for jamming down the lid. I couldn't carry her in my arms because I had that huge doll box.

It was Uncle Reuben who brought me back to Brooklyn; he said he had business to take care of in the city. "You will tell our dear once up in Montreal," he told me on the train, "how Aunt Fanneh turned herself inside out to give you a good time."

My good-bye with Ben had been aloof. He shook my hand, without a hug. It was as if both of us were being punished for I knew not what.

My birthday party Monday was not particularly pleasant either. The cake Aunt Daisy baked for me had turned out lopsided, the white icing hadn't hardened, and there was too much shredded coconut. Nevertheless, the Hitzig boys enjoyed it.

Uncle Reuben wasn't at my party, though he had stayed overnight in the house. I know all the grownups had been up late talking because I heard Reuben's loud voice coming up from the kitchen while I tried to fall asleep in Aunt Daisy's bed.

She didn't take me to the depot. A relative of my father's friends had an automobile; he drove to Brooklyn to pick me up to meet the other Montrealers at the railroad station. Aunt Daisy's good-bye to me had an absent-minded sadness to it, as if something weighing on her mind had tempered the warmth of her feeling toward me. I might have been more affected by the difference had I not been so excited by the prospect of riding in an automobile.

My visit to the States had had so many new experiences.

3 ✳

MR. MAURICE ROTHKIND requested the honor of our presence at the marriage of his sister, Sophie, to Benjamin Kuper at the Broadway Central Hotel in New York. The honor was requested of Mr. and Mrs. Samuel Samuelson *and family*.

"Leave me home," I said.

"With who?" Papa asked.

"With Bram. I'm ten and a half. I can take care of us."

"I want to go," Bram piped up. "Millie was in New York. I never was."

"New York's nothing much," I said.

"Aunt Fanny will be very insulted," Mama said. "She wants our whole family. To show off with the *mispochah*. She wrote me in a letter she is in seventh heaven: the girl is American-born, refined and educated. She plays piano; she reads books from the public liberry. And brings a nice piece money."

Papa said, "Pish-pish."

"I can't miss school," I said.

"One day you can miss. Saturday night we take the sleeper. Sunday night is the wedding. Monday Papa brings you home. Me, myself, maybe I could stay a couple days, a week, with the family. My sister Hannah wrote she heard from Daisy Papa doesn't feel too good; he has little *swindles* in his head."

My father chortled. "You bragged to me your father always was an honest man. An honest man has little *swindles* in the head?"

62

Mama frowned at him. "*Swindles* is dizziness; don't make believe you forgot already speaking Jewish. Hannah wrote it could be blood pressing. I could take him to a doctor, a professor. Kill two birdies with one stone."

Kill two birdies! What a thing to say! Two lovebirds being slaughtered. And my big mouth did it. The heat of guilty conscience suffused me. Promptly, I tried to shift the blame.

Ben, you false and fickle creature, you spooned with my Aunt Daisy, you toyed with her affections, then you jilted her. "Deserted and forsaken," like Ella—or was it Marietta?—in *Hid from the World*. Or was it Daisy jilted you and this Sophie Rothkind healed your wounds? Whichever, Aunt Fanny is, tee-hee, delighted, but I will not watch you take another for your bride. "You go," I told my parents. "That wedding's not for children, anyway."

"Fanny wrote they will have a children's table," Mama said implacably.

"And I'll sit with the Hitzig boys." I made a snoot. "I can't stand those kids."

"First cousins," Mama answered. "And very smart in school. Bram could take a good example. Even you, Millie. Your report card marks last month I wouldn't brag about. Special the arithmetic. . . . The brother of the bride, this Maurice—Morris, whoever—Fanny wrote, has fine children, too. He is a high school teacher."

"Pish-pish," Papa said.

"This time," Mama said, "I will not sew a gown for myself; I am calling in a dressmaker to make for me. For Millie, too. Fanny wouldn't need to be ashamed of Reuben's family."

"I'm going to throw up," I said.

I did. Mama followed me to the bathroom; she felt my forehead. "No fever. You ate something didn't agree."

In the morning, having discovered how helpful it was to stick your middle finger down your throat, I threw up my breakfast. Mama began to worry.

"Maybe I should give you castor oil."

"That's for rubber plants," I said.

"If you're making jokes, you are not a dying person," Mama said. "You will live. Only clean the system out." She put me on milk toast and weak tea and kept me home from school. I moped around the house, wondering should I tell my mother about Aunt Fanny's threat about over her dead body. However, if I did I'd have to tell her I had watched her sister spooning, and I'd have to ask her what a *nafke* was, and girls my age were not supposed to know about or think about certain things.

The dressmaker saved me. She arrived to measure Mama for her gown, and she brought along an American Butterick book to select the style. Mama had decided on velvet—purple, the royal color—to be trimmed with bands of fur. Not ermine, merely mink. I had never owned a velvet dress; I had always wanted one. Mama, the sly puss, saw envy in my eyes and began to think out loud: now if the seamstress cut the material this way and that, they could save enough material to make me a jumper. And with a lace blouse—

I grabbed the bait. "I'd rather have blue," I murmured. "Purple is too old for my age." The dressmaker agreed with me. Mama winked at her.

All right, they seduced me with a sapphire velvet jumper. But actually what made me agree to go was curiosity: to see with my own eyes the piano-playing paragon for whom Ben had jilted Aunt Daisy.

Bram got a new blue-serge sailor suit. Papa rented a tuxedo and a collapsible silk hat. He also bought Mama a platinum-diamond lavaliere to wear with the diamond earrings he had given her for their tenth wedding anniversary. Buying the lavaliere was a surprise; he had promised it but had halfway taken back his promise, saying maybe it would not look good, with Canadian boys going off to die in that war against the Kaiser, for people to be sporting diamonds. Yet if the jewelry store was selling them, they must expect Canadians to buy. And anyway, Mama would be wearing her diamonds down there in New York, so they couldn't cause hard feelings up in Montreal. Mama announced she didn't plan to wear her glasses at the wedding. "If the bride is beautiful, you will tell me; if she is homely, better I shouldn't see."

We went directly from the train to Brooklyn. There was no breakfast waiting at the house. In fact, Aunt Daisy wasn't out of bed. Grandpa, distraught and disheveled, his *yarmulke* askew, greeted us. "Daisy is sick, I don't know what."

"Fever?" Mama darted anxious looks at Bram and me, wondering had we blundered into measles or diphtheria.

Grandpa spread his hands helplessly. "The head hurts; the food don't stay in the stomach. . . ."

"She coughs?"

"Terrible. The whole night I couldn't close my eyes."

"So she catched a cold. All right, Papa, no more worrying. I am here; I will look after."

Mama shed her hat and coat and headed for the kitchen. "I'll make the oatmeal and the coffee, then I'll see to her. . . . No, Millie, not you. All I need is you should catch a sickness from Daisy."

I saw Aunt Daisy after Mama had sponged her, fed her milk toast and tea, changed her sheets, aired her room, and combed her hair. The person in the bed was hollow-eyed and hollow-cheeked, her freckles like rust on her milk-white skin. And she couldn't or she wouldn't smile. All she managed to say—laboriously—was, "Go to the wedding. Go," before she turned her face toward the roses on the wall.

How could we go? How could we leave her all alone? Mama pondered. "I will stay," she announced. "Sammy will take the Grandpa and the children."

I saved the situation. I reminded Mama about Mrs. Fitzsimmons, the neighbor, the one who'd taught Aunt Daisy to drop gs. She might help us out. We went next door, and Mama said, "You remember me, Mrs. Fitztsimmes? I am Ada, the oldest from the Springer girls. . . . Yeh, yeh, the one that moved to Canada." She went on to explain how we had all come down on the night train to attend a wedding. No, not immediate family, a brother of a sister-in-law. "Yeh, yeh, the wife of Mr. Reuben Springer; you remember them?" Well, in a small family, you consider relations of relations your relations, too. We had planned to sleep overnight in a hotel, because for four extras there weren't enough bedrooms in the Springer house. But when we came, early in the morning, straight from the train, we found Daisy sick abed, no one to look after her—

"I knew it, I just knew it." Mrs. Fitzsimmons interrupted Mama. "Myself did see her in her yard, hangin' out her wash, no coat on, no shawl. And takin' out the ashes, in the snow, in a summer dress. 'Daisy, darlin', you'll be sick,' I said to her. She paid me no mind. Distracted. Like somethin' was botherin'. Whatever it was, she never said one word—"

Mama interrupted *her*. "Mrs. Fitztsimmes, I come to ask a favor, two favors, it would be a *mitzvah*—that's a blessing in our language, Mrs. Fitztsimmes; the One Above Himself would reward you—if tonight, when we go to the wedding, you would keep an eye on her."

"No sooner asked than done. I love her like my own."

Mama gripped the woman's hands and squeezed them. "An angel from heaven. And Mrs. Fitztsimmes"—Mama hesitated before she asked a larger favor—"if you could find a small little space in your own house . . . I have my two children with me, this Millie you know, and our son. Supposing my sister, God forbid, has a catching sickness, the diphtheria, God forbid! If the children could sleep this night in your place, I would bring over the feather quilts we have from the old country. The children could maybe sleep on your parlor floor."

"Now, Mrs.—what is the name?—Mrs. Samuelson. No need to be upset. My son, Jimmy, he's a sailor; he is off to sea, God keep him safe from them German submarines. And there is Jimmy's room. And 'twould be no trouble, none at all, to put on the clean sheets. . . ."

Mama kissed her cheek. Her tears were rolling down. "What a darling neighbor! What a friend!"

" 'Tis my pleasure. And my duty before God," the darling neighbor said. "And I love your sister, she's a darlin' girl. Yourself and himself, Mister Samuelson, now where do you and him plan to sleep?"

"We will manage," Mama said. "A couple chairs. A couch."

In our best clothes, we went into the subway, five of us including Grandpa, and off we rode to the wedding. Uncle Reuben, a plump penguin in a tuxedo and a stiff white shirt, was waiting for us at the Broadway Central's ballroom door. "Daisy didn't come?" I thought he looked relieved. "She has a cold? Too bad. . . . The hat check is over there, Sam, no charge, everything is paid. . . . Fanneh is inside. She will introduce."

Aunt Fanny was wearing a very ordinary dark blue taffeta, over corsets pulled so tight she panted between words; her only jewelry was a gold chatelaine watch above her left breast. Though her country wasn't in the war, and wearing diamonds couldn't be out of place for her, she hadn't even a tiny lavaliere. When she saw us in our elegance of velvet, fur and lace and Mama's diamonds, her florid face got redder, and her nose went out of joint. Which was, as I now recall, my only truly happy moment at Ben and Sophie's nuptials. It made up, in a minor way, for the smirk and sniff with which she greeted me. "You see, Millie. Who was right?"

In sequence, as they happened, I'll put down some high spots. First, the Samuelsons were presented to Maurice Rothkind and Bertha, his wife. These were thin, neat, nervous people, both wearing gold-rimmed spectacles. Mrs. Rothkind told Mama, "Call me Birdie, please, everybody does." Mr. Rothkind told Papa, "It is an honor for us to have these splendid guests come from so far for our sister's wedding." Papa put on his pish-pish expression, though he didn't say the vulgar words but merely waved a deprecating hand. "To tell you the honest truth, Mr. Rothkind, I am only a ladies' tailor in Montreal." Mr. Rothkind, matching candor with candor, hurried to explain that, although he was on a high school faculty, he didn't consider himself an *echt* intellectual since he taught commercial subjects only: bookkeeping, business correspondence, et cetera. They both laughed over that.

Birdie Rothkind gushed to Mama about how pleased she was we had made the trip safely; everybody knew how dangerous it was to travel wintertime. She turned briefly to me. "We have new young friends for you." She had two daughters, Rosalind and Beatrice; I would meet them later, they were inside with the bride; their Aunt Sophie chose them for her bridesmaids, she loved them, they loved her; oh, they were going to miss Sophie, the house won't be the same. Being the perfect hostess, she even noticed Bram. "I am sorry we do not have a boy playmate for you. But, maybe, who knows? The young couple—"

She may or may not have been about to address Grandpa before her husband pinched her arm. "Birdie, don't forget Grandma Rothkind."

Birdie Rothkind led us over to an old, old woman, propped in an armchair against the wall. Her skin was brown and dried out like a mummy's; her eyes were like milk glass; her thin lips were blue; her black dress had a high neck and long skirt, as in the olden days. "This is Grandma Rothkind," Birdie said. "The happy grandma of the bride. She is rejoicing she lived to this day to see her dearest Sophie under the bridal canopy. Maurice's parents—the bride's parents, may they rest in peace—till their last days they hoped and prayed—"

Unexpectedly, Grandpa Springer plunged into the civilities. He grasped the clawlike fingers of the mummy's hand. "*Mazel tov*," he said.

The bleak eyes seemed to search his face. "Who are you?"

He was abashed. "The father from Reuben."

"Who is Reuben?"

"The brother-in-law from Ben," Mrs. Rothkind told her.

"Who is Ben?"

"Mama, Ben is the *chusen*. The bridegroom from Sophie."

"What are you telling me?" The blue mouth gaped. "Sophie found a *chusen!*"

Mrs. Rothkind changed colors, pale to blush. "Grandma is so old—Maurice says ninety-four—she forgets from one minute to the next."

My father clucked sympathetically. "They should only live and be well," he said.

"And happy," Mama added.

Suddenly, a hush descended on our little group. Aunt Fanny had borne down on us to introduce, with breathless pride, her prize package, the legendary aunt and uncle, Herschel and Lily

Goldmark. They were round and rosy-cheeked and full of smiles. She glittered with diamonds that made my mother just a poor pretender to the throne; he wore a Prince Albert, black silk vest, stiff white shirt, wing collar, and white tie. Yet with tufts of snowy hair sticking out beneath his silk high hat, he looked like Foxy Grandpa of the funny papers. Not like Mr. Millionbucks.

Mrs. Goldmark clasped my mother, lavaliere to lavaliere, crying, "Chayele, you I didn't see since your own wedding day!" She looked over Mama's head to give a quick and affectionate glance to all the Samuelsons. "Did we do a bad day's business when we brought to Brooklyn a young man from Canada?"

Mr. Goldmark flung his arm around Grandpa's shoulders. "Yankel, of you tonight I am jealous; they didn't make you dress up in a monkey suit."

Aunt Fanny steered her Uncle Herschel to the Rothkinds. She didn't bother to present the Hitzigs after they arrived—Uncle Davy in blue serge, shiny at the seat, Aunt Hannah in a batik sack, and three boys, wearing suits that were too long or too short in the sleeves and too loose at the knicker knees. My father pumped Uncle Davy's arm and scooped the boys into an all-inclusive hug. The Rothkinds, the Goldmarks, and Aunt Fanny had disappeared.

Someone cried, "Shh . . . *sha!*" Someone else cried, "Please take seats." We moved up and arranged ourselves on chairs facing a crimson-velvet bridal canopy. Then I saw Ben Kuper. His uncle, Herschel Goldmark, and his brother-in-law, Reuben Springer, were leading him, each holding an arm. Ben's face was flushed, his eyes were glazed, he walked unsteadily, lurching into place beneath the canopy.

Papa and Uncle Davy traded glances. "*Shikker,*" Papa whispered to Uncle Davy.

"Too much Moxie," I whispered to both of them. Uncle Davy goggled at me. "Well, Uncle Reuben said he was a little wild," I defended myself.

"*Sha!*" Mama hissed at me. Then musicians began to play that tune that greets a bride, and she came in.

All brides are beautiful, they say. And so Aunt Fanny said,

pressing her clasped hands against her diaphragm, exhaling, inhaling. "Sophie is *so* beautiful!" My mother, not having her glasses on, nodded to agree with her.

Ninny on your tintype. This bride was no beauty. She was bean-pole skinny, with a long nose so sharp it could puncture holes in the veil that couldn't hide a sour face. The two young girls in white China silk with wide sashes of baby blue who followed her looked happier than the bride. Her sister-in-law, Birdie Rothkind, and some other woman whom we hadn't met led her round and round the canopy, where Ben Kuper waited with glassy, bloodshot eyes.

A *chazan* began to chant. It sounded sad. Aunt Fanny whispered to Mama, "*El Mole Rachamin.* For her parents. May they rest in peace." Mama dabbed her eyes.

I began to feel sticky hot in my velvet dress in that overheated, crowded room, and so I shut my eyes and tried to shut my ears while a rabbi droned. I didn't open them until I heard a crack of breaking glass and saw Ben raise that veil and touch his lips to the pale cheek beside the long, thin nose. Around me my relatives were yelping, "*Mazel tov! Mazel tov!*" pushing back chairs, and stampeding toward the canopy. Mama seized my arm. "Come up and give them *mazel tov.*"

"I'm going to be sick," I said.

She gave me a look. "I should have left you home."

Yes. Undoubtedly.

It wasn't too bad at the children's table. The Rothkind girls were friendly. They admired my dress; I admired their dresses, saying, however, that though I thought China silk was sweet we did consider it more suitable for June than January.

Rosalind was the same age as I and in the fifth grade, too. Beatrice was twelve and smart enough to realize that, though I lived in Canada, I was not an Eskimo. She said she understood, it being cold up north, we had to wear warmer things like velvet and like mink. Tactful. Wanting to be friends. Nevertheless, not meaning to, I'm sure, right off the bat she said something that made me lose my appetite. "Uncle Ben is so handsome," Beatrice Rothkind said.

Uncle Ben. She'd got him for an uncle. I didn't even have him any longer for a friend.

She poured salt on my open wound. "What relation is he to you?"

"He's my Aunt Fanny's brother. Aunt Fanny's married to my Uncle Reuben. Uncle Reuben is my mother's brother."

Rosalind's forehead crinkled. "Why, you're not even in his family," she said.

Might have been, if I hadn't opened my big mouth. Nevertheless, I opened it again. "I know Mr. Kuper very well," I bragged. "Last summer he took me swimming at Coney Island."

"We don't go to Coney Island," Beatrice said. "We go to Brighton Beach. It's more refined."

"He took us to the Hippodrome," Rosalind said. "One day when Aunt Sophie was shopping for her furniture."

What the Hippodrome was I didn't know, but I could imagine what had taken place, Ben giving this one a little hug, that one a little squeeze, and buying ice-cream sandwiches for them. And maybe kewpie dolls for souvenirs.

A waiter towered over, balancing a tray. He set down my soup plate, spilling some, barely missing my velvet lap. "Eat," the waiter ordered me.

I spooned indifferently. I should have been famished—we'd eaten sketchily all day—but the ceremony had destroyed my appetite. The Rothkind girls, not having my problems, went straight to business, eating steadily but daintily. No slurping or speaking till their plates were empty. Then Rosalind laid down her spoon to tell me gleefully, "They have a beautiful apartment. In an elevator house. Five rooms. Right near Prospect Park. Aunt Sophie bought a walnut bedroom set."

"She didn't want a three-piece parlor suit," Beatrice interrupted. "She told Mama three-piece suits are going out of style. Odd pieces is what she's getting. Made to order. Aunt Sophie has taste."

"*Ych!* So *she* thinks," Rosalind said.

"Anyway she has packs of money. She can buy anything she likes," Beatrice said.

"Mama let her take the piano. Aunt Sophie said it was really hers; she was the only one ever played on it," Rosalind said. "She used to give us lessons. She said we would never be any good because we didn't practice."

"I'm getting her room," Beatrice said. "I won't have to share with Roz."

"We still have Great-Gramma," Rosalind said.

"*Ych!*" Beatrice said. "Who wants to live that old?"

The waiter took our soup plates, set down roast chicken, *kugel,* carrots, and green peas. The Rothkind girls devoured. I pecked, waiting till their chicken bones were stripped; then, hoping my tone of voice would not reveal too much, I said, "I suppose your Aunt Sophie loves Mr. Kuper."

The girls looked at one another. Rosalind giggled. "She'd better," Beatrice said and leaned across to me. "Mama was sure the best she'd ever get was some humpback old man." And blushed. "Mama'd kill me if she heard me repeating this, but I heard Mama telling Papa she couldn't believe her eyes when Mr. Kuper came to call. Some man brought him to our house. A man with a beard. Some man Papa met some place. We were downstairs, and we heard him introducing. 'Mr. Kuper, this is the wonderful young girl I have for you.' "

"Young!" Rosalind snickered.

"Then he came a second time on a Sunday with your Aunt Fanny and your Uncle—what's his name? The one with the Kaiser mustache—and they all had dinner at our house and then Mama said Aunt Sophie was engaged to Mr. Kuper and we should congratulate her." Beatrice pushed back her plate and rested her elbows on the table. "He gave her a ring. A tiny little diamond, just a chip. He doesn't have a lot of money, Mama told us. He's just starting out in business. His uncle, Mr. Goldmark, who is wealthy, said he'd put some money to Aunt Sophie's money to open up a store for him. Haberdashery, whatever that may be."

"Aunt Sophie wished he was a teacher—or a dentist—or at least a druggist," Rosalind said. "She was hoping she would get to marry a professional man. Uncle Ben isn't educated, really."

I couldn't bear it any longer. "He's a lovely man," I blurted.

They seemed startled by my vehemence. "He's good enough for anybody. I hope she appreciates him."

"She'd better," Rosalind said.

"She does, she does," Beatrice added. "And they'll live happy ever after."

"You hope," I said.

Bram was getting a hard time, too, from the Hitzig boys (Snooky, I'd been pleased to note, was not a wedding guest), though the badgering hadn't affected my brother's appetite. His hard time was about his sailor suit. "Militarist!" Karl had jeered at him, wondering out loud how soon Bram was going to enlist and go out on a ship to save the British Empire and the royal parasites and be blown to pieces by the German submarines, like the *Lusitania*, which was carrying ammunition. "Everybody knows it's a big lie to keep saying, 'Oh, those poor innocent passengers.'"

"We're pacifists, our family is," Eugene added. "President Wilson *says* he is. We don't believe one word of it."

"He knows the people are against the war," Karl informed Bram. "He wanted another four years in the White House. So he said he'll keep us out of it."

"'I didn't raise my boy to be a soldier,'" Walt began to sing. His voice was rather sweet; Karl shushed him sternly.

"Boys like Bram," Karl said, "end up cannon fodder. For the kings and the capitalists."

Bram kept eating, saying nothing. After all, he was barely seven, and all war meant to him was seeing parades now and then around Dominion Square.

Mama came over while we were finishing our orange ice and sponge cake. She took Bram's hand and mine. "Now we will go and say a nice *mazel tov* to the young couple," she said.

The memory of shame lasts longer than the memory of pain. I am trying not to remember our march to the head table, the fixed and mirthless smile on Ben Kuper's mouth, the emptiness of his eyes that met my mumbled "*mazel tov*." Nor the cold bony fingers his bride offered me, while I kept thinking, She's so ugly. She's ugly as sin. And I should like to forget the triumphant glower Aunt Fanny (between the mummy grandma and the brother of the bride) flung in my direction. What does stay sharp and clear in my memory is Mama's loud and cheery voice.

"Mr. Kuper, this is the first time I had the pleasure to meet you. We live far away, up in Canada. We don't come together often with our dear ones, only for a big *simcha* like this. I want to thank you for the good time you gave my daughter Millie, at Cooneyilan. She told me all about it, how nice you were to her, with the kewpie doll and everything. And I wish you and your bride a lotsa happiness and maybe sometime you will come on a trip and visit us." And then she leaned across the table and kissed—actually kissed—the bride's sallow cheek.

Luckily, we left shortly after—no more mingling, no more hypocritical pretending to be joyful. Grandpa's age and our fatigue after all-night-on-the-train were our excuse. The Goldmark chauffeur drove us back to Brooklyn in a Pierce-Arrow limousine. Bram dozed off against Papa's shoulder; I stayed enough awake to hear most of the adult conversation.

Mama: "So where did Fanny's brother find the *matzeah*? A big bargain."

Papa: "A homely girl could make a first-class wife."

Mama: "So your wife is homely? She is not a first-class wife?"

Papa (sighing): "Who else could be lucky like me? A first-class wife who is also beautiful. Like a queen you looked tonight."

Mama: "Reuben went and found the *shadchen*. Fanny made him go."

Papa: "So what is wrong? Did a *shadchen* do bad for us?"

Mama: "We were old-fashion people. From the old country we just came; we didn't have a big acquaintance here. A *shadchen* had to find the right person for you and me, everything equal on both sides."

Papa: "Who's complaining? They should only have our *mazel*."

Grandpa: "Sophie brings a nice piece money. Ten thousand dollars in the bank, Reuben told me."

Mama: "Fanny told me the Uncle Goldmark is putting up the money for a business."

Grandpa (disagreeing mildly): "Reuben told me Sophie is giving half."

Mama: "What good is the money without *mazel?* To me, that Sophie looked sickly, a consumptive. . . ."

Grandpa: "Reuben told me the family guaranteed the girl is healthy."

Mama: "Girl? A old maid. Maybe older than me."

Papa: "Maybe she didn't catch a bargain neither. Fanny's brother likes his *shnapps.*"

Mama: "If the husband is a *shikker*, the wife don't have a picnic."

Grandpa: "My Daisy should only have a little *mazel.*"

Mama: "What's the matter, my brother Reuben couldn't find somebody for his sister?"

Grandpa: "He is looking, he is trying."

The house was cozy warm; that Irish angel, Mrs. Fitzsimmons, was in the kitchen, drowsing over a newspaper. "I gave her a soft-boiled egg and strong, hot tea, and a hot-water bottle to her feet, and I looked in: she's sleeping like a babe, not one cough out of her this last hour. Now, if your young ones will come along with me . . . what time would you want me to be waking them? I'll set the alarm. . . . No trouble, no bother at all, at all. What's a neighbor for if not to help?"

We were awakened at the crack of dawn to catch the train, and so I saw Aunt Daisy only long enough to say good-bye to her. She looked like a child, propped on those goose-down pillows. In a hoarse whisper, she said, "I am sorry to make everybody trouble. I am glad your mother will stay a couple days with me." Drawing a limp hand from beneath her quilt, she offered it. "Be a good girl," she said to me. At that time I didn't know those were the last words her own mother had said to her. And I didn't know she thought that she was going to die and was hoping it would happen soon.

Mama remained in Brooklyn longer than we'd planned, two whole weeks, in fact, and Papa had to arrange for our char to come in every day to cook for us—pea soup mostly, which I used to love when we got it for a treat but came to hate when it was on the supper table practically every night. Papa went around looking worried, and not because of what Therese dished up for us but

75

because of why Mama had to stay in New York. "Bad trouble, sickness trouble in the family," I heard him tell Therese.

At last he got a letter, telling him what train Mama planned to take, and all three of us went to Windsor Station to escort her home. She looked exhausted, and not altogether from the trip. She had nursed Aunt Daisy; she had cooked and cleaned the halls, the stairs, the roomers' rooms; she had shoveled coal into the furnace, carried ashes out—chores she hadn't done in her entire married life. When she took off her coat, we saw she had lost weight, which those days was a matter for distress, since plumpness was a hall-mark of prosperity as well as of good health. Consumptives were thin; poor people were thin, not well-off people like ourselves.

"Like a hoss I worked," Mama said and paused. "Like a hoss my sister works; no wonder she got sick. A man is needed in that house."

"*Nu?*" Papa answered her.

"In his whole life did my father lift a hand?"

"Who speaks about the father?" Papa said.

Mama sighed, indicating that she understood to what he referred. "My sister is not an ordinary person. Her feelings she keeps in herself. I asked her, and I asked her many times, and only once she answered me. 'I would marry only if I loved,' she said, 'and for that it is too late.'"

"Pish!" Papa said. (The number and inflection of his pishes, I had come to know, indicated varying attitudes. One pish meant disbelief; pish-pish was derision; pish-pish-pish was mocking admiration.) "How old is your sister Daisy?"

Mama calculated silently, adding and subtracting. "A young girl yet," she lied. "Maybe twenty-seven, twenty-eight, not yet thirty years."

Papa didn't argue. "So let your brother, the big *knacker,* find for her somebody."

Mama cradled her face between her hands. "My sister is sick, she is very sick. I took her to a doctor, a big professor in New York. He said the lungs is weak, it could come to consumption."

Papa blanched. For once, he didn't have a wisecrack ready. Consumption was the dread, the horror, of their generation.

76

"The doctor said she should go to the mountains, breathe in the fresh air, eat fresh eggs, drink fresh milk, and rest herself."

"And she said?" Papa tapped the table top impatiently.

" 'Who will take care of my father?' my sister asked the doctor. More trouble." Mama rocked her head between her hands. "Papa's blood pressing is high. He must keep a strict diet, no red meat, no salt. No cigars smoking, positively. And also rest, not run around collect the rents for Herschel Goldmark. A hospital we could have in that house." She raised her shoulders, shrugging hopelessly. "Go change those two stubbren people. What I could do, I did. I made for her the *guggle-muggles,* the egg, the milk, a little cognac I put in to make her strong. For him, I boiled chicken. Like a hoss I worked. My sister said positive she cannot go to stay in the mountains. Not leave Papa by himself, not leave the house. Who would clean for the roomers, make heat and hot water, take out ashes and garbage? So I said, 'Then get a servant girl to do the heavy work.' "

"*Nu?*" Papa brightened. "The talk begins to be sensible."

"Money," Mama said. "I talked with Reuben. He complains he had to hire a salesman, pay big wages, his brother-in-law got married. And his business now is off. The war is coming to them, sure. Who knows what is going to happen there? But a little he will help. Ten dollars a month he promised. Hannah can't help nothing; Davy is a small-salary man and four boys to buy shoes—"

Papa scowled at her. "Money is the least, stop worrying. What is needed, we will send."

Mama laid her hand over his; he drew her toward him, pressed her head down on his shoulder, and when her tears began to drip, he shook out his handkerchief, saying to me with his chortling laugh, "A crazy woman, foolish, your mother is, Millie. She cries because her husband makes a little money."

Afterward, during supper (Mama cooked it, and it was delicious!), in a more cheerful mood, Mama told us she had been to Ben and Sophie's flat. "They invited for Sunday me and Fanny and Reuben—not Hannah with the boys. The furniture was beautiful; the dinner was terrible. Old-maid refreshments."

"Tea and biscuits," Papa prompted.

77

"On a doily," Mama added. "And a small piece chop meat on the plate." Her nose crinkled, in disdain. "But the dishes was pretty —not real English bone, like us, more like a imitation. And Sophie played for us on the piano. Fanny was in seventh heaven."

However, when the table was cleared, the dishes done, Mama's somber mood returned.

"My sister worries me. What got into her, I don't imagine. The Irish neighbor—that woman, Sam, is from heaven an angel, nothing is too much to do for Daisy—tomorrow I go down to the factory, pick out a beautiful suit for her. Forty-four, she says is her size. Ask, Sam, who is going to New York, to bring down the present. . . . That woman told me before Daisy catched the cold, she was acting funny, acting like she wanted to be sick."

I needed a deep hole in which to hide. All this, I had not the smallest doubt, was the consequence of my blabbering. If I hadn't told Aunt Fanny what I'd seen and what I hoped— Yet I had to stay and listen to each word my mother said and to linger, all ears and guilty conscience, whenever Aunt Daisy was discussed.

The family dinner table is where a child's attitudes are shaped. What is there discussed, or not discussed, decides the sort of adult he—or she—is going to be. At our family table, through that winter and the following spring, most conversations I remember dealt with our obligations toward our kinfolk in the States. A family is all for one and one for all. I heard that over and again.

I know Papa sent regular remittances, and I know, because he mentioned it, that the extra expense worried him somewhat. We were deep in the war: the Huns kept sinking British ships; woolens had become scarce; their price had gone up. The future was uncertain. We hoped, hurrahed, and prayed, yet we couldn't be absolutely certain our side would win the war.

There was all at once a spate of letter writing—something new for us. Grandpa wrote he'd had to fire the servant girl; she mixed the meat and milk dishes up. Daisy could manage now; she had only a small cough. What they needed was a man—to tend the furnace, carry out the ashes, do the heavy work. Naturally, this he himself couldn't do; he still had those *swindles* in his head; the doctor's medicine had not helped him much.

"So let them get rid of the damn house." Papa so seldom used profanity, we realized he was upset.

"Where will they go? Where will they live? A home they have to have."

"And it is killing them."

"From the tenants they have a little income."

"And a lot of trouble," Papa retorted. "Let them come live here, both of them."

"While Papa is alive, he needs to have his home." Mama was firm. "In Brooklyn he is a person, a landlord. Here he would be an old man, eating on our charity."

Aunt Fanny also wrote to Mama. She and Reuben had visited Daisy and Grandpa, and everything seemed fine. Reuben had taken his father to the doctor; the blood pressure was down twenty points. She was sorry she hadn't gone along; she had been thinking about giving that professor, the big-mouth, a piece of her mind, giving out a report that Daisy had weak lungs. When a girl still is single, even to hint her health is not A-one, that she is damaged goods—especially when Reuben was trying to find the right person for his sister. If, God forbid, the father died, how could Daisy manage by herself?

Even Aunt Hannah wrote. She had been over to visit Daisy and Grandpa. She had taken the boys. Daisy had enjoyed the visit, though it seemed to tire her—Walt and Snooky were so active; they ran around and made a lot of noise. Hannah thought, too, that it was a pity they were stuck with the big house, just the two of them and so much responsibility. Sam and Ada, try, try hard, to talk them into moving into a flat.

As far as I knew, Daisy didn't write, not even to answer Mama's letters. Could she, after all? Aunt Fanny had assured me she was an uneducated girl. Didn't even finish the night school.

Then, early in the new year, that fateful year of 1917 when the United States finally decided to join us in the war, Aunt Fanny wrote again: Sophie, thank God, was pregnant and she (Fanny)

79

was in seventh heaven. And Reuben was in that seventh heaven, too; he had found someone for Daisy, a Hebrew teacher, a scholar. Papa was overjoyed. Ezra Magid, the prospective groom, was a strong, good-looking young man, not interested in money, in a dowry, looking only for a good wife and a kosher home. His family—the mother, father, sisters, brothers—all were on the other side (in what kind of trouble nowadays, you could only imagine!). He had nobody here except a couple of cousins. He lived in a furnished room with a relative. The same *shadchen* who introduced Ben and Sophie had found this Ezra Magid. (And Sam is not to worry; if he can't see his way to help, Reuben will personally pay the *shadchen*'s fee.) The wedding will be before Pesach, in the father's house in Brooklyn; only the family, so they all must come. Reuben wants his dear ones present; he has a proposition to make to them. Reuben's mind was always busy, thinking about the welfare of his family. God didn't bless them with children, so the sisters and the sisters' children are their nearest and their dearest ones.

Aunt Hannah, the family cynic, put in her two cents. "So at last our father gets one religious son-in-law, a *tzaddik*. Papa gives thanks to God. Woodrow Wilson and the Kaiser he should thank. The bachelors are running quick like cockroaches to get married, they shouldn't be drafted for the war. The *shadchen* business is booming."

Grandpa also wrote, enthusiastically, for him. The One Above had heard his prayers: He had provided a fine *chusen* for his youngest daughter, a young man, strong and healthy, learned and pious.

Again, Daisy didn't write, though Mama wrote to her and told us what she'd written. "I said to my sister she should be happy our papa found for her the right person, like he found for me, and she will now have *mazel*, like it was with me. The main thing is the person should be suitable; the love comes afterward."

Papa wagged his eyebrows, making no comment.

Mama went down to the States a week early. It seemed that the simple home wedding required expert management. Aunt Fanny was inaccessible as well as unwelcome, Aunt Hannah was inept, and Aunt Daisy, the bride, was too frail to do everything herself. Mama didn't have a new gown made, and she left her diamond lavaliere in Papa's factory safe. However, she wore her eyeglasses. A simple home wedding is not fashionable.

By the time the rest of us arrived, early on Sunday morning, tired and dirty from the all-night train, the Brooklyn house was fragrant with great cooking aromas and noisy with the bustle of assistants: Aunt Hannah and her eldest boys, who had come to move the furniture.

I was amazed, and covertly delighted, to see how the boys had changed. Black-haired like their father, browned-eyed like their mother, they had always been; neat, polite, and manly they'd become. Karl was wearing longies—his first, Aunt Hannah whispered, nudging his ribs affectionately and simultaneously giving me a wink to take notice, please, this is a young man, not a snot-nose kid. I'd already seen in his eyes a certain flattering brightening, a surprised dilation of the pupils when he caught sight of me. There was a half-shy drawing back before he offered to shake hands. Eugene wasn't shy. He said right out, "Hey, the kiddo's pretty!" He was wearing glasses, which gives you clearer vision.

"Millie is a little beauty," Aunt Hannah agreed.

"Takes after her father," Papa said.

"Where's Aunt Daisy?" I inquired.

"Upstairs." A worry frown creased Mama's forehead. "She is resting. Do not bother her."

There was an aproned stranger at the kitchen sink, scouring pots. And on trestle tables that filled half the kitchen a banquet was spread: platters of roast spring chicken, stuffed *derma*, chopped liver, potato *kugel*—enough to sink a battleship—a big bowl of home-made *mandelen* for the fragrant chicken soup that simmered in the copper pots on the old coal stove. And in a special corner of its own, fenced off by polished wineglasses, was the three-tiered, white-iced wedding cake.

Mama mopped her brow with her apron. "Some work, but we did it, me and Daisy. Everything strict kosher."

"And how is the *kalah* feeling?" Papa asked.

"Tired. We came home very late last night from the *mikvah*," Mama said.

There was a sharp rap on the basement door. Eugene ran to answer it. He ushered in two portly women, wearing *babushkas* and carrying satchel pocketbooks. "We come to cut the hair," one of them announced.

Aunt Hannah flushed with anger. "He makes her wear a *sheitel!* A wig! Like in the old country!"

"*Sha!*" my mother answered her. "Papa wanted it."

"Who is getting married," my father asked belligerently, "Daisy or the father?"

"Sit down, everybody sit down in the dining room." This was Mama's way of answering him. "Hannah will bring you breakfast." She dried her hands on the kitchen roller. "I will go up with them to her." I noticed that she didn't offer the portly women tea or coffee, as she would have ordinarily to those toward whom she felt friendly. "Upstairs. Come," was all she said to them.

I stared at the ceiling, wondering what was going to happen in Aunt Daisy's room. My father and Aunt Hannah muttered to each other, somewhat incoherently.

Later that morning, we were allowed to go up to Aunt Daisy's room. It was different. The dainty bird's-eye maple furniture was gone. In its place was a dark walnut double bed, a man's walnut chifforobe, a lady's walnut dresser. "Fanny and Reuben's present," Mama told Papa. The bed was covered with a white Marseilles spread. On it, on a sheet of tissue paper, lay two long, lustrous braids of earth-brown hair.

I looked at them and looked away and back again, because the only other thing to see was Daisy, and I could not bear to see what had been done to my darling aunt. A cap of artificially glistening dark-brown hair, center-parted, matronly, had been fitted to her skull, to a head that seemed all bones. The tiny nose looked pinched; the skin, drawn taut, was as white as the Marseilles spread. And her eyes were red-rimmed, as after steady weeping.

Yet she let me hug her, as of old, and she hugged me back,

kissed me, and kept holding me until Mama said, "She has to rest. Come, everybody. Get to work."

Make no mistake, a simple home wedding is a backbreaking enterprise. The Hitzig boys and my brother, Bram, ran in and out, to and fro, fetching chairs, whatever the upstairs roomers and the neighbors on both sides could spare, carrying these and the dining-room chairs up to the parlor, where my father aligned them in rows.

Papa and the boys brought table leaves from the cellar and stretched the dining table. Mama concealed the wood with bed sheets, covered the sheets with a handsome heavy linen cloth, embroidered, she announced, by her own mother's golden hands. In the middle of the table, she placed her mother's candlesticks, so highly polished they seemed to be throwing sparks. We could see emotion bubbling in her—the cheeks flushing, the facial muscles quivering, the eyes glazing, filling up. Needing the safety valve of something to be furious about, she blurted out, "That chandelier! The gas! Tell them, Sam, put in the electric; you will pay for it."

"Old-fashion people," Papa said. He was oddly subdued as if this hubbub in the house contained something alien and, in its way, offensive to him.

Mama brushed her eyes with the back of her hand. "Millie, help me set the table. Let me count how many we will be? Reuben, Fanny. Fanny's brother, Ben, his Sophie. Four—"

"Here? At Daisy's wedding?" I couldn't help myself.

"Why not?" Mama answered coldly. "They invited us to theirs. . . . Hannah, Davy, the four boys, makes ten. My father makes eleven. The Samuelsons, four more, is fifteen. Ezra . . . he has two cousins and their wives he is bringing. That makes twenty. Right, Sammy? And the rabbi and whoever Papa brings from his *shul* to make up the *minyan*."

"And Daisy," I said.

"You know, I almost forgot Daisy," Mama said.

"I didn't," Papa said.

Mama didn't hear or notice him. "Too many for this table. We will fix for the children in the kitchen. They will come in here after eating. Reuben wants to make a little speech. He has a proposition to make to the family."

"How much will it cost me?" Papa asked.

She ignored him again. "The Goldmarks are not coming. They are in Mount Clemens. Lily Goldmark drinks the water for her gallstones. . . . Millie, napkins goes inside the glasses. Watch me, how I fold. See! Stand up in the glass, open up the corners, like a flower. The Goldmarks sent a Liberty bond, one hundred dollars, for the wedding present. . . ."

Karl and Eugene traded glances. Hannah held a warning finger to her lips. "No war talk. No *Sozialismus*. This is a wedding."

"Fanny wanted Sophie's family. The Rothkinds. I said there is too many already. I bet she brings them anyway."

Hannah said, "Come in the kitchen, whoever is hungry. We can *nosh* a little."

The day extended into afternoon. Uncle Davy arrived with Walt and Clarence, called Snooky still, because it didn't seem appropriate to call a chubby, giggly little monkey Clarence. Aunt Hannah hustled both of them into the bathroom to make peepee and wash up after the subway trip. Next the Samuelsons took turns sponging and changing clothes in the bathroom. (No bathing, Mama warned us sternly; the hot water is needed for the dishes.) Then Karl and Eugene washed and brushed their hair and put on jackets.

Aunt Daisy's door remained shut, though Mama, trailing the scent of her lily-of-the-valley talcum, kept popping in and bringing out bulletins: "She is weak from fasting." . . . "She tried on the veil. It is beautiful." . . . "I have to take a couple stitches in the dress. Daisy got terrible thin."

Primped and scrubbed and restless, we milled in the cupboard-lined passageway between the bedroom and the parlor until Mama emerged from Daisy's room and shooed us away. "Downstairs, everybody. The bride is coming out to bathe herself."

We strolled through the kitchen to the yard—Bram and I and the older Hitzig boys (Walt and Snooky, hand in hand, tagged after us), and we marched around and around the rectangle of grass and talked about going to school and what we planned to do when we grew up.

Karl said he was just now finishing first year high. I said that was remarkable since he wasn't yet Bar Mitzvah. Karl said he wasn't having a Bar Mitzvah; his family didn't believe in it—it was just a racket to get fountain pens for kids, and he already had a fountain pen. Eugene said Karl knew more than most boys of thirteen, even fourteen years; he was in Townsend Harris High, where only the brightest boys were enrolled. Loyally, Karl said he was sure Eugene would also get in there, the kid was no dumbbell; did I know he was already earning spending money by tutoring the neighbors' kids in long division and fractions? Eugene said math didn't really interest him, science did; he'd already bought himself a microscope; he'd probably be a doctor. Karl said, naturally, he was also planning on college; he expected to be a lawyer, to defend people like Bill Haywood or Tom Mooney; you didn't make a lot of money defending those people—your reward was serving your ideals. Since Bram and I didn't know who those people were, we kept silent, listening, awed.

All at once, behind us, Walt began to chant: "Biddlum sitting on a sturbcone gooing a chad of wum. Along came a big molicepan and said let me goo your wum? Ninny on your tintype said the biddlum."

Bram swung around, puzzled. "What's he saying?"

Walt, shrugging, said, "Can't you understand plain English?" and Eugene gave him a friendly shove.

"Pig Latin. Little bum sitting on a curbstone." And giggled. "Walt's a poet and he doesn't know it."

Karl said, "He should be a poet. He's named after one. Who you're named after is supposed to inspire you." He puffed his chest out. "Karl Marx, who I'm named after, was a great man. The greatest of his century."

"What do you plan to be?" Eugene asked my brother. Bram said he hadn't thought about that much; maybe his father would take him in his business.

"I suppose you don't have any idea what you'd like to be,"

85

Karl said to me. I recalled how he'd badgered me when we were kids up in the Laurentians, and I said I certainly knew what I'd like to be: I'd like to be a queen and have people bowing down to me.

Karl dropped to his knees, right there on the grass, and said, "Your Majesty! The Queen of Sheba!"

I blushed, and Walt giggled, and I said, "Get up, idiot, you're getting your pants dirty."

He got up, brushing his knees, but quite seriously he went on to say, "Queen or no, first you ought to get an education. You should plan to go to college. Lots of girls do, nowadays. If you would move down to New York—"

Eugene jabbed his brother's ribs. "Karl thinks you're the cat's meow," he said. It was Karl's turn to blush.

Then we heard Aunt Fanny's strident voice, calling from the kitchen doorway. "Children, come inside, say hello. Uncle Reuben is here."

Uncle Reuben, who had been announced, wasn't *here* in the kitchen, but Sophie Kuper was, and the bride of the Broadway Central looked terrible. A bean pole to begin with, now she was fat, but in one place only, in the middle. The bulge was covered with a kind of dark wool apron on a dark wool dress. Her long nose was shiny red, and her eyes were sunk in purple hollows. "I made your acquaintance at my wedding," she said to me politely, but we didn't kiss. A sister-in-law of an aunt-in-law doesn't require cheek pecking unless you happen to be friends.

Aunt Fanny said, "Sit, Sophie, rest," and looked around for a chair.

"Upstairs," Eugene said helpfully. "All the chairs are up." We followed—we watched her haul herself up the staircase. Fanny seated her on the parlor sofa, and there she sat, alone and dismal, the first wedding-guest-in-waiting. I didn't see Ben. Apparently he hadn't come with her. For that I was grateful.

But I did see Uncle Reuben. He had Papa pinned against the wall in the cupboard corridor, and so absorbed was he in his monologue to Papa he gave me just an absent-minded shoulder pat. When I sidled over to my father, Papa hugged me hard. "Where were you, little sweetheart?" He seemed relieved I'd turned up to interrupt, but Uncle Reuben just kept talking.

"The father is not young, he is not well, we must be prepared...."

Papa, who was listening with his how-much-will-this-cost-me? air, gave me a gentle shove. "Go, sweetheart, go talk to your cousins."

Their conversation broke off, anyway, because Grandpa arrived just then, not through the basement entrance but directly to the parlor floor, by way of the front staircase. He ushered in an entourage of graybeards, all wearing broad-brimmed black felt hats. Papa and Uncle Reuben hurried forward. "Sammy! Reuben!" Grandpa scolded. "Hats!" Papa looked annoyed; Uncle Reuben looked abashed. Grandpa saw me, but he didn't greet me or present me to the bearded gentlemen. (One, I gathered, through the big ears we little pitchers have, was the rabbi.) He led them through the cupboard corridor, back to his bedroom.

"You see," Uncle Reuben told my father, "he is a very happy man. What he always wanted, now he gets, a religious son-in-law," and added, "Let us find our hats, he shouldn't be ashamed of us. Where is Davy Hitzig? Does he have a hat?"

The upstairs doorbell rang. I answered it and opened the front door for a brawny, black-bearded man and two middle-aged couples, none of whom I'd ever seen before. "Here is the *chusen*," one of the women said. "We are the cousins." Thus it fell to me to welcome Daisy's bridegroom, tongue-tied and with a twinge of fear, because Ezra Magid was overawing; his bulk and his shifting, darting eyes intimidated me.

"They're expecting you," I managed to say before I fled to call my father, who would summon Grandpa or whoever was supposed to welcome them, then to find myself a refuge with the Hitzig boys. By instinct, rather than by thought-out reasoning, I had come this afternoon to realize that my cousins might be a bulwark against Uncle Reuben and Aunt Fanny—against Grandpa, too. Not just because they were clever, but because they didn't care. Being poor and irreligious, they already were beyond the pale. The family couldn't bully them.

The sun went down. The gas lamps were kindled in the parlor. Silver candlesticks appeared from somewhere and were lighted on the table near the mantel. A wine bottle, two glasses, and a linen napkin were set out there. And wedding guests arranged themselves on the close-packed chairs.

A red-velvet canopy was unfurled. My father, Uncle Reuben, and two of Grandpa's entourage each took a stick to hold it aloft. Ezra Magid took his place beneath it; Grandpa and the rabbi stood in front, waiting for the bride. Mama and Aunt Hannah led her in, a stiff-jointed doll, her face blurred by the white mist of the veil. They walked her around and around, the seven times, holding her arms. Twice she swayed and faltered—I was afraid she might fall —before they placed her under the canopy alongside her groom. He was tall and she was small. "Mutt and Jeff," my clown-cousin Walt whispered. "*Sha!*" someone hissed at him. Grandpa's friends, black-bearded, black-hatted, surrounded the canopy. I could no longer see the bride.

The rabbi began the chant that mourns the dead. My mother dabbed her eyes. Seeing her, I groped for my own handkerchief. The groom's mouth was open, making singing motions. Yes, that high-pitched voice probably was his, and it sounded rather sweet.

The rabbi stepped closer to the canopy; his voice, alone, was heard, droning on and on. Bored, I began to wriggle like Snooky on his father's lap. Then, for the first time, I noticed Ben. When he'd come I didn't know, and how he'd dared to come I couldn't guess. Yet here he was beside his Sophie on the couch, with Aunt Fanny on the other side of him. But this was not the Ben I'd known two years ago; this man looked old and worried, the juice of playfulness drained out of him. Why did I, at that instant, in my mind's eye, see a merry-go-round, Ben astride a tiger, leaning out, to grab a brass ring for a free ride? Anyway, everything is straightened out. He is married; she is being married; no one is left out. All four of them are going to live happily ever after, I suppose. I hope.

The droning ended. I saw the groom lift Daisy's veil, touch his mouth to her cheek. I believe I saw a shiver racing through her, but maybe I imagined this. The shiver might have been my own if those whiskers had brushed me. I heard the crackle of the stamped-on glass, the yelps of *"mazel tov,"* and everyone was getting up and pressing forward to congratulate the pair. By the time I came up front, Aunt Daisy was sobbing in her father's arms, and he was stroking her back and murmuring, *"Mein kind, mein kind."* My mother took Daisy's arm to lead her off, telling whoever was near, "She'll be all right, a little weak from fasting." The groom stood by himself, towering but pale, perhaps from fasting, too. He's my uncle now, I thought. I ought to kiss him and say *mazel tov.* I won't. I can't. Not yet.

Instead, I joined my cousins. We carried chairs downstairs, placed them around the extended dining table, and helped Uncle Davy and Aunt Hannah set up the children's table on sawhorses in the kitchen.

Mama, Aunt Hannah, and Aunt Fanny bustled in and out of the kitchen, serving food. Walt cut Snooky's chicken and mopped up what Snooky spilled. Karl, Eugene, and I tried to work up a conversation, but it wasn't possible with traffic moving in and out. "Some circus, eh, kiddo?" Eugene said.

Mama came to the kitchen door. She wigwagged for us to go into the dining room. "Reuben is going to make a speech," she said.

We arranged ourselves against a wall, a phalanx facing our elders, Walt holding Snooky's hand, Snooky holding a chicken drumstick he'd refused to leave behind. We watched our uncle rising from his chair, one seat removed from the bridal couple. He rose a bit unsteadily, gripping the chair back. His face was red from the room's heat or too much wine. My father struck a water tumbler smartly with his fork, commanding silence.

Uncle Reuben's mustache and his heavy eyebrows bristled. He hawked to clear his throat and gulped to swallow phlegm. "My dear once," he began, "this is for me a werry heppy occasion." He twiddled with the seals on his watch chain. "I should maybe speak in Yiddish so the older people all would unnistand. But there are young ones standing here, back there by the wall. Look at them, everybody, how beautiful and smart they are—I want them special to unnistand what I have to say. Because for them and their future it is important."

89

He paused to clear his throat again.

"It is for me a wunnerful occasion to be here in this house, enjoying the wedding of my baby sister to the learned and high-talented Ezra Magid. Daisy—Dvorele—and Ezra—from today you are my brother, Ezra—to the both of you I wish the highest heppiness." He raised a wineglass, veering toward the bridal pair. Daisy did not lift her head; the groom stared at him, expressionless. "I wish for you long life and many children." He touched his wineglass to his lips. "Children! This is the main thing in life." He set the wineglass down. "My dear wife, Fanneh, and myself, we have not been blessed. So all the young once of the family, those beautiful young people, you can see for yourselfs standing up, decorating this room, them we hold dear, and we worry about their future like they were children of ourselfs."

Again he halted, possibly waiting for applause. All anybody heard was Snooky saying, "Wally, take my bone. I don' wan' it any more." Uncle Reuben harrumphed to silence him before he began again.

"It was me, myself, that met my sisters, my dear once, on Ellis Island, greenhorns coming off the ship. And me that brought them in a horse and carriage to this house. A home my Fanneh and myself made ready to get them settled in the *goldene medina*. This house. This home. Here in this house, my oldest sister, Ada, met a wonderful young man, who came down all the way from Canada, looking for a wife. And in this house they got married. And the One Above has blessed them with prosperity. They make a fine living, thank God, and they raise a lovely family—a hensome boy and a beautiful girl, a queen."

Eugene poked my ribs. "God save the queen!" I poked him back, whispering my father's favorite "Pish!" Uncle Reuben glanced in our direction and crossed his finger on his lips.

"And so, when Fanneh Kuper said she will be my wife, where did we live our first year while we were struggling and saving every penny to make good? We lived here in this house. The Springer femily home. And Daisy—Dvorele we used to call her when our sainted mother was alive—she stayed in this house, taking care of the father, who is not young any more, looking after him like a little mother. So now she has somebody else to take care of. And him to take care of her. In this house, this home, this Springer femily home, where we have come togedder all of us and enjoyed an enjoyable occasion. The second wedding in our family home—the first was our oldest sister, and now it is the youngest. And my sisters, all togedder, have made for us a banquet, like the finest caterers."

He had begun to sweat. He had to stop to unbutton his vest and mop his forehead with a napkin. Also, he had begun to bore his audience—chins and cheeks were propped by elbows all around the table. Grandpa seemed to be dozing—his head jerked now and then, forcing himself awake; my father drummed the table top; Uncle Davy was busy rolling little heaps of crumbs; only Aunt Fanny, at the table's curve, sat bright-eyed, expectant. She had Ben and Sophie next to her.

The throat was cleared again, the napkin dropped. "Now I come to the reason why I am standing here in front of all of you to make a spitch. I have a proposition to propose. My dear wife, Fanneh, who is my partner in every single thing, we have talked this proposition over, and we have decided this is a correct thing to do, and now in this evening when we are all togedder, celebrating an important occasion, is the time to bring it up and get it going. The proposition I want to propose is we organize ourselfs to bring our near and dear once close together for now and for forever. Amen. The proposition I propose is we create here, now, the Springer-Kuper Family League or the Springer-Kuper Family Circle, whichever one you want to call it. Fanneh said we should call it the Springer Family Circle, but I said no, Kuper belongs in the name—you, Fanneh, when you were only a young girl, a kid, you found for us this house, this home, this shrine-to-be. We want your family's name in our Circle. And your brother, Ben, will be in it, too, and Sophie and all the wonderful children they will bring into this world."

I don't know whether Ben and Sophie became ecstatic at this prospect, because Snooky was jiggling up and down, repeating, "Wally, I hafta make—Wally, I'm gonna—" And Walt, hustling him out of the room and their shoes clattering on the steps, distracted me so that I missed several sentences, which was luck for me, because Uncle Reuben was no orator, and the room was steamy hot. When he caught my attention eventually, he was explaining why we had to have that Family League.

"To help one annudder, with advices, with encouragement— even, when and if it is needed, with financial assistances." He turned to look directly at Aunt Hannah; I saw her jaw jut forward bellicosely. "We have some smart young fellers in this family. Maybe they have some funny ideas now, not practical, that they will outgrow when they get a little older and they know the value of a dollar. They might want to go in college, to be doctors, to be lawyers, we could all be proud of them. Money help they could use to get them started. The Springer-Kuper Family League—or Family Circle, whichever name you call it—would be here to help them out. Heh, Karl! Eugene! What do you say now to my proposition?"

Both boys were red-faced, looking furious. I answered Uncle Reuben for them, muttering, "Pish!"

"Hey, Millie, what did you say? You feel bad I didn't mention out your name? A girl like you wouldn't need no college money. Maybe only from the Family League a nice wedding present."

I was blushing now, as angry as my cousins. Uncle Reuben heehawed like a jackass.

"Anyhow, that is for the future. I bring up another point. Maybe this is not the exact right moment to bring this matter up in a time of *simcha*. But a Family League must think ahead and be prepared. Like our President Wilson tried to get us good-prepared to fight the Hun over there, only certain redicals—" He stared at Uncle Davy, who glowered so portentously that Uncle Reuben took to twiddling watch-chain seals for whatever time it took for Davy's wrath to simmer down. "So, my dear once, what I'm getting at is the Family League, as soon as it is organized—I myself would be willing to act as chairman or secretary or treasurer or whatever you would want, to get it started—what we should do right away is buy a piece of property—okay, Sam, you call it a cemetery plot; I say a piece of property—a Springer-Kuper piece

92

of property. Where our dear once, when the Almighty sends for them, who can know how soon—" His gaze was directed now toward Grandpa, sitting straight, though with eyes closed. "This should be our first piece of family business. I talked it over just before with Sam, my brother-in-law from Canada. In many things Sam is a practical feller, only here he talked a little skeptic. He says, for himself, it could happen he would pass away up there in Montreal; why should he buy a property in Brooklyn? I explained him, I made him unnistand—"

Papa scraped back his chair. "Enough, Reuben." His voice was loud and unusually harsh. "This is not the place, the time. You want a Family Circle, have a Family Circle. You want to be a president, be a president; I give you gladly the privilege."

I helped Mama and Aunt Hannah clear the table; they washed the glasses and the silverware, stacked the plates, before Aunt Hannah decided the hour was late, she and Davy had to take the children home, they had that long ride to the Bronx. Mama said, Go ahead, she'd do a little more then come back early the next morning and finish up; she didn't want Daisy to have to wash dishes on her wedding night—it was too bad they hadn't arranged for the helper to stay after the dinner. They told each other Daisy's dress and veil had been beautiful, and then they started to cry on one another's shoulders until Aunt Fanny came in to announce that she and Reuben would have to be leaving; they'd have to hurry to catch the last train to Grady's Mills, Reuben had to get up early to open the store, and Ben and Sophie would be leaving, too—didn't we want to say good-bye?—she expects in a month, they didn't want to come, it was too much for her, but she, Fanny, made them come out of respect for Reuben. Sophie wants a boy, a name-after her father. And how did the *chusen* impress us?

"A good voice," Aunt Hannah said.

"Papa Springer is in seventh heaven," Aunt Fanny told her.

They were gone, Ben and Sophie with them, by the time we three emerged from the kitchen. Ben hadn't spoken one word to me, not hello or good-bye. My Hitzig cousins did say good-bye and with enthusiastic handshakes. I said I hoped I'd see them soon again and please come up to visit us.

When Mama and I went upstairs, we found the bride and groom together on the sofa in the parlor, making conversation with his cousins. Daisy's veil was off. She looked ghastly pale, I thought. Grandpa and his cronies were off in a corner, talking in Yiddish, and Grandpa, too, looked ghastly, as he had the right to, being old, and with those little *swindles* in his head. Bram was snoozing on the golden chair I'd earmarked for my own. Papa shook him awake, and we all hugged Aunt Daisy, shook hands with the groom, and got blank, bleary glances from his peculiar eyes. Daisy rose and followed us out of the room. She clung to my mother with a kind of desperation. Mama said, "Dvorele, be happy," and, "Don't work tonight. Tomorrow Millie and I will come early to clean up."

Outside the house Papa spat furiously on the pavement. Mama didn't rebuke him. We walked in silence down the street, looking for a taxi. In the cab, riding to the hotel where we were to spend the night, my parents talked a little.

Mama said, "Hannah and Dave were insulted. They understand what Reuben meant. They are the poor relations. The family might need to give them charity."

"Your brother, the fat *putz!*" Papa said. "He knows the old father's health is not good. So a Family League he needs, to make sure he won't need to put up the whole sum to buy a plot."

"*Sha.*" Mama placed her hand over his mouth. "My father will live to a hundred-twenty years."

"From your mouth to God's ears," Papa said. "Tomorrow, I get home, I send Reuben a check for the down payment."

In my presence they said nothing whatsoever about Daisy and her groom, though I kept thinking about them, about her so pale and sad—and shorn—left alone in that house with Grandpa and those bearded strangers and that Ezra Magid with the peculiar eyes. I wished someone had told me that she loved him dearly or that he was in love with her.

Papa and Bram left us very early to catch the train. Mama decided to rest in bed later than usual; she'd had trouble falling asleep last night, she told me, in the strange bed, with her bones and head aching. "Papa and I talked a long time," she said.

"About what?" I asked.

"Not children's business," Mama said.

The Brooklyn house was dusky and quiet when we got there close to noon. The borrowed chairs had all been stacked in one corner of the dining room, and we heard dishwashing noises in the kitchen. Sure enough, Aunt Daisy was at the sink. A white towel was bound around her head; her movements were jerky, as though she was numb.

"I told you not to," Mama scolded. "I said I would come finish up."

"I have to do something," Daisy said.

"Where is Papa?"

Her shoulders rose. "Maybe in *shul*."

"And Ezra?" Mama looked toward the ceiling.

Again, the shoulders rose. "Maybe sleeping."

Quickly, Mama said, "Millie, what you should do is carry the chairs to the neighbors. We made a mistake to let Hannah's boys go before they took back the chairs."

"I'll show you which goes to who." Aunt Daisy brightened a little, pleased and relieved, I think, to have us in the house.

And so, for an hour and more, I dragged chairs, to the neighbors, both sides, and up two flights, three, to the roomers' rooms, while in the kitchen Mama and Aunt Daisy washed the dishes and talked out their hearts. What they said to one another that morning, I never did find out. All I know is that during the long conversations both of them did considerable crying, because when I saw them after my chore was finished, their eyes were red and their cheeks moist. "Now, go upstairs, Millie, wash your hands," Mama ordered me.

I was coming from the bathroom, going through the long, dark, cupboard-lined passage to the parlor, when I heard footsteps behind me. I turned. A huge man figure loomed in the passage, filling it. The man took hold of my shoulders; he swung me full around. He stroked my hair, my face; his big hands began to crawl, over my chest, my belly, down, down, down. He raised my skirt. I wriggled, squirmed, and tried to pull away. One hand held my shoulder tightly; the other, with a swift and sudden motion, opened up his pants. And he pushed a swollen penis hard against my body. A scream started in my throat—his hand covered my mouth.

Terror gave me strength. I wrenched myself free and ran. Through bead portieres that jingle-jangled, into the full light of the parlor. There I stood an instant, shaking, before fear drove me toward the stairs. He'll follow me. Be quick before he catches up.

I managed to get down and, insane with terror, I gripped the heavy brass pestle and held it brandished, waiting in the dining room. If he comes, when he comes, I'll brain him. I will kill him with this pestle.

He didn't come. I let the pestle drop into the mortar. Mama heard the clang. She looked in. All she noticed was my pallor. "Carrying chairs was too much for you," Mama said. "Sit down. Take a rest."

I said, "Get finished, Mama. I want to go home." But I knew I could not tell her why. I could not tell her because those days you did not tell your mother things like this. And if I told her, Aunt Daisy might find out that the man to whom she was married had done this shameful thing to me. And if they faced him with what I had tattled and he said it wasn't true, they might call me a dirty-minded kid.

Early in July we got a telegram. Mama began to shiver before she opened it; everybody knew telegrams were dispatched only to convey bad news. "My papa," she faltered. "It's the end."

"Open it," my father said.

Mama tore the yellow envelope. "From Reuben," she said.

"Read," Papa said.

"EZRA DROWNED CONEY ISLAND. FUNERAL TOMORROW. COME AT ONCE," she read.

I began to laugh.

"Stop it, Millie. It's no joke." She slapped me across the mouth. I started to bawl. She huffed off, to find a black dress in her closet and pack a valise, but Papa put his arms around me.

"Why did you laugh, Pussycat? What got into you?"

I kept on crying.

96

"Sweetheart, Mama didn't mean to hurt you. She was all upset. Daisy is her dear, loving sister. They are like one, the three sisters. She is all choked up with sorrow for her sister Daisy."

"Good riddance to bad rubbish," I muttered.

"What did you say, Millie? Why did you say it? You never even knew the person," Papa said.

I let my breath out in a long, sobbing sigh. "God knew him," I said.

There wasn't much talk after my parents returned from New York. What they did say seemed cryptic to me.

From Mama: "He was a strong swimmer."

From Papa: "With the crowd hollering—"

Mama: "He got excited, he forgot how to swim."

Papa: "Good we already bought the plot. Reuben didn't want. He said who could be sure—"

Mama: "My father gave permission."

Papa: "Ezra wanted a home. So now he has a home. With the Springer-Kuper family."

Mama: "A funeral in the house. *Ai, ai.* First weddings, next a funeral. *Ai.* I was a little surprised at Daisy, how she took it, I don't know. The shock. She will feel it after."

Then she brightened and addressed herself to me.

"Fanny's brother, Ben—you remember him?—his Sophie gave birth to a boy. Arnold, they call him, a name-after Sophie's father, Aaron. Fanny is in seventh heaven. She has another baby to give prickly heat." By the way she'd turned the conversation around so fast, I got the impression that the family was less than grief-stricken over the transfer of Ezra Magid from the Springer-Kuper Family Circle to the Springer-Kuper Family Plot.

Before the year ended, Grandpa joined him in the plot. I didn't go down for that funeral either, although when I heard the news I managed to shed some respectful tears. I had not hated Grandpa. Nor had I loved him. The truth was I had been afraid of him. That mysterious authority that emanated from him had been as troubling to me as the stench of his cigars. And not precisely knowing why, I held him to blame for what Ezra Magid had done to me. He'd welcomed that filthy pig into our family; he'd chosen that monster to marry my Aunt Daisy.

As my anger seethed, it grew. And became distrust of older people, generally. My parents? Yes. They don't know everything, they cannot know because I haven't told them certain things that I alone know.

When Daisy came to us for Pesach, her hair had grown out and she wore it in a short bob. Bobbed hair was just coming into fashion. My aunt was up-to-date.

As always, I was glad to be with her, though now I felt constrained, since I had come into my teens freighted with a distressing secret, centering around her. A shame had sullied both of us, a shame too horrible for me to mention it.

Daisy brought us snapshots of Ben's baby boy and spoke of Ben and his child so fondly that I felt even worse. Had it not been for me and my foolish tongue, that might have been her baby.

4 ✼

ON A SATURDAY NIGHT in June my cousin Karl introduced me to Jay. It was on the Hotel Astor Roof, at a precommencement splurge by members of the class of 1925 of the College of the City of New York. Dance orchestra. Cover charge. Hip flasks around.

Our table, however, was ginger ale straight, for Karl and me, Karl's friend, Morry, and Morry's girl, Ruth. Morry and Ruth wore horn-rimmed spectacles and smoked cigarettes. Morry was amiable, though he did not ask me to dance. Ruth had decided I was Miss Rich-bitch, slumming. Her hostility was visible. She'd gained that impression, I chose to believe, from the way I was dressed, in a "formal," my first, of sapphire chiffon, made by my aunt. "The color is squisit for you," Aunt Daisy had said, while she fitted and pinned. "You'll be the prettiest girl at the party."

Did it occur to you, dearest aunt, that being the prettiest girl at a party can make trouble, too? The other girls, being jealous, are sure to resent you; hence to keep peace in each twosome their escorts will have to ignore you, while your escort is embarrassed because you're conspicuous, overdressed.

Moreover, I had compounded the original blunder. I'd dropped in at Wanamaker's and bought long white kid gloves. Back home young ladies wore long white gloves with formals. However, this wasn't back home; this was New York and the celebration a once-in-a-lifetime extravagance by boys who squeezed silver dollars till the eagle screamed.

99

Morry's girl was suitably dressed. She wore an "afternoon" of black crepe, with iridescent beads at the neck. It reeked of moth balls.

Karl hadn't warned me—he was too intellectual to concern himself about how his girl should be dressed. It was the curl of Ruth's lip and her loud whisper, "Should I curtsy, Morry?" that told me I'd made a *faux pas*. I shucked off the gloves as soon as I'd taken my seat, but the damage was done. No one except Karl asked me to dance, and my cousin's talents were not in his feet.

My slippers were mashed, my toes were sore, my disposition curdled by the time Jay meandered over to us. He greeted Karl and Morry, whom he knew; they greeted him: "Hiya, Jake!" He eyed me. I noticed that sharpening of pupils that tells a girl a man likes what he sees.

"Who have we with us tonight? Royalty?"

Karl was scowling. He seemed reluctant to introduce us. At last: "Mildred Samuelson, Jake Barrymore Bernstein," adding, "Jake is our gift to Broadway."

Jay pressed his hand to his middle, bowing. "My pleasure, Princess." His voice was resonant, rich. He pulled a chair over and straddled it behind me. I perked; the evening was coming alive. He sniffed at my hair. "Shalimar." A statement, not a query. He noticed the gloves—"You wear these, Princess?"—and reached across my bare shoulder to pick them up, to fondle them sensuously. "White gloves at the Astor. Good title. Let's write a song." He dropped the gloves into my lap. "Put them on, Princess. I crave elegance." Before I could say yes or no, the orchestra started a fox trot. Jay scraped back his chair. "My dance, I believe."

I looked at Karl, for consent—it's a courtesy you owe your escort. He scowled again, though he nodded yes. "Watch your step, Millie," he said.

I didn't need to. I was a good dancer; Jay was better. He danced as if he'd invented the art, with natural grace and perfect rhythm, shoes where they belonged—on his feet, not mine—and he held me the way I prefer to be held, no sweating palm on my

100

spine, no bumping against my bosom, no cheek-to-cheek. Yet all the while he kept smiling an odd, aloof half-smile, as though reserving judgment about me. Likewise, I about him.

His face was piquant rather than handsome: a pointed chin; hazel eyes, bright and intense; mouth full-lipped and mobile, though by no means gross; dark hair untidy, a forelock straggling down a high forehead; and conspicuous ears. There was about him a bold playfulness that made him arresting and therefore attractive to me. He had on white flannels and a navy-blue jacket, rather warm for an evening in June in New York, though in its way appropriate for occasions like this. In all candor and modesty, I have to say we were the best-dressed pair on the floor.

The music stopped. We stood clapping for an encore. "Where do you live, Princess?" he asked.

"Montreal. Canada."

"Aha!" Tapping his temple. "The gloves. Climate, *n'est-ce-pas?* Visiting?"

"Going to college. Barnard."

"Live in the dorm?"

"No. In Brooklyn."

His jaw fell. "That does it. We can't have a date."

" 'Nobody asked you, sir,' she said," I said.

"I do the asking, when, as, and if," he replied.

The orchestra wasn't playing the encore. Strolling back to the table, he tried to explain. "I never date girls who live in Brooklyn. Because I live on the Heights—Washington Heights, if you know where that is. Take a girl home to-hell-and-gone in Brooklyn, ride all the way back to the Heights—" He spread his hand in an eloquent shrug. "Waste your youth on the subway."

"Oh," I said airily. "My date always stays overnight."

He gave me a sharp, calculating glance. "I should have guessed."

The truth, the absolute truth—but torture me, sear with white-hot pokers, I will not tell you, Jake Barrymore B.—is that the only young man who has taken me out this year in New York has been Karl, on Saturday nights, and it's the most natural thing in the world for him to bring me back to Aunt Daisy's house where I live and to sleep overnight on the parlor sofa. She would have the couch made up with fresh sheets, as well as sandwiches, cake, and cocoa for two, waiting in the kitchen. In the morning, she'd prepare an elaborate breakfast, after which Karl would dash to the subway, off to the Bronx, to do his homework. A prodigy, an intellectual giant, he had romped through college as he had through high school, and Columbia Law had said yes to him.

"What's this about Broadway and you?" I asked Jay.

"Yes. No. Perhaps." He made a snoot, belittling himself. "You like the theater?"

"Very much."

"Me, too," he said.

Karl was mooning over his sandwich crusts when we returned to the table. Jay asked Morry would he mind pushing his chair closer to Ruth's. Morry said he would mind, yet he pushed. Jay wedged a chair in beside mine. Karl poured ginger ale. Jay produced a flask.

"Ginger for the ale?"

"Rotgut! Don't touch it, Millie!" An order from Karl.

"Don't worry, I won't. I go for real stuff. Weaned on quality, dear."

Jay's eyebrows twitched. "The princess is full of surprises," he said.

The orchestra started again. Karl and Jay rose simultaneously. "This one is mine," my cousin Karl said. "Unless Millie . . ."

His wistfulness made me say, "Certainly, Karl."

"You'll regret that, Princess," Jay said.

Karl danced silently, sullenly, for a moment or so, then, "Watch your step with Jake Bernstein, kiddo."

"So you said. There's nothing to watch. He didn't even ask for a date."

"How come? Why not?"

"He doesn't go to Brooklyn, he says."

"He will. He'll go any place where there's something he wants."

"I'm not what he wants." I felt Karl's moist paw through

the chiffon. "Not jealous, are you? Why, if you weren't my cousin—"

"Because I'm your cousin, I can say watch your step. The man is an actor. Actors I do not trust."

"Why not?"

"Dance," Karl replied.

"The same to you, cousin. And not on my toes."

Jay was not at our table when we came back. Morry's girl, Ruth, stamped her cigarette out, studied her wrist watch, and announced it was late; they should be starting uptown. Morry said if we wanted to hang around, Karl could settle the bill (if he had enough money, that is), and he'd settle with him Monday morning. Karl's glance consulted me: stay or depart? I took up my gloves, ready to leave, and made insincere chitchat with Ruth ("Charming evening" . . . "We must get together again"). The boys argued over how much to leave for the tip.

While I waited for Karl to fetch my wrap from the check room, Jay appeared at my side. "Have a phone?" He had a tiny notebook and a pencil in hand.

I gave him Daisy's telephone number; he wrote it down. "I might call you," he said.

"I'll be going home soon," I said.

"And I might not call you," he said.

"I'll not hold my breath," I replied, adding, "It was nice meeting you."

"Likewise, I'm sure," he mocked me.

On the subway, riding to Brooklyn, I asked a few questions (sounding offhand, I hoped, though necessarily shouted above the train's rattle and roar), and I received some answers. Yes, Jake Bernstein did live on Washington Heights. With his family. The father was an insurance agent, a modest living, no better than that. They'd have to scrimp and sacrifice to put Jake through law school. . . . Yes, he'd applied. . . . No, Columbia had turned him down; N.Y.U. had accepted him. But the crazy guy turned *them* down. He wanted the stage, nothing else. And the worst thing of all was his mother encouraging him. Stage-struck, a frustrated actress herself, probably. . . . Yes, he had talent, a little of it.

103

"How far can a little take you on the stage? He hasn't the looks, you'll agree, will you not? No Valentino. No Barrymore. And the theater, Millie, is a hard road, one of the hardest there is. One week your name's up in lights; next week you're on the bread line. When you think, with his assets—his voice, his gall—what a trial lawyer he'd be—"

When I kept nodding noncommittally, my cousin lowered his voice, so that I had to strain to hear him.

"Kiddo, I am in a way responsible for you. I talked you into coming down here. You could blame me."

"For what?"

He blushed and began to stammer. "For nothing, I hope. All I ask is, don't take him seriously. Because he is not a serious person. An actor can't be, is what I mean. Not a real person. Not a whole person. An actor is parts, only parts. One week he's this, next week he's that. Which part really is him, nobody knows. Not even himself. So, Millie, I hope—"

"Forget it," I said. "I danced with him once. I enjoyed dancing with him. I don't expect to see him again."

"Promise," Karl said. "Promise me you won't take him seriously."

And so while the train rushed through the tunnel underneath the river, I promised my cousin that I did not now and would not in the future take Jake Barrymore Bernstein seriously. "Dear Karl, don't worry, he's far from my romantic ideal."

But, cousin, you do not know and I shall not tell you that a tall, slender man with light-brown curly hair, a cleft chin, and a presence that makes me think of a lance of sunlight has been It for me since I was ten.

Next morning, the very next, while we were at breakfast in Aunt Daisy's kitchen, my ideal appeared. This wasn't coincidence, it was custom: Ben dropping in at Daisy's with Arnold, his son—two natty gentlemen, the boy in a tweed Norfolk jacket and Buster Brown collar, the father in serge, coat double-breasted, trousers knife-creased, both with gleaming, high-polished shoes. In

104

certain ways they were look-alikes—the fair, curly hair, the indented chins, the engaging sweetness—with these differences: Ben was becoming paunchy; there was puffiness beneath his eyes; Adonis still, possibly out of my memory of him, though slightly shopworn. And the boy, the young Kuper, was too skinny, too pale, too worried-looking, too like a little old man. He reminded me, though he shouldn't have, since surely there could be no reason for this, of that dismal, unwanted child in *Jude the Obscure*, the one they called "Father Time."

Well, if Arnie Kuper had worries when he was a tyke, they must have been about his health. The first time I saw him, he had a runny nose; the next time there was cotton batting in both of his ears, catching the glop from draining abscesses that had been lanced. "The poor darlin' has bad tonsils and adenoids," Aunt Daisy explained. "The doctor says he should have an operation, but Sophie is afraid. I do not blame her." Also, his digestion was poor.

"No, thank you, my mother doesn't let me eat between meals," he'd say when Daisy offered cake or cookies, though eventually he would give in and suggest that if she put two cookies into his brown paper bag he might have them with his lunch. Such a lunch! Buttered whole wheat bread, waxed-paper wrapped, a lettuce leaf (also waxed), and a small apple. Wholesome. Nonfattening. Poor kid!

Whenever Aunt Daisy fussed over him the way she used to fuss over me, he'd stand stock-still, accepting affection, acknowledging it with a vestigial smile, but never trading a hug for a hug. And when Ben was with us at the table, enjoying the cake and coffee, Arnie would sit next to him, a princeling, mannerly and silent, hands clasped on his lap. Those hands were remarkable, the fingers long and supple, a pianist's hands. He was taking lessons, we were informed, from an expensive teacher, the best in Brooklyn, and Sophie kept him at practice every day after school. Arnie didn't mind; playing piano indoors was less hazardous than playing with kids on the block. They called him "sissy." He was. On Sundays Ben would coax him out to Daisy's yard to play catch.

105

"Pitch to me, Arnie. Throw the ball. Throw hard." Arnie threw like a girl, underhand, and ducked when it hurtled toward him. Even a rubber ball terrified him.

I had been startled when Ben and Arnie appeared at Aunt Daisy's on a September Sunday morning shortly after I came to live in the house. I thought it was cruel as well as tasteless for Ben to flaunt his offspring here. It took a while for me to understand that he was sharing with Daisy the best thing he had. And if she could welcome his gift, why couldn't I? What's past is *fini*.

Thus I believed, in my immaturity, not having yet learned that there is no *fini*. Every experience, every emotion, is recorded and registered inside yourself, and it remains, dictating, corroding, driving, creating, throughout your life. Nevertheless, on those Sunday mornings I decided my aunt was either a fool or a saint. I did not then know that there are a few—an elite—who feel demeaned by bitterness.

With Ben's wife, Sophie, Aunt Daisy had an adequate relationship, no more than this—they were, after all, merely in-laws, once removed. They met at family gatherings, as when Uncle Reuben and Aunt Fanny came to Brooklyn for Seder. They exchanged telephone calls, Daisy to ask about Arnie's health, Sophie to advise Daisy about getting a public library card. And on the Sunday visits, Daisy observed the amenities. "Arnie, how is your mother feeling?"

"She has a bad headache." Or "She is very tired. She couldn't sleep one wink last night." With that Father Time worry look. Daisy would glance at Ben to verify this; usually, Ben would nod, yes, though seeming discomfited, as if, in some way, he was to blame for Sophie's poor health. He'd snap up the lid of his gold watch.

"Whee! It's late. Come, Arnie, let's go." This is Father-and-Son Day.

"My mother likes me out in the fresh air," the boy would say gravely, departing—to the zoo in the Bronx or to Ebbets Field, though if the weather was foul they'd take the trolley to Ben's haberdashery, where Arnie busied himself rearranging the necktie displays, making rainbows out of the four-in-hands, while Ben worked over accounts in the cashier's cage at the rear.

In September, shortly after I arrived in Brooklyn, Ben asked me if I'd care to join them at the ball game. Not having ever seen a baseball game, I said yes. I went. I found out I had the soul of a fan.

Baseball can be a grand passion, though the heathen say it's a bore. True, the action is measured, the thrills are subtle, the partisanship irrational. And from high in the stands the players resemble midgets, idling on the greensward. Yet in each of them rests the potential for valorous deeds that will raise ten thousand adults, roaring, from their seats. That first afternoon I saw a double play and a man stealing home. And I became an addict and a Brooklyn fan.

The Dodgers of that year (I mean no disloyalty—look it up in the book) were mediocre hitters. Hence, a three-base hit— even a double—could send the fans into paroxysms of ecstasy, hugging one another, madly embracing. Nothing personal, mind, just let me hold on to you before I explode with rapture. Whenever that happened, Arnie watched Ben and me, startled, shocked. And disapproving.

Ben had outlined the rules to him, had explained the daring of the stolen base, the split-second timing of the double play, the strategy of the sacrifice bunt. Ben had recounted team legends to Arnie, the fabulous prowess or the colossal ineptitude of this player or that, to capture the princeling's interest. But Arnie continued to gape whenever we sprang from our seats, and he covered his ears against the cheers and obscenities around us.

And so, to keep Arnie busy, Ben taught him how to mark a scorecard. He called out each play to his son and supplied a running account of the action, all to be neatly penciled in on the card. Ben also bought Crackerjack and peanuts. Occasionally, Arnie accepted a single peanut. "Don't tell Mama," Ben admonished him.

I believe, though I cannot be certain, that Arnie was pleased when the Dodgers won, and this was because his father was happy.

107

He'd pat Ben's arm as we strolled from the park, as though he were the indulgent parent and Ben the fun-loving kid. A prissy child, really, an obnoxious prig. Why, then, did Daisy and I love him so much? Because he was Ben's. And neither of us had stopped loving Ben.

Daisy never went to games with us; she said she had work to do—dressmaking for neighbors and friends of neighbors as well as the care of the house—though actually she had less work than when Grandpa had been alive.

There had been a brief period after Grandpa's death when she had not been sure she would be able to have a home here. Grandpa had not left a will. Like so many other things he had neglected during his life, he had left the consequences for others to worry about. Uncle Reuben had demanded that the house be sold and the money divided among the four siblings—since the mortgage was small, there might be a fair amount of cash to invest in the stock market which was going up. However, my father pointed out that real estate, too, was on the rise, and an income-producing building was a sound investment. Papa also reminded Reuben of his speech at Daisy's wedding when he had called this the family shrine. A family sell its shrine? Shame on you, Reuben, shame!

Next, Reuben, nudged by Aunt Fanny, no doubt, announced that since he was the son, the male heir, it was proper that the deed be recorded in his name. Papa was too quick for this. Ada was the eldest; if any single one of Yankel Springer's descendants was to pre-empt the inheritance, she had the first claim; women do have equal rights nowadays; all right, maybe not in the Province of Quebec—well, then, he as Ada's husband represented her. He came down from Montreal, had a conference with the venerable Herschel Goldmark, that shrewd tycoon, and produced a compromise: the deed and mortgage would be transferred to a family corporation in which each of the four Springer children would have equal status. A Goldmark son-in-law would be a fifth member of the corporation, protecting the mortgagee's interest and available to break a tie, in case of a disagreement. Whatever income the building yielded, above taxes, interest, heating, repairs, and miscellaneous expenses, would be divided equally among the four

Springer children, but Daisy was to have a home there as long as she wished. She'd be the guardian of the shrine.

What eventually mollified Reuben was Papa's offer to pay for renovating the building: wiring it for electricity and installing modern bathrooms, a gas range in the kitchen, a new furnace and an instantaneous gas hot-water heater in the cellar, radiators, fresh paint, and wallpaper throughout. The two topmost stories were turned into floor-through apartments for substantial on-a-lease tenants, not fly-by-night roomers. Aunt Daisy would collect their rents and supervise the premises; a part-time janitor would clean the halls, take out garbage, trash, and ashes, shovel snow from the sidewalk in winter, and trim grass in the yard through the summer.

"She is a lucky person," Aunt Fanny said. "She lives like a queen. In a palace. If not for us, she could be living in some small furnished room."

By the time I came to live in the house, Daisy had bought, out of her dressmaking money, a Frigidaire and a console radio, and she had installed a telephone. She also had removed the bead portieres, wallpapered, and illuminated a certain cupboard-lined passage of evil memory on the second floor. The walnut double bed had been sold, the bird's-eye maple furniture was back in her room, and Grandpa's fusty, dark room had been aired, papered and painted, and transformed with chintz draperies, an armchair, and a day bed into a pleasant room for me. The tiny gilt chairs were still in the parlor. I took one into my room.

It was Karl who had persuaded me to move to New York. We had been corresponding since we'd met at Daisy's wedding, and through my final years of high school he had been writing, "Plan on going to college, Millie. Get an education, do something with your brain, don't figure on just getting married and being a pot wrestler forever. The world is changing, Millie. Look at Russia. Over there women are working alongside their men, equals, partners. Not parasites."

I had graduated from high school with high marks but no clear idea of what I wanted to do with myself. For a whole year I drifted and lazed, sleeping late, lying on my back, reading books,

109

getting up to help Mama with housework, going out with her to inspect dwellings to which we might move. The time had come, she believed, for us to make a big change, from Outremont which was middle class to Westmount which was upper class. "You will be having company in," Mama told me, meaning, We must get ready; Millie is in the market, on the auction block. I played mah-jongg and bridge with girls drifting, like me; I played tennis with Bram; I went to teas with Mama and her friends; I went to dances, under Jewish auspices and chaperoned. Papa bought a car. I took lessons, learned to drive, became Mama's chauffeur. I wasn't un-happy, I was merely bored.

Karl's letters nagged and titivated me.

"You'd like living in New York, Millie, there's so much go-ing on. The theater is very exciting these days. New playwrights with social ideals, new directors with fresh ideas. We have a great new playwright, Eugene O'Neill; he is writing strong plays. You would like his work, I am sure. And I would be glad to take you to shows." When I nibbled, he went on to ballyhoo Barnard Col-lege. "I hear it's snobbish, Millie. The tuition is high, so most of the girls are from well-to-do families. But if you could get in— the entrance requirements are stiff—you'd get a first-class educa-tion—or so they tell me. Actually, it's a part of Columbia Uni-versity. Some of the same professors teach Barnard girls. . . ."

Without telling my parents, because not for an instant did I believe Barnard would consider me, and it was senseless to have Mama and Papa ask "*Nu?*" each time I got mail from New York, I applied to Barnard. My high school principal and teachers wrote glowingly about me. However, when I showed my parents the letter saying I would be admitted, hell broke loose.

"So you want to move to New York and marry a *goy*," Mama accused me.

"I don't, I won't, I'll only go out with Jewish boys. Karl said he'd introduce me—"

"Karl!" Mama snorted. "What kind of boys does Karl know? *Bolsheviki.*"

"Pussycat," Papa said quietly, "it would be lonesome here without you."

110

"You won't miss me, you have Bram."

"Bram!" Mama sniffed. "All he knows is from skiing. Sam, how many times did I tell you you shouldn't buy him the skis? Jewish people have enough trouble without breaking legs from skiing."

"Pussycat," Papa said, "Bram is Bram. He is somebody for the tennis, the skis. You are somebody for the house." The way he said that, the sound of his voice like a caress, brought tears to my eyes.

"*Meshugah*," Mama scoffed. "All her life Millie has crazy ideas what she wants. Remember, Sam, one time she was yelling and crying she wanted the ocean? So what did she get? Salt water in the nose and a kewpie doll."

"Pussycat," Papa went on, as if she hadn't spoken, "your Mama and me, we would never refuse you something worthwhile. For you we want only and always the best. So you go to New York, and we start in to worry. In what kind of place are you living? With what kind of people do you come in contact? And supposing it happens you would get sick, who would bring you two aspirins and a cup of hot tea? . . . No, I would only consider the proposition if you would live with your auntie. Then we would know you are safe."

Safe! That's a bad joke. For an instant, I felt the tweak of remembered terror, I heard the jangle of bead portieres. This passed with the surge of elation at knowing I would be getting my way.

Ever practical, my father went on to say, "I don't know if Daisy will agree; you, Ada, must talk her in. We will pay board for Millie. A guest in that house she can't be."

"I think Daisy will agree," Mama said. "A nice few dollars would help out my sister; she has to figure with a short pencil. *Mazel* she never had."

It was more than the checks for my room and board Aunt Daisy welcomed. "Millie, darlin'," she said, "you do so much for me, you don't realize. You bring young life to this house."

I brought her books, too, and some contact with the life of the mind. She herself had discovered good reading before I'd

111

moved in. She had used the library card to sample Dickens
—*A Tale of Two Cities*, for instance—and Tolstoy—*Anna Karen-
ina*—and Scott's *Ivanhoe*, romances all. She'd even purchased a
book, Mary Antin's *The Promised Land*, an immigrant's outpour-
ing of love for the country that had taken her in. My contribution
was merely to spread her horizons somewhat with poetry—
Browning, Ruskin, Matthew Arnold—out of my English Lit
course. She pored over my texts like a hungry child, and I think
she grasped all she read, though I cannot be sure since she was
too humble to try to discuss literature. However, in one book of
mine she did leave a mark that I took for a statement about herself.

Jean-Christophe was the book. Karl had induced me to buy
it, though the book I'd intended to get with my Chanukah money
from home was *The Sun Also Rises*, which some of the girls in
my class had been raving about.

"You're buying a book, buy a great book," Karl said. "Ro-
main Rolland won the Nobel Prize."

And so I acquired *Jean-Christophe*, but I laid it aside to read
at mid-term. Aunt Daisy got to it first. I found her mark there, a
V on its side, like a bird on the wing, penciled lightly beside a
line at the end of a chapter. "Life is a tragedy. Hurrah!" was what
she had marked.

Uncle Reuben was also pleased that I was here. He and Aunt
Fanny came down from Grady's Mills the Sunday after I'd settled
in. They were obese and short of breath. Uncle Reuben's bushy
mustache had silver threads among the brown. He sat me down on
the parlor sofa to receive instructions.

"Millie, now you are here in America, and you are an educated person, I appoint you secretary of our Family League. When
we have correspondence with our dear once, you will write the
letters to them." He had located cousins—third, fourth, or fifth,
he hadn't figured this out—in the state of Ohio; they had put him
in touch with additional cousins in Michigan. When he outlined
the advantages of our miniscule league—i.e., the well-off to help
the not-so-well-off in times of distress, and glory to rub off on all

from the attainments of the successful few—they agreed to add their addresses to his brief mailing list.

"The first letter you will write, Millie, will be with the news to the cousins that you have come here to go to Barney's college and also your cousin, their cousin, Karl Hitzig, in next June he will graduate from the City College, at the age of nineteen years which is werry exceptional. In the family *yiches* each cousin should share. You will write the letters in an intelligent way, and you will mail them to me, and I will sign my name as the president."

Aunt Fanny also had instructions for me. "You should meet refined Jewish young people. I will ask the Rothkind girls to invite you to introduce you to a nice crowd." She phoned the Rothkinds while I was setting the dinner table. The girls were out; she left an explicit message for them to call me.

Rosalind Rothkind called back in the evening. She was amazed I had been accepted by Barnard—they were so anti-Semitic, a Jewish quota and everything; she herself was taking an art course at Pratt; no point in wasting time and money getting a college degree when what you really wanted was to meet a fellow who made a good living. She invited me to a Halloween party. I accepted and went. Of that social event let me merely remark that the nice young crowd was more interested in drinking applejack than in bobbing for apples. Some of them spattered the bathroom with vomit. Also they turned on the phonograph and danced cheek to cheek, which I considered repulsive. And the young man who offered to drive me home in his Ford had halitosis, a bad case of acne, and such pushy thighs that I practically fell out the side door of the car.

When he let me out at Aunt Daisy's, he denounced me as a prude, a tease, a coward, and an inhibited Victorian (which I was), because I wouldn't let him kiss me good night.

Rosalind called me next night and asked how I'd liked Henry Kugel. I answered "*Ych!*" and "Is that really his name?"

"He's a very fine fellow. And a good catch. He's studying to be an accountant."

"That's no reason for me to kiss him, is it?"

"Did he?" She giggled.

"He didn't."

"Why not?"

I could have mentioned his pimples or his halitosis, but I chose to say, "I don't go in for that stuff."

"Why not?" she repeated. "What is the harm in a kiss? Some of my friends thought you were stuck up, but I think something else is the matter with you. Honest, you do not get pregnant from one little kiss. Really, don't they know about sex up in Canada?"

"They know, I know." I know so much my flesh crawls whenever a man's body is thrust against mine. "Excuse me now, Roz, I have homework to do." You won't ask me again, Rosalind, and if you do, I'll say no. I *am* a Victorian prude, and I'll go out only with my cousin Karl. He drinks nothing stronger than ginger ale, he keeps his thighs to himself, his complexion is clear, and his kisses—hello or good-bye on the cheek or the brow—are brotherly.

Karl was not only companion and guide; he was also my mentor, determined to make something noble and wise and class-conscious of me. On Saturday evenings, I'd meet him at Gray's Drug Store on Times Square; we'd examine the cut-rate ticket listings in the drugstore basement to see what second-balcony seats were available. If there wasn't anything on Broadway we wanted to see, we'd travel downtown and try for cheap seats at the Provincetown or the Neighborhood Playhouse. After the show, if we were uptown, we'd hike to Columbus Circle for wheat cakes at Childs, or, if we happened to be in the Village, we'd go for a sandwich at Polly's or Three Steps Down. Karl preferred the Village tearooms; he could smoke a pipe there, which he could not at Childs.

In the beginning I had volunteered to go Dutch, but Karl insisted that in this respect he was old-fashioned; a man pays when he takes a girl out. He made clear it was his own money he spent; he'd earned it tutoring and being a summer camp counselor. On the rare occasions when Eugene tagged along, he paid his own share. Those Hitzig boys called themselves Socialists, but they seemed to know more ways of earning a dollar than any capitalist boys I had met.

Nevertheless, on our Saturday evening outings, my cousin attended faithfully to the indoctrination of Mildred: I got Soviet Russia in massive doses; I got Sacco and Vanzetti, Tom Mooney, and the Palmer Raids ordered by President Harding, with earnestness, indignation, and abundant detail. Karl would have badgered me into reading *Das Kapital*, I am sure, if he'd thought me capable of grasping it.

No, teach the girl by examples, not by the book. As on the evening when the cut-rate board had no show we hadn't seen: "Millie, how would you like to go to Night Court?"

"What for?"

"Education."

"I presume if you're planning to be a lawyer you need to visit the courts."

"*Your* education," Karl said. "See what a capitalist society does to its women. That court is the shame of New York."

We decided to walk to Greenwich Village where the Night Court was. It was a bright-starry night with just enough snow on the pavements to remind me of home. I linked my arm into Karl's, feeling adventurous. I was going to see those fallen women I had read about; I was going to glimpse a forbidden world.

The building surprised me: it looked like a church. Policemen in the foyer glanced at us dubiously, a pair of college kids, neat, clean, yet they let us pass into a stuffy, badly lighted room, to sit on slippery wooden benches, shoulder to shoulder, thigh to thigh, with furtive, sharp-eyed, flashy, sleek-haired, bay-rum-scented men. Now and again one of them ogled me. I inched close to Karl and stared straight ahead, at a robed judge at an elevated desk. And at the wicked women.

They were young, most of them no older than I. They weren't pretty or elegantly dressed. Their nubile breasts strained against sleazy satin. Sometimes their lips were rouged; sometimes their eyes were touched with mascara. Yet for the most part they were drabs, teetering on high heels, waggling their buttocks when they walked. Bovine-eyed, they stood in front of the judge and listened impassively while a man—"Vice squad detective," Karl whispered to me—rattled off the squalid details of their immorality.

115

"She came up to me and she said, 'How about a good time, Buddy?' . . . She took me up to this room. She took off her dress. I took off my pants. And I gave her the five dollars. . . . Then she took off her slip and her bloomers, and she lay down on the bed. Then I put her under arrest."

From the judge: "Did you notice any distinguishing marks on the defendant's body?"

"Well, she had this brown mole on her right hip."

From the judge: "Thirty days."

I felt sick. "Please, Karl, let's go." He seemed reluctant to leave —this exhibition fascinated him, I believe—but while we walked again in the crisp, cleansing air, he gave me the Marxist explanation.

"You've seen it for yourself, Millie, how capitalist society degrades its women. It compels them to sell their bodies in order to eat. Then it punishes them for its sin. *Its* sin, Millie. Not their sin. Thirty days in a cell. Then what? Out to sin again. And again. . . . Hard to take, isn't it? Now in Soviet Russia—only the Soviet Union has abolished prostitution, you know—their women have dignity; they have an opportunity to find decent work. No girl needs to prostitute herself to have bread. Oh, sure, sure, there are some women, a few, relicts of the old regime, or badly educated, ignorant girls, who still ply the trade. It's mostly for foreign visitors. But there's no police entrapment, no persecution, no prison cells. They've established prophylactoriums where the women are comfortably housed, taught respectable trades, so they can return to society and be accepted without shame. Only in Russia, Millie—"

"Karl, dear," I interrupted him, "tell me something. Why do men want that so much they have to buy it from sluts?"

For a long minute he remained silent; I don't think he knew what to tell me—he was, after all, a full year younger than I. Finally: "Well, Millie, some men simply cannot control themselves. Their physical urges, I mean. They have to have intercourse; they're scared of masturbation—you don't mind my speaking this frankly, do you? If this frankness bothers you—but after all, you were the one who asked—"

116

"Go on." I was glad the streets were dark.

"Well, these men with strong sex urges don't care to ruin a respectable girl, and they can't afford to get married—of course, in Russia, where there's work for everyone, there isn't the economic factor in it— Or if a man is married and his wife happens to be cold. Or she's afraid of getting pregnant. Those are just some of the excuses men give for going to prostitutes. But another reason, it's the real one, I'd say, is simply they are animals." He paused; he sucked in his breath, let it out, inflated his chest. "As for myself, I intend to keep myself pure, for the right woman, for the woman I'll choose for my wife, the mother of my children. . . ." His voice was rising, growing shrill and thin, breaking like a nervous adolescent's. "And I hope and pray she will have kept herself clean for me."

He looked down at me, in a querying way. This had turned out to be hard for him, more so than he had expected, especially since I hadn't responded with a single word, agreeing or disagreeing. In an effort to make his monologue impersonal, he began again, on a new tack.

"What you wouldn't know, I am sure, is there are certain types of men who have to go to prostitutes. There are degenerates, perverts—"

"I know," I breathed. It was the first time I had spoken.

He stopped short on the icy street, stopped walking and talking, to stare hard at me. "How would you know, a girl like you?" But shrugged and laughed, a short, mirthless laugh. "Happens in the best of families." And strode ahead, now speaking low and fast. "I'm not supposed to tell you this, not breathe it to a soul; it's our family's deep, dark secret. A certain gink who was married to someone we know, I won't mention names— It happened at Coney Island. Two little girls were changing their clothes, putting their bathing suits on, under the boardwalk—they're not supposed to but people do that all the time when they haven't the money for a locker. Well, this gink saw them, and it seems he grabbed hold of one, and both kids started to scream, and people heard them and began to chase him, and he ran to the ocean and started to

117

swim. He could swim but not good enough. The brother of one of the girls, the police said, was swimming after him. And he got so far out, he got tired. He sank like a stone. When they pulled him out, he was dead."

"Good riddance to bad rubbish," I said.

He broke step to stare at the sidewalk. "I agree."

"Did they tell her?" I asked. "His wife."

He shook his head. "I don't think they did. I understand they only told her he drowned, got a cramp, swimming far out. I heard my parents talking about it. My father—he's a journalist, you know—he got the details from a reporter he knew."

"Did he know—the wife's father, I mean?"

"Why, no, they couldn't tell him. An old man, a very religious man. Why, he picked this gink for his daughter himself. He picked him because he was so religious. Orthodox. And that is what burns me up. The hypocrisy. . . . Millie, your teeth are chattering. Gosh, you must be freezing. I thought you were used to cold weather. Let's get into the subway, quick, quick."

That night's conversation kept haunting me. I guess it bothered Karl, too, because after that, in our long talks in Village tearooms or Aunt Daisy's kitchen, he never again obliquely referred to Ezra Magid or so much as mentioned sex. Instead, we discussed books and plays, ideals and Life, meaning the purpose thereof, and what we planned to do with our own lives, in, for instance, the next dozen years. The Hitzig plans were all set. Eugene intended to study medicine. Walt, the family comedian, had announced he was going to be an organizer—trade unions first and, when the time was ripe, the proletariat, for the revolution. "He's a nut, Millie. Immature. It sounds great and glorious to him to lead the workers on the barricades. But I don't agree. We can get social justice through the law, I'm convinced. The law can be made to work for us all. Clarence Darrow's my model, Millie; he was the famous lawyer my parents named my brother Snooky after. Poor Snooky!"

Poor Snooky, indeed! That bouncing, bumptious baby had been crippled by polio in a summer epidemic right after the war.

He dragged himself around on heavy braces and crutches. *He* never spoke about *his* future. Nor, for entirely different reasons, did I.

"Kiddo, what are you going to do with your life?" That's Karl's routine question, posed in a serious tone and manner.

"Honestly, I do not know."

Teacher? Librarian? Social worker? Secretary? Nurse? Millie Samuelson is not intrigued. Writer? Well, no, she's a reader, rather than a writer. No talent, no urge. The theater? As one of the audience. Again, no talent, no drive.

The single ambition she has ever voiced—as a joke, as a joke—was to be a queen, and her cousins had picked that one up and kept reminding her. "Born to the purple," Eugene said. "She carries the throne wherever she goes."

"With the potty beneath," Walt added. "Nah, Mildred never pees. Not refined. That's for the common people."

Stop, boys. Quit teasing me. Can't I convince you I am not a snob? "You are somebody for the house," my father had said. Meaning? Why, you will get married to a nice Jewish boy; you'll fix up a house, with Oriental rugs, matching upholstery and drapes, two sets of dishes for all year round, two other sets for Passover, and bone-china cups and saucers to serve tea to the ladies who drop in for mah-jongg. You'll raise two children, one boy and one girl. Healthy, with perfect manners. Is this a life? A full life?

It's my mother's life, and she seems to enjoy it. Then, how about my aunts? Hannah's grown heavy and shapeless. Her pox-pitted face is ravaged; it looks like the relief maps we used to make out of papier-mâché. She dyes her hair to look youthful; you can see the white at the roots. The weight of her burdens has made her old, raising a large family of boys, doing housework, scrimping on Davy's small salary, worrying, running hither and yon, trying anything, everything, to help her youngest. Would you call that a life? She chose it. Did she? Which woman chooses to suffer?

Daisy didn't choose. Her destiny was delivered to her by her

119

father, her brother. It gives me a start when someone calls her "Mrs. Magid." She still looks young, and pretty, too, with her bobbed hair. But she's in a shell. The shell of that house, the cleaning, cooking, and the dressmaking. This is what fills her days, though once a week she goes to a Hadassah sewing circle, to make layettes for the newborn of Palestine pioneers. And she does take walks: to the public library, and in Prospect Park. And she enjoys having company—that is, she enjoys serving guests. Do for others, don't demand for yourself, is how she was and is.

But in one way she has changed. She's not as Orthodox as she was. She still blesses the Sabbath lights in her mother's candlesticks, but that's as far as she goes. We have butter with our meat; we use the same dishes for milk and meat meals, except when Fanny and Reuben come to the house. Daisy is afraid of them, I think, especially of Fanny's loud mouth.

Fanny and Reuben came to Brooklyn for the Seder—Reuben demanded that Daisy make one. "For Millie's sake. She is far from the mother, the father, the brother, she should not be lonesome on *yom tov*. You will invite Ben and Sophie and the boy. You will tell Hannah she should bring the family. Maybe Dave Hitzig has a friend could lend him a car, they could bring the cripple boy. How old is he? . . . Already eleven years? So Arnold will read the Four Questions. He is the youngest. Very smart." And added lugubriously, "For Fanneh it will be a little *mitzvah*—a good deed, unnistand. Since the Uncle Herschel Goldmark died this winter, she is down in the mouth. A second father, like, he was to her."

Aunt Daisy and I worked like dray horses. We took her rosebud-patterned Bavarian china Passover dishes from the top shelf in the pantry; we soaked her glassware in a wash tub for forty-eight hours; we even plunged the cutlery into the damp earth in the yard to make it kosher for Pesach. "But Daisy, dear," I complained, "how would Uncle Reuben know if we did or didn't?"

"*She* would know," Daisy replied. "*She* would ask. For me it is easier to do than to lie."

120

We brought the dining-table leaves out of the basement and stretched the table to its fullest length; we took down the plump goose-down pillows, for Reuben to recline at table like an Oriental potentate. We prepared *gefüllte* fish, chicken soup, *matzoh* balls, roast chicken, *tsimmis, kugel,* stewed fruit. One million calories.

Arnie stuttered through the Four Questions. Uncle Reuben patted his head; Aunt Fanny hugged him. "An angel. A diamond." Reuben droned through the long Haggadah. Walt Hitzig propped his cheek on his palm and made snoring sounds. Snooky rootched on his chair and whimpered about his braces pinching. Eugene and Ben drained all four glasses of wine and started to look glassy-eyed. Karl barely sipped a single glass. My calves ached from running to and fro, serving food.

Sophie Kuper cornered me in the kitchen where I was stacking dishes. "My son, Arnold, told me you went with him and my husband to the baseball games."

"Last fall. A couple of Sundays."

"Why did you go?" A peculiar question, implying what?

"Because I like baseball."

"A college girl likes baseball games? My son says the crowd is rough. They say dirty words."

"Not all the time," I said. "Sometimes they say complimentary ones."

Her expression doubted me. "My son didn't tell me. Arnold tells me everything. We are best friends."

"As it should be." I was remaining polite, though growing curious. "I wouldn't worry if I were you. What Arnie might hear at Ebbets Field, he'll hear in school, in the street, wherever kids—"

"Not my son," she said. "His father should know better than take him to such places. I'm surprised a girl like you—"

"The spring season's starting," I said brashly. "I can't wait to go again."

"With my husband," she said, and added, "A young, pretty girl."

Uncle Reuben said, as he prepared to leave, "Now you have

had a beautiful Seder with your dear once. It is something you will remember all your whole life."

I remember that Seder. . . . I remember it as the last time I saw the oak table in the basement fully extended to accommodate relatives. And I remember it as a strained, tepid gathering, an uninspired droning of an ancient ritual. One more disappointment in a disappointing year.

College had been no more than fairly good—the classes mildly interesting, my schoolmates amiable but aloof. One or two did ask would I care to join them for tea dancing and did I have an escort? However, after they learned I lived with a widowed aunt in Brooklyn, those parties never materialized. I spent lonely mid-week evenings doing homework on the dining table while Aunt Daisy sewed beside her radio. Saturday nights, I went to shows with Karl, Sundays to ball games with Ben and Arnie, and on holidays to the Bronx to play checkers with Snooky. I spent a lot of time on the subway. Yet pretend otherwise as I might, I felt alien in the city. And that was, I told myself, because I was Canadian. A foreigner, a country cousin, dismayed by the jazziness, by the sneaky guzzling of inferior liquor, by the flouting of manners, the defiance of moral standards. We're Queen Victoria's children, we who grew up in the north. We've not left the nineteenth century. Perhaps we want to stay in it. It's cozier in our settled ways.

Yet I had begged for this; I had bludgeoned my parents into letting me come. Like the Atlantic Ocean before, New York had disappointed me. Was this to be my pattern? Whim, fantasy, and letdown?

Well, suppose I went home and stayed, what would there be for me? The teas and mah-jongg, the tennis with Bram, the shopping at Morgan's and Eaton's. Making much out of trivia and waiting till a young man with good prospects and antecedents became available; then an engagement party, a diamond solitaire, an elaborate wedding in the synagogue. Furnish a house, hire a French char to keep it polished and tidy, have the two babies, the boy and the girl, send them to a Jewish school. Do the same things, the right things, into infinity.

122

No, siree-bob, it's not enough. So do not give up, don't quit. Not so fast. Go home in June, stick out the summer, return in September, try one year more. Something interesting may come of it.

This was my plan, my projection, up to the June evening when Jay danced into my life on the Astor roof.

Arnie Kuper slipped two cookies into his brown-paper bag and took his father's hand, to accompany Karl to the Bronx. Ben was taking his boy to Yankee Stadium this time, to see the great Bambino, George Herman Ruth. He had invited me to go along. I'd had to refuse. My European history final was coming up, and I had cramming to do.

I spread my books on the basement dining table and snapped on the light. Aunt Daisy kissed the crown of my head before she carried her sewing out to the yard. I was deep in the Austro-Hungarian Empire (and not enthralled by it) when the telephone rang. I answered it and heard *his* voice, repeating our number, querying, "Is Miss Samuelson home?"

"This is she."

"How do you do? Bernstein. Jay. Remember me?"

"The chap who never goes to Brooklyn."

"How did you guess?"

Aunt Daisy poked her head in, saying, "I thought I heard the telephone."

"For me."

"Is something wrong?"

I shook my head, wriggling my fingers, please-go-away, at my aunt, with Jay saying into the receiver at my ear, "And I do not intend to *shlep* to Brooklyn. This nickel has been invested to ask you to come to New York."

"Can't. Up to my ears. Studying for a final."

"Not today, Princess. Next Friday evening. Look, see, I am in a play. . . . No, it is not on Broadway. It is downtown. I work with an experimental group. Friday night our first production. Name *Potpourri*. If you are interested . . ."

"I might be."

123

"Swell. I'll leave a ticket for you at the door."

I hesitated, turning coy. "But you never take girls home to Brooklyn."

"That is correct. And so I will leave a pair of tickets. Take somebody. Anybody. Take Karl. See if I care." His tone changed, mocking me. "Take whoever stays all night."

"You're generous."

"I can afford to be. Look, Princess, I can't kid around on the phone, used up my nickel's worth. I'd like you to come. If you're interested, that is."

"Yes. No. Maybe."

"Which is it? Make up your mind."

"I'm interested."

"Settled. Here's the address." He added the nearest subway stop, the curtain time, and "Clap loud, will you please?" before he hung up.

I decided to invite my aunt. "A young man I met last night, a classmate of Karl's," I told her, "is acting in a play. On Friday night. He invited me to come to it. And bring a friend."

"You're asking Karl?"

"I'm asking you."

"Me!" Her eyes widened, her color rose. "To a theater!"

"Not exactly." From the address he had given me, I assumed this was an auditorium, a meeting hall, rather than a regular playhouse. "I don't know how good the show will be. Or what kind of actors. They're amateurs."

She wasn't listening to me. "Once I was in a theater," she was saying. "Only one time. In the first years after we came to America. My brother took us, my sisters and me, before he married Fanny. A Yiddish theater. It was *King Lear*. You heard of it? An old king had three daughters. And nobody to take care of him when he was old. . . ."

Oh, Reuben, you fox! Sisters, listen to Shakespeare, don't abandon your father. You especially, Daisy, you petite Cordelia, with your gentle ways. . . .

"This play will be different," I assured her.

124

She dressed in a black taffeta suit, the jabot of her lace blouse spilling down the front of it; a veiled small straw hat was perched on her head. I hadn't known she owned such pretty clothes. A dainty little lady walked beside me into a fusty auditorium, where wooden folding chairs had been set out in uneven rows. The programs were mimeographed.

Unaccustomed as she was to playgoing, nevertheless Aunt Daisy looked disappointed when she scanned the amateurish play sheet. "Which one is your friend?"

I ran down the list. JAMES BURNS. That must be Jay. A stage name. Not bad. JAMES BURNS will sparkle on Broadway marquees. The name was halfway down the cast of characters. A major role, undoubtedly. In order of appearance, minor characters head the list usually: the butler, the valet, the maid. Naturally he has a leading part; he wouldn't have asked me otherwise.

"James Burns is my friend." I indicated the name and marked Daisy's frown. "Jake Bernstein," I hurried to reassure her.

The lights dimmed; the curtain divided jerkily; the wooden chairs rasped and squeaked as the audience settled. The stage was starkly furnished and poorly lighted; actors entered, talked at each other, sometimes shouting, sometimes whispering; you heard some too well, some not at all.

At last, enter James Burns, matured by make-up and a small mustache. Burns speaks. The voice is familiar; it is rich, resonant. He's confident, poised. Professional.

The curtains closed. I clapped so hard my palms tingled. A peroxide blonde near the end of the row turned to eye me. I blushed and dropped my hands on my lap. Aunt Daisy leaned to me, whispering, "Which one was your friend?"

"The one with the mustache."

"Oh! An older person?" Again the faint disapproval.

"Make-up," I said. "For the part."

"Good-looking he is not," she said, but quickly, to mollify me, "The voice is nice."

"He's the only one up there with talent." I must have spoken loudly, for the peroxide blonde leaned across a rotund man to

125

inquire, "Are you discussing James Burns? The actor? He is my son."

I blushed again, mumbling my name, adding, "And this is my aunt."

"Mrs. Bernstein, his mother," the peroxide blonde told us. "This is the father, Mr. Bernstein."

"I am no critic"—Aunt Daisy spoke carefully—"but in my opinion your son acts his part very good."

"A little talent," Karl had said. A genuine talent, I decided, while I watched Jay moving around that stage as if it were his habitat, speaking lines as though they had been composed by him, solely for his purposes. A lump filled my chest and throat. I was on a cloud, and then and there, in that auditorium, I revoked the promise I had made to Karl; I began to take Jay seriously.

We saw him in the lobby while we were making our way through the crowd. He emerged from a side door, still wearing the make-up and mustache. The peroxide blonde lunged and hauled him against her bosom. Across her shoulder he saw us. He broke away and reached my side.

"You liked?"

"You were wonderful!"

He gave my aunt a quick glance, but before I could tell him who she was, he bent to me and whispered directly into my ear, "Princess, you *are* beautiful!" It was as if he had been debating with himself and had finally settled the argument. Then the crowd pushed us apart.

We didn't talk on the subway riding home. Aunt Daisy's voice was too light to compete with the noise of the wheels, though in the few seconds of relative silence while the train was at a station, she did begin diffidently.

"I did not exactly understand what the play was about."

Yet when I tried to outline the plot, the tightness in my throat left me short of breath, so that I had to complain, "Can't talk with this racket," and she accepted the excuse. Only after both of us were undressed and ready for bed did she ask.

"Is he your feller?"

126

"Just a young man I danced with," I said.

On Sunday afternoon, he telephoned. "Well, Princess, how was it?"

"It was great."

"Don't kid me, it was stinko. Mort Hoffman—he directs our group—he can't make up his mind. One day he thinks he's Stanislavsky; the next day he's Max Reinhardt."

Since those names meant nothing to me, I said, "But you were wonderful."

"You have good taste," he replied.

A pause, both of us trying to improvise dialogue. I came up with "I look forward to seeing you in many plays."

"I look forward to being in many." Another pause. "I give you news. I leave town next week. For Provincetown, Massachusetts. For the summer. A theater there. On a wharf. And O'Neill is in town; he lives there."

I caught my breath. "You'll act in his plays."

"I doubt it. I'm still an amateur, Princess. An apprentice. I will be hanging around, listening, watching, learning the ropes. With luck, I'll meet him, and I will meet others who know what acting is. I'll sweep floors for them, paint scenery, run errands, do anything, everything, just to breathe the air—" He broke off. "Princess, let me have your address, where you'll be for the summer. I might get in touch."

"Montreal's further than Brooklyn," I said.

"I don't want to lose you," he said.

Aunt Daisy came into the room while I was packing. "I will be lonesome for you, darlin'." She seated herself on the gilt chair. "I got used again to somebody in the house. Since my father passed away, it was—" Her empty arms spread to finish the sentence.

"Aunt Daisy, dear"—I turned from the valise—"you are still young, you are pretty"—stumbling toward where angels should not tread—"you could still meet the right person."

Pain swept into her eyes. "I would never. I could never." She

127

was struggling for control. It took a while before she could say softly, "What was *beshert* was *beshert*." What was ordained was ordained. She got up, distracting herself by folding a skirt and a blouse for me, before she could add, "I have my health. I have my home. My life is quiet. My nerves are quiet." Then, folding another blouse, she moved to a different topic. "I spoke with Hannah on the telephone. I asked her to lend me Snooky for the summer. The yard is here, it is cool, it is clean; he can be in the fresh air, not on a hot, dirty sidewalk in the Bronx. My poor sister Hannah, she works so hard, she can get a little rest. And I will have the pleasure from Snooky. And"—she brightened with additional news—"I heard Ben Kuper is buying a car, a Maxwell. He will drive Sophie and Arnold up to the Catskill Mountains; they will stay there in a hotel for two weeks; then, when their vacation is finished, on Sundays Ben could come here with Arnie and the car and they could drive Snooky to the beach."

"You, too," I said.

"No." Fingers, pressing her lips, told me I had blundered. She recovered quickly. "You see, darlin', I do not go in the ocean. It is too cold. Since my pneumonia, since the sickness in my lungs, I gave up the swimming. And the beach. . . ." Pain was in her eyes again, a different pain, of quiet desperation. "It would not be sensible for me to tag along. Take Sophie's place. No." She shook her head. "The two boys together would be fine. Arnie does not like to jump around. He could sit with Snooky on the sand. It would be good for the two of them."

I put my arms around and kissed my aunt, aware that I had never known and would not know again another person as selfless as she.

"Hannah is considering the proposition," she went on to say. "This would make the summer pass for me with pleasure. Till you come back." Her chin rose, her eyes searched my face. "You will come back? Promise, darlin'."

I promised, as glibly as I had made Karl a promise. By September, I assured her, I would be delighted to return to New York.

"The young man, the actor?"

"Just an acquaintance. Not important." Yet even while I

128

flipped my wrist, dismissing him, I knew I lied. James Burns—
Jake Bernstein—had become important. However, to admit this
after one fox trot, two telephone calls, and one whispered compliment was childish and, accordingly, embarrassing.

Karl and Walt came to carry my valises to the midnight
train. "See you in September. Don't take any wooden nickels,"
Walt said. "Don't do anything I wouldn't do."

"That goes double," Karl said.

5 ⚹

WHEN WE JUMPED DOWN from the *calèche*, the driver winked, saying, *"Bon chance."*

"Not at all, Bub, not at all," Jay retorted with New York aplomb. "It's a sure thing."

The driver cocked his head, grinning. *"Oui,"* he said, *"oui, oui."* To a foreigner's ear that may have sounded like, "Why? Why? Why?" Jay got red in the face; I doubled over, laughing.

People from the States who think they know French are often misled by patois. I tugged Jay's sleeve, whispering. "He wished us luck. Say *merci*. And tip."

"But what did I do wrong?" Jay wanted to know while we walked up Sherbrooke to where his tin Lizzie was parked.

I squeezed his arm. "Nothing," I said. "You were perfect." From my point of view. Yet up to the moment when we climbed into the *calèche* to go up the mountain, practically everything he did had been wrong.

To begin with, he'd come uninvited. Granted, I hadn't asked him—would I have dreamed that a chap who refused to travel to Brooklyn would go to Montreal to see me? Out of sight, out of mind, for Mildred. The most I had hoped for was a picture post-card saying, *The weather is fine, wish you were here.*

Moreover, he hadn't alerted me that, invited or no, he would be driving this way. "But, Princess, how could I know my friend would come down with the pip, lie sick abed, leave his jalopy standing out in the road? I traveled, believe me, faster than a letter could."

I remarked that he might have stopped on the way to make a phone call: "Jay Bernstein is coming; don't bake a cake; store cookies will do."

He held my hand and looked into my eyes. "Princess, it is one hell of a drive from there to here. Push the jalopy over forty an hour, it shimmies and shakes, 'twill fall apart sure. I kept praying, 'God, don't give me a flat, I don't have a spare.' Stopped ten minutes to buy a hot dog, take a piss, that is all. I needed to get here. I had to see you. . . ."

Worst of all, he hadn't cleaned up before Mama saw him. It took her years to get over the shock of the sight of a man in paint-spattered corduroy pants, sweat-stained khaki shirt, and sandals open over dirty toes, sprawled on our front steps, a disgrace to a fine neighborhood.

While I had been in New York, my parents had made the move to Westmount. "You wouldn't be ashamed to invite high-class company," Mama said. Meaning prospects for matrimony. Millie's not homely; her father is well off; she's had a touch—just a touch, don't be afraid she's too intellectual—of higher education at a college in New York. She might catch a doctor, a dentist. With luck a K.C.

Mama had waited for me to help her decorate. That afternoon we had been downtown, selecting fabrics for living-room drapes. As we came up the street, we saw a dusty and rusty tin Lizzie at the curb in front of our house and Jay on the steps. He saw me and waved, not getting up.

"You know this bum?" Mama gasped.

"A friend of Karl's." My heart bounced.

"Aha! A Bolshevik!" Mama said.

"An actor," I said. She gave me a look of complete bafflement.

Jay uncoiled and got up but did not approach.

"What are you doing here?" I cried.

"Bootlegging." White teeth flashed in his bronzed face.

My mother scowled ferociously.

"Mama, this is Mr. Bernstein."

"From New York?"

"Most recently from Provincetown, Mass. Come close. Smell the fish." He raised one arm and sniffed his armpit. It was disgusting. "I would have washed before we met. Unfortunately, your front door was locked. Modom, would you give me a bath?"

That introduction would prejudice any mother, let alone a fussbudget like mine. While Jay was soaking upstairs in our tub, Mama, eyebrows arched and lips pinched, wanted to know, "This is your feller, Millie?" meaning, For *that* we sent you to college in New York?

"Just an acquaintance," I said. "Not even a friend."

"Some nerve!" Mama said.

He came downstairs, golden and shining and with a clean shirt, presentable and in his own way beautiful. He bowed to us and strode into the parlor, his nose tilted arrogantly, his right-to-left glance critical. So this is how the princess lives, his manner seemed to be saying. Not elegant, not exotic, merely bourgeois-conventional. Even Mama's Georgian silver tea service and her unmatched tea cups drew no admiration from him.

Mama, hospitable in spite of herself, said, "Millie, ask your company would he care to have a cold drink."

"You bet," Jay answered before I could ask. "Cold beer would be great." In our breakfast nook, he emptied two bottles. "Genuine." He smacked his lips. "God bless the king!"

"*Shikker*," Mama muttered, glowering at me.

He said, "Hello, Sam," when my father, home for supper, was introduced. Papa took the informality in his stride, though it rattled Mama. ("No respect," she grumbled to me.) I was biting my nails. If the tension hadn't let up, I might have scraped bone.

Papa, bless him, behaved sensibly. He inquired about Provincetown, what it was like, what kind of people were there, what their occupations were, but after Jay answered in detail, zestfully, Papa shrugged. "From this you expect to make a living?"

"God and the Theater Guild willing," Jay said.

Mama sniffed. "Our family are business people. Only my sister Hannah, she married a journalist. He makes a poor living."

"Karl's father," I amplified for my guest. "Papa, Mr. Bernstein was a classmate of Karl's."

"My nephew Karl is being educated for a lawyer," Mama bragged.

"You are a tourist, on your vacation?" Papa asked.

"No, sir. I came for one purpose—to see your daughter."

This time Papa scowled.

("But, Princess," Jay said on the mountaintop. "I had to come exactly this way. Unexpected, unannounced. To find out who and what. I'd met a girl who bowled me over. She was different from any female I had known—and I've met many, Princess. For the moment, ignore those blue eyes, those silken coppery curls, the peaches-and-cream complexion—ignore, but do not belittle. Concentrate on the unique quality. The regal air. The grace. A certain spirit and sparkle. 'Tis quite a girl! Is she real? Or an illusion? I had to find out for myself what else you were. If you also had patience and tolerance. And a true sense of humor. I had to know, before I committed myself." On the mountaintop he committed himself to me. And I to him. The preliminaries, however, were nervewracking.)

After supper, he kept yawning, dozed off in the middle of sentences—his own as well as ours—jerked his head to force himself to wake up; no doubt he was exhausted after ten hours at the wheel of the jalopy. Mama and Papa exchanged uneasy glances. Mama ventured, "Maybe your friend would excuse himself and go to his hotel."

I spoke up recklessly. "Bram is away. His room is empty. Mr. Bernstein can use Bram's bed."

I know, because I heard him pacing, that Papa patrolled the upstairs hall all night long. There was no need. Jay slept like a log. I sat at my window, too excited to sleep. Young Lochinvar had come riding out of the west—young Bernstein out of Massachusetts. To me.

Papa went off to his factory with no more than a mildly

sarcastic query. "Your friend came to Montreal to take a good nap?"

Mama cleared away our breakfast dishes and departed to do marketing, with an over-the-shoulder mutter. "Your friend is making a big mistake if he thinks I will stand around in my kitchen a whole morning to fix a breakfast for him."

I stood around, riven with ambivalence: the pride and elation of knowing he'd come all this way just to see me, and the dread that his conduct had antagonized Mama and Papa. They'd want to know, they had a right to ask—I couldn't deny them this right—why, out of the enormous population of the city of New York, only this crazy would-be actor had appealed to me. "Millie is *meshugah*," Papa'd declared when I was ten. "Millie's *meshugah*," he'll say again. I'm not. I merely am, I merely am . . . What am I merely? I am their daughter. But I am myself.

It was nearly noon when Jay came down, bright-eyed and bushy-tailed. "Two fried eggs," he ordered. "Turn 'em over. I don't suppose there's a slice of bacon on the premises. . . . No, no, don't run out to the store. It was just a wild hope that maybe you weren't that kosher. Toast. Two slices. Butter on the side, a spot of strawberry jam if it's available. I take coffee black." No "please," no "thank you." No kiss on my cheek.

I bristled while he ate with voracious appetite.

"Now, Princess"—he threw down his napkin—"climb into my chariot. I trust your backside is not delicate. And off we go to find a place, the perfect place. . . ."

Assuming sightseeing was what he meant, I led him to Bonsecours, down by the river—the St. Lawrence, *my* river. I thought the market stalls and the picturesque market people would amuse him. They did. He gave my arm a small squeeze of shared pleasure. I led him up the winding staircase into the steeple of the old church. The narrow passage was dark; I thought—and in a way, dreaded—he'd attempt an embrace. He did not. He kept a proper sightseer's distance, one step behind me, and when we came down, he said, "I detest dark places; do better by me, Princess."

"We'll go up Mount Royal," I said. And I thought, If that doesn't please him, nothing here will.

I like to believe that I set the stage, selected the perfect background for romance. High above the sparkling river, surrounded by lush, fragrant pines that sifted sunlight and sprinkled gold on our heads, snug on a sagging seat worn down by amorous couples, behind a sympathetic driver and a patient horse, we acted the charade of declaring love.

Jay used a long moment to absorb the vista, before he drew his breath deeply in and let it out slowly. He turned to me, his eyes intent, and folded my hands between his. " 'Behold thou art fair, my love! Behold, thou art fair!' Whose words do I speak, my princess? Come, come, has no one wooed you before with the Song of Songs? Solomon to his Queen of Sheba."

The name my cousin had called me—Queen of Sheba! I inched toward Jay. He raised my hands and kissed the tips of my fingers, each separately.

"Would you rather hear from Romeo? 'It is my lady; O, it is my love! O, that I wish she were! She speaks, yet she says nothing: what of that? Her eye discourses, I will answer it.' " The balcony scene, throbbing with passion, poignant with discovery. " 'Love goes toward love, as schoolboys from their books.' " He spoke the lines exquisitely.

Not having memorized Juliet's part, I couldn't respond in character. All I remembered was, "O Romeo, wherefore art thou Romeo?" and "What's in a name? A rose by any other name would smell as sweet," which in this situation was irrelevant.

Thus, then, he won me, with borrowed lines, from Shakespeare and the Song of Songs. There was no grossness of thigh pressing thigh, no lecherous groping for my breasts. My body remained inviolate, so that I had no fear of him or of the love he offered me.

He dropped me off at our house, not taking the time to stop for refreshments or amenities. He shifted gears with a grating and grinding and blew a kiss back to me before the jalopy rattled out of Westmount. He departed with my firm promise that before the summer was over I would come to him at Provincetown and bring along an imperial quart of whiskey. How I would manage this I'd not figured out. All I knew was that I had been caught up in

135

the madness of a sudden love and I would need to convince my parents that I had the right to it.

"So where is your friend, the slob?" Mama demanded when I entered the house.

"On the way to the border."

"He couldn't stop for a minute, say pleased to of met you, Mrs. Samuelson?"

"He asked me to thank you for him."

"Not enough. A gentleman says personal thanks to the hostess."

"It was me he came to visit, Mama."

"Your family counts for nothing? Is he your feller, serious, Millie?"

"He is."

She eyed me with open hostility. As I expected, she said, "*Meshugah.*"

"I'll set the table," I said.

Papa had barely started on supper when Mama began. "Sammy, guess what is happening here in this family. Our Millie says she is serious with the *matzeah* who came in the tin Lizzie."

Papa put down his spoon, looking solemn. "We knew someday we will lose you, Pussycat, but what is the hurry?"

"It happened fast," I replied.

"You could give yourself a little more time. Look around. A girl like you, I guarantee positive, wouldn't sit an old maid."

"Find a substantial person," Mama said. "Not a slob actor that don't make a living."

"He will, Mama, he will. And some day you'll go around bragging he stayed overnight in your house."

"Took a bath in my bathtub. *Gottenu,* he needed the bath. All the way from the corner I smelled him."

"Oh, that!" Please, Mama, don't be crass. "Mama, the poor man had been driving all night and all day to get here."

She snorted. "So tell me, tell us, where did you find the *matzeah?*"

"At a college dance. Karl introduced us."

"You met his family?" Papa asked.

In a way, I thought. "Yes, I did," I said.

"What does the father do?" Papa asked.

"He sells insurance."

"Thank God, a respectable business," Mama said.

My father was saying little; he had been watching me with a kind of sadness, a preliminary loneliness, possibly. Now, he spoke. "Why must you grab, Pussycat? When somebody grabs, they could get a *potch* on the hands. Take your time. Be friends with him; nobody is stopping you from being friends. But be friends with different fellers also. Then ask a little advice from older people and pick the right one."

I rose and went to him; I twined my arms around his neck. "Dear Papa, I am no baby. I am twenty-one. I should know what's right for me. Papa, dear, when you met your girl, you knew she was right, didn't you?"

"I don't know if I did," Papa said.

Mama hurried to amplify what he'd said. "It was arranged for us, the right person for the right person. Everything has to be equal on both of the sides. What your family is is what you are. People are not alone in this world; everybody comes from somebody. Okay, Sam didn't have no relations here, they were on the other side; so the *shadchen* who brought him to our house, he had inquired what kind of reputation Sam Samuelson had in Montreal. Then he arranged Mr. Samuelson should come to our house, like a gentleman, to make acquaintance with my family. And my father talked over with him, and he decided this would be the right person for Ada. Then, after, when we got to know one the other, we could talk about love. . . ."

I stared from one to the other; I looked at them together. I saw a middle-aged couple, solid and stolid, hair turning gray, out of the same province in Russian Lithuania, out of the old country and its old-fashioned ways, brought together by a stranger, joined together and left together, to make a living and a home, together to create a daughter and son. But never to hear the poetry, never to know the fever in the blood. I burned with the fever, lightheaded with it. I was in love, believing sincerely and completely that I knew what love is.

The arousal of love employs various instruments: the cadence of a voice, the touch of a hand, the mysterious chemistry. And the imagination.

I took my chair again and dipped my spoon into my soup. "The times have changed," I told my parents. "Today's generation makes its own choice. The older generation should not interfere."

"Who's interfering?" Mama cried. "We are only discussing."

"Pussycat," Papa said, "maybe sometimes older people, from their experience, know what is better for young ones than the young ones know for themselves."

"Reuben and Fanny knew better!" I blurted. "Grandpa knew better!"

Mama glanced up, eying me, saying nothing, waiting for me to continue.

"Two lives were ruined." I rushed ahead. "Don't tell me—I know, I saw it. I was just a kid but I saw. I could tell Daisy and Ben were in love. It was like a fairy tale, they were so happy together. They could have lived happily."

Mama's eyes started to tear. "Reuben wanted only good, the best for his sister. Always he tries the best for his dear ones." She gulped. "Reuben is a prince."

"Pish-pish!" Papa muttered.

My eyes met his. We smiled. From that trading of smiles, I might have sensed victory was heading toward me, yet there was an additional barb to be hurled to crown my triumph. "Those brilliant people, those know-it-alls, they picked a husband for Daisy—Grandpa, Uncle Reuben, I'm not sure which one picked him. And you know, you know well, how that—" I couldn't go on, I was hearing the jingle-jangle of bead portieres, and so I started to weep. My father rose and dried my eyes with his big handkerchief.

I had my way. Had I not always gotten my way with my parents? Storm and rage my mother might, protest my father did, yet by next evening Papa told me I could visit Provincetown. Provided Mama accompanied me.

"You don't trust me! Your own daughter! You treat me like

138

a baby. You act as if I were an idiot. Or"—I gulped, gathering up my temerity—"as if I were a common prostitute."

That last word stunned them into silence. I pressed my advantage.

"Remember, I have my own money." Thinking of the gold and silver nestling in flannel in a candy box. "Grandpa sent it to me to spend how I wished." A bluff, nothing more. I didn't know the price of train tickets, and I had no notion whether there was enough in my box. Here's Mildred, aged twenty-one, who hasn't earned a dollar in her life. They held me in the thrall of an allowance, the petty cash that is doled out to kids. The clever move would be to try appeasement. "Provincetown is a summer resort. At the seashore. Fine families go there. . . ."

"There is a respectable hotel?" Papa asked.

"Naturally." I answered, not knowing whether or no. "Several. All high class."

"I will inquire." He rose, ending the dialogue, and with a warm hand on my shoulder said, "Pussycat, don't think for a minute your parents are your enemy. For you we want only the best."

Papa inquired; the Provincetown Inn was respectable. He sent a telegram, reserving a single room, with bath, for me. And I agreed with Mama that, if spending a holiday with Jay did not change my mind, the Bernstein family would be invited to meet mine so that an engagement might be announced.

However, before that could take place, my mother had written Aunt Hannah, whose son Karl had told *his* mother, who had sent Karl's message on to *my* mother, that Karl hoped Millie realized what she was letting herself in for.

Jay and the borrowed tin Lizzie met me in Boston; we drove the length of Cape Cod, I in euphoria. I checked into the Inn, opened my valise, and presented Jay with the imperial quart—U.S. customs, I had correctly surmised, would not be so crude as to grope for contraband beneath a young lady's sanitary napkins.

Jay uncorked the bottle while I changed my clothes in the bathroom. He had poured for two. He flung his whiskey down;

139

I refused the drink. "Lightheaded," I said, "just being with you."

" 'Drink to me only with thine eyes,' " he replied. " 'And I will pledge with mine.' " I held the bottle while we drove to his room.

It was an attic, littered with clothing, shoes, books; a bare floor, gritty with sand; a dormer window open to the sound and the smell of the sea.

He opened his arms for me, and standing in the close embrace he disrobed me adroitly, a fumbling with hooks till my skirt dropped, a flick-flick down the buttons of my blouse, a light-fingered pushing of shoulder straps and waist-band elastic until I stood naked in his arms.

The bedsheets were clammy.

"You are trembling, love. Don't be frightened. I'll be gentle, love. . . . Let me kiss you . . . here and here and here. . . . Let me taste those nipples. . . . Let me touch you, stroke you . . . here . . . and here . . . and here. . . . Don't be afraid, don't tremble. You're so beautiful, love. . . . My love. . . . My love. . . . Now . . . now, I'll try not to hurt you, dear . . . dear . . . dear. . . ."

I clung to him, wanting desperately to listen, to hear only the words of his love, to dim, to diminish, drown the jangling of the bead portieres.

Afterward. "That wasn't punishment, was it, love? If you'd let yourself relax . . ."

After that, drowsily, "Bathroom's yonder. Better mop yourself, my pet. You virgins sometimes drip."

Then sleep, his arm flung across my belly, his snoring an un-romantic buzz, an incongruous counterpoint to the foghorn on the dark sea. I lay wakeful—one moment feeling proud and emancipated, another riddled with shame and a nameless fear.

In the morning, over coffee, he said, "But, Princess, we can't marry yet. I don't have a job. Or a dime in the bank. And who knows how long it's going to be before I can support you in the style you're accustomed to? God knows nothing would delight me more than to cover your hands with jewels, to swathe your exquisite body in silk and velvet and sable. Ah, just to hold you in my arms night after night, to see your beauty when I wake! But, love, be practical. We're not cut out for poverty, either of us. Starving in a garret—you'd be wretched; I would be too, knowing I'd done that to you. So what's the point? We know we love each other; a license, a ring won't change anything. You'll come back to New York or Brooklyn or wherever; I'll be in the city working. Don't worry, I'll find something or other—worst comes to worst, there is radio. And I'll get a place where we can meet, be together. I'll arrange it. Trust me, trust, dear heart. And you will not get pregnant. Knock wood." He rapped his skull. "I'll take the precautions. I did last night. Were you too scared to notice? And really, Princess, why were you scared? It's pleasure, dear heart, believe me, it is. I'll teach you. I'm an excellent teacher, darling."

I had a splendid sunburn when I returned to Montreal; undeniably I was the picture of health. I told my parents I had had a lovely time. The Inn had been comfortable, the town fascinating, and Jay a perfect host. He had lots of friends who were charming and interesting. They had been pleasant to me—one of the women decided my name should be Mimi; Mildred was too prosaic.

No, I went on to tell her, Jay and I had decided not to be engaged formally. I was still a schoolgirl, wasn't I? The wise thing, we believed, was to get to know each other better. Marriage is a serious step; you want to be very, very sure of each other before you take that step. So please don't start making plans to bring the families together.

I spoke with assurance, as Mimi, a woman of the world, passionately loved, initiated, and without shame. The only guilt that troubled me in Mama's presence was that I'd eaten clams and lobster on the Cape. The dietary sin might have shocked her as much as the carnal one.

The first week of September, I returned to New York, carrying along Grandpa's gift coins (in case of emergency) and another imperial quart. I hung my clothes in the closet and waited for telephone calls.

"Darlin', it was a nothing summer," Aunt Daisy told me.

"Snooky stayed just the one week; the stairs were too hard for him to climb up and down. Hannah took him home. And Ben and Arnie never came; Sophie said now they have the Maxwell, Sundays they will all go riding, her and him and the boy."

I traveled up to Barnard, paid the bursar's fees, met a couple of girls I'd known last year, had a soda with them at Oelker's, agreed, "This term we positively must see more of each other," admitted I was still living with my aunt in Brooklyn. It was inconvenient, but my parents wouldn't have it any other way. Guarding my virginity, saving it for my old age.

"You should live in the dorm," one of them suggested. "That is a nunnery."

Exactly what I need. "Get thee to a nunnery, go. . . ." But Jay was Romeo, not Hamlet, and he had not rejected me. "Romeo, Romeo, wherefore art thou?" When he crooks his little finger— "Love is merely a madness." Shakespeare wrote that, too.

Jay didn't phone. I would have put pride in my pocket and called him, but I didn't know where, and the listing of Bernsteins in the Manhattan phone book was no help—there were dozens and all around town. Which one of these might be Papa B., the insurance agent? Perhaps Jay had his own telephone. Under what name? Burns? Or Bernstein? Or suppose I hit the right number for his family, and his mother answered, and I had to explain who I was—a girl, the girl who had slept with him at Provincetown. My cousin Karl might have known how to reach Jay. I couldn't ask him, because I had broken the promise I had made.

Karl didn't phone either to ask for a date. Nobody called, not even my Uncle Reuben, the head of our Family League. My kin, I felt, were behaving peculiarly. Was I being ostracized? How fast, how far, had gossip spread? Millie, the loose woman, ran after an actor. She lost her virginity in Provincetown.

Sunday came. Sunday went. Not even Ben and Arnie dropped in, to invite me to a ball game. The imperial quart lay in my emptied valise, also waiting for the phone call. I began to feel cheap, a giddy girl who gave herself to an elocutionist. A tawdry summer romance. I'll bet he's bragging all around town. "Listen,

142

guys, there was this girl who rushed down from Canada to crawl into my bed." Yet *he* came to me first. To my house. "Trust me, Princess."

Aunt Daisy noticed. She couldn't have been unaware that I inquired as soon as I entered the house, "Any phone calls for me?" and that always I found an excuse to stay in the dining room where the phone was, pretending to study though never turning a page. My appetite was capricious; I dined chiefly on my fingernails.

"Darlin'," Aunt Daisy said on a sunny Sunday morning, "come sit in the yard, the fresh air will do you good."

"I am not sick."

"Come," she persisted. "Enjoy the sun while it lasts. Soon, it will be winter—dark, cold." She carried chairs out to the yard, waiting on me, as though I were an invalid.

"Darlin'," she began again when we sat side by side, "you had words with the parents?"

"Nothing unusual."

"Ada wrote to Hannah. . . ."

I knew Ada had, and I knew what Hannah had answered. "Does everyone in this family have to discuss my personal affairs?"

She laid her hand over mine. "We are a family, darlin'. We worry one for the other."

I thrust my chin high. "I wish they would mind their own business. Is that too much to ask?"

"No." She was silent, braiding her fingers. Then, "Is it the actor?"

Reluctantly, I nodded yes. She paused again, thinking with me and for me. "You wait for him to call up. He does not call." She drew my head down to her breast. "Cry, if you want to," she said.

Stubborn and proud, I pulled away. "There's nothing to cry about," I said. "Everything is okay."

She sighed, a soft, yearning sigh. There was envy in the sigh. Or perhaps I imagined that there was.

Another week passed. Each day, when I came from classes, Aunt Daisy met me with a careful smile and a headshake that said no one had called. Then, Saturday, before noon, while I was upstairs washing my hair: "Darlin', phone call for you!" with a jubilant lilt in her voice.

I snatched up a towel to swathe my curls and raced down the stairs.

"Hello! Oh, hello!"

"Princess, you're out of breath."

"From holding it, waiting for you."

"Sorry. Sorry. Sorry. I couldn't call. Too busy running around. Seeing people. Arranging things."

"They're arranged?"

"I have a job. Radio."

"Great! Wonderful!"

"Don't go overboard. It's just so-so. Chicken feed. I bring you better news: a friend of mine is off to Rome for the winter. He's left me his flat. In Greenwich Village. For the two of us."

I gasped, then swallowed hard. He sounded so exuberant, I wanted to make sounds to match. Yet the implications of clandestine couplings in a borrowed bed were troubling me. Faint-voiced, I answered, "Perfect! Wonderful!"

He didn't seem to have noticed how I'd said what I said. "Princess, I assume you've returned to Barnard. What time is your last class over Monday? . . . Half past three. Bit early. . . . Tell you what. Walk over to the Columbia campus. Wait at the Alma Mater statue. I'll be along soonest possible."

"I have a bottle for you. How can I drag that to class?"

He laughed. "You think of more problems. Relax, my love."

Aunt Daisy said, "Everything is all right, I see it in your eyes." And, again, I caught the hint of envy.

Monday was one of those autumn days when the sun is sharp, the air like wine, though as the afternoon stretched I had to keep moving around Alma Mater to warm myself in the patches of sunshine. My briefcase was heavy—books and a bottle make a load.

Jay was late, but he'd said he might be. I tried not to fret that he might not come. Or that Karl, hurrying from his law-school classes, might find me loitering. Why, Karl, I'm just waiting for a friend. True, is it not? Jay *is* my friend. He's more than a friend. Is a lover more or less than a friend?

But my cousin despises my lover. For reasons of his very own. Montague and Capulet. My jealous kinsman, Tybalt. Dear Romeo, do not kill Tybalt. Please don't.

Jay came running, taking the stone steps two at a time. "Princess!" He kissed my mouth, took my briefcase, seized my hand. We raced toward the subway kiosk. And again I felt happy and chastely innocent.

On the train, he said, "It's been too long."

"Much too," I echoed him. "I was afraid you were going to stand me up."

His eyebrows quirked. "Learn to trust me," he said.

The borrowed flat was above an Italian grocery on Bleecker Street. The halls, the staircase stank of garlic, must, and mice. Jay swung the door open. A mammoth roach scudded across the sill. I squealed. My lover scowled.

"I was told we'd have the place to ourselves. No other tenants. Out, you miserable bastard! Out!"

Jay's friend, whoever he was, had been a pig. He'd left an unmade bed, littered newspapers, dishes in the sink, and dust scum everywhere. Jay glanced at me, apprehensively. "You mind?"

"Yes, sir, very much." I circled him with my arms.

He tilted my mouth up to his but released me quickly. "For everything there is a time. I will not carry my princess to a dirty bed." He shucked off his jacket. "Now where in hell did that son of a bitch hide the sheets?"

It was after ten o'clock when I remembered that Aunt Daisy might be worrying, and I telephoned to say, "Don't wait up for me. I'm staying overnight with a friend in New York."

There was a too-long silence before my aunt said, "Sleep well, darlin'."

Next afternoon, when I returned to Brooklyn, Aunt Daisy didn't ask where or with whom I had been. Her smile seemed slightly forced; possibly my guilty conscience saw it that way. Silently, she carried our supper to the kitchen table. We sat down together. I shook out my napkin, trying to decide whether to tell her truth or a complicated lie. Well, part of the truth, anyway. . . .

"I was with my actor friend, you remember him, don't you? And we were talking and talking—it was in the apartment of a friend of his down in Greenwich Village—and he had to tell me all that has been happening to him—in the group he's been re-hearsing with, and the radio job he has. If you tune in at three tomorrow afternoon, you can hear him. In *Blue Fire*. It's a kind of ghost story. Well, we simply lost all track of time. And when we realized how late it was, he refused to let me go home alone on the subway. And he couldn't escort me all the way, then go back to Manhattan. . . . Oh, I like living here with you, dear Aunt Daisy, you make it very pleasant, but for busy people, it *is* inconvenient. And he *is* so busy. The radio's a regular job. And his group—the ones that acted in the show we saw—are very serious people. They hope to form a repertory company. To do at least four plays a season. Important plays, like Galsworthy's *Justice* or Chekhov's *Cherry Orchard*. They'll put their productions on wherever they can find a stage—a settlement house, a union hall. And they'll keep going till the critics take notice of them and they can move to Broadway. One of their problems is their director, a man named Hoffman, Mort Hoffman. He studied abroad, and he can't de-cide which technique he prefers, Stanislavsky or Max Reinhardt. Besides, he's writing a play, a comedy. And he's tied up in knots. So he's difficult, temperamental at times, and they have to be patient with him. Also, they themselves have to earn money to pay him and pay production costs. You can't imagine how much worry is involved! That's why Jay was so glad to get that radio job, al-though it pays chicken feed. And when your ideals and ambitions are high, when you know you have acting talent, radio is sort of degrading. But it's regular work. And a foot in one door. In the mornings Jay runs around to producers and agents to see if anyone is casting a Broadway show. He's determined, Aunt Daisy, and he's going to make good. He knows it, I know it—"

146

She interrupted—she had been listening politely, letting me prattle. "You, darlin', what are your plans?"

Without hesitation I answered, "To be his wife, as soon as that is practical."

Her glance went to my left hand, a reflex to check the ring finger. "We don't believe in formal engagements," I hurried to say.

A worry crease sprang between her eyebrows. "Do your parents know how it is with you?"

I began to bristle. "Whose life is this, theirs or mine?" But quickly penitent: "They've met him. And I know they'll like him when they know him well."

She put her hand over mine. "Millie, darlin', don't hurt them. They should be proud, not—not ashamed. . . ."

In her gentle way, she'd touched the sore. They would be ashamed, as, when I stopped to think, I also was. Because in its surrender, my body had found no pleasure, though at his bidding, I spread my thighs and pretended to welcome him. For had I refused, I might have lost the other joys he offered me: his tenderness, his adoration, his poetry—the verbal coin with which he paid for intercourse. " 'Thou art fair, my love.' "

"Darlin'," my aunt was saying, "you are not alone in the world. You belong to somebody, to a family. . . ."

I flared, being edgy. "Family! Family! How does a family know what is right, what is wrong?" And, growing reckless: "See what the family did to you! You could have been happy, Ben could have been happy, if the family had left you alone."

Her head was down; I couldn't see her eyes, nor she see mine, which was fortunate, since I was remembering and trying so hard to forget the ten-year-old who had made mischief with a careless tongue. I put my arms around her.

"Don't you see, Daisy dear, when two people are really in love, families should never butt in. How can they know what's right and what's wrong?"

Her chin tilted up. "Ben is happy." Her lower lip trembled. "He has a beautiful son." She drew off from me. "What shall I tell your mother, my sister, if she asks me questions?"

147

"Tell her I am well and happy. And past twenty-one."

Neither of us, I later recalled, had mentioned Ezra Magid. We had spoken only of Ben.

In October, Aunt Hannah decided to give Snooky a party. He had reached the age of thirteen. None of the other Hitzig boys had had Bar Mitzvahs—Hannah and Dave didn't follow the Orthodox customs—yet because this youngest son had been cheated of so many pleasures, his parents decided a party and presents might compensate a little for the loss of the use of his limbs.

I decided I wouldn't go—not fence with prying relations, not face my cousin Karl. I decided I had to go—not going might make matters worse; Karl would build my absence into an admission of sinning. Moreover, I liked Aunt Hannah and Uncle Dave; I liked all the Hitzigs, including Karl, whose intentions, I told myself, were probably good, though he certainly would never admit he was simply jealous of Jay.

I swung back and forth, one day yes, one day no. When the party was first mentioned, I paved the way for a refusal by complaining to Aunt Daisy that I had so much homework I didn't see how I could spare a Sunday afternoon. She said nothing, but through her unsmiling silence I could read her thoughts: if Millie didn't spend so much time with that actor, she wouldn't be behind in her schoolwork.

I wondered whether I could say at the last minute that I didn't feel well, had a cold coming on. Fat chance. Not a sniffle, an aching tonsil, or a sinus twinge. When I was younger, I could stick a finger down my throat and vomit. Yet even that hadn't excused me from attending a certain wedding. My mirror told me I looked supremely healthy. Love does more for you than cod-liver oil.

My parents took it for granted I was going to the party. Papa sent a money order in U.S. dollars, asking me to buy a watch for Snooky. If they were to purchase it in Montreal and mail it to him, his family would have to pay duty. "Millie, write on the card we hope and pray he will be rewarded for his sufferings with a happy, successful life. Something sweet and loving."

Aunt Daisy was making a sweater for Snooky. She sat beside her radio knitting. I knew she listened to *Blue Fire*, because she mentioned it. "He speaks good, your friend. Only the words he says . . . a little foolish, in my opinion."

"Dear, an actor doesn't make up the words he speaks. He plays a part; he says whatever words are written for that particular part."

"An actor is parts, only parts." Yes, Karl, you said that. I remember it well.

"Darlin', would you like to invite him to Snooky's party? He could meet the family."

Good lord, no! "He's much too busy. You can't imagine all he has to do."

"If you expect to marry him, he will need to meet your family."

Not in Aunt Hannah's flat. With Karl glowering. And Reuben making speeches.

"Fanny told Hannah to invite the Kupers. I don't think Sophie will go; she says she is not well, something with her insides, I don't know what." My aunt blushed. "Ben might come with Arnie. If they go, they could give us a lift in the Maxwell."

I bought Snooky a handsome gold wrist watch with my father's money, and I used my own allowance to get a personal gift, a book, I decided. What would boys his age be reading? *"Bomba, the Jungle Boy,"* Jay suggested. I turned up my nose. "Okay, the plays of William Shakespeare. There's nothing between." I countered, saying possibly a fountain pen would be appropriate. "Got six for my Bar Mitzvah," Jay told me. He was no help. The very notion of a Bar Mitzvah that was not a Bar Mitzvah amused him. "I thought that family was dyed-in-the-wool Socialist," he said. "You know, Princess, I never dreamed Karl was your cousin. I couldn't imagine where he'd met a doll like you."

"Someday you'll have to meet my relatives. All of them."

"Someday you'll have to meet mine. And God give you strength."

Someday. The distant dream. Meanwhile, the reality: sitting in drafty rehearsal halls, waiting in the wings, the cast brushing

149

by, flicking wrists. "Hello, Mimi. How's the kid?" All of them knowing I was waiting for Jay and a bedroom in Bohemia. I had a key to the flat. I'd go there straight from classes and wait for him to come from the radio station. I'd fix a simple supper, eggs or spaghetti usually. On his paydays we'd go out to dinner at an Italian speakeasy. Often, on the day before his payday, we would divide a Hershey bar. He wouldn't let me share the expenses. "Poor but proud, Princess. A temporary condition. However, with you by my side—"

Some Saturday evenings we went dancing, which was a delight. Some evenings, we lounged in the borrowed apartment and he read to me—*Hamlet, Othello,* and his *Blue Fire* scripts. Whatever, invariably the evenings ended on the mattress.

There were times when he was busy with personal affairs, professional affairs, family matters. Then I'd go directly home to Brooklyn. I spent Sundays with my aunt, doing my grooming chores and looking after my clothes. But always with warring emotions, both powerful: the anticipation of tomorrow with him and the nagging guiltiness I had not resolved.

Before the party, a lot of baking and phoning went on in the house. Daisy phoned Hannah: "Don't buy cake or cookies. I'll bring everything." Two cakes, one with coconut icing, one with chocolate frosting; two apple strudels; a half ton of cookies. Hannah phoned Daisy: "Don't bother roasting capons. Davy decided we'll buy delicatessen."

Sophie Kuper phoned Daisy: "I can't promise we will go. Depends how I feel."

I fretted over how we'd carry the baked goods to the Bronx if the Kuper Maxwell did not call for us. At one o'clock, Ben telephoned: "We are leaving right now. Please be outside in front of your house."

Sophie was in the Maxwell's front seat, rigid as the feather on her cloche. Ben was at the wheel, Arnie alone on the back seat, a blanket over his knees. Daisy and I and our bundles surrounded him. We hugged him; he did not hug back.

Sophie's feather swung part-way around. "Arnold, move to

150

the other side, it will be more comfortable for you. Take your blanket. Mildred, please be good enough to help him cover his legs; all I need is he should catch a cold. Arnold, don't touch the handle on the door! Don't fool with it—you could fall out."

"I'll keep my arm around him," I volunteered.

"It is not necessary. Arnold obeys."

Pish, my father would have said. Pish, I said to myself.

Ben started the car. "How was your summer?" I asked Arnie.

"Pleasant, thank you."

"Go to many ball games?"

Ben cleared his throat, as though warning me.

"We didn't go," Arnie said. "My mother didn't want us to."

"What did you do?"

"I went to the Catskill Mountains with my mother."

"Aha! And what did you do there?"

"Arnie rode on a pony," Ben answered for him.

"Let the boy speak for himself," Sophie said.

"They had a black pony," Arnie said. "His name was Marko. I had one ride on his back."

I patted his arm.

"And there was a dog. A collie." His voice was thinning with excitement. "And a gray mama cat. With kittens."

"A zoo," I said, nudging the conversation.

"No." He corrected me gravely. "A farm is not a zoo. It has only domestic animals." He laced his thin fingers. "My father wanted to get me a kitten."

Sophie's feather cut a threatening arc. "All I need in my house is a filthy animal." I believe that is what she said. Yet I cannot be sure the word "another" did not precede "filthy animal."

Aunt Fanny and Uncle Reuben had arrived before us. Fanny hauled me against her bosom; then she thrust me off and held me at arm's length. "You look healthy. I was thinking maybe you were sick—you didn't have the strength to come visit us, not even to lift the receiver up to ask on the phone how we are feeling."

Aunt Hannah embraced me, too, but diffidently, as if she wasn't

151

certain that she should. Uncle Davy wiped his hands on the dish towel, apron tied around his middle, and pumped my hand. "Glad to see you, glad to see you. Excuse me, I'm chief cook and bottle washer."

Snooky's eyes bugged when I gave him the watch.

"Capitalist!" his brother Walt jeered.

"I approve," Eugene said. "The proletariat should wear gold watches; let the capitalists wear the Ingersolls."

Aunt Fanny snatched the watch from Snooky, examined it, slipped the band over her fat wrist, admiring it. "Too expensive for a child. They should change it for something practical."

"Give it back!" Snooky screamed.

"Okay, okay, Aunt Fanny isn't stealing from you," Reuben said, propitiating. "Show the people what the uncle brought. Show." When Snooky, busy strapping on his watch, made no move to show, Reuben rummaged among the gift boxes. "See!" He held up a white silver-trimmed scarf. "I was sure, positive, Dave wouldn't buy a *tallith*. So the uncle provided, the boy should know he is a Jew."

"He knows," Eugene said. "A crippled Jew. Double trouble."

Arnie, edging forward shyly with his present, stopped and stared at Snooky's braces. He flushed, yet he managed to stammer, "My mother thought you could use a painting set." He thrust a tin box at Snooky. "There are brushes in there, but you have to use water for the colors." He retreated, stood a small distance off, staring down at his own skinny legs, his eyes, all at once, full of tears.

"See how your dear ones love you!" Aunt Fanny cried. "They bring you wonderful presents."

"My father got me the best present," Snooky said. "A puppy. We named him Yankel."

"After Grandpa." Walt snickered.

"Shut up, idiot!" Eugene put a hand over Walt's mouth. "Show some respect."

"Karl's paper-training him," Snooky said. "In the bathroom. Go take a look."

Karl kept his head down, pretending to be fussing with the newspapers on the bathroom floor, to avoid looking at me. "Hello," I said. "I came to meet Yankel."

He pointed to under the tub. When I didn't bend, he reached beneath and hauled out a ball of fluff as black as Grandpa's summer mohair suit. He handed the puppy to me, saying acidly, "Another bad actor. Look out he doesn't mess on you."

"He won't," I said. "Nobody does." I set the puppy down and spread my palms. "See? All clean!"

"Quit bragging," Karl said.

"How was it?" Jay wanted to know, when we met Monday after my class and his broadcast.

"A nothing afternoon," I said. "Only the birthday boy enjoyed it. His loot was wonderful. Gold watch. Puppy dog. Just one fountain pen—mine. All of us milled and tried to act as if we were friends. Uncle Reuben lectured his brothers-in-law on the stock market. Buy blue chips. Don't sell. The market will go up, up, up."

He yawned and stretched his arms for me. "Did you give Karl my regards?"

"Certainly not," I replied.

Jay invited me to his mother's house for Thanksgiving dinner. Regarding that, a general statement will do: all families are horrid when you meet them en masse. When you arrive, they offer you fish-eyed stares, and they ignore you afterward. You sit or stand, like a dope, against a wall. Now and then someone ambles over, asks an inane question, but drifts away before you're done answering.

I had to assume they were nice people—all families, including mine, do have members whom you might want for friends. And in any case you can bicker with your own, because you belong. But here, thrust into a swarm of boisterous men, women, and children who were Jay's relatives, I was just the girl he had happened to bring. I'm sure they were sure I was sleeping with him, which I was. However, that gave me no status. On the contrary.

"This is Mimi. She's a foreigner."

"I am pleased to meet you."

"Oh, you speak English!"

Jay's mother, the peroxide blonde, said, "We have always welcomed our son's lady friends."

His father, the spectacled insurance man, said, "So you're from Canada. How do you like America? Some difference, eh?"

His teen-age sister, Janet, asked, "Are you in show business? ...No. Then where did Jake meet you?"

The cat dragged me in.

Ladies, notice my English tweeds, splendidly tailored in my father's workrooms. And please mark my manners: I praise your turkey, which is dry as a bone, and your soggy Brussels sprouts —I was raised by superb cooks, yet I pretend you're offering a Lucullan feast. . . . It is important to make a good impression on those whom you might someday call your "dear ones." That bath-tub gin, that homemade wine, that rotgut whiskey you pass hand to hand and smack your lips over—"No, thank you. I do not drink."

"An old-fashioned girl," Jay's mother said. "For a change."

Jay, my hero, was their hero, Jake. He sat beside his mother at the head of the table. His girl friend, Mimi, sat below the salt. There were twenty, elbow poking elbow, at the feast—uncles, aunts, cousins—and each was compelled, separately, to advise my lover that he or she listened to *Blue Fire;* the script was *gestanko,* but he, their wonder boy, was marvelous, too good for the common people—glancing briefly down the table toward me, to see whether I agreed. I did, I did; I kept nodding, yes, yes. It limbered my spinal column.

"Poor Mimi," Jay said recklessly. "She's never heard the program. She has afternoon classes at Barnard."

"You're missing something exceptional," his Uncle Seymour hurried to inform me.

"I wouldn't go to Barnard if they paid me," his sister, Janet, said. "They're anti-Semitic."

"But you do go to the theayter?" his mother asked me.

"Theayter!" his Aunt Reba sneered. "Saturday night my husband and me, we came home from a show, and I said to him, 'Seymour, if I had a half an hour to spare, I could write a ten-times-better play.' You'll see, Jake, one of these days I'll write you a show; you'll act in it; you'll be a big hit."

"Families are horrible," I told Jay on Bleecker Street.

"Don't bother them, they won't bother you," he said. "My father ignored you because he didn't consider you a prospect for a Twenty-Payment Life. My mother ignored you because she figured the least I would bring home would be Mary Pickford."

"No glamour," I said. "Just a little Jewish girl who goes to Barnard and resides in Brooklyn."

"Suits me fine," he replied.

I didn't go home for Christmas holidays. The play Jay's group had been rehearsing was scheduled to open during Christmas week; it didn't, on account of running short of money to pay the electricians and other mercenary individuals. Jay was desolate. Naturally, I had to spend considerable time on Bleecker Street, consoling him.

In January, I missed a period. I'd always been regular as clockwork; there could be one reason only. I had an idea of when and how it had happened. On New Year's Eve, Jay and I had gone out with his group; there had been considerable drinking. Most likely Jay hadn't been sober enough after we came back to the flat to notice that his condom had split. I believe I did—the act of sex absorbed, preoccupied him, but in me it induced a tense wariness. I believe, too, that I mentioned it and heard him mumble, " 'S all right. Trust me," before he fell asleep.

When I told Jay my suspicion, his face went slack with shock. "You sure? It couldn't be a cold or something? Shouldn't you see a doctor? For your own sake, I mean?" Then switching roles, contrite, cradling his head in his hands: "My fault. I must have been careless." His lower lip thrust forward, not pugnacious, merely thinking of how to handle the problem. "Not on the schedule, not this particular season." His head cocked, studying

155

me. "If I could arrange it, would you—?" He shook his head sharply, dismissing the notion—"Hell with it. Where would we get the money?"—thrust back his shoulders, assembled a lovely smile, and folded my hands into his. "Princess, do not worry, do not be upset. I made you a promise. 'Trust me' is what I said. Whatever you want, that's what we will do. Say the word, tomorrow morning we'll go down to City Hall."

All I could say, and this weakly, was, "How can we get married? Our families haven't even met." And we exploded into crazy laughter, after which he rubbed my belly, saying tenderly, "Who would believe it, in there is a tadpole. And I made it; it's mine."

I wrote a long letter to my parents, saying Jake Bernstein and I were in love, truly, deeply, sincerely in love, and we wanted to get married and live together in a place of our own and work out our future. It was true that right now he wasn't earning much, but he had talent and wonderful prospects. And so, if I didn't register at Barnard next semester—there wasn't any point in my going on with college, was there? I didn't plan to be a teacher or anything special, did I?—why, with the money they would have sent me for tuition and living expenses, and with what Jay earned from radio, we could get married. And can they imagine what it would mean to us both for me to be at his side, inspiring and encouraging him? I'd be a full partner in his success; they'd be proud of us. I was sure, very sure, that this was what I wanted more than anything else in the world. Jay realized he'd made a peculiar impression on them when he had dropped in last summer, but that was for a reason, a good reason they ought to know: he was testing me, making sure in his own way that I wasn't just a spoiled kid from a bourgeois home; what he was looking for was a real woman with tolerance and patience, who could be a genuine partner, for better or worse. We had considered eloping, but we decided this would not be fair to those who loved us. They had every right to want to share our happiness. "And, Mama and Papa, I know what you want for me is my happiness."

I showed Jay the letter before I mailed it. He said it was

156

brilliant; he was afraid he wouldn't have that easy a time with his own parents—they'd been expecting a Mary Pickford. And he added, with an anxious hopefulness, "I don't suppose you've come around yet, have you, Princess?"

Instead of writing or phoning, Papa took the sleeper down from Montreal. He turned up, red-eyed and unshaven, at Daisy's before I was out of bed. When I came down to have breakfast with him, he kissed me, then held me off, his glance dropping to my middle where the tadpole lodged. No bulge. Of this, I was certain.

"Pussycat, you gave Mama and me a surprise," he said, over Daisy's oatmeal.

"After last summer you might have expected it."

"We figured you would give yourself a chance. Think it over, consider carefully."

"I did." Papa received a sweet smile. "This is a thought-over decision."

He stirred the mush in his bowl. I glanced at Daisy, sitting with us. It struck me that she looked frightened—how much had she told my father about the nights I spent on Bleecker Street? Did she blame herself for what was happening? On whose side would she be, theirs or mine? I thought I'd detected a certain envy in her. Would it, could it, turn into malice?

"We have nothing personal against the young man," Papa was saying. "Okay, Mama thinks he is fresh, a smart aleck, the way he was behaving when he was with us. But I explained to her, I made her understand: nowadays young people—some young people, not all; I would break my son's, your brother's, neck if he acted fresh like that in a strange person's house—some young people don't speak with respect to older people, like in our day. To an older person they speak like an equal; more than an equal, a show-off. It's a style nowadays, I explained to your mama. But maybe in their hearts they do have respect."

It was a long speech for my father, the longest I had ever heard him make. He halted to swallow a spoonful of mush, laid the spoon down, and continued.

"Your mama wanted to come to New York with me, only we agreed sometimes she gets excited, she talks more than is needed, so I am here by myself to have a talk-it-over with our daughter."

I smiled again. I said Jay and I had talked it over; after all, we were the ones most involved. Jay had even suggested we go down to City Hall, get married without any fuss—marriage is a private affair; neither of us wanted a big family circus. I stole a glance at Daisy, the third at that breakfast table, silently crumbling a roll on the cloth. Aware I might be giving her pain, I stumbled over my next words. "Why, we even talked about eloping. But then I felt since I had parents—and I loved my parents—I should at least discuss this with them."

"Thank you for the big favor," Papa said. He paid a little attention to his oatmeal, two scanty spoonfuls swallowed, while he absorbed what I had said. "And what do his people say to this?"

I blushed. "I don't know."

"You have met his family?"

"I went to them for Thanksgiving dinner."

"And they received you nice?"

"Oh, very nice."

"He has talked over with his parents what he plans to do?"

Not knowing whether he had or hadn't, I said, "Of course he has."

"And they said?" He was driving at me in a way he had never previously done.

"I can't give you their exact words, I never asked. Because I trust Jay. He's a man, not a kid; he's on his own, earning his living—"

"How much?" Papa asked.

"Oh, Dad!" I bit my lip. "That is beside the point. Remember he's just starting out in his profession."

"Call Bernstein up. Tell him I am here. I wish him to come right away for a talk with me."

It was, I was beginning to think, like a Victorian novel. And why not? Papa was out of Victorian Canada. Yet I was out of my times: a free woman and past twenty-one.

158

The young man who turned up before noon was Jake Bernstein of Washington Heights. He was perfectly costumed for the role of suitor for a daughter's hand: clean-shaven, hair trimmed, well brushed, well pressed—suit and overcoat, white shirt, modest four-in-hand, gray fedora. We exchanged smiles and handshakes, but we didn't kiss. He shook hands with Aunt Daisy and told my father, "Sam, it's good to see you again, though you shouldn't have gone to so much trouble."

Papa drew himself up—it is hard to make a roly-poly impressive. "Nothing is too much trouble for us for our daughter. By us, she is a somebody."

"By me, too," Jay said.

I was in and out of the room while they conversed. I did need to get dressed. This was a significant occasion, the most important one in my life; it deserved better than a flannel bathrobe. Aunt Daisy, as I recall, kept out of sight and hearing, busy in the kitchen. The situation, I have reason to think, was embarrassing to her; she was fearful she might be blamed for her lack of supervision.

A month of madness followed: a desperate madness, fighting against the time when the tadpole would become a bulge; an exhausting madness, making plans and changing plans. Then Jay's professional world collapsed: *Blue Fire* folded up. He was promised another show in March. And Mort Hoffman, who had been coaching the Group, decided to call off rehearsals for two weeks, to concentrate on the comedy he had been rewriting. All this left us time enough for a honeymoon. "An abortion and a Bermuda cruise cost about the same," Jay said. "I'd have to beg or borrow for one or the other. Choose, Princess, choose." I chose Bermuda, as any impractical woman would.

We were married in a rabbi's study. Those present were my parents and my brother, Bram; Jay's parents and his sister, Janet. And Aunt Daisy. Jay's mother fumed over Daisy's presence. "If her aunt is invited, why not his?"

"She's my second mother," I said.

The bride wore a suit her father's factory had made, a small hat with a veil her mother had assembled, and a purple orchid on her lapel that the groom had purchased. The rabbi was beardless; there was no canopy, no shattered wineglass on the floor, not even a ten-male *minyan*. "*Goyish*," Mama muttered.

"We do not follow those old-fashioned customs," Jay's mother explained to her. "We are Reformed."

Afterward, the family group drank bootleg champagne and ate nonkosher chicken in the private dining room of a mid-town hotel. Both sets of parents were sullen. There had been protracted arguments before about the sort of wedding it would be. I had settled the matter. "Look, Mama and Papa," I told them, "I know you'd love to have a big affair for your only daughter. She'd love that, too. Every girl dreams about marching down the aisle in a white gown and veil with the soprano singing 'O Promise Me.' But look at how much that would cost. Jay and I at this moment are poor as poor. If you'd consider giving us a check for what a big wedding costs, we could use it to buy furniture."

They were so startled to find me being sensible that Papa wrote a check at once. It was so substantial that the groom didn't need to beg or borrow for the Bermuda honeymoon, though he did insist he was disappointed. "I had looked forward, Princess, to seeing you in the white gloves. That was the original attraction. Remember?"

"I'll save them," I said, "for your Broadway openings. They'll get lots of wear."

Of my wedding day, I remember only tidbits which are choice: Jay's father, speaking earnestly to mine in a corner of the private dining room, and Papa coming away, grumbling, "Some *machuten*. He picks this time to try to sell me a Twenty-Payment Life. For the couple's benefit."

And Mama muttering into my ear, "At least today he wasn't dressed like a bum. Ashamed for his mother, maybe."

And Jay's mother, shrilling to my mother, "Naturally we are relieved he is marrying a respectable girl. Not a peroxide-blond floozie."

And Mama, eying the woman's coiffure, answering coldly, "Peroxide-blond I know, but what is a floozie?"

And my brother, Bram, a handsome, ruddy redhead, trying to explain the sport of curling to Miss Janet B.: "I am a sweeper. A sweeper has to keep the ice smooth in front of the goalie. . . . Yes, he sweeps with a broom, like a regular broom."

I don't remember Daisy saying or doing anything, though I know she was among those present.

As we prepared to depart, I saw Papa shaking his fist beneath Jay's nose, saying, "Be good to my daughter. You hear, be good to her." And I heard Jay answering, "Trust me, Sam. Mildred does."

I miscarried that night off Cape Hatteras, where the sea is turbulent. It was a mess. Jay and the ship's doctor were both panicky, the M.D. having had more experience with seasickness than with obstetrics. Luckily, the waves calmed, and there was no hemorrhage. Confused and contrite, I lay on the berth, while Jay, sitting beside me, held my hand. "Darling, I don't feel imposed on," he assured me. "I would have married you anyway. I adore you, Princess. Someday we'll make another tadpole. When it's the right time." His voice was so lugubrious, I insisted he go up on deck, get some sun and sea air, enjoy himself. It was, after all, also his honeymoon. By the time we reached Bermuda, he had a sunburn, I had a pallor, and I needed his arm to help me down the gangplank.

From a steamer chair on the hotel lawn I watched Jay playing tennis with a brisk, bright young girl; I read magazines while he went swimming with a group of guests. I had to retire early, yet generous to a fault, I'd say, "Dear, don't sit here moping; go down to the bar, go dancing. Anything. I'll be all right. I'll be fine." Though I dripped a few tears before I fell asleep. The Atlantic Ocean, for the second time, had brought me misery.

My color had improved, although I was still shaky when we got back to New York. We saw both mothers waiting for us on the pier. Jay linked his arm into mine. "Be strong, be steadfast, be snotty, darling. Confess nothing, pet."

His mother hugged and kissed him, remarked how well he

looked, pecked me on one cheek, asked had I been seasick, I looked so green. My mother hugged and kissed me and shook Jay's hand mechanically. She stared at me hard, and while we walked down the pier she managed the intimate question: "Millie, are you already ...?"

"No," I could answer truthfully, "I am not in the family way."

In the fortnight of our absence, each mother had been planning for us, deciding where we would live and hunting for an apartment for us. My mother had found one on Eastern Parkway, over in Brooklyn, not far from the Kupers; Jay's mother had her eye on a place on Washington Heights. They had also decided where we would lodge temporarily. Mama said my old room at Daisy's was waiting; Jay's mother said she had fixed up his old room, adding a folding cot for the bride.

Jay piled our valises into a taxi and told the driver to take us all to Bleecker Street. On the way to Greenwich Village, he spoke firmly to both mothers, making clear he and his wife would decide where to live and how to manage their lives. Both of them became red-faced angry, and my mother retorted with spirit, "The way you two managed already is nothing to be proud about. Two families insulted, aunts and uncles not invited to the wedding."

Next morning, I telephoned to her at Daisy's. She said she was taking the midnight home; I shouldn't bother to come to the depot; I'd need all my strength to clean up the dump to which my husband brought me; it was hard to imagine how a girl like me, raised up in a clean home, could move in with dirt and cockroaches; I must be crazy.

At the end of the week I received Papa's check for one thousand dollars. Whether this was a wedding gift or a final payment he did not specify.

We found three rooms and bath on West Fifty-seventh Street, near Central Park, not far from Broadway. I scooted around, hunting for cheap furniture, and Jay ran around to producers' offices, looking for parts.

Thus I began a new life, an adult life, separate from my parents, in which I would no longer need to wheedle permissions from them or cope with their wraths. In one way it was restful, in another frightening. Where would we turn if Jay failed to find work and we ran out of cash?

Trust me, Princess, he kept saying.

6 ❦

IN THE FALL OF 1929, stocks went down, down, down, everyone's, including Uncle Reuben's blue chips and Papa's Canadian minerals and mines. Perversely, at that very time my husband's stock went up: the movies had begun to talk, and all at once Hollywood was hunting for photogenic actors who could speak. Like Burns of the golden larynx, the vibrant, audacious, and ambitious kid.

However, by the time the godsend came, he was James Burns, an established professional, attested by a few small clippings, pasted in a large book. For nearly two years Jay had been featured (not starred) in a Broadway hit. I would like to claim that marrying me had brought him luck. That wasn't so. Mort Hoffman was the instrument. The Shuberts had bought Mort's comedy, and Mort had let Jay read for a part, a light and lively character, tailored to his personality, possibly inspired by it. The third act had a cabaret scene where he'd need to dance a Charleston. From personal experience, I knew Jay had talented feet.

Matchmaking is tricky. If we had not danced that fox trot on the Astor Roof—

Farewell to radio: rehearse, rehearse. Endure the out-of-town tryouts: Atlantic City, Philadelphia, wherever. Pray. Sweat. Have faith. We will not, we must not, be defeated by a bad second act. Mort Hoffman rewrote and rewrote, his cast relearned and rehearsed.

In our flat on Fifty-seventh Street, I waited for Jay to come

164

home, limp with exhaustion, to snatch a sandwich before he buckled down to memorize fresh lines, work out the business for new scenes. Tense weeks. And penny pinching. ("Mildred, do you happen to have a few simoleons in your purse? . . . I thank you, my mother thanks you, my father thanks you!") Thank *my* mother and *my* father, Jay. I've stretched their gift check, counted pennies, scrimped and slaved. (If I don't send his shirts to the Chinaman, if I wash and iron them myself . . .) Was it worth the struggle? To my husband, yes. He was an actor; this was his purpose and fate. And because it was to him, it was to me.

Sometimes I worried about money while I scrubbed floors or pressed shirts. And sometimes I brooded about Bonnie Granger, with whom Jay danced that Charleston in the third act. "She is a scarecrow with broomstick legs," he assured me. "No competition, pet." He wouldn't let me observe and judge for myself. No loitering in the wings during rehearsals, you'd be in the way, and no hanging around the dressing room. Would you want them to think your husband is henpecked? Never, love, never. All I want is what you want: a hit.

On opening night, I wore my white gloves, and I sat with Jay's parents in fourth-row house seats. All of us clapped like maniacs; so excited were we about what was happening on-stage we forgot that we were natural enemies. When the curtain finally closed, we swept down the aisle, worming our way backstage, to his dressing room. I let his mother embrace him first, his father pump his arm and slap his back. Over their heads, Jay winked at me. I blew him a kiss.

"Jake," Papa Bernstein announced, "Mama and me would like to go somewhere with you, to a restaurant. Celebrate."

"Impossible, Dad. Mort wants us—the cast—over at his place. Post mortems, et cetera." Again, the wink in my direction. "Sorry, Dad. Sorry, Mom. No celebration till the reviews are in." He picked up a towel to wipe make-up off.

"We'll see Mildred home," his mother said.

"*I'll* see Mildred home," Jay said.

In Morton Hoffman's apartment, I met Bonnie Granger—saw

her, that is. She acknowledged my presence with the briefest of nods before she sprawled on a couch. "Bushed! Oh, thank you, thank you!" to the maid who offered her champagne. "Mmmmm! Saved my life!" She was spirited, she projected charm—assumed or authentic, I couldn't say. She had pre-empted the only sofa; the rest of the cast stood around, drinking and jabbering in a language shorthand of their own. I stood on the edge of the crowd, waiting to speak when someone spoke to me. Nobody did. Someone brought newspapers in. Mort read the reviews aloud. The show was a hit. There was wild laughter, clapping, more champagne.

Four papers had mentioned Jay. "James Burns is a young performer of striking personal and vocal attributes." . . . "James Burns' acting has a fresh and spontaneous quality." . . . James Burns, a promising newcomer whom we hope to see again and often," and "Bonnie Granger, a sprite, a dewdrop with bobbed patent leather hair, is a delight to watch. Her Charleston with the versatile James Burns stops the show."

When that one was read, Bonnie jumped up, flung her arms around Jay, and kissed his mouth. Mrs. B., watch out and worry, I said to myself. Nevertheless, alone on the rim of the crowd, I made myself smile while I waited for Jay to come home with me.

In the morning, I clipped the newspapers, red-circled the name of James Burns, pasted the clippings into a book, and in my mind strung them out like pearls. I got duplicates, mailed them to Mama and Papa. My father's acknowledgment was perfunctory. "We received the newspaper items. Thank you."

What did I expect? What could I expect? My parents live in their own narrow world. Broadway success means nothing to them. Nevertheless, I hoped and kept hoping for a hint of approval, an admission that maybe, maybe, Millie wasn't a nut, she knew what she was doing, marrying a versatile man of striking attributes. Their silence was such that I began, in my mind, to accuse them of wishing he had failed. That would have proved

166

their point: Millie should have married a doctor, a lawyer, a rich businessman. Dear parents, this is love. It's real. You were brought together and mated, like cattle—it's amazing you've gotten along as well as you have. If love is blind, luck is more so, *n'est-ce pas?*

The show settled in for a long run, and I settled down to being an actor's wife. That's a backstage role. It gets no applause.

Jay worked two afternoons and six nights every week. He came home after midnight, beat. I had a sandwich, a cold bottle of near-beer, waiting for him, and a pan of warm milk, to cosset his throat and encourage sleep. He slept until well after ten while I skimmed the morning papers, glanced through the mail, sitting close to the phone, snatching it up at the first ring, and speaking, low-voiced, not to disturb his last moments of rest. We breakfasted together. He read his mail and *Variety* in pajamas and robe, then showered and dressed, his attire including a Borsalino, a flamboyant ascot, and a light cane to be twirled. He kissed me before he stepped out on his rounds: seeing people, *his* people (agents, press agents, managers, producers, playwrights); keeping in touch with old contacts, developing new, in case—bite your tongue, cross your fingers—you never know when they may decide to post a closing notice. He stopped at the barbershop—a daily store-bought shave was his luxury, a once-a-week manicure and a hair trim, necessities. He dropped in at the Lambs and the Players, not as much for bridge or billiards as to stand in with his peers and to collect trade gossip. Whether or not he also stopped in at Bonnie Granger's apartment he did not say, nor did I ask, though I wondered, intermittently. And wondering about it, I squirmed (mentally), remembering a miscarriage off Cape Hatteras. Without the pregnancy would Jay have married me? Yet *that* was his fault. . . . Come, come, a woman is partly to blame. By being available. Yet I didn't go to him at Provincetown, looking for sex. Truly, that was not on my mind. Well, then, was I seduced? Yes. By lofty, lovely phrases. By inevitability.

I filled my days with marketing; with prowling department stores, looking for household furnishings and inexpensive clothes;

with sewing bedroom and kitchen curtains; with doing piddling chores. ("Mildred, take my black shoes to the shoemaker, please. New rubber heels.") Evenings, I thumbed magazines while I listened to the radio. And I was lonesome, because one thing I had neglected to do was to acquire playmates in New York. Whether that was due to snobbishness or to a stranger's shyness is anybody's guess, yet the fact is I had not felt a lack of companionship. The first year Karl was squiring me and the relatives were hovering; the second year began with Jay and ended with him.

But now, noon to midnight, I was alone. Jay's family continued to resent and ignore me, as my family did him. And to his colleagues in the cast, I did not exist.

We did have our Sundays together. Most of them were good, lolling abed, reading the Sunday papers, giggling over the funnies. On fine days we walked in the park, we rowed on the lake. In the late afternoons, we'd take a taxicab down to the Village, dine Italian, with a pitcher of wine. And once Jay took me to a ball game. At the Yankee Stadium. It was different. I missed the raucous bonhomie of Ebbets Field; I missed Arnie, diligently marking a scorecard; I missed Ben's excitement and his shouted advice to the team. Jay lacked the true fan's passion; he had come for a look at the stars: Gehrig and Ruth. And to be seen. He kept craning, standing up, turning around, making himself visible. It would have made him exceedingly happy if someone, anyone, had stopped by and asked, "Aren't you James Burns? . . . Didn't I see you in . . . ?"

Not vain, exactly. Just being young, an apprentice celebrity.

One spring Sunday, a mild afternoon of brilliant sunshine, we took the ferry to Staten Island: we gawked at the maiden with the torch, at the squat Ellis Island buildings where Reuben had met the Springer girls; we listened to the creaking gulls; we felt salt spray on our cheeks. And we watched—as I had watched when I was little—ships moving majestically to and from the ocean. It was a delicious outing, until, while we stood at the rail, Jay started to sing, softly, as though to himself. Then, I froze. Because he was singing, " 'My Bonnie lies over the ocean, my Bonnie lies over the sea.' "

"Don't!" I put my hand over his mouth.

His eyes met mine. They sharpened and turned hard. "Come inside," he commanded. "Sit down. Sit. Listen to me. Listen good. You're jealous of Bonnie. Cut it out. Unless you're an idiot, which I refuse to believe. Kiddo, as long as I am an actor, which God willing, will be as long as I can draw my breath, there will be Bonnie Grangers around. I'll dance with them, make love to them. On-stage." He smiled that half-smile he had worn while we danced on the Astor Roof, the smile that was a sort of measuring stick. "It may even happen, if the mood is right, I'll make love to them off-stage. And you're not to get your bowels in an uproar over it." He took my hands, held them tightly. "Because whatever happens, I will come home and I'll put my shoes under your bed. Because it's *you* I married. *You* I want for my wife. I like the way you talk; I like the way you walk, the way you hold your head —the queenly quality. And I like your looks. I don't think you know how gorgeous you are—that lack of vanity is part of your charm. . . . True, true, in bed you're not so hot. Too inhibited. Victorian. Remember that queen—*your* queen—believe me, she went for it, my pet. See how many kids she had. But you will improve; I have hope, I have faith. Because I love you very much. And shall I tell you why I love you? Because with you I feel safe. You trust me; you're loyal. You're my girl; I'm your man. And that's the score, my pet. Take it or leave it, that's how it is, how it has to be."

The hard line, testing me, as on that summer day in Montreal. Take it or leave it, these are my terms.

The ferry's horn tooted above our heads, the crystalline day had turned into gray fog. Symbolic? "My Bonnie lies over the ocean." Out in the fog.

But he is here and I am here, his fingers meshed with mine. And he's made a vow that whoever, whatever, whenever, he will not leave me.

Nevertheless, it rankled a little that he never took me dancing. A minor complaint, actually, yet you do need an excuse now and then to feel sorry for yourself. He dances with Bonnie each night and two afternoons. Am I, or am I not, as good a dancer as she?

No, I am not. Oh, let her have her little whirl. His shoes go under my bed.

On matinee days, Jay found it more convenient not to rush home for dinner between performances, and so, frequently, I would ask Aunt Daisy to come in and go shopping with me or to a matinee. Afterward, we'd stop for cake and coffee and we'd chat, about the show we'd seen or the items I had bought. Daisy wasn't wild about what I chose. Everything had to be ultramodern, straight lines and angles, chromium tubing, sharp reds and blues. "My husband likes this," I told her.

"And you go along?" A pause, a searching glance. "You are happy with your new life? Yes, I see your eyes, they are happy eyes."

But *your* eyes, Aunt Daisy? They're dark, still pools. They tell me nothing about how you feel. Are you angry? Are you sad? Mrs. Magid. A widow. Were you ever truly a wife? Did you feel grief when he died? Or was there only shame? A shame I shared. A shame I'm afraid to remember, and I can't forget. Your family did that to you. Or did you do this to yourself, letting your father and your brother choose a husband for you?

I chose for myself. And I am happy. You say you see happiness in my eyes. Yet I'm not entirely sure I am. You see, I threw myself into a life that now and then scares me. So much has changed. Well, for one thing—this is so trivial you'd laugh if I told you—Jay doesn't call me Princess any more. I'm "Hey, Mildred!" who washes his BVDs.

I need a woman to talk to, a confidante. Much as I love you, Aunt Daisy, you aren't the listener I need.

"Darlin', if you want summer curtains, choose your material. I'll run them up on my machine."

Right, Daisy dear, I'm a housewife. Like you.

Some evenings when I sat alongside the radio, I wondered whether Aunt Hannah might be the confidante; she'd been a rebel, she had chosen her man. Made her bed, as they say, and was lying in it, with poverty and a crippled son. Aunt Hannah, do you have regrets? Tell me the truth. You won't. We never were close. And more than before we're now estranged. Because of Karl. Did he want me for himself? That wasn't possible, he ought to know; we're first cousins, our children might be idiots. Besides, Karl, the It wasn't there, the chemistry. Karl, don't be angry, please do not be. I want us to be friends, "dear once," as Uncle Reuben says.

After our basic furniture had been bought and placed, I decided to have a party, a buffet supper on a Sunday evening, a housewarming, a get-acquainted for my family and Jay's. He fancied the role of a host so much that he went out and purchased a costume: a brocade smoking jacket, with crimson velvet lapels and *soutache* trimming, and he provided a list. I wrote invitations, including one to Montreal. Bram replied for my family; they didn't think it was practical to make the long trip for a social gathering. Signed, "Sincerely yours, your brother, Bram Samuelson." Nothing personal, not even "Regards to Jake Bernstein—James Burns—whatever he is called."

Aunt Fanny was also formal. "Mr. and Mrs. Reuben Springer accepts your invitation to be among those present at your social gathering."

Not only "among" but the first. The Springers arrived before I had garnished the cold-cuts platter with olives and parsley sprigs. Fanny came bearing a grudge and a monstrous cut-glass bowl. She pushed my floral centerpiece aside and plunked her atrocity in the center of my table. "Gorjus, no? Believe me, you didn't deserve it, Millie. Us you didn't invite to your wedding, your mother's only brother and his wife."

Uncle Reuben pinched my cheek. "You should learn and remember, Millie, a family should come together always for *simchas*. The weddings so much as for funerals."

Aunt Fanny asked were the Kupers coming. When I said they'd not been asked, she scowled. "But Sophie knows you are having the party; I told her on the telephone. Now she will be insulted." She glowered at Jay, as if blaming him.

He asked, "Who are the Kupers? Should I know them?"

"He was my first love," I said. "When I was ten."

"My brother," Aunt Fanny added. "A businessman. I am Mrs.

171

Reuben Springer; Millie didn't introduce us. The gentleman is Mr. Springer, my husband. He is also a businessman." She fingered the smoking jacket. "Dressed up like an actor," she observed astutely. "This number we don't carry in our store. Our trade don't go for fancy stuff."

"Pleased to meet you, I'm sure," Jay replied.

She did a rapid inventory of our living room. "Modren! You like modren!" Her tone implied our taste was not only preposterous but somehow obscene.

"Would you care for a drink?" Jay asked Uncle Reuben, using the smirk that implied we have bootleg gin and whiskey on the premises.

"Ginger ale if you have it," Aunt Fanny replied. "But he could wait till Millie serves the crowd."

Aunt Daisy arrived, loaded with cooked corned beef and tongue, a lemon chiffon pie, and strudel, reinforcements in case I hadn't provided enough. Then Aunt Hannah, with Eugene and Walt—Davy worked Sundays, Hannah explained, and Karl had to stay home to look after Snooky and walk the dog. Her glance followed Jay when he led the boys to the bedroom to drop their caps and Hannah's coat. I wondered what Karl had told his mother about my husband. See for yourself, Aunt Hannah. No cloven hoofs, no tail, one head.

Finally, Jay's relatives: the parents, the sister, the uncles and the cousins and the aunts, in a swarm, loading down our bed with their coats and hats, jamming our living room, spilling into the foyer, swamping the handful of my relatives. So many of them, so few of us. We were numerous when we last assembled in the Brooklyn house: Grandpa Springer, my mother, my father, my brother, Hannah, Dave, their four boys, Reuben and Fanny, Ben and Sophie, their name hyphenated with ours in Uncle Reuben's Family League. Here, now, milling among these strangers, were the remnants: Hannah, gray, stooped, and shabby, with her middle sons; Reuben and Fanny, grotesquely fat; and Daisy, sweet but lusterless, like a—like a wilted morning glory.

Passing a canapé tray, I tried to single them out to say the words, offer the gestures and the smiles to make them feel welcome. Hannah touched my shoulder gently. "Forget about us, Millie. Look after his family." But Reuben seized my arm, pulled me over to where he had trapped my father-in-law against a foyer wall, and went on with the lecture he had been delivering.

"So, Mr. Bernstein, I say you should go, take a look how beautiful our plot is kept up. I send a check regular—I am the President from our Family League—to pay the grass should be cut. Only two places are taken. My father, he should rest in peace, and the husband from my sister Daisy. A sad case. Died young from a accident." He gave Jay's father a searching look. "A accident," he repeated.

Mr. Bernstein clucked sympathetically. "No insurance, I bet."

"Think over," Reuben persisted. "You could sometimes say to yourself, it was my lucky day I met that Springer feller in my daughter-in-law's apartment—Millie's apartment—and he invited me to join his Family League so my dear once would not need to worry, they will have a place when the time comes."

My father-in-law cleared his throat to meet earnestness with sincerity. "Mr. Springer, it was farsighted of you to provide this final resting place for your family. But I might say too farsighted, or perhaps not farsighted enough. Have you considered maybe the location will not be convenient for some when their time comes? And then you are stuck with the real estate. But if every person in the family carries a policy, the survivors can buy a plot in whatever place is convenient. And have something left over to pay for the stone. . . ."

It was macabre but terribly funny. I moved away—I had to before a giggle broke loose. Then, as I moved on with my tray, I heard a few sentences that congealed the mirth in my throat. Jay's Aunt Reba was talking to his Aunt Jennie—their backs were toward me. "My dear," Reba was saying, "she got him by the oldest trick in the world. Told him she was pregnant, he'd have to marry her. And after they were married, he found out she wasn't pregnant." Maybe they were speaking of me, maybe not. But the final sentence floored me. "Paula told me herself." Paula was my mother-in-law.

173

I hurried to the kitchen. Jay followed me there. "Uncle Seymour is asking for hot coffee," he began. "Cold drinks don't agree with him." He noticed my face. "What's up? What happened?"

"Jay, did you tell your mother—"

"Tell her what?"

"About us. That we had to get married."

"I did not," he said. "Don't be a jackass." He kissed my forehead. "Put on the coffee. It's not a bad party. They're all enjoying themselves. Me, too, in an odd sort of way."

Jay's mother said, as I handed her a cup of coffee, "I'm surprised your parents are not here." She stared at my face, not my figure, which considering what I had overheard was gracious of her.

"Too bad your brother didn't come, I liked him," Jay's sister said. "Is he still twirling?"

"Curling," I said. "Yes."

"Oh, is he a hairdresser?" Jay's Aunt Jennie asked. She, too, didn't stare at my body—it may have been some other female they had gossiped about.

"Curling's a sport, a game. Played on the ice," I told them.

"They live such a different life up there," Jay's mother said.

"Cream and sugar?" I said.

My cousin Walt said at departure, "Kiddo, you look perfectly swell. I'll tell Karl."

"Too bad he couldn't come to see for himself," I said.

While we were washing the dishes—I washing, Jay leaning against the refrig and kibitzing—my husband remarked, "I liked those kid brothers of Karl's. Especially Walt. He's smart as a whip. He knows a chap who's written a play about the Sacco-Vanzetti case. I told him to have the chap get in touch. If our show closes —God forbid!"

"God forbid!" I said. We laughed. He kissed the back of my neck.

"It was okay; you were okay. And don't worry about my old lady's big mouth. She's a half-wit."

But then and there, I made my mind up (though I did not tell Jay) that never again would I ask her to my house, nor, if

174

invited, would I go to hers. Collecting grudges, chewing them over, storing them, is the normal way of families.

Walt's friend phoned and came up on a Sunday with his script. He had a bad case of acne and a violent habit of flailing his arms while he talked. Jay assured him he'd read the play sympathetically. I served iced tea and cookies while he and Jay discussed the case. In the evening, Jay read the script, grunted, tossed it on the floor. I stooped for it. "May I?"

"Don't waste your time."

I wasted time; the play was terrible. "Soapbox speeches. No drama," I said.

"You have taste," he said. "That case deserves something great —something to stir the world's conscience, get into its guts."

"I didn't know you cared," I said.

"I care," he said. "When there's something worth caring about."

In any event, there was no current need for Jay to look for a new vehicle. Mort Hoffman's merry masterpiece had survived the summer slump; after Labor Day it was SRO. I had survived the summer, mostly on benches in Central Park. Jay had suggested I run up to Canada for a holiday with my folks. "And leave you sweltering in the city?" Sincerely meant, though my family hadn't been pleading for the pleasure of my company. Technically, there was no breach, since there had been no trading of insults or ultimata, not since that suppertime in Montreal when I had asserted my right to go to Jay. Yet a breach did exist; it had come from the simple fact of my adulthood. They no longer fed me and housed me, no longer paid my bills, hence no longer could they tell me what I should or should not do. And in spite of them, I had married the man of my choice. Hence, apparently, I had forfeited their concern, their love.

That is preposterous. Parents don't stop loving children, nor children stop loving their parents. The condition of loving is inborn. We can disagree, can't we, yet remain good friends? Not they. They're sulking in that house in Westmount because Millie married an actor and he turned out not to be a bum. Your elders hate to admit that they were wrong.

I could have—this I conceded only to myself—enjoyed a spot of family bickering; it would have helped me pass the time. For the truth was I was bored. By the second year of my marriage, I knew I would have to make a drastic change: I'd either need to return to college or become pregnant.

Jay arched his brows high when I asked him to make a baby with me. "No kidding? Ah, well, we aim to please."

His casualness surprised me. Weren't young husbands supposed to be reluctant to assume new burdens? A baby needs all sorts of things: diapers and gocarts, Grade A milk, cod-liver oil, and Teddy bears. Do we—will we—have money for all this? And are we mature enough to guide a young life? It should be discussed, shouldn't it? "We aim to please."

We chose a Sunday afternoon, with sunshine streaming through our bedroom window. And for the first time since I had been having intercourse with Jay, I didn't tighten up with dread. And when I held him close, it was an embrace, not a fearful clutching.

"We'll have a son," I announced. "His name will be William. After Shakespeare. Romeo and Juliet started all this."

"I knew," Jay said before he dropped off to sleep, "once you got the general idea, you'd be okay in bed."

At last, I was busy, sewing and knitting, shopping for maternity and infant clothing, studying Dr. Holt's baby-care book, visiting the obstetrician and the dentist.

Jay's mother had recommended the doctor after her son had phoned to say, "Mildred has news. Take it calmly. . . . Come on, Mom, you expected this, didn't you? You advertised it before it happened. . . ."

"My husband and me"—Paula Bernstein had asked to speak to me—"are very young for grandparents. Why, if he didn't take the precautions, we could still have one of our own. Are you sure you are ready? This wasn't an accident? . . . Well, Dr. Lorwin is wonderful; he delivered Jake and Janet, and he believes in helping you with a whiff of chloroform at the end. Not let you suffer the

176

way some doctors do. He will be absolutely, positively flabbergasted to hear Paula Bernstein is going to be a grandmother."

Dr. Lorwin took the news phlegmatically. He was late-middle-aged, heavy-set and gray. He had kept me sitting in his Manhattan waiting room for an hour before his nurse ushered me to the desk side. He asked the date of my last period, wrote down an approximate date of delivery, recorded my blood pressure, perched me on his scale, hooked my feet into stirrups on the examining table, announced, yes, I was pregnant, slapped my buttocks lightly. "Get dressed, we'll talk." At desk side again, he asked my preference for private or semiprivate at the hospital, admonished me to watch my diet, not gain too much weight—it's an advantage for first babies to be small—patted my cheek, shook my hand, said, "See you in three weeks." The nurse took the fee and instructed me to bring a urine specimen—the morning's first leak—next time I came.

I hadn't mentioned my previous pregnancy. Nor had he asked. What they don't ask, you needn't tell. Possibly I was misjudging my mother-in-law. At that stage of my life—it is true—I mistrusted all parents, my own as well as Jay's. Middle-aged people are not as smart as they think. They've forgotten what it's like to be young.

The dentist was Dr. Weinbaum. Aunt Daisy had recommended him. His office was in Brooklyn. He was jolly.

"Mrs. Bernstein? James Burns, the actor, is your husband, eh? . . . What's it like to be married to a Broadway star? . . . I bet you know lots of celebrities. . . . Wait till I tell my wife I have Mrs. James Burns for a patient. Know what she'll say: 'Aha! Oho! Ask her to get us passes.' Two cavities, Mrs. Bernstein. Burns. Which name shall I call you? . . . Doesn't matter, eh? A rose by any other name. . . . Don't forget to drink milk, protect the teeth, build strong bones for the baby. . . ."

One afternoon in Dr. Weinbaum's waiting room I ran into Arnold Kuper. He was going out when I came in; he was carrying a black leatherette music roll.

"Are you—aren't you Arnie Kuper?"

"I am Arnold Kuper." Spoken uncertainly and with a blush —my bulging figure might have disconcerted him.

"I'm Millie. Millie Samuelson, Millie Bernstein now. We used to go to the ball games. Remember?"

He remembered, and he smiled. The smile was like his father's—sweet—but smaller, less spontaneous.

"And how are your parents?"

"They are well, thank you. . . . Excuse me, I'm late for my piano lesson."

"I see the Kuper boy's your patient," I remarked to Dr. Weinbaum while he clipped on my bib.

"I have the family." He paused to correct himself. "Used to have. The father came only once." He wadded my gums with cotton rolls and reached for his drill. "The mother used to bring the boy. Now he comes by himself. Nice kid. Except he looks down in the mouth. Like me. Ha-ha! Ho-ho!"

He looked down in my mouth and tortured it with the drill, so that until he halted to change the burr I could not retort. "What can you expect from a Dodger fan?" I remarked.

"Aha! Oho! You're a Yankee fan!"

"Not particularly. I used to go to Sunday games at Ebbets Field. With Arnold and his father."

"The father?" The drill was in my tooth again. "What is with the father?"

I shrugged, silenced by the wadding and the drill.

"I pulled a molar for him. First I advised we try to save the tooth. A good-looking man, I would expect—you would expect —he'd want a nice-looking mouth. . . . Relax, take it easy, Mrs. Bernstein, Burns; just a couple more seconds. . . . He said, 'Pull it out, get the pain over with.' We spoke about a replacement. He asked me how much. I try to keep my bills fair and reasonable— it's one price for a pivot tooth, for a removable bridge it's another. I don't know if it was the money worried him. He never came back. . . . Okay, Mrs. Burns, rinse, spit out. . . . That family related to you?"

"Mr. Kuper is a brother of my aunt," I mumbled through cotton rolls, before he again started to drill.

"Of Mrs. Magid? The one who recommended you? . . . Don't be so jumpy, Mrs. Burns, the nerve's not exposed."

On another afternoon when I had come for the professional cleaning that completes the job, I saw Sophie Kuper in that waiting room and went toward her to say hello. Her icy stare froze me in my tracks, before she picked up a battered *Collier's* and opened it to read.

Dr. Weinbaum emerged, saying cheerfully, "You ladies know each other, don't you?" Sophie rose without a word to me and followed him in.

The dentist's chair was still warm from her when I sat down in it. "What goes on?" Dr. Weinbaum demanded while he clipped on the bib. "I mentioned to her you mentioned you used to go to ball games with the father and the kid. And she got—well, she acted as if—" He held the drill, menacing, above my head. "It's none of my business. But was there something between you and Kuper? Hanky-panky, maybe? Nothing serious. A pretty young girl . . . a man could get ideas. Especially a man who's married to a —to a —"

I seized the instant before he started working in my mouth. "I used to love Ben Kuper madly," I said, "when I was ten. He won me a kewpie doll, and he bought me Crackerjack."

"That's why you had those cavities," he said. "Lay off the Crackerjack."

In September, when William Shakespeare Bernstein had begun to bounce beneath my ribs, I wrote my mother and father to expect a grandchild early in the coming year. My father answered they already knew, Daisy and Hannah had informed them; they had been wondering why they hadn't heard directly from me. "Pussycat, we are your loving parents. For you we wish prosperity, health, happiness. Mama thinks you should come here for the baby to be born; we have good doctors, and this big house was your home. It would make Mama happy to take care of you and the little one."

I answered I was grateful for their offer but the baby's father wished to be on hand to welcome his first-born. That meant I'd have my baby in New York; he, she, or it would be a U.S. citizen, and I hoped they would not hold the nationality against a helpless child. Naturally, if they cared to come down to the States, they could be among those present to welcome their American grandchild. I was feeling flip, the world was merry, everyone was prosperous, and I was round with a lively unborn child.

My parents were on hand to welcome the baby. Jay was not. He was on the other side of the continent.

In October the stock market crashed. Jay's father's insurance firm was busy investigating claims of families of men who'd leaped from apartment windows or turned on the gas. The show limped for a few weeks; in November the closing notice went up on the board. Jay put in a fortnight of heavy drinking, of rocking his head in his hands. "My God, Mildred, what have we done? Picked the perfect time to start a family, didn't we?" Then, ruefully, "But it was a beautiful notion, wasn't it? Who could have dreamed the U.S.A. would go broke?"

In the morning of an early December day, Jay's agent phoned, and when he hung the receiver up my husband had changed: his cheeks were flushed, his eyes were shining. He grinned, ear to ear. "They want me on the Coast. Screen tests. Pinch me, Mildred, pinch me hard. Make sure I'm not dreaming."

I pinched him hard. "When?" I asked.

"Now. Immediately. 'Hop on it, buster,' the man said. 'Not later than tomorrow. Grab the Century to Chicago. Pick up the Chief to the Coast.'" He squeezed my hands. "Kiddo, this is kismet."

"Wonderful, wonderful," I managed to say, though my glance went down to my middle where the almost-finished baby squirmed.

Jay's glance followed mine. "This is no time to leave you," he said.

"Kismet," I said.

"Mildred, if I shouldn't, if you think— If they really want me, they will wait. . . ."

A lump was rising in my throat. "Go," I said. "It's your big chance." I swallowed the lump. "Our chance," I said.

"You'll be okay?"

180

"I have a good doctor. And a telephone."

"I could ask my mother, my sister, to come stay with you. . . ."

"Don't you dare."

"You could ask your aunt, the one you like."

"Darling, I'll be fine. William isn't due for months."

He was not reassured. "Suppose you came with me, we did the trip together?"

I stroked his cheek. "Pregnant women shouldn't travel," I said.

He said what was in the back of my mind: "We *want* this kid."

A charming, domestic scene, affectionate, considerate. Practical details, however, can wreck a mood.

"Mildred, what's in the bank?"

"Peanuts," I said.

He began to pace, thinking hard. I had a brain storm.

"Dear, I have some gold pieces, some silver. My grandfather gave them to me. I've been keeping them for William."

He managed a grin. "A hell of a note, robbing a piggy bank to get to Hollywood." He kissed my cheek. "You're such a good kid," he said. "You're a doll."

I brought out the old candy box and poured the coins into his hands. He jingled them, doing arithmetic. "Wouldn't get me to Buffalo, Princess. Thanks, anyway. I'll call my agent; he'll finagle something."

"Take them, use them," I said. "They will bring you luck."

Yes, fans of James Burns, it is the truth: your idol traveled to Hollywood in an upper berth paid for by Grandpa Springer's Chanukah *gelt*. The rest of the cost of his trip came out of a loan his agent finagled for him.

Before Jay went out to pick up the ticket money, he asked me to wash and iron his shirts; there wasn't time to get them to the laundry. After he had left, I wrote to my father, asking if he could tide me over with a loan until Jay got a contract on the Coast. His check came promptly, with a letter suggesting that, if I wished, Mama would come down and stay with me; in my condition I should not be alone. He added that he wished my husband luck; he didn't know much about the business side of the movies, but he'd been told there was big money in it. He didn't mention that he himself had had to borrow to make this loan to us.

At the end of a week, Jay telephoned. The ringing woke me at one in the morning; he'd not yet become clear about the time difference. The connection was poor. All I learned was that so far nothing had happened; all he learned from me was the same.

"Take care of you and William."

"Take care of yourself."

The next week I received a letter from a gee-whiz kid.

Garbo walked by the other afternoon, her beauty defies description. Saw Norma Shearer on her set. Not bad, not bad, she has class. Harlow was pointed out to me, I don't go for that type. Mildred, the abundance of female pulchritude in this place is stultifying. Beautiful girls are a dime a dozen. Don't worry, kid, don't start getting jealous. I notice them, they don't notice me. A cat can look at a queen, but this cat is nobody yet. Until you're under contract—

That'll come, they tell me. But when? How soon? Two studios have tested. Rumor is, tests were okay. But nothing counts till the check has cleared the bank. And they've got the stock-market jitters here. In spades. Nothing's likely to happen quickly, I'm afraid. And unless something does, I may have to drive a taxi, look for a busboy's job. Anything for eating money. But one thing is sure, I am not rushing back. I will stick it out. So stick by me, kid. And try not to feel badly if you have to spend Christmas alone.

Christmas Eve and Christmas Day and New Year's Eve and New Year's Day, alone, beside my radio, knitting an afghan for William's crib. Then, on a bitter January night, twinges changed to rending pain. I had barely time enough, before hysteria arrived, to telephone to Dr. Lorwin, beg him to leave his bridge game, and to call Aunt Daisy to ask her to find a taxi and come to take me to the hospital. Hurry, hurry, please hurry. I'm having a baby, and it hurts.

Night was turning into morning when Dr. Lorwin, in a white

182

butcher's coat, held up by one skinny leg something that looked like a plucked chicken—"This is your daughter, Mrs. B."—in such a contemptuous tone that I had to protest through the chloroform haze, "What do you expect from an amateur?" before I was lifted off the table and trundled to bed.

"Some amateur!" Dr. Lorwin said when he stood beside my bed. "An old hand couldn't have done it better. No fuss. No complications. Of course, it helped that she's small. Three pounds, one ounce. And she'll lose before she starts to gain. Don't let that worry you. She's perfect, she's healthy. What name shall I put on the certificate?"

"I'll have to consult the father," I said. "He's in California."

Aunt Daisy sent my telegram to Jay: WE HAVE A THREE POUND ONE OUNCE DAUGHTER. WHAT IS HER NAME?

At noon a nurse carried in two boxes of roses: a dozen red for me, card reading, *Great performance, Princess. Congratulations;* a dozen pink, card reading, *For Greta, a new star.*

Greta. After Garbo, undoubtedly.

But Jay, dear, I hate to admit this, your daughter is no beauty. She is a red-faced nothing, although what's astonishing is how well she's equipped. Fingernails, eyelashes, eyebrows. Everything except hair and teeth.

Jay's mother dropped in during the afternoon, when my cubbyhole was full of roses. "My crazy son!" she exploded. "Spends a fortune on flowers when he doesn't have a job. No sense, no practical sense whatsoever. Two of a kind, you and him. You need a baby now, in this depression, like I need a hole in my head."

My parents came straight from their train. They had just enough time to kiss my forehead before a nurse shooed them out, saying, This patient has been up all night; she has to get some sleep. Right after breakfast, they returned with decisions made and plans worked out for me. They had slept in my apartment— Daisy had my keys—and they had decided the place would never do: no space for the crib, the dresser, the carriage; no place to dry diapers; and the landlord was a *momser*, a bastard, all night there was not a drop of steam heat, the flat was like an icebox. Naturally, details like these would never occur to Millie. From past experience they knew how impractical . . .

Forget the past, let's have no recriminations; the important thing is what's best to do now. Mama and Papa had decided the best thing for me and the baby would be to go straight from the hospital to Daisy's house. Daisy would help with the baby—yes, she had offered, she would be delighted. And there was a yard for drying diapers and airing the infant in her carriage—they'd buy the perambulator, this was the grandparents' privilege. Naturally, it would be only a temporary arrangement. Temporary can be as long as it has to be. Maybe, later, we will go to Westmount.

I wired Jay; he wired back: OKAY IF YOU CAN STAND IT. GOOD LUCK.

At four-hour intervals, Greta was brought to me to be taught to nurse. She couldn't suck: too puny, too weak, or too drowsy. The nurse carried her out, hungry and yowling. She lost three ounces. I wept. Dr. Lorwin tried to comfort me. "We'll keep trying, though maybe you never will be a cow. Those breasts. Decorative but not useful, possibly. We'll put her on formula. Calm down, behave yourself, or I'll tell Paula Bernstein on you."

His threat dried my tears. That and the fact that Greta gained a half ounce, an ounce, on the formula. Her stools, I was assured, were of normal color and consistency. I still saw her at regular intervals and held her in my arms. Her color began to change, from the angry red to the pink porcelain of the females in my family, and her eyes, when she deigned to open them, were blue. This, Jay's mother informed me, meant nothing whatever; all babies were born with blue eyes; they change. An old wives' tale. I was born blue-eyed; blue-eyed I remained. And my daughter, resembling me, will grow up and fall in love. With an actor who is far away.

At last, Dr. Lorwin said, "Go home, both of you. See me in four weeks."

Mama rewarded the nurses with boxes of Whitman's Sampler before she picked up the blue-blanket cocoon that held my sleepy-head. Aunt Daisy carried my valise and the emergency supply of

184

formula the hospital had made up for Greta. Papa juggled a potted plant Jay's parents had sent. He paid the cashier. Straight up and down and empty-handed, I sat between the ladies in the taxi, riding back to Brooklyn, into the bosom of my family.

Greta's Uncle Bram was waiting at the house with his Kodak to snap pictures of the infant for whom it might concern. I was allowed to hold her for two photographs before Mama ordered me to bed in Daisy's room.

I was a *kimpetorin*, a woman who had just given birth, hence presumed to be a physical wreck, who must stay off her feet, gain strength, while in truth I felt strong as a horse. Mama and Daisy changed Greta's diapers, powdered her, oiled her, bathed her, powdered and oiled her afresh, swaddled her in blankets, tucked her into a beribboned, lace-hooded bassinet. Daytimes, they wheeled the bassinet into the parlor bay, which was sunny, nights to the corridor between the parlor and the bedrooms, "So we can hear our baby if she wakes up," Mama said.

"*Our* baby." Not Millie's baby. Not Jay and Millie's baby. *Ours*. A family treasure. We will feed her and bathe her, cuddle her, sing lullabies. Millie? She is a child. What does she know?

I resented this until it dawned on me that Mama's slavish doting was a sort of atonement for her indifference to me after my marriage: we allowed our daughter to struggle and suffer and to worry all alone. We have reclaimed her; hereafter no Bernstein–Burns will come between us.

When Mama and Daisy slept, if they did, I do not know. I'd catch glimpses of them in the middle of the night, wraiths in flannel bathrobes, hovering around the bassinet, changing, turning, tucking, conferring, admiring; tiptoeing to shut my door tightly so my sleep would not be disturbed. At dawn they went to the kitchen, to sterilize bottles, mix formula, measuring the ounces meticulously; soaking, boiling, scrubbing diapers, hanging them in the yard to freeze and flap, like white boards; afterward, warming the flannels on the radiator tops. Busy, bustling. Mildred, the mother? Oh, no, she can't lift a finger. She must rest.

If I had been very good and had finished my oatmeal, rice

pudding, or chicken soup, I was permitted to hold Greta for her afternoon bottle while my mother clucked. "Be careful. Hold her head steady."

Honest, I won't break my baby's neck. Can't you trust me? I made her, I love her. At least I believe I love her. In those moments when she lay in the crook of my arm, I groped for the sensuous thrill, the mystical bond that's supposed to tie a mother to a child. Not yet. Later. When she learns to smile, to cling to my finger. When she begins to know me. And to trust.

And so I lolled on the goose-down pillows in Daisy's bed and fretted about my husband. We had talked on the phone, but the long-distance call had been slurred and blurred. A present and a future can't be arranged in three-minute dialogues.

However, the main thing, the good thing, was that he had work. In a picture. "Not exactly what I hoped for. Will write the details." Which he hadn't done. Busy at the studio, no doubt. Not occupied, I hope, I hope, with those dime-a-dozen beautiful girls.

Nevertheless, we had decisions to make: whether to keep our apartment, and if to give it up, to where shall we move?

Nothing, some wiser person has observed, is more permanent than a temporary arrangement. The plush comfort of Daisy's house was fine and dandy. And seductive. However, it had to have its limits. An imposition on Daisy, and on Mama, who had begun to remark that Papa was feeling neglected, she'd been away so long. Nevertheless, as long as *our* baby and *our* daughter need her . . .

By the middle of February I had grown fat and restless. My wedding anniversary was approaching; it's hard to celebrate that event without a husband. "The mountain can't come to Mohammed," I told Mama. "Mohammed must go to the mountain."

She blinked. "What Mohammed? Who is Mohammed?"

"Me and Greta. We have to go to California."

"A newborn baby travel on a train in the wintertime? You must be *meshugah!*"

Aunt Daisy said, "If Millie would give me the pleasure—our

darlin' baby doesn't make one minute's trouble—I would be happy to look after her. You could go, have a visit with your husband."

"I was getting ready to go home," Mama said. "Sam was complaining already. But how could Daisy take care by herself?"

"Daisy could, by herself," Daisy said.

"Maybe Sam would let me stay another week, two weeks." Mama began to compromise.

"I heard in California it is always summer," Daisy added. "A vacation in the sunshine would be a tonic for Millie."

"I will stay; you can go," Mama decided. "Our baby wouldn't miss you. Does she know you are the mother? How much do you do for her?"

Thus, all my life, my mother had given in, though with a barb, a small knife thrust. I telephoned. Jay received my news ecstatically. "You can't know how much I've missed you. . . . I'll do my damnedest to meet your train. In case I don't—those jokers at the studio can make things difficult—grab a taxi, go straight to my place, the door will be open."

Papa sent a money order to pay for a Pullman ticket and a handsome suit of English tweed in which to travel.

"You look like a college girl," Daisy said.

Mama sniffed, "Some college girl! Take off the skirt. I'll move the button. You gained."

I gave Greta a tender hug. "I'll tell your daddy you are beautiful." She yawned in my face.

At parting, Mama admonished me, "Tonight on the train, take a tablespoon mineral oil, you shouldn't get constipated."

On the subway, riding to Manhattan and the railroad station, it occurred to me she hadn't said, "Give my regards to Jay." Not yet admitting I was a married woman, with a living husband, or that "our baby" had a father. Immaculate conception by Madonna Mildred, who, flat in the middle and resembling a college girl, was off on a romantic journey, like a once-upon-a-time departure for Provincetown.

The Pullman porter hovered and fussed: straightening the head-rest towel when it didn't require straightening; fetching a footstool I hadn't asked for; removing it ruefully; asking half a dozen times, while he made up my berth, whether there was anything else I needed, another pillow, another blanket, perhaps; brushing my jacket and coat before he hung them up carefully—working for the tip he counted on and prayed for, since there was just one other passenger in that Pullman car. And, in the morning, I breakfasted in a dining car where the white table linen on the empty tables was dazzling as snow. And eerie, lonely. While I'd been hid from the world in Brooklyn, Depression had moved in on the land. Bypassing me.

Jay didn't meet me at the Los Angeles station; I had to find a taxi. It was pouring pitchforks; the air was murky and raw. I forded a running gutter stream to climb into the cab. The ride was monotonous, endless: block after block of low, pastel-tinted buildings, crude and impermanent; intervals of ugly palm trees, with wind-whipped, shivering fronds. Rain slathered the windshield; it leaped from puddles in the road, spattering the fenders. California, where is that golden sunshine, where is the beauty you have advertised? In the distance, I saw hills, brown and barren, crouching like moth-eaten lions, and my memory began to play tricks. It flashed a picture-postcard view of Montreal, in this winter month: the dark green pines crowning the snowbanks, the solid splendor of the gray stone mansions, the mellow warmth of old red brick. For a moment, I was homesick and sickened by the sodden shoddiness of this place to which I had come. I am an alien, I don't belong. Will I remain a stranger because I married Jay?

The taxi stopped in front of a pink stucco hut, one of several huts around a grassy rectangle. Purple flowers, whose name I didn't know, were plastered against the wall; yellow blossoms on a bush, whose name I didn't know, dripped beside the door; palm fronds swayed and hissed above the roof. The knob turned at my touch; the door was unlocked.

It was a square, white-washed room, holding a couch bed, a chest of drawers, a table, two wooden folding chairs, a sagging armchair, a bridge lamp. The floor was bare. It was Spartan but immaculate.

In the middle of the table stood a bowl of crimson roses; propped against it was a note. *Welcome, Princess! Welcome home!* True, where my husband lodges is my home.

I hung my dresses in a narrow closet, next to his familiar suits, his gaudy smoking jacket, and those shirts I had ironed in New York. I ran hot water into a tub, soaked off a long journey's grime, powdered and perfumed my flesh, put a kimono on, then went to look for food in the kitchenette. Two oranges on the counter, an inch of coffee in a canister, half a box of graham crackers. I opened the Frigidaire beneath the sink. No bread and butter, no eggs or milk. Only a quart of champagne. I was touched, and I was torn. Dear crazy husband, red roses and champagne—such wild extravagance! But exactly what we need for a reunion scene. The perfect props.

I found a percolator that was shining clean. Is some woman housekeeping for him? Stop! Stop that jealousy! It's you he married, you and no one else. I set the percolator on an electric plate. Hot coffee warmed me while I waited for him to come home.

It was almost dark when he arrived. "Dear heart, I came on wings!" I flew into his arms. His coat was damp, his hair slicked wet. He held me off, arm's length, smiling the odd, appraising half-smile of the Astor Roof, as if making up his mind about me. And I, at the same time, making up mine about him. Because, in these last months, we had traveled alone on separate roads, and important things had happened to each of us. We had to make certain we were all we had been.

"I've missed you," he said finally. "Let's have a drink."

"Let's talk," I said. "I need to know everything."

"Drink first," he said. His thumb pried off the cork; he poured the cold and sparkling wine into water tumblers, raised his glass. "To you," he said.

"To us," I said. "Our glorious future."

He grimaced before he drank.

I set down my glass. "Now tell me, tell me everything."

He waited to finish his wine. "They are idiots. The stupidity here is abysmal. . . . Mildred, when you first saw me on a stage—remember?—the play was sophisticated, lively, meaningful, was it

189

not? And I, I played a worldly, mature man. Now speak the truth, was I adequate?"

"You were marvelous."

He managed a smile. "And when, for more than a year and a half, I played in a Broadway hit, a comedy—"

"The critics raved," I told him. "It's pasted in my book." Yet I thought, The part you played best was Romeo. For an audience of one.

He drained the dregs in his tumbler. "But how do these morons cast me? As a gangster. A sleek, sleazy member of the mob." He paused, waiting for horror to show on my face. " 'Grab it,' my agent said. 'Take anything, whatever they offer. Get your foot in the door. You're in no position to pick and choose. Not how things are nowadays.' " He reached for my hands. "Mildred, I'll make it. To the top. You hear me? The top. Trust me. Trust me, kid."

"I do, I do. You know I do."

"Let's have another drink," he said.

While he poured, I ventured, "But how long—how long before we know for sure?"

"I'm goddam lucky—so they tell me—to be signed for anything."

"Jay." I spoke gently, reminding him. "We're a family now, we have a child."

He set down the bottle. "So we are. So we have. Perfect timing."

My eyes began to fill. He noticed and became contrite, leaning over the table to brush them with the flat of his hand. "I didn't mean that, Princess. I'm on edge. It's not a picnic, kid."

"Let me show you Greta's pictures. Our baby. Ours."

I got the snapshots from my purse and spread them on the table. He shuffled and thumbed rapidly. "Much ado about nothing," he said.

"Monster! She's a Dresden doll. Her eyes are blue, like mine."

He looked up, into mine. "Pretty. I agree. But I cannot get excited about very young girls."

190

"I'll tell her what her father said."

"Drink," he said. "Then we'll lock the door and close the blinds." Impatient, shifting on his chair while he finished his champagne, then rising to yank off his shoes and slide them beneath the sofa bed—the gesture, the symbol of what he meant to me and I to him.

He stripped the kimono off; he pressed me down on the bed, moved the bridge lamp close, and stood leaning above my nakedness. "Looking for landmarks," he explained. "Places where I used to go. . . . No lumps, no bumps, no streaks. Amazing. By God, if I didn't know otherwise, I'd say this is a virgin, luscious, ripe." And he went down, stroking my breasts and thighs, while an old fear, an old shame, crawled over me.

"Please, Jay, not now, not yet."

"Sweet, I've been counting the days, the hours, the minutes."

And so I listened to his panting breath and to the hiss of palm fronds that was like a distant surf. Only when he had finished could I hold him tightly within my arms. And then he squirmed as if he wanted to be free.

He slept; I did not. I was hungry. Evidently, my husband hadn't remembered that a visiting wife might also want a sandwich and a glass of milk.

In the morning, very early, he rolled out of bed, moving cat-soft so as not to wake me. But I pulled the sheet around my nakedness and sat up. There was lemon-yellow sunshine around the edges of the window blinds.

"Sleep, Princess, sleep all day if you like. There's an orange, coffee, crackers for your breakfast. We'll go out to dinner."

He kissed my forehead, swung the door open. "A pretty day," he told me. "Get out in the sun. Beauty treatment. Not that you need it, pet." He closed the door, opened it to say, "There's a market two blocks down, if you're in the mood to buy some groceries." After he had shut the door again, it occurred to me that he had not offered me money to buy groceries. He's spent whatever he had, I decided, on red roses and champagne. And this, I told myself, is why I married him.

Around noon, I propped a chair outside the door and faced the sun. The purple flowers on the wall were blooming blatantly, the grass in the patio gleamed like emeralds, and the blue, pink, and yellow stucco huts around the open space had a certain playfulness.

People emerged from their huts: a man with a Fu Manchu mustache and Chinese pajamas; a skinny blonde with wrinkled parchment cheeks, leading a stiff-legged white poodle who wore a lavender bow; a blowsy red-haired woman, swathed in a Spanish shawl; a cadaverous oldish man in baggy tweed knickers. They eyed me as they hurried past, with quick, suspicious glances, before they averted their eyes, as if—so I thought—by greeting me, by offering casual friendship, they might expose themselves: their secrets, their disappointments, their defeats. They couldn't guess I had no wish to know their failures and their fears. Because those very things might be in store for Jay and me, and I preferred to hope and not to know the worst.

Thus, for a week, I watched these strangers scurrying past while I sunned myself, read motion-picture magazines, and waited for Jay to come from his studio.

I found a market, bought bread and butter, eggs and milk; I washed my husband's socks and BVDs in the bathroom basin; and occasionally I took walks, away from the immediate neighborhood. On one of those walks, I met an elderly man who, on his knees, was trimming the edges of a flourishing lawn. He stood up, rubbing his back. He noticed me and said, "Hello." I said, "Hello," and asked him would he tell me, please, what were the names of the flowers I was looking at.

"The purple sprawl is bougainvillea. That showy flower is the hibiscus. No, not the one you're pointing at—that is oleander. The yellow is called acacia. This spiky red thing is named bottle brush—looks like what it's called, don't it? And over there is my lemon tree. Ever see a prettier sight than the yellow lemons with the shiny green leaves? You know roses, don't you, Miss? They keep blooming here winter and summer, all year."

I thanked him. I said knowing the names of what I looked at made me feel less alien.

"Just come out? Not in pictures, are you? Want to be? You're pretty enough for it. . . . Don't want to, eh? That's good. Excellent. You move out here, you get yourself a garden, grow some flowers. That's the best. The flowers. You ask me, that's the best thing anywhere. I don't mean only just because they're pretty and smell sweet. Because they got roots. Roots! The moom-picture people, they come and they go. People without roots. Nothing good grows without roots."

On Sunday, Jay rented a car. I saw the Pacific Ocean; it looked gray and quieter than the Atlantic, which had once frightened me. I saw the outside of the studio where my husband worked, the locked gates and the warren of buildings behind them; I saw white-stucco haciendas with red-tiled roofs and stone palaces behind ornate metal fences, where the rich and famous dwelt. "Princess, I promise, take my word, one day, one day soon, we'll live in a mansion like these."

Evenings, when we went out to dinner, I noticed that Jay counted his money carefully. How much he earned he didn't say; I didn't ask. "They didn't start me at the top" was all he told me.

He introduced me to no one. I met no celebrities. The phone in the hut rang occasionally in the evenings. Jay's conversations were brief and businesslike. I gathered he hadn't acquired any intimates.

I grew restless, and I realized he was restless, too, mildly complaining that dinner out every night was costly, grousing that the studio couch was a tight fit for two; and, more significant, he seemed relieved when I thrust his probing hand away, saying, "Not now, not tonight, please." And so I announced, "I have to get back to Greta and let you concentrate on your career. I'm a nuisance here." Then we talked sensibly: I was to give up the apartment, send our furniture into storage, stay in Brooklyn with Greta until Jay had a good contract and could provide a home for us out here. "A temporary arrangement, pet. We have to be practical. If your folks could see their way to helping out . . . you trust me, don't you?"

I put my hands over the backs of his. "I do. You know I do." And trusting is the best gift that I have for him. Yet it struck me we talked too much, too often, about trusting. Between a loyal husband and a loyal wife, trust should be implicit.

I called Brooklyn. My mother answered the phone. She told me Greta was an angel, no bother to anyone, she had gained four ounces and had smiled. A pity her own mother hadn't been around to see that first smile! No, no, it wasn't gas, it was a real smile. Positively, absolutely. "Ask Daisy if you don't believe me." I told her I was fine; I'd been having a rest, a pleasant time. And I added, though she hadn't asked, that Jay was also fine. I said I'd send a wire to let them know when my train would arrive. A brief conversation. Three minutes. Precisely.

The Chief was two hours late. In Chicago, I missed my connection with the Twentieth Century and had to take a slower train, sitting up all night in a filthy day coach. It was Sunday noon when I arrived. No one met me at Grand Central Station, and when I opened the basement door to the Brooklyn house I heard my baby crying and Uncle Reuben bellowing.

7 ❧

THEY WERE around the table in the basement: Uncle Reuben in the middle, Aunt Fanny beside him, my parents on a curve, two empty chairs between Mama and Fanny. Opposite, facing Fanny, Ben Kuper sat by himself.

The chandelier dropped a pool of light, a centerpiece for the table; beyond, in the penumbra, Reuben and Fanny were purple blobs, my parents crude sketches in black and white, and Ben—he who had been debonair and shining-tall—seemed gray and diminished.

Aunt Daisy stood in the kitchen doorway, leaning against the frame, a fist pressed to her mouth.

"Bummer! Low life!" Reuben was yelling before he noticed me. He stopped, mouth gaping, like a dying fish.

For an instant I heard no sounds except Greta's thin wails on the floor above. Then Papa rose and came to take me in his arms— "Pussycat! Hello! Hello!"—with false cheeriness. "I was going to meet you by the depot. Only—" his head gestured toward Reuben and Fanny.

Mama bustled over, pecking my cheek. "You got a sunburn. How was the trip?"

"Terrible," I said. "I'm pooped." I squirmed out of my coat.

From the kitchen doorway Daisy said, "I'll make you a cup of tea." Yet she stayed leaning against the frame as if lacking strength or will to move.

195

Reuben and Fanny said nothing. They waited, glowering at me.

"This *is* a surprise," I said. "I didn't expect a family gathering. How is everybody?"

Ben raised his eyes. His lips moved, soundlessly, trying to shape words.

"You had a vacation. Go tend your baby," Fanny said.

I ran upstairs and lifted Greta from her bassinet. She was soaked to the ears. "Darling, what's going on?" I asked her. Being so young, she couldn't answer, though her wailing abated to whimpers when I took off her diaper. Her tiny fingers searched for her mouth. She's starved; they've neglected my child!

I had her in my arms when I came down. Mama said contritely, "I put the bottle up to warm. I forgot to give her." Daisy inched aside to let us go into the kitchen. "Early today, in the morning," Mama began to explain, "Reuben calls up. He says they are coming; Daisy should fix a dinner for them—something light, Fanny don't feel well. She is in hysterics; Sophie called her last night on the phone." Mama took the baby's bottle out of the water in the saucepan, dripped milk on her wrist, gave the bottle to me. I tested it on *my* wrist; the milk was ice cold. I put the bottle back into the pan and lighted the gas.

"Why's Papa here?" I asked.

"He came last night to meet you today by Grand Central Station. A quick hello, how are you, how is everything? Then tonight he will take me home on the sleeper. It's a blessing he is here. My brother has respect for Sam; he quiets down when your papa talks."

"About what?"

"About Ben," Mama said. "Sophie threw him out."

Surprised yet not altogether surprised, I asked why.

"She is right, and he is right," Mama said.

I tested the milk again; it dripped lukewarm on my wrist. I thrust the nipple into Greta's mouth. She sucked and gulped avidly.

"Stay in the kitchen," Mama said. "Better you shouldn't go in."

Nevertheless, I went in, cradling Greta, holding the bottle for

196

her, because I had to learn why Sophie had thrown Ben Kuper out. One corner of my romantic mind began to hope this was because Sophie had learned Ben was in love with Aunt Daisy. If so, this might be for the best.

I took the chair beside my parents. Fanny flung a word at me. *"Nafke!"* The Yiddish for whore. I felt heat sweeping to my toes.

Papa's chair crashed; he lunged toward my aunt.

"Sophie said," Aunt Fanny hissed. "I tell only what Sophie said: 'The *nafke* Mildred, the one that got mixed up with the actor, only a schoolgirl, a beginning college girl, she had the *chutzpah* to go out with a married man.'"

"Which married man?" I managed to ask.

"Him. The bum." My uncle pointed at Ben. "To baseball games, she went with him."

"Who goes to baseball games?" Aunt Fanny jeered. "A cheap crowd. Only bums."

"Gott in himmel!" Papa muttered. "Sophie was an idiot. You are worse."

Ben raised his head; he glanced toward me. The ghost of a smile flickered on his lips.

"A terrible crime, a sin," my father continued, "to sit a couple of hours in the fresh air to watch a ball game."

Fanny's eyes sharpened. "And the hugging and the kissing that went on—that, by you, is a joke?"

Ben stared at me, I at him. He shook his head, bewildered, but I laughed out loud, because I was remembering those moments of rapture—a three bagger, a stolen base, those triumphs over ineptitude, rare, all too rare, at Ebbets Field—when fans flung their arms around each other, in ecstasy, exuberance, joy. In the full view of the multitude.

"The boy told Sophie." Fanny was glaring at me. "He told the mother everything. First is this one. Millie. Then the other one. The one in the store. Sunday afternoon. When it is raining, snowing, too cold to be on the street. The boy told the mother what went on in the back in the store."

"Nothing went on," Ben Kuper said.

"No?" Fanny shook her index finger at him. "The boy is a liar, maybe?"

"She was a friend. From in the neighborhood. She helped me sometimes in the store."

"On Sundays? When there is no customers? What kind of help?" Reuben unbuttoned his vest, readying to deliver a speech. "He tells the boy, 'Go play up front, do what you want—don't bother us, the *nafke* and me; we make monkey business back in here.'"

Fanny elbowed him. "Not only in the back in the store. Upstairs in her flat."

"That was a cold afternoon, freezing cold." Ben was speaking slowly, dragging out his words, as if reluctant or weary. "The steam was off in the store. She says, my friend says, 'Bring Arnold up to my apartment. I'll make a hot chocolate for him.'" He spread his arms in a hopeless shrug. "If I was doing something I could be ashamed, why would I bring Arnie with me?"

"To learn him," Reuben said. "How to be a low life. So Sunday afternoons, in the back of the store, is only small monkey business. In the nighttime goes on big monkey business. Mister Benny Kuper comes home one o'clock, two o'clock in the morning. His wife is going crazy, worrying: maybe he is run over by a truck, maybe he is killed by bootlegger-gangsters. So he comes, he opens the door, he takes off the hat, the coat; he don't explain her one single word; he lays down on the sofa in the parlor—"

"Don't take off the shoes," Fanny broke in. "Dirtied up the expensive upholstering."

I smiled. I may have giggled, also, because my aunt turned on me.

"By you it is a joke. You know from a decent married life? The husband goes away—God knows where—the wife, she—"

Reuben nudged her; my mother was trading Fanny glare for glare. "Come to the point," Reuben said.

"The point? The point is a respectable husband sleeps in the bed with the wife. Not on the parlor sofa."

"Unless she has a cold, he could catch it," Reuben said.

"Unless she locks the door." At last Ben raised his head to look directly at them. He hadn't shaved; the stubble made his face somber and shadowy. "To her I am a dirty animal." His hands were knotted so tightly the knuckles were white. "She screams, she yells. The minute I come in the apartment, she starts in to holler. I tell her, in a nice way, 'Please, Sophie, you will wake up the neighbors; they will call the police.'" A thin smile touched his lips. "When I ask her 'please,' she hollers more. 'You will wake up Arnie,' I tell her. She answers me, 'Let him hear, let him know.' And she opens up his bedroom door; she brings him out. And he stands there in pajamas—the apartment is cold; he has no slippers; he will get sick. I think she doesn't care what happens to him, she cares only for herself. 'Look at him,' she yells to Arnie. 'Look at your father. The dirty animal.' And Arnie starts in crying; he cries like a baby. I go to him; I touch him on the arm; I say, 'Stop crying, Arnie, she is nervous, excited, it's nothing.' She pulls him away. She takes him by the hand; she takes him in the bedroom —to sleep in the bed with her. And she locks the door." He was speaking fast, as though a dam had been sprung, words long held in, gushing out. "I am not an animal. I am a human person. A human person needs a little friendship in his life. Not cursing, screaming, every night. Complaining from everything. I don't make enough money for her. This is one complaint. Another complaint: when I close the store, I enjoy to play a game pinochle with my friends. Not come home to hear her *kwetching*—it hurts her here, it hurts her there. 'So go to a doctor,' I tell her. 'Take an aspirin, two aspirins,' I tell her. . . . No, I am her sickness, is what she says."

My father rose to pace around the table, impatient and embarrassed, too. "Enough! We heard enough already. What goes on between a man and his wife we do not need—"

"Mr. Samuelson," Fanny interrupted. "By you this is a nothing. By me, by the Kuper family, and by my husband, Reuben Springer, it is a something. It is a disgrace for our family. I thank God my uncle, Herschel Goldmark, he should rest in peace, he did not live to see his nephew that he loved like his own son, that he led under the *chupa* himself, that he loaned a big sum money to start him in business, he should have the shame that the nephew makes monkey business with a *nafke* in the store in front of his

199

little boy and he runs around to *nafkes* in the nighttimes—hokay, hokay, he says he is playing pinochle with his cheap friends, so he is a *cortesnick*, a cards player. I ask you is this something for a businessman, he should be doing, when the wife, a refined, educated American young woman that we picked out ourselfs for him . . ."

I looked toward the kitchen doorway. Daisy's glance met mine. "I forgot," she hurried to say. "I told Millie I would make her tea."

"Make for everybody," Reuben said. "And bring a piece cake."

Greta had fallen asleep in the crook of my arm. She'd taken barely an ounce of formula. Crying has exhausted her, I told myself, and it struck me as ironic that a tragic drama was being played in this house, yet the only one who'd wept was a babe who had heard none of it. These adults were full of self-righteousness —yes, Ben, too, was full of it—but not one was shedding tears.

I should cry, I thought; I'm the one who ought to be crying. The blabbing child I used to be pushed Ben Kuper out upon this road to misery. Yet did he need to marry Sophie because Fanny told him to? Who gave Fanny—who gave them all—the right to play God? What was wrong with Ben; what made him listen to Fanny? Daisy, too. They had no spunk, those two, no courage to lead their own lives. Why, they're to blame, as much as anyone.

Suddenly, I realized I was too tired to try to unravel this, and so I rose with Greta, saying, "I'll put the baby to bed and get some rest."

"Rest, she needs." Fanny shrugged. "Comes sunburned from vacation, she needs to have rest. All week I work like a horse, Sunday I run to the train—"

Ben turned to me. "You look good, Millie," he said. "Where were you?"

"In California. With my husband. He's acting in the movies." High time, I decided, to make the family aware of Jay.

"Makes big money, huh?" Reuben asked.

"Packs," I said. "Piles of it."

"Maybe he would lend me some," Reuben said. "He is, after all, a member of our family."

"Dear once," I said.

"Exactly," Reuben said.

I put Greta in her bassinet, and I stretched out on the parlor sofa, trying to nap. The wrangling voices were so loud below I could not fall asleep, and so I went down again. There were empty teacups on the table, and plates, sticky with chocolate frosting. Except in front of Ben. His cup was full; his wedge of layer cake had not been touched. He was leaning forward, speaking in a calm and serious way to his sister and brother-in-law. "The business is something different. Sophie says she put her money in; to her the store belongs; she will sue in court. So let her take the business, I don't give a damn."

"From my brother, such language!" Fanny said.

Ben ignored her. "The business is rotten," he continued. "I don't need to tell you, Reuben; you know yourself how retail business is today. So gladly I give Sophie the store. Let her sell the stock and fixtures, let her keep what she gets. Let her pay off the creditors, let her break the lease, settle up with the landlord. Let her have the headaches, it makes me no never mind. This way or another way, I am bankrupt."

"Bankrup'!" Fanny rocked her head between her hands. "My brother, Benny, is a bankrup'. In my family, our whole lives, never was a bankrup'. If my Uncle Herschel Goldmark—"

"Herschel Goldmark!" Papa broke in. "Let him rest in peace. I am sick and tired of Goldmark, Goldmark, Goldmark!"

"He makes a nothing from my uncle." A malicious smile squirmed on Fanny's mouth. "If not for my Uncle Herschel, would Ada's sister Daisy have a home in this house? Would the daughter, Millie, have like a hotel, she could eat and sleep, no charge, leave a newborn baby somebody else should look after, she has to run for vacation in California?" She paused to catch her second wind. "And would the Springer family be landlords from a high-class piece of property, rents collected from tenants upstairs? From my uncle everything came, all he did for Reuben's family. . . ."

Daisy emerged from the kitchen, carrying a cup of tea for me; her hand shook as she set the cup down. I managed to seize the hand, press it against my cheek, before she slipped away to lean on the frame of the kitchen door.

My father rose to march around the table, hands clasped behind his back. "Enough already, Fanny. I give your uncle the credit. The money I spent for improvements—Ada, *sha!*—we do not mention this. And Daisy's hard work, cleaning, taking out the garbage, fighting with the tenants—*sha! Shtill!* We don't mention it. Some day we will make a reckoning; now is not the time. Benny Kuper is in trouble; we are here a family, to see what we can do to help him. So let us talk, like good friends, like business people with a little sense." He sat down again and leaned over the table, addressing Ben. "Sophie hires a lawyer; the lawyer puts in her claim for what she says she loaned to the business. You say the store you are ready to give her, without a trial in a court. Fine. Good. Maybe, also, she can hire a manager, an honest man, he could squeeze out a little income for the boy and her." Papa scratched his temple, looking doubtful. "All the same, a father has a duty to support a son, a young boy, not yet Bar Mitzvah. So Mr. Benny Kuper, how will you do this? What is your plan to make a living for yourself and provide a little something for the son? Maybe you have a couple of dollars put away."

Ben turned his pants pockets inside out. Their gray linings flapped like patches on his hips.

"He bought on margin," Reuben jeered. "My smart brother-in-law!"

"*You* bought blue chips, I bought mines. All in the soup," Papa said.

"Don't worry," Ben said. "I'll find a job. A salesman with my experience—"

"From your mouth to God's ears," Papa said.

"I would not hire you for my store," Reuben said. "In good times, you were not a bargain. Now, in a depression . . ."

Ben lowered his eyes; he ran his index finger under his shirt collar, as if it was choking him. "The boy, Arnie," he said slowly, with pain. "He is the main worry for me. She says I can't come to him, he can't come to me."

202

My father pursed his mouth, thinking. "If you go to a court, a judge would give you—"

Ben spread his hands, hopelessly shrugging. "He would give me nothing. She would tell her stories. She would tell her lies. On me and my family."

Fanny's head snapped up. "What could she say on this family?"

"She already said." His brief glance was toward me, his faint smile apologetic. His glance moved on, to Daisy in the kitchen doorway, and I began to wonder whether Sophie Kuper had made an obscene something out of those innocent Sunday *Kaffee-klatsches* in this kitchen. Surely, Daisy's offense was less than mine. I *had* hugged Ben in the grandstands at Ebbets Field.

"The boy. She tells the boy"—Ben was staring at his knotted hands—"she gives him an order he must never see his father's family; they will poison his mind. I am rotten; so my family, everybody, is rotten."

"My heart!" Fanny pressed a plump hand against her navel. "It pains me in my heart. Reuben, you hear me, I am getting a stroke."

"Bring Fanneh a glass water!" Reuben cried.

Nobody stirred to fetch water. Somehow, I felt—we all must have felt—she'd be revived by her own bile.

Reuben shook his fist at his brother-in-law. "You are killing your loving sister with the shame you brought. Benny Kuper, here, in front of witnesses, I will tell you something: we are finished, you and ourselfs. So long as you live, you are not welcome in my house, in my Fanneh's house. We have no place for bummers. Tramps. Bankrup's. And I tell you something else: in the Springer-Kuper family plot, for you we will not have a place."

"This is my lucky day." Ben rose. His gaze, sad and uncertain, moved around the table, as if seeking a trace of something generous and kind from one of us. "So, good-bye." His lips were quivering. "Good-bye, everybody. *Seit gesundt. . . .* Keep well. I make you all a promise: Ben Kuper won't make more trouble for this family." He wheeled around, the gray pocket linings flapping, and strode from the room. Daisy stirred, one single step, as if she meant to follow him, before we saw his face again, at the hall entrance, leaning in, asking, "Where is my overcoat? I laid it down some place in here." And all at once there was a buzz of concern, a bustling around the table, a homely anticlimax to Ben's theatrical exit.

Fanny found the coat. It seemed, when he had come in, Ben had flung it on a chair directly back of where she sat. She waited until he had thrust his arms into the sleeves before she waddled over to him. She buttoned the buttons; she fluffed out the knot of his four-in-hand tie, she raised the coat collar to surround his ears. Then she slapped his face, a hard, stinging blow on each cheek. "Go, *shlemiel!*" she cried. "Where is your hat?"

He smiled, a small, pathetic smile. "In Sophie's apartment," he said. He bowed to the table, to all of us, and in a faintly mocking tone, he said, "Good-bye, dear ones."

Fanny sat down heavily and began to sob. "My brother. My poor brother. She took away from him the hat. He will catch a cold. He will be sick. Who will take care of him?"

My father shook out his handkerchief, hawked into it, and spat. I smothered a giggle. The show had turned into farce. Penniless, homeless, cut off from his son, branded a moral leper, yet here was his sister weeping for him, because, hatless on a windy Sunday, he might catch a cold.

Reuben pulled out his turnip watch and snapped up the lid. "Quick, bring supper, Daisy," he ordered. "We make the seven-fifteen."

Fanny dropped her sodden handkerchief into her lap. "Half past seven," she said.

"Quarter past," Reuben said.

"Who knows better, you or me?" Fanny asked.

When they had departed finally, my mother, who had been silent while they were here, began to talk. "I am ashamed. I am ashamed from every side of it. I am ashamed from Ben, and I am ashamed from Sophie. A husband and wife, they have trouble between them, they should not make a *tarraram* in front of a child. They should go private to a rabbi; he would speak with them and explain who is right and who is wrong and what the Talmud says. But most I am ashamed from my brother and Fanny: they bring the dirty business to this house; they spread it on this table; they hold like a trial. Whose business is it what goes on between Benny and Sophie? Is it my business? No. Is it Sam's business? No. Is it Millie's business? No. Is it Daisy's business?"

"*Sha. Shtill!*" My father's elbow nudged her.

She wouldn't stop. "That Fanny is a Sarah Bernard. On a theater stage she should act. She makes a drama in this house, carrying on, everybody clap the hands. And after the show, Daisy, the sister-in-law, should make a supper for her. You saw, Sam, the appetites? Like pigs they *fressed*, the both of them. She chases the brother out like a dog. Then she starts the crying, he will catch a cold. *Feh!*" She paused, wrinkling her forehead, before she added thoughtfully, "So think about it, where will Ben go? Who will take care of him if he gets sick?" Her glance strayed toward the kitchen, where Daisy was washing the supper dishes.

"You know what I think, Ada?" Papa said. "I think you talk too much."

She reddened, yet she flared at him. "My sister-in-law insults my daughter, I should keep the mouth shut? Sam, you are the father; you could tell Fanny, Apologize to Millie." Yet, in her tone, there was uncertainty, as though there might be a reason why Fanny should not apologize.

"I didn't mind," I said. "It was just foolishness."

"A crime, a sin," my father said. "A feller puts an arm around my pussycat." He drew his own chair close to mine and squeezed me hard. "Enough Fanny, enough Reuben, enough Ben. Let us talk about you. For you we are here, Mama and me. Only you. So tell us, tell us everything."

"We had a happy week," I told them. "My husband is working hard, but he doesn't mind hard work. He knows he's lucky to have anything; they've got the depression there, the same as here. The part Jay has is small, but it's in an important picture, and of course his pay isn't much. He lives in a tiny bungalow—it's all he can afford." I saw anxiety on their faces. I tried to reassure them with a smile. "So we talked things over, and we decided it wasn't sensible for me and the baby to move to California, not till he could provide a proper home for us." I watched their expressions changing, an expectation, an eagerness entering. "And so we decided," I added, "if Daisy is willing, for the present, Greta and I should stay where we are, in this house."

They had mixed feelings, I could judge that by their darting glances at each other. It occurred to me they might be wondering whether there had been a rupture between Jay and me, a possible breakup of our marriage, and they were not certain whether to be glad or sad.

"There's no problem between us," I hurried to say. "This is a temporary arrangement. No more than that."

"How long is temporary?" Papa asked.

Mama lifted her chin. "Come to us, go back with us," Mama said. "Our home is your home."

I gave her a frivolous answer—"An infant does not travel in the wintertime"—but there was, I sensed, a peril in what they offered me. If I went back with them, they'd surely try, directly or subtly, to wean me from Jay. No, let this house be my way station, my shelter, until Hollywood came through for us.

Daisy said she was delighted; I was doing her the favor; I couldn't imagine how much it meant to her. And the baby was no trouble. On the contrary, she was a joy. The baby and I could have the big bedroom; she would take Grandpa's room, the one I used in my brief college days. And spring was on the way. The yard would be ideal for airing the baby. Moreover, I was not to think of this as Daisy's home; my mother was, in fact, a part owner of the property. Without my asking, Papa said he would mail a monthly check for my share of the household expenses.

And so I became Penelope, waiting for an absent husband, though without suitors or a loom on which to weave. In any case, Mildred–Penelope was far too busy for weaving. With all she had to do, she needed a third arm.

Dismantling the apartment on Fifty-seventh, emptying, destroying, the first home I had made, the cradle of our hopes and

dreams, the tasteless product of our inexperience, was not a pang
—I had disconnected from it—it merely was a picky and backbreaking chore.

The January *Delineator* lay on the rug where I had dropped
it when labor pains started. The phone bill envelope, with Dr. Lorwin's telephone number scribbled on it, was beside the telephone,
the bill inside unpaid. Tell the company to disconnect; we won't
be taking calls here any more. Empty the garbage pail—that January night things had happened so fast I hadn't had the time or
mind to put my garbage out. Roaches, fattened on fetid trash,
skittered across the sink, in the kitchen I had kept immaculate. A
home, must be tended, constantly and lovingly. Like a marriage.
Remember this, Mildred. Yet I am here, and he is there. Can our
marriage survive a separation? It can. I love him; he loves me. And
this is temporary. How long will temporary be?

I took down the curtains I had sewed; they were grayed with
city smut. I soaked them in the bathtub while I emptied kitchen
cabinets. I hung the curtains on the shower rod to dry while I
sorted our clothes and packed in tissue the blue baby things I had
made for William. In whose box shall I pack the clipping book, in
Jay's or in mine? Those strips of newsprint look so lonely—the
opening night seems so far away, as far, as far, as California. I'll
take the book with me, to have it handy when our ship comes in.

While I was packing crockery, my fingers turned all thumbs.
I had an accident—let me say "accident," though Freud might
not agree—I dropped the cut-glass bowl Aunt Fanny had given
me. It shattered into a hundred chunks, crumbs, slivers on the
parquet floor. I began to stoop to sweep them up before I stopped
myself. This much I will not do for her. *Nafke!* Indeed! Because
I'd hugged a certain member of our Family League, in the ninth
inning of a baseball game.

I gave the janitor a dollar bill to sweep the place and take
discards away. The movers—heavy, sweating strangers—carried
our bed and dresser, our chairs and tables and cartons, off to
storage, to wait in dark and airless rooms for when we might send
for them.

Storage is a gap, it's not an abyss.

The last thing I did was remove our name card from the door. J. Bernstein (Burns) doesn't live here any more.

In April, Jay mailed me a check for one hundred dollars; he said he had won the money in a poker game. "Lady Luck is smiling. Buy yourself pretties." I didn't, because we had a money problem at the Brooklyn house.

The couple in the second-floor apartment had moved out. The man had lost his job; they were going upstate to live with her parents. (Another "temporarily.") Daisy nailed a "To Let" sign beside the basement entrance. She and I grew footsore running up and down the stairs, showing the vacant apartment—many lookers, no takers: too expensive; everyone is short of cash these days. Daisy reduced the rent, five less, then ten, then fifteen, and finally we got new tenants, an older couple with an adult son who worked nights and slept days. His parents banged on our ceiling whenever Greta cried. Babies need to cry now and then to let you know they're hungry, wet, or bored. I had to spend a lot of time rocking Greta's carriage or carrying her around in my arms, which, according to the books, was how you spoil infants.

The new second-floor tenants also ran the hot water day and night, so that the third-floor tenants began to complain there wasn't enough for their baths. The instantaneous gas heater ran up alarming bills. Our money was so tight Daisy decided she'd have to let the part-time janitor go—reluctantly, because the man needed the job. I offered to sweep the halls and take the rubbish out but she wouldn't hear of me doing janitor's work, though she let me take on more and more of the regular chores in the house. With that and washing the baby's clothes, the hands of the princess of the white kid gloves grew red and rough.

Evenings, I wrote letters: to my parents to thank them for the latest check, and to repeat that I did not wish to move to Montreal, Greta and I were comfortable here; and to my husband to tell him that his child and I were well and that I loved him and I always would. Daisy and I listened to the radio, but drowsily, because we were tired. Occasionally, she sewed, though her dressmaking trade had fallen off. In these hard times, her ladies made do with last season's clothes.

The phone seldom rang, and when it did, frequently Aunt Fanny was the caller. "How is things? How is the baby?" And with affected casualness, "You heard from Benny? . . . What! He didn't come around to the house? I'm surprised; I was sure and positive he would visit you." One afternoon, Uncle Reuben telephoned and asked for me. "Millie, I am calling from the store, Fanneh shouldn't hear what I say. She is going crazy, where is Benny? She is sure he comes to Daisy's house, only Daisy wouldn't tell her. For spite Daisy is keeping a secret. Millie, you are an intelligent girl, you can understand a sister's heart. So tell me the truth: Benny comes? You see him? How is he? What does he do for a living? Your uncle you can tell."

"He hasn't been here," I said. "He hasn't called up. We don't know where he is."

"I have to believe you, heh?" sounding dubious, before he sighed. "When you hear from him, when Daisy hears from him, be a good girl, call us up right away. Fanneh gets crazy worrying."

We had not seen Ben, we'd not heard from him. What's more, we did not speak of him; our conversations were exclusively about domestic matters and principally about Greta. What to do for her loose bowels: take her off orange juice, put her on barley water, or take her to a doctor? (Ten dollars for the office visit, plus two taxicabs!) Does her dribbling and drooling mean she's cutting teeth? Is that why she cries? All I knew was what I read in Holt's book, which offered no clear explanation about Greta's eyes. When she was awake in her carriage in the yard, reaching for the sunbeams that played hide-and-seek in the ailanthus tree, it struck me that she had a squint.

Passover came and went without a Seder in our dining room. Reuben had telephoned, hinting, but Daisy was firm: she had too much other work to do the holiday cooking.

"Millie could help you?"

"Millie has the baby to tend to."

209

"Fanneh could come and help you."

"Not this year," Daisy answered with a sharpness I never had heard from her. "I do not want a family affair."

We bought a box of *matzohs;* Daisy made chicken soup with *matzoh* balls. We ate in the kitchen, out of the all-year-round dishes; we went early to bed. It left a bleak feeling in me, since the Seder is a family festival, a night for a gathering of kin. If Daisy also felt as I did, she chose not to mention it. There was about her nowadays the taciturnity of a person on short tether, overstrained and overburdened. My fault and the baby's presence? Sometimes I thought yes, but more often no, because in the moments she snatched for rest in the kitchen or the yard, the old, soft, loving look returned to her eyes.

In June she had a happy week. Hannah phoned to say Karl was graduating from law school. He had been given two tickets for Commencement, just two. Dave said he'd give up his ticket if Daisy wanted to go. Daisy's face was flushed with pleasure when she came out to the yard to tell me about the call. "My sister Hannah has a hard life," she said. "And now she has a little *naches*, she wants to share it with me. I said, 'Let me make a party for his graduation, we could all enjoy.'" Her forehead wrinkled, her mouth pursed. "Hannah said, 'If you make a party you must ask the family. Reuben. And Fanny. No.'" Daisy paused, as if deciding whether to say more. "My sister said, 'Why should I share my *naches* with my brother? What did Reuben do for me? A greenhorn, he sent me to sew buttonholes in a factory. I have a sick boy. Does he say, "Let us take him to us for a week, give him a change, give you a rest"? No, Reuben does nothing for nobody. Only for himself, to make himself big.'" Daisy clapped two fingers on her mouth, silencing herself. "I have become a *yenta*," she said. "I talk too much."

Remembering an earlier graduation and a party on the Astor Roof, I kept silent, too, until, after a brief pause, my aunt began to speak again and in an altered tone. "I wanted this party for Karl. To give him pleasure, also. He was so busy with his college, his jobs to earn spending money, nobody saw him at all. You remember, darlin', how good it was those Sunday mornin's after he slept overnight; we all had breakfast in the kitchen. Laughin', talkin', enjoyin'. And Ben came with little Arnie. . . ." Her eyes blurred, her voice grew faint and distant—"I wonder, I wonder what . . . I wonder how . . ."—before it dribbled into silence.

I broke the silence, saying briskly, "There have been lots of changes." A banal statement, concealing the turbulence that roiled up in me.

Daisy met it with a sentence as brisk as mine and more irrelevant. "I will make a dress for Hannah to wear to the graduation," she said.

Jay arrived on a July afternoon, unannounced and unexpected. He was begrimed and exhausted, having traveled day coach all the way from the Coast. He went to bed immediately and slept around the clock. When he woke, refreshed, he took Greta from her crib, kissed her forehead, held her high, announcing, "Pipsqueak, this is Daddy, don't look cockeyed at me." He put her down and turned to me, asking, "Is she really cross-eyed or is that her opinion of me?" before he went on to other matters. He expected to be around awhile; the picture was finished, nothing else was on the fire out there for him. He'd give New York a whirl, see what was cooking on Broadway for the fall; if the best the Coast could offer him was minor gangster roles, he might as well try to get back on the stage. "And be with my wife," he added. "Princess, I have missed you. The situation was ridiculous."

This situation was awkward. I found it vaguely embarrassing to have intercourse with my husband in Aunt Daisy's bed. At least I blamed my distaste on the bed. Jay didn't comment. Other problems occupied the front of his mind. Each day he headed for Manhattan to make rounds. Sometimes he was home for dinner, sometimes not; we never knew beforehand, though a place was set for him. Occasionally, he returned with little presents: a Raggedy Ann doll for Greta, a small potted plant for Daisy, a string of bright beads for me. I scanned his face when he arrived, seeking clues. Usually, his face showed nothing, he said nothing, though a tautness was visible in lines around his mouth and in little forehead creases.

211

Together, we took Greta, prettied up, her wisps of golden hair done up in a kewpie curl with a pink bow atop, to an ophthalmologist. The doctor verified what I had suspected yet not admitted to myself: my blue-eyed daughter had a squint. Later, we could try corrective glasses, not yet; a tiny tot can't adjust to wearing spectacles. If glasses didn't help, surgery would. That night I cried as I had not wept since I was a child. "I want her to be beautiful. A girl has to be. She won't get married if she is not beautiful." Jay stroked my arm and shoulder wordlessly. There was nothing he could say, since, apparently, he agreed with me.

We took Greta on the subway to visit Jay's family. They fluttered around him and badgered him with questions—"How much did they pay you? . . . Did you save? . . . What offers do you have?"—the mundane questions I had feared to ask. And, as previously, they ignored me. And seemed to resent the baby—an encumbrance, an impediment. Did Jake have to be burdened with a family? His mother suggested Jay might be more comfortable in his old room in their flat—it was on a direct subway line to Broadway; also he would not be beholden to Mildred's family. Jay didn't answer her.

Aunt Daisy had accepted him as she had accepted me: *entitled*, a member of the family in the family's house. She blushed whenever he put his arms around her and gave her a hug, and she giggled when he mocked her Irish lilt, "You do like havin' a young man around the house, do you not, darlin'?" She did. His presence gave a fillip, a completeness to our lives. When a man is expected home for dinner, you take extra pains. Nevertheless, he remained a guest, neither asking with what coin we bought our bread and butter, meat and eggs, nor offering to help to pay for them. However, he didn't ask for pocket money—he seemed to have sufficient for his personal needs.

On an afternoon just before Labor Day, he took me into Manhattan to a preview of the film in which he'd worked on the Coast. A score or so of people were scattered through the dark projection room. We sat by ourselves. My heart was pounding; I chewed my nails. Jay took my fingers from my mouth; he held

212

my hand, his thumb pressed to my thumb. At last, I saw him on the screen, dark, saturnine, one of several in a group, but so alive that his presence registered before I heard his voice. I must have made a sound, an "oh" or "ah," because he whispered "Ssh," squeezed my hand, and held it till the picture ended.

The lights went up. Tingling with the thrill of seeing James Burns—the now and future name—on the roster of the cast of characters, we started up the aisle. A man came up behind us, gripped Jay's shoulder, slapped his back. "You've got it, kid," he said. "I'll call you in the morning." And was gone before Jay could introduce him to me.

Jay said, "We should celebrate. Where can we buy a drink? Don't know my way around town any more." We strolled down Broadway, pretending to be looking for a speakeasy that might let us in. We walked on air, beaming, bubbling, intoxicated by elation.

In front of Roxy's or the Capitol (I don't remember which) I noticed a little crowd around a peddler who was demonstrating a wind-up toy, a painted tin clown that wobbled, waddled, staggering crazily across the pavement. While we strolled toward the crowd, a policeman appeared. He argued briefly with the man, nudged him with a night stick, collared him. The peddler stooped to pick up his clown. The night stick prodded him.

"Bastard!" my husband grumbled in my ear. "Lousy cop! There's a Depression on. Let the poor jerk earn a buck."

I said nothing, since I had seen the poor jerk's face. It was Ben; seeing him like this had hurt too much.

The agent telephoned before Jay was out of bed. The sleepy actor rubbed his eyes and, listening on the phone, turned wide awake. "Get ready to go back," he said the agent said. "Had one call last night, expecting more today—they're still asleep on the Coast. . . . You made it, boy! You're in! . . . No, Christ, no! Hold your horses! We'll settle for a featured part. . . . Sorry, Buster, sorry, seems for now you're typed."

"Keep your fingers crossed," Jay said to me.

213

"How long?" I asked.

"Not long, not long. I said, 'Trust me,' did I not?" First, I'll get the debts paid off. I'm in hock to that agent—he staked me, you know."

I, too, in a way, I thought, but we won't mention it.

"He was sure I'd make it big."

"I, too," I said and hugged him hard.

"The minute I see daylight, I'll start looking for a house for us. Sit tight. Stand pat."

He assumed—and blandly—that I could stay in limbo, dependent on Aunt Daisy's hospitality and my family's remittances—an adult in independent spirit, a child in fiscal helplessness. Each letter of my father's wondered when I would come home to them, surrendering that independence, admitting the man I had chosen could not provide for me. And because the implication of mistrust was in their letters, I returned resentment when they should have had my gratitude.

For three days, until Jay left, we were in a whirl of answering the telephone, making hurried expeditions to Manhattan to buy him clothing, shoes and shirts and underwear. Not till Jay had gone did I find a moment to tell Daisy I had seen Ben Kuper on Broadway. And all I told her was he'd been selling toys, and he seemed to be healthy. She sucked in her breath; her lips moved soundlessly, as if in prayer, giving thanks.

"You said hello to him?"

Could I tell her I did not, that I could not because a policeman had him by the scruff? "We were in a hurry. Jay was in a hurry."

"You were ashamed?"

"Why should I be ashamed? I'm not even positive that it was Ben. It could have been someone who resembled him."

"The store where you saw him selling toys? You remember the address?"

"Greta's crying," I answered. "Let me get her before upstairs starts pounding on the floor."

She saw through my evasiveness. "Something happened; you

don't want to tell me." But brightened. "At least we know he is alive."

One afternoon she left the house, not telling me where she was off to or when she would return. She was back after four, tight-lipped, grim. She went into the kitchen to start the supper preparations without saying where she had been. Next afternoon she went out again. And the next day and the next. Then, after the next-next-next day's expedition, she slumped on a kitchen chair and began to weep.

"Daisy, dear, is it Ben you go looking for?"

Her eyes met mine. "Arnie," she replied. "I see him; he turns his head away."

"Where, Daisy? Where do you see him?"

"In the street. By his school. I got the idea after you told me you saw Ben, at an address you didn't remember where. But Arnie we could find; I knew where he goes to school. . . . Millie, Millie, darlin', when someone is dear— So I stand in the street, and I wait till the boys come out of school. Oh, Millie, Millie, he looks so sad . . . ashamed."

That week rains came, the lashing equinoctial rains. Nevertheless, she went out each afternoon, to stand in a schoolyard, under a dripping umbrella, watching for Arnie Kuper and waiting for him to acknowledge her. Then came a mellow October; the waiting and the watching were less difficult.

I was in the kitchen, straining Greta's spinach, when I heard two sets of footsteps in the dining room, and Daisy's voice, with the lilt: "Darlin', we have company." I rushed in; I draped Arnie with my arms. Through his jacket, I could count his ribs. He stood like a skinny scarecrow, unyielding, though tears welled in his eyes. "I can't stay but a minute," Arnie said. "My mother would worry." He snuffled, the perpetual cold.

"Milk and cookies, Arnold?" Daisy said. "You always liked my cookies. Millie, darlin', take Arnie to the yard, show him our baby. I will bring refreshments."

He stopped on the door sill, opening to the yard. "He played catch out here with me," I heard Arnie say. Daisy came behind

215

him, bearing a tray, and then he remembered to whom he belonged. "No, thank you, my mother doesn't like me eating sweets. I have to run home, hurry up."

"Arnie, you'll come again," Daisy said. "You can find this house by yourself. You used to enjoy comin' here."

"My mother wouldn't like it."

"Do you have to tell her every place you go?"

"She knows what time I get out of school."

"You could say you stopped to visit with a friend," I said. "That wouldn't be a lie. We're friends, aren't we?"

"Used to be," Arnie said. He turned and began to run.

Daisy helped me feed Greta before I carried her upstairs to her crib. My aunt and I ate supper in the kitchen, without conversation. Each of us was thinking, thinking hard, and about the situation. A step had been taken, a breach made in a wall.

Yet when Fanny phoned, as she did at least once a fortnight, I overheard Daisy telling her, "I do not know one thing about Ben or Arnie. If I was worried like you, I would call Sophie up." My aunt was growing crafty. Something, I told myself, might come of this new attitude.

However, it was I who brought the next news of Ben, out of a blustery February day. I ran into him on Thirty-fourth Street, near Macy's department store. I had been shopping there for Dr. Dentons—Macy's had advertised a sale; Greta, having become plump and energetic, was kicking her blankets off. I was hurrying toward the subway when I noticed Ben, ambling with the shuffle of men with too much time to kill. His overcoat collar was turned up to his ears; his nose tip was magenta with the nipping cold. He'd seen me, too, there was no doubt of that; there had been a flicker of recognition before his pace had quickened, moving so fast I had to run after, pluck his coat sleeve, and call out, "Ben, it's Millie. Millie Samuelson. Millie Bernstein. Don't you high-hat me."

His face melted, then, with the smile that had been so much of his charm. He gripped my hand. "Millie, you look wonderful," he said.

"You, too," I lied. Actually, he looked terrible: pale as ash, unshaven, pouches underneath his bloodshot eyes. The neckline of his shirt was dirty, frayed; the overcoat, missing a top button, was wrinkled as if he slept in it. Hurstwood. That name flashed through my mind. Hurstwood of Dreiser's *Sister Carrie*. Broke. Degraded. On the skids. Except that Ben was no Hurstwood—he'd never been wealthy or trapped, consumed by passion. He'd never been more than a *shnook*, a personable, amiable chap, who liked pinochle and baseball and had the misfortune to be married to a bitch. Moreover, in the Depression winter of 1931, many—too many—men were wearing threadbare overcoats and cracked shoes.

"Let's go some place and talk," I said. "Let's get a cup of coffee."

He mumbled, unconvincingly, about being on his way to meet a man on business.

"Oh, come on," I said. "I haven't seen you in a year. There must be an Automat in this neighborhood." Again, I saw his hesitation, a wanting to say yes, a need to say no. For a particular reason, I guessed. But coffee only is a nickel, surely Ben has a nickel, everybody has a nickel. . . . Ben, the openhanded spender —let me buy you Moxie, let me buy you Crackerjack, I'll shell out my dimes till I win a kewpie doll. . . . Ben's broke; he doesn't have the nickel. I watched his hand, rummaging in a coat pocket, as though seeking coins. . . . Yes, he has a nickel, his pride is salvaged.

We found an Automat. I left him at the coffee spout and scooted to the sandwich and the pastry windows. I put two Swiss cheese sandwiches and a pair of jelly doughnuts on my tray. Ben had staked out a table; he was seated there, behind two cups of coffee, still wearing his overcoat. He rose to hold a chair for me and eyed my tray with naked greed. "I didn't think—you said just a cup of coffee, Millie."

"My eyes are always bigger than my appetite," I said. "You'll have to help me eat."

Fakers, two of us, neither fooling the other. He wolfed the sandwiches, with merely a self-conscious smile when he reached for the second. "You don't want it, Millie? Sure?"

I managed half a doughnut; he managed one and one half. I

didn't try to talk to him. Just looking at him, seeing his ravenous hunger, had told me more than I wished to know.

At last, he whipped out a grayed handkerchief and wiped his mouth. "How's your baby, Millie?"

"Fat and sassy. When are you coming to see—?"

"How's your husband, Millie?"

"Fine. He's in Hollywood, you know."

"Making moving pictures?" He looked at me oddly. "So why—?" He was having trouble framing his question. I helped him out. "Why am I in New York? A temporary arrangement, till he gets established. It's something like—like when my Grandpa Springer came to the United States. To get settled here, then send for his family." Yet his wife died before she saw the Promised Land. A bad analogy. Skip it. "Jay was here last summer," I hurried to add. "In September he was called back to the Coast." I remembered a scene on Broadway and bent my head to my cup. Could I ask: Were you arrested? Did you go to jail? No more than he could ask: Has your husband walked out on you?

He must have misunderstood my embarrassment since he changed the subject promptly. "How are your parents?"

"Fine. Everybody's well."

His eyes brightened, an inspiration dawning. "Just now it occurred to me, if I could get up to Canada, maybe it would be easier to find a position. Maybe, maybe, your father could use a salesman."

I hated what I had to say. "It's as bad up there as here. People shuffling up and down St. Catherine Street, the unemployed."

He stayed silent, nibbling a ragged pinkie nail, resigning himself to this disappointment, then shifting his thoughts. "How is your auntie, the one with the crippled son? How is the boy?"

"The same, I understand. I've not seen them lately."

"Don't you see the family any more? Not even your Aunt Daisy?"

He was jumping to another wrong conclusion—a movie actor's wife gets too *fancy-shmancy* for her relatives.

"We live with Daisy," I told him, "the baby and I. Daisy looks after us."

He laid a hand over mine. "You are a lucky girl," he said, though I could tell he still was puzzled by my situation.

"Daisy helps me, I help her," I told him. "It's a big house, you know. A lot to take care of: the tenants, the building."

"She has a janitor?"

"She had to let him go, can't afford one."

"She does the heavy work herself?" He shook his head, emphatically objecting. "That's too much for her; she should have a man to do it."

In the funny papers, when a brilliant notion hits a character, the artist draws a lighted bulb above his head. Probably it was my imagination, yet I would swear there was a light over Ben. Help her, she needs you, I thought; God knows you need her. For loving-kindness, shelter, food. And a button for your overcoat.

This wasn't mentioned, not by either one of us. All he said was, "Millie, tell her she should spare her strength."

Tell her yourself, I wanted to say, come back, come home with me, though I hesitated, fearing to speak now because long ago I had said too much.

"Tell me something, Millie. Do you know: has anybody of the family seen Arnold?"

I nodded. "I have."

"When? Where?" His face brightened with the old-time smile that had been so beautiful.

"He came to the house. Daisy met him near his school, and he walked home with her." Said that way it sounded like a chance encounter, a casual, friendly act, without the agony of her watching, waiting in the schoolyard. Why hadn't Ben done that himself? Or had he?

"How did Arnie look?"

"He's grown tall. He's thin."

He grimaced. "She never makes a decent meal. One carrot. One lettuce leaf. Never an egg, not a piece of steak. A growing boy needs substantial food."

A man, too, I thought. Come back with me. Daisy will treat you like a human being. I didn't say it. Ben has pride, he's pretending he's the Ben he used to be. A man is doubly poor when you take his pride away.

"My boy is well?"

"Sure, oh, sure. Just a sniffle. Stuffed-up nose."

"The tonsils. He has lousy tonsils. The doctor said he should have them out; he wouldn't be catching colds all the time. She knows more than the doctors." Ben drummed the table top, tapping some anger out. "What did my boy tell you, Millie?"

"He told Daisy he gets good marks at school. He told her he won't have a Bar Mitzvah. His mother doesn't believe in it."

He shrugged. "If a boy has a Bar Mitzvah, there should be a father present, to hand him the Torah. That's why she denies Arnie the pleasure—I shouldn't have to be there." He paused to let his anger ebb. "Did he mention me, Millie?"

"He did," I told Ben. "He remembered you used to play catch with him in the yard."

A flush swept his face. His eyes marbled; he brushed them furtively and forced a laugh. "He was a lousy catcher. I'm surprised he remembered it. We had some good times together, he and I. Not the baseball, Millie. He never liked that. I found a special pleasure for him. When we would go in the subway, him and me, I would take him to the first car to stand and watch the signal lights—the red and the green, the yellow and the blue. He learned quick what each one stands for. You would think his big ambition was to manage the IRT. . . . And animals, Millie. Not only he enjoyed to look at them in the zoo. But to touch. A dog. A cat. Whatever was soft." Remembering was etching pain grooves in his face. "Tell me, Millie, did he look happy? . . . No, how could the boy look happy? What kind of home does he have? No cheerfulness. No pleasures."

"No father," I said.

He stared at the far wall. "What kind of father did he have? Ask Sophie. A tramp, a low life, a bum. And a lousy businessman. He didn't make money for her. Money, money. I tell you, Millie" —his fists clenched—"if I made big money, Sophie would never, never in this world, throw me out. She would complain, she would

220

holler, but keep the husband in the house; let Ben be how he is, come home late, take the boy wherever he takes him Sundays. . . . But comes the Depression, he doesn't bring home enough money—" He flung his hands wide. "Finished. . . . Millie, good it never was between us. We were different natures. I like to live, to enjoy, to have different kinds of pleasures. . . ." He stopped speaking and sat staring at his clenched hands, until he could say, with desperate earnestness, "Millie, I lie awake nights, and I think and I wonder with what kind of eyes my son will someday look at me."

"Brown. Wide open," I replied.

He shook his head. "He will look at me with his mother's eyes. Her poison will be in my boy. He will be sick with the poison, Millie. Maybe this I deserve, this I earned. . . . Maybe not." He began to rise, bracing himself with the heels of his hands on the table top. "I have to get going."

"Where to? Give me your address so we can get in touch."

He evaded my eyes and my question. "I just got back from out of town."

"Are you working, Ben?"

"Off and on. A few days here, a few days there. Remember, I am not the only one."

We walked side by side to the door. "Come home with me," I said. "It will make Daisy happy."

"I would be glad to see her. Only not"—he glanced down at his overcoat—"not like this." And reddened. "Tell her you saw me, Millie. Do not tell her—"

I put out my hand. "Come, Ben, come. You would be so welcome. She worries about you."

"She is a sweet woman. Please give her regards."

Then, abruptly, he wheeled, moved swiftly, and was swallowed up by the crowd. On the subway, riding to Brooklyn, it occurred to me that possibly one reason why he hadn't come with me was that he had spent his last nickels for two cups of coffee and was ashamed to reveal he lacked subway fare. I would have been glad to pay that and more to bring him to Daisy. It occurred to me, too, that in all our conversation he had not mentioned Fanny.

221

I'd have been delighted to tell him how often conscience—or curiosity—drove her to the phone. That might have cheered him. Or enhanced his bitterness.

However, I did tell Daisy I had seen Ben and had had a cup of coffee with him; he had sent his regards. But I lied about his appearance—"Same old Ben"—and about his situation—"Part-time jobs. He's managing, getting along." And I added an invention: "He said he would phone as soon as he had a chance." Not for an instant did I dream this would happen. It did.

On a May Sunday morning, one of those spectacular late spring mornings when the last sharp thrust of winter has been blunted, the blue sky is undiluted, the new foliage is lush, and fat robins are strutting on the grass, I heard the phone and answered it. "Millie? This is Ben. Ben Kuper. How are you? How is your Aunt Daisy?"

"Fine, just fine." (A trifle dazed.) "And how are you?"

"Pretty good for an old man. Millie, I am wondering: it is a nice day; would you ladies care to take a little walk in Prospect Park?"

"What an idea, Ben!"

Aunt Daisy's head poked in. She had heard me say the name; her eyes bugged. I nodded, yes, it's he, and, handing over the mouthpiece, urged, "Talk to him."

"I can't." She shook her head.

I said, "Ben, come on over. We'll have lunch and decide about the walk." Trying to sound as if this took place every day. "It will be a pleasure to see you."

"It was really Ben?" My aunt was by turns white and pink. She sat; her knees had gone rubbery. "He is coming here! How did he sound? Tell me again, what did he say?" Incoherent with excitement. "What will we give him for lunch? . . . Oh, Millie, if we knew before. All we have in the Frigidaire is chop meat, for us. . . ."

"He'll be pleased with whatever we have, I'm sure."

"I'll bake a pie. Do we have time? . . . Where was he when he phoned? . . . How soon will he be here? . . . I could make stuffed cabbage. . . . No, that would smell up the house. . . . Plain chop meat is for the family, not for a guest. . . . Millie, please go upstairs, straighten up the parlor; I will do the dining room. . . . Please open Greta's kiddie coop in the yard; she could stay there, not creep underfoot." Daisy Magid, widow, middle-aged, was dithering like an adolescent.

I grasped her by both arms. "Listen to me. Go upstairs, comb your hair, put on a pretty dress. I'll fix lunch." I gave my aunt a gentle shove. "Up. Up."

In minutes, Ben was ringing our basement bell—he must have phoned from a nearby store booth. A stripe of sunlight made a path for him through our downstairs hall. He was different from the man I had seen in the Automat. His cheeks and chin were freshly shaved, his thinning hair was brushed, his shiny blue serge suit had been pressed, and his cracked shoes were glossy. Presentable. Personable. Almost the charmer he used to be.

My aunt came down the staircase slowly; her cheeks were rosy apples, her eyes alight. Ben stretched both hands to her, she hers to him. I turned away and left them there, to say what they had to say to one another, in whatever way they chose. They passed me at the kitchen sink, going out to the yard, to the ailan-thus tree. Decorously, they sat on kitchen chairs and talked. Near their feet, Greta crawled and cooed in her pen, playing with her blocks and ball, with Raggedy Ann and a glass-eyed Teddy bear. It was a charming domestic scene.

I set our table in the kitchen. The round oak table in the dining room held evil memories; the sunny kitchen had the happy ones. Nor did we, after lunch, go for a stroll in the park—instinct must have warned Daisy that Ben's presence at her side might prove embarrassing—on a Sunday in Prospect Park who knows whom you'll meet? We were walking on eggs, sensitive and wary, for this visit might be a turning point, might heal, might lead. To what? To a fairy-tale ending. Naturally.

He left before dark, telling me, "The lunch was delicious," pumping my hands enthusiastically. ("Delicious!" Hamburgers fried hard as rocks, lumpy mashed potatoes, a lemon pie with a cardboard crust and a meringue that wouldn't fluff. I have cooked excellent meals in my day. This time my mind was not on my work.)

"Four o'clock," I heard him telling Daisy. "How can I thank you!" But not an embrace, not a kiss, not even a handclasp. Such refinement! Such restraint!

Later, when we were washing up, my aunt said thoughtfully, "He didn't look bad, don't you think? If he could find a steady job —he has a day's work now and then, Saturdays in a store—he could buy a new suit for himself. And did you notice, Millie, the cracks in his shoes, worn out, walking, walking, looking for some work?"

I said, "Daisy, if he got a divorce—"

"Sophie wouldn't give him."

"Sophie doesn't want him."

"She wants him. To punish him."

"For what?"

"For nothing," she said.

I said, "Daisy, it's none of my business, but I always wanted to know. . . . You loved Ben, he loved you. . . . Don't deny it, I saw and I knew. . . . Why didn't you? Why did you—?"

Her chin firmed. "My father," she said. "My father said no." She noticed my outthrust lip, my angry headshake, and she put a hand on my arm. "Millie, I am different from you. I was raised with *derheretz*. You know what that means? Respect. Respect for the father, for the older person; he knows better than you. My father decided for me."

"He decided that Magid . . . that . . . that . . ."

All color drained from her cheeks. "Let us not talk about him," Daisy said in a painful whisper. "I was never his wife, the way a wife is." Then, with a peculiar expression, with a flat tonelessness, "The way I was when I knew Ben before, so now I am still."

Which wasn't true. Virgin or no, Aunt Daisy had changed. She was her own woman, strong and seasoned by grief.

"It was wicked," I said. "They were all wicked—"

"It is past," Daisy said.

Before we closed our bedroom doors, she said, "Millie, if Fanny should call up and I am not in the house, please, please do not tell her."

"Trust me," I said.

I woke to the fragrance of coffee cake baking. My aunt had risen with the sun. She bustled through her household chores, raced upstairs and down with the tenants' trash and garbage. She swept, scrubbed, and polished; she dashed to the grocer and butcher, not talking, saving her breath for four o'clock. By half past two, she was dressed and gone from the house.

I put Greta in her crib for a midday nap. The silent house was clean and expectant. At three o'clock, the top-floor tenant rang our basement bell. Where was the janitor? A toilet was stopped up, a bathroom flooded. I found a rubber plunger and went up to try to clean the mess. By the time I came down, Greta was awake and howling. I had her in my arms when I heard the basement bell and went down to let Ben Kuper in. He peered around and behind me. "Nobody here?"

"Daisy went out," I said. "She didn't say where."

"She went to bring Arnold." He laid a package on the kitchen table. "I brought a present for the baby."

"A wind-up clown that walks," I said.

He gave me a startled glance.

"I'm smart," I wisecracked, but hastened to reassure him. "A wild guess, that's all."

"Let me show you how it works," Ben said.

We were on our knees watching the clown wobble on the linoleum. Ben's back was to the door and so, at first, Arnie was not aware of who was there—the clown had caught his eye. "Cute," he said, approving it. Ben scrambled to his feet; he faced his son. The sweetness that used to be—the sunny, ingratiating smile, the youthful *joie de vivre*—brightened his face.

The boy backed a step, growing pale.

"I told you I had a surprise," Daisy said, watching Ben, only Ben.

Ben's arms extended. The boy kept backing off.

225

"Arnold, this is me, your papa. Say hello?" A hint of impatience, a trace of irritation. "Come. Shake hands. Shake hands like a gentleman."

Arnie's right arm slowly rose, the uncertain start of greeting. Ben seized the hand. He drew Arnie to himself, held his son against his body, kissed the boy's face and hair.

Arnie wrenched himself free. His face was crimson, his eyes desperate. "I can't," he cried. "I can't! I can't!" and veered toward Daisy, sputtering, "Why did you—? How could you—?" Frantic, he screamed at Ben, "Don't touch me! Let me be!" wildly staring, head veering side to side, as if hunting a way to escape. Greta and I blocked his path.

They looked so stricken, Arnold, Ben, and Daisy, I had to try to help them out. "Arnie, dear," I said, "this is just a little visit. Your father was worried about you. He wanted to see you. He missed you." Gratuitously, I added, "He loves you very much."

"My mother will kill me," Arnie answered me.

For an instant, the notion of Sophie's anger stunned us, left us wordless—we hadn't thought of her. It was Daisy who recovered first—my genteel aunt who in these last months had learned the art of dissemblement. "Do you have to tell her, Arnie? Let this be a secret, a pleasant, nice secret. What harm is that? Your father wanted to see you. Very much. Very."

Arnie stared beyond us, toward the kitchen wall. "I didn't want to see him." His lips were quivering.

Ben said nothing. The joy had drained from his face, leaving it waxen and perplexed. One hand groped in his jacket pocket; we heard the jingle of metal. The hand emerged, extended. "I wanted to bring you a present, Arnie. I didn't have a chance to go to a store. Take this money, buy yourself—"

The boy stood rigid, arms at his side, refusing the coins as he had rejected his father's hand. "We don't need your money," Arnie said.

"I th-thought, I wa-wanted . . ." Ben had begun to stammer. He stopped, forcing a smile, while he paused. "So answer me one question—only one—it wouldn't kill you to answer one question. How do you feel?"

"I am well," Arnie said. Then he slewed around and, dodging, ducking, slipped past me. The door banged.

We had an instant of puzzled silence, no one so much as breathing, before we heard the crunch of tin. "The son of a bitch!" Ben cried. On his face there was shame and fury. And while we stood stricken and shocked, my aunt and I heard Ben say with cold earnestness, "I have been trying to make up my mind. I have been trying to convince myself one way or the other: was my son a rotten little son of a bitch? Now I know. . . ."

"Ben, Benny." Daisy was pleading. "The boy was upset. He didn't know, he didn't realize—"

"He knew. He realized. He told her. He snitched. Is that rotten? Tell me, yes or no?"

"Ben, the boy was afraid of the mother. She dragged words from him. She twisted, she made from the words . . ."

He shook his head at Daisy, denying what she said. "Maybe yes, maybe no. My son hates me. This much I know." He drew a ragged handkerchief out of his jacket pocket, dabbed at his eyes, and balled the damp rag in his fist. "What do I have to live for?" he asked.

Why, at this moment, did Daisy not go to him, put her arms around him, offer comforting? I would have done that myself, except that her compassion—her remembered love—gave her the priority. But then it dawned upon me that, in his gush of anger, Ben had hurt her, too. Tangentially, he had admitted the truth of Sophie's accusations. He had made the boy, willy-nilly, a witness to what my uncle called the "monkey business." And this was worse than indiscretion. It was stupidity.

"I am going, ladies. I will not bother you more."

"You will have coffee. We will have supper," Daisy said, but unconvincingly.

"I have to see somebody." He forced a smile. "A man about a dog."

My aunt slept poorly. All night I kept hearing her bedroom door and the bathroom door opening and shutting. I heard it because I, too, was not sleeping well. What I had heard and comprehended in the kitchen had told me what Ben Kuper was—a weak and stupid man. He had jilted Daisy, who loved him; he had married Sophie, whom he did not love, because his bullying sister had demanded it; he had been unfaithful to Sophie—promiscuous, yes, and lecherous—No, that is not fair; what actually happened, I do not know. Yet he was unbelievably, unutterably stupid to do whatever he did in Arnie's presence. Trusting the boy, relying on Arnie's affection, on his loyalty. But how much had been exaggerated, how much dirtied up by the boy's imagination and Sophie's viciousness? For instance, that exuberance in the grandstand at the baseball games, those innocent embraces. . . . Innocent? His breast against my breasts, his hands lingering and caressing me. Remembering, I grew hot with a new shame, and it occurred to me that the blabbing, blundering child I used to be might, after all, have done a kindness to Daisy.

But then I thought of Sophie, and I realized that however weak and foolish Ben's conduct had been, Sophie's behavior was monstrous. She had taught her son to hate his father, and by that she had orphaned him.

At the end of the summer, Greta and I moved out of Daisy's house. Jay had a good contract with a major studio; he was ready to provide a home for us. He came to New York to fetch us and to help me sell the furniture I'd put in storage. "Junk. Not worth shipping to the Coast." My parents came down from Montreal to say good-bye to me and Greta, and there was a sadness in my father's voice when he said to Jay, "Take care of them. Take good care," though he did not shake his fist beneath my husband's nose as he had the day I married him. I said I hoped they would come and visit in California. My mother sighed and shrugged and said, "God knows. It is so far." The parting was solemn, though without the finality that Ben Kuper's departure had had.

When Ben walked out through the basement door, he walked out of my life. The clown had been smashed on the kitchen floor. It hadn't been a proper toy for Greta anyway; the tin had sharp edges, and the paint probably was poisonous.

Which one of us had smashed the tin clown, I have never been certain, and now and then I've replayed the scene in my mind, trying to fit pieces together, as in a jigsaw puzzle. Arnie had gone; we were just three. I know I stood rooted, with the child in my arms. Daisy—I am not sure about Daisy—I would like to believe it was she, finding her spunk, writing *finis* to a romance by crushing a tawdry symbol of it. But I believe it was Ben, destroying himself, though not meaning to.

8 ❄

BILLY WAS CONCEIVED in the master bedroom beneath the red tile roof of the white stucco hacienda that tourist guides pointed out as "where the Star James Burns resides." Not adding, With his wife, Mildred, his daughter, Greta (called "four eyes" and "the cockeyed kid" by sadistic juniors in the neighborhood), Greta's wire-haired terrier, Mac (short form of Macbeth), a middle-aged couple named Olsen (she, housekeeper-cook; he, houseman-butler-chauffeur), and a sequence of nursemaids named Marjorie, Alma, Nicole, Bridget, Della, Pearl, Josephine—satellites, all to the Star. The nursemaids, in particular, became so attached to that Star I had to fire and replace them frequently.

Harry, our Japanese gardener, born on this coast, came three times a week, to weed the flower beds, manicure the lawns, and scoop eucalyptus leaves out of the pool. Harry watered and sprayed enthusiastically. He ran up prodigious water bills.

The house sat atop a canyon. From its master bedroom we saw the sprawl of Hollywood; from the nursery at the rear, the brown hills that reminded me, always, of moth-eaten lions, crouching. When fog rolled in from the Pacific, we saw nothing whatever, not even pinpoints of light from the Gruening house below ours.

Billy was conceived on one of those foggy nights. I had steered our Cadillac through the cotton-batting mist: Jay and I, returning from a party, he dozing or pretending to doze while I fought the fog and a full gut of anger. Once inside the house and upstairs, my anger spilled. Jay stared, bleary-eyed, until the barbs of my fury reached him. Then he lunged, ripped off my dress, and pinned me on my bed. When he rose, I caught a glimpse of his face, smug, self-satisfied, as after a great performance. Take a bow, Sir Jake. Pity there is no applause. Not from this audience.

Hours later, after a studio car had driven him off to work, I lay abed, wondering whether the hour had come to give up my tinsel heaven.

"Millie lives like a queen, her home is a palace," my mother had written Aunt Daisy, who had relayed it to me, though neither of them had journeyed west to see for themselves where Her Majesty—that frigid princess from the frozen north, so dubbed by James Burns of the cinema—dwelt in elegance, beauty, and discontent.

Tourists, peering through our iron gates, saw only the beauty, the flowers, and the emerald grass. A landscape architect had helped with the shrubbery—helped but not dictated, since, as always, I had whims. Bougainvillea draped our walls, hibiscus crowded the front door, and red begonia, continuously flowering, flanked our driveway. But off to one side, we had a rose garden, whose blossoms, crimson, pink, and white, were fat and exquisitely fragrant, while on the opposite side of the house, across the lawn, there was a miniature grove of lemon trees. The yellow fruit, amid the shiny leaves, looked so pretty it seemed a sin and a sacrilege to pick it. Out back, beyond the swimming pool, at the far edge of the wide lawn where Greta played, we had a stand of graceful eucalyptus trees. They had been on the property when we bought the place, original inhabitants like the hummingbirds and mourning doves. There were no palms. The landscape architect had raised his eyebrows when I declared that, to my mind, these were the world's ugliest trees; their scaly bark, the grotesque swellings on their trunks, and their pointed fronds repelled me. No cactus, either. I am disturbed by nature's sharp thrustings. I would have liked oaks and maples, to enjoy their autumnal bronze and scarlet. However, in Southern California, seasons show up nowhere except on calendars.

You can't have everything, Mrs. Burns. Make do with an ermine wrap for gala evenings, a ruby-and-diamond dinner ring, and an "authentic" Spanish interior that had been a photo layout in a national magazine. The downstairs, that is. There, I had let a decorator have her way; she had done our dropped living room with rough plastered walls and dark ceiling beams, had outlined our fireplace with Spanish ceramics, had put up black wrought-iron sconces to hold candle bulbs. The sofas and chairs had carved wooden frames and red velvet cushions, with ball fringe and tassels; the grand piano, on which neither Jay nor I performed, was draped with Carmen's shawl, though atop the embroidery were silver-framed photographs, inscribed to James Burns by Norma, Gloria, Jean, Shirley, et cetera. There were red-velvet draperies to draw and close for a privacy the room seldom craved. However, aside from the sconces I have mentioned, the walls were bare. That was due to a brief contretemps with the decorator. Somewhere she had acquired a large wooden crucifix. (Mrs. Sponduliks, or whatever they call you, do you know we are Jewish people? . . . Correct, we don't flaunt our religion; our cuisine includes bacon and shrimp. And our name? You know about Hollywood names, do you not? There's more box-office appeal in Burns than Bernstein. . . . Don't be ridiculous, a crucifix does not become nonsectarian when it's an antique. . . . If my parents or Jay's turned up, they would be horrified. . . . Pictures? Why, yes, a picture gallery between the living room and the dining room would be just great. A Rembrandt or two, don't you think? . . . Oh, oh, I forget, our motif is Spain. El Greco, then. Or Velasquez . . . Well, now that you mention it, they do cost a lot and—surely you know, nothing is secret here—ours is *new* money, exceedingly new. We can't afford masterpieces. Not yet. Give us a few years. You're right, I agree, bare walls do show an independent spirit.)

Adjoining the living room—the connecting wooden door had worm holes, adroitly contrived—was our paneled den, where the couches were upholstered in butter-soft leather, coal-black, the

232

books locked behind diamond-leaded glass, the Victrola, the bar, hidden in ornate cabinets, and Jay's clipping books (leather bound) displayed on a refectory table.

Up a step from the living room, in which we did not and could not live, was our formal dining room, whose mahogany table alone had cost more than all the "modren" we had bought for the flat on Fifty-seventh Street. The chairs had purple-velvet cushions and a tendency to tip.

The decorator had sensed I despised the Spanish *drek*—I wore my disdain openly—yet she'd plunged ahead as if she had had orders from the studio heads. A rising star must live like a star; he owed it to the industry.

One concession she made to our personal needs: a family dining room, large and sun-swept, at the rear of the house; a wall of glass, opposite one of brick, a long trestle table, benches, and shelves, crowded with Mexican tinware, straw gewgaws, clay pots, and colored glass. Strings of red peppers and magenta onions hung from the ceiling beams. The effect was lively and cheerful. But alien to us. (Mrs. Shnitzelfritz, or whatever you are called, we are a Jewish couple, out of Brooklyn and Washington Heights. People might get wrong impressions, seeing this. Okay, okay, you claim it's a perfect background for Burns, though I can't guess why. We pay our money, and you make our choice. Nevertheless, keep your hands off upstairs—that's my *lebensraum*. My bedroom —so huge that back home we might use it for a curling rink—must be pink and white, with sheer, airy curtains, ruffles on the bedspreads and glazed chintz (with rosebuds) for the wing chair. Yes, ma'am, I am a romantic, an old-fashioned girl.) Greta's room had a rocking chair and a wicker bed for Mac, her wire-haired terrier.

The Olsens had a suite above the garage that held our four-door Cadillac, our Buick convertible, and our two-door Essex for the staff's use. Gus Olsen had suggested we buy a Ford, but Jay had refused. "That anti-Semite can't get a plugged dime of my dough." Howard Gruening had told Jay about Henry Ford; Howie kept up with the world outside Hollywood.

I used the convertible for my personal errands and to drive

Greta and her nursemaid to the beach. The child was mad about the ocean, as much so as, long ago, I had thought I would be. A fearless tyke, she romped in the surf and the spume while I, on the sand, watched with my heart in my mouth. A pretty child, too, except for that squint. We planned to operate. Eventually. I tried to get Jay to help me set a date. "Later, later," he kept saying. "Leave the kid alone." He left the kid alone, not hostile exactly, or indifferent, merely wrapped up in himself.

Whenever I snapped pictures to send to my family, I removed Greta's glasses and photographed her in profile. Vanity. Vanity. Let's not admit that anything we have is less than perfect.

A studio car picked Jay up every morning and brought him home in the evening. A valuable property, this gifted young star, one of the galaxy of romantic toughs that included Bogart, Cagney, Garfield, Raft—reluctant members of Capone-type mobs; victims of a miscarriage of justice, rattling prison bars; young avengers, stalking evil in the city slums; secret agents, haunting cheap cafés in tropical ports, foiling plotters against the U.S.A.; cool and wisecracking, noble beneath rough exteriors, brave and loyal (no doubt whatever of that) to flag and country and the dame with the padded shoulders and the cast-iron permanent. Certainly, Jay played romantic scenes, but oddly they did not trouble me as I had been troubled by the Charleston he had danced with Bonnie Granger on Broadway. This is celluloid, I told myself; that other had been warm and vibrant flesh.

Jay would, no doubt, have liked a shot at Romeo or Hamlet, but the clink of coin at the box office said loud and clear, "Your public likes you in these parts." My husband's fan mail kept a staff busy, mailing out his photographs. And the salary the studio paid James Burns seemed astronomical to both of us. In the East they were singing, "Brother, can you spare a dime?" while in the West we lucky few were suddenly rich.

Suddenly? Not truly so, if you add together all Jay's years of single-mindedness: the yearning, first, the ambition, mocked by his peers at City College; then, the learning, the apprenticeships at Provincetown and in Mort Hoffman's group. Add these to his natural gifts: his talent and capacity for work. Add those to the magic of personality, the *je ne sais quoi* that travels across footlights and off a flickering screen. In no conventional sense was James Burns handsome—I'd acknowledged this the night I met him—his features were irregular, the chin too long, the ears too large. Yet anywhere and everywhere, the women swarmed like ants around the honey spill. "Trust me, Princess." How long? With whom?

As on Fifty-seventh Street, I kept the home fires burning; that is, I told the domestic staff what I wished them to do. I made sure that Jay's personal wardrobe was cared for and replenished. I purchased his after-shave lotion and his razor blades. I handed him aspirin for hangovers and ordinary headaches. And well-dressed, poised, amiable-seeming, I greeted his guests, smiled indulgently when Jay scintillated in the living room, joined conversations when I was addressed, gave parties, went to parties, mingled with crowds around a pool, ours or someone else's, nursing a martini—only one drink; keep a clear head. "No thanks, I don't smoke. Of course, I don't mind if you do. But please, please don't blow cigar smoke in my face. I had a grandfather who liked Pittsburgh stogies; he reeked of stale smoke. That may have conditioned me." What happens to you in childhood persists in odd ways.

Mine was a glamorous existence—ask any reader of fan magazines. Mrs. Burns, President Roosevelt himself has said it: "You have nothing to fear except fear." And the fear that nags you is irrational. A thousand housewives, coast to coast, dream of living like you.

Get up when you please. If it's early, breakfast downstairs with your child, kiss her, pat her on the head, send her outdoors to play. If it's late, ring a silver bell; Mrs. Olsen will come with orange juice, coffee, the morning newspaper, and a single rosebud on a tray. After breakfast, sit at the phone and order: groceries, meat, liquor, services. Make appointments with the hairdresser, the dentist, the dress shoppes; accept invitations or extend your own, for dinner or cocktails; tell Mrs. Olsen how many we'll be for dinner tonight and let us have squab for a change, rib roast is so ordinary. Write checks to pay bills, balance the checkbook, write to the family, and mail them snapshots of Greta.

It was peculiar about my family: we were *dutiful*. I wrote to them, they wrote to me, at spaced intervals. We asked each other: How are you? How do you feel? We told each other our healths were okay, our activities proceeding in their normal ways—"Jay is starting a new picture" . . . "Mama thinks my new fall line will be a big success" . . . "Greta and her nurse and I drove down the Coast as far as San Clemente, the scenery was beautiful" . . . "Mama and me are going on the train to Ottawa; I got the idea in my head I would like to take a look at the Parliament." Staying in touch. Perfunctorily.

Time and distance alienate, even when there has been no open break. I live my life, you live yours; all we have in common are our genes. Never did they indicate a wish for me to visit them, or they to visit me. Nor did I press my invitation on them; their presence here might be uncomfortable—for all of us. Especially for me. I'd have to try to explain why Jay behaved as he frequently did and why I put up with it.

Some of Jay's relatives did write, suggesting that if we would supply Pullman tickets (lower berths) they'd be pleased to receive our hospitality. And Jay once showed me a letter from his father, thanking him for a check he had sent. "Your sister, Janet, has to have a whole new wardrobe. She's going to the mountains for vacation—a swanky hotel. Maybe she'll meet somebody. Your mother is anxious to see Janet settled." And asking Jay's opinion of the plan he was mulling: to relocate in Los Angeles. "Your mother says she would never want to live in Hollywood, with all those phony types, and she wouldn't want to be in a position where your wife and her fancy friends could snub her. I figure Los Angeles is not too near, but not too far, to get some good out of your connections."

I'm not sure why Jay showed me this letter—it contained pinpricks and rankles, in addition to the fact that the check he had sent had not been drawn on our joint bank account or discussed with me. Not that I would have refused—Lord! we had enough

236

to scatter largesse. However, he might have talked this over with me. But the fact was he rarely talked anything over with me. Naturally laconic, now busy and preoccupied. Studio demands. And a social life lived in crowds. A minimum of privacy, save in the bedroom, where, late at night, we wrapped ourselves in fine percale in separate beds. "G'night, Mildred." "Good night, Jay."

A marriage needs dialogue, doesn't it?

It was to Thelma Gruening I did my talking, while we sprawled on chaises in the patio alongside the pool, in the afternoons while Greta napped. Thelma was the best friend, the female confidante I had yearned for in the first years of my marriage, a sophisticated, forthright, attractive woman—dark bobbed hair (with bangs), mischievous eyes, and an irreverent tongue, older than I by ten years, which put her midway between parent and contemporary. She'd been a dancer—a student of dance—at the Neighborhood Playhouse. We shared memories of New York—its sights and smells, the roar and rattle of its El and subway, its Greenwich Village speakeasies—and we argued about Romany Marie's. Thelma said the wine was terrible; I said the coffee was. Thelma called me naïve for believing Marie was a gypsy; she was just a *yenta* in a peasant skirt. I said in any case the place gave me a romantic feeling; candlelight and drippings on wine bottle necks do that to me. "What idiots when we were young!" Thelma said. "Speak for yourself," I told her.

The Gruening house was smaller than ours, and it had no gates, since tourists were not curious about Howard's domestic life, he being merely a writer, one of those whose names appear in smaller type among the screen credits. Like Jay, he had gone to City College, and he, too, had met his bride at a dance—a Halloween masquerade in Webster Hall in the Village. "Howie wore a leopard loincloth—that's all; the rest of him was naked. Hairy. Chest. Arms. Legs. Disgusting, Mildred. And me, neck to ankles in chiffon, the seven veils. He dared me to dance with him. Beauty and Beast. A natural alliance, no?"

And an easygoing marriage, trading jokes and tag lines of jokes instead of sarcastic jabs. "Howie jokes to keep from crying," Thelma said. "A *Weltschmerz* kid." In his student days Howard had written verses of social significance. They'd been printed—without payment—in "The Guillotine" in the Socialist *Call* and in "The Conning Tower" of the Republican *Tribune;* he had known the two Maxes, Eastman and Bodenheim, personally, and had nursed an ambition to be pointed out to uptown tourists as a genuine radical Bohemian. "Fate was his enemy," Thelma told me. "Fate set it up while he was in his cradle. She gave him talent. A small amount. Just enough to give him the itch. So he surprised himself and everyone by writing a novel. Searing and scathing. With some dirty words. Realism. Sensational. So Hollywood said, 'Genius, come, write crap for us.' "

The Gruenings mocked at Hollywood, yet through the stock-market crash and the Depression they had clung to it. "The oranges are so cheap," Thelma said. "Where else can you afford to feed kids?" They had two strapping boys, who rode bikes up the canyon road without huffing and puffing and swam like seals in our pool. Only occasionally were they cruel to Greta.

Jay liked Howard Gruening. He liked Thelma, too, in an offhand way—she wasn't, thank the Lord, pretty enough to make me uneasy. Once a week, usually, Jay went down to Gruenings for poker with Howie and his cronies, who were mostly writers, also from the East. After the game, sometimes during, names cascaded through the room: the key names of the nineteen thirties—Lenin, Trotsky, Selassie, Mussolini, Roosevelt, Hitler, Franco, Father Coughlin, Litvinov—and the key words—New Deal, *Putsch, Dearborn Independent,* Fifth Column, Fascism. The voices were loud and positive, the gestures sweeping, with table poundings. In the babble, I rarely heard my husband's voice—it seemed to me Jay preferred the role of a listener, interested and possibly flattered to be at a table with dabblers in *Weltpolitik.* They *did* know more than he did; they read an enormous array of publications that never came into our house, and they honed their minds in debate. Hence, though his salary far exceeded any of theirs, James Burns was humble, awed to silence by how much they knew and how positive their opinions were.

As for Thelma and me, we were bored rather than cowed. The quotes from Marx and Lenin drove us to the kitchen. Let the men repair the world while the women fix the sandwiches. Alcohol was never served at the Gruenings', not even beer. Howie had the start of an ulcer; Thelma preferred he'd not be tempted, which was fine with me. Jay became difficult after he had been drinking, which he did too frequently.

My night-table phone was ringing, its burr like a dentist's drill. I picked up the receiver. "How do you feel?" Jay wanted to know.

"I'll live, I guess."

"I seem to recall I was rough last night."

"And so?"

"And so you want me to apologize?"

"I hadn't thought of it."

"You will." A pause. "You had it coming, pet. Long time overdue." Another pause. "I'm not in the priesthood, Mrs. B. No vow of celibacy."

"I don't want to talk about it."

"Eventually you will. And I hardly can wait."

He hung up, I hung up. I started to cry. Jay, why are you cruel to me? I've tried, it's not my fault. Okay, whose fault? There's no simple explanation for how we behave. . . . It's Mama's fault. Mama, I blame you. You shouldn't have let me marry him. I was just a kid; what did I know? Mothers should protect their daughters. Why didn't you? You were jealous, that's why. Because I was Papa's pet. Competition for you. . . . Where do I get ideas like this? Why, out of books. Fathers lust after their daughters; mothers resent them. Stop this, Millie, it's ridiculous. You were a pigheaded brat. "Thou art fair, my love." Also you were pregnant, let's not forget this small detail. You felt guilty; he felt guilty. Guilt is sticky. Oh, he had glamour and glitter. He had gall. He seduced a foolish virgin. We started married life with a secret, with a sin. One thing led to another. Now to this, my drunken husband raped me in my bed.

My dress lay in a heap on the bedroom floor, where it had

239

fallen when he yanked it off; the shoulder strap was torn, along with a chunk of silk. A two-hundred-dollar creation good for nothing except the rag bag. More where that came from, Mrs. B. One thing you have, if you have nothing else, is charge accounts.

I saw myself in the bathroom's full-length mirror. There were purple bruises on my arm, his fingerprints below my vaccination scar. Greta is going to see this; the help will notice it. By tormorrow morning all Hollywood will be gossiping: Burns is beating his wife.

I sat on the bathtub's edge, trying to think. What's wrong with us? What's wrong with *me?* Jay wants me—at least I believe he does. And I want him—I think I do. But I'm the princess from the frozen north. A word is missing. Say it; come on, speak the word. Frigid. He comes to my bed like a beggar. Princess, please! While I shrink and shrivel, tied in knots. All you have to fear is fear. The fear is enough.

I pulled on a robe and went back to the phone. "Thelma, dear Thelma, come over, come early, please."

"Something wrong?"

"Come for lunch." A guest for lunch means wear something with sleeves, not a bruise-revealing bathing suit.

While Greta and her nursemaid, Josephine, were at the trestle table with us, we traded mild chitchat.

"How was the party?" Thelma asked.

"Okay, I guess."

"Who was there, Mrs. Burns?" Josephine asked.

"The usual crowd."

"I mean celebrities," Josephine said.

"James Burns."

"Of course. Who else?"

"Mildred Burns," Thelma said.

"Bless you, sister, for the compliment. Mrs. Burns is no celebrity. She's merely someone for the house."

"What did they serve?" Thelma asked.

"Scotch and rye, I believe. And champagne."

"How original!"

"Didn't they give you supper, Mommy?" Greta asked.

"Baby, they were stingy-mean. Not even a small piece of cheese."

"We had hamburgers," Greta said. "I gave Mac some of mine. Josephine said I shouldn't, he could get sick on people food."

"Not exactly, Mrs. Burns. I just don't think a dog should be encouraged to beg at the table. He has to learn manners."

"Correct. Manners are important. They're a way of being kind. Everybody should have manners. Even pups."

Greta giggled. "Know what you said, Mommy? You said pops. Is my Pops-Daddy kind?"

"Drink your milk, baby. And one cookie. Only one. Your teeth will get cavities from too many sweets."

"Mommy, would you drive us to the beach today?"

Josephine backed Greta up. "It's such a perfect day, I told her I thought you might."

"Not today. I have a splitting headache."

"The troubles of the rich," Thelma said.

"Upstairs, Greta, baby. Scoot. . . . Mrs. Olsen, no company for dinner. Something simple, please. . . . No, I'm not sure when— or whether—Mr. Burns will be home. . . . Thelma, let us go out. I need to breathe air."

I pushed twin chaises to the far side of the pool, away from the ears of the house, and set them close. Thelma opened her knitting bag and took out balls of colored wool. "Argyles. Working on my Christmas list. For the freezing New York relatives. Howie says knitting is my masturbation."

"Don't be vulgar!" I said.

She gave me a quick, sharp glance. "Okay, Mill. What happened at the party?"

"The usual," I said. "In spades."

The usual, Thelma knew as well as I, is that at the parties the studio bigwigs throw, an actor's wife is a decorative nobody. She trades small talk and gossip with other wives; she fends off passes from repulsive drunks, using finesse so as not to make an enemy of someone who has power. And she keeps a wary eye on her husband to be sure he doesn't step far out of line. Scenes and scandals must be avoided. The box office objects.

"Thelma, last night Jay humiliated me."

"*Mah neshtanah?* . . . Wherefore is this night different?"

"Okay, okay, he's done it before. Time and again. He likes the girls; the girls like him. Hungarians, Scandinavians, Bulgarians. No race prejudice. Except last night it was worse. Fritz Scheller's blonde."

"A distinguished man," Thelma said. "They snatched him out of Berlin. He's okay. Politically."

"What's politics got to do with it? His blonde is a tramp. A mistress—believe me—never his wife. Oh, he wasn't there; someone brought her to the party. Dropped her off. Sequins, spangles, dingle-dangles. She came through the door and spotted Jay. 'The vunderful, chahming Meester Buhrns!' First, it was him on the arm of her chair, massaging her knee. Then it was two of them drinking out of one glass. Then it was nuzzling on a couch in a corner. Everyone watching. And watching me, and me pretending . . ."

"Good girl," Thelma said.

"Good girl, my eye! My husband is smooching a floozie. That's what he does at all the parties. People, please pay no attention, I do not mind it in the least. But then it got late. Very late. And people were saying good night. And looking at me, wondering what I was planning to do. Because Jay and the blonde had vanished."

Thelma was untwisting the colored stands of yarn. "What *did* you do?"

"I went to look for him."

"Oh-oh!" Thelma said.

"I found them," I went on to say. "Upstairs. On a bed. Oh, her skirt was down, his fly was closed. But lipstick was all over him."

"Aha! And what did he say?"

" 'A lady knocks before entering' is what he said."

"And you said?"

"I was a lady—he'd said I was, hadn't he?—I said, 'It's time to go.' And he looked at his watch; he leaned over her to hold his

wrist to the lamp near the bed—he had to make sure I was right—
'So it is, so it is,' he said, and he rolled off the bed and stood up and
saluted her with his hand to the side of his head. *'Fräulein, Danke-
schön,'* he said, or something like that, and she, stupid or brazen or
whatever she is, said something like, 'Who will see me home?' And
I said, 'The vice squad,' and Jay looked at me and pretended to
shudder and said, 'Cheese it, the cops.'"

"Crazy! Crazy! Crazy!" Thelma laughed fit to burst. "I must
tell Howie. He could use that. Excellent dialogue."

I flared like a match. "Don't you dare. It was stupid. Rotten.
And I had to drive the car home. Because he was tight as a tick—I
couldn't trust him at the wheel. And the fog was awful. He didn't
talk. And I had to concentrate on the driving. Oh, Thelma,
Thelma, it was a nightmare!"

"Then, you got home," Thelma continued, for me. "You
drove the car into the garage. You went into the house, upstairs
to your room. He followed you, a little bit sheepish. He began to
undress. Then you opened your mouth. You let him have both
barrels. And he grabbed you, and he nailed you to the bed...."

I gaped. "Were you—how did you—?"

She smiled crookedly. "Certain glands, when aroused, by
whatever, whoever—what the *Fräulein* started—"

"Stop it!"

She took up her needles. "Par for the course. I should
know—"

"Not you. Not you and Howard."

She shrugged. "Is Howie's libido a raisin? He is a male. And
susceptible. Millie, when we first got here, he was like a kid in
Macy's toy department Christmas week. So much pulchritude!
Dolls with round heels! My *shlemiel* had himself a time!"

"And you let that go on!" (In my family, I thought, that is
the high crime; Ben Kuper walks the streets of New York with
holes in his shoes, Ben Kuper's son eats his heart out with hate, because, just because— And I—one day soon I shall have to decide.)

Thelma jabbed her knitting needles into a ball of wool. "Millie, Millie darling, what should I have done? Castrate Howie? Or

243

play the game, tit for tat, what's sauce for the gander?" She shook her head stoutly. "I'm not the type. Was not, am not, beautiful, like you. No wolves at my door. And some women have pride; they do not care to be laid out of charity. Moreover, Mill, I knew what I was—an old-fashioned wife, a one-man female. A lucky girl who'd found what she likes. Of course"—she squeezed the wool ball—"I could have threatened a divorce." Her slim shoulders rose. "He might have said, 'Okay.' It scared hell out of me he would. Because—see—I loved my *shlemiel*. I loved him and no one else. And we had too much between us to break our marriage up. Not just the kids—forget what the books say, the kids could have survived divorce. I'd have protected them from some of the mess; Howie would have, too. No. It was me. I'd be the loser. I'd lose our good conversation, the jokes we shared. We can talk in tag lines, you know—'Just like in Cincinnati' when you roll out of bed."

She caught the blank look on my face. "Heavens, don't you know *anything*, Millie? That is a very old joke. The middle-aged man from the Middle West who's sure he's been missing out on sex. So he goes abroad, and he demands the most talented whore in Paris, pay any price, get the fancy work. . . . And it turns out just like in Cincinnati."

I didn't think that was funny. Nor at the moment did she, for she went on to say, "As far as I'm concerned, the silences we share are better than the talk. You understand things; you feel things the same way; you communicate without words. Just the touch of his hand on the nape of my neck when I'm worried or tired or mad at the kids. Small gestures of tenderness." She looked up and over at me, questioning.

I must have blushed. "That's not in the script."

"Who wrote the script? You or Jay?"

I spread my hands. "I've done my best."

"I doubt it," she said and sat, still and silent, staring across the turquoise pool toward the ragged eucalyptus trees, while I rubbed the bruise beneath my sleeve and stared, too, at *my* lawn, *my* trees, *my* flowers, *my* swimming pool. Millie Burns lives like a queen, in a palace, I told myself, with a black and blue arm and a pain in her heart.

"Millie, do you love Jay?"

"I married him."

She shook her head. "That's not what I asked. Put it another way: do you want to keep him? Do you care for him enough to take him as he is?"

I hesitated too long. She answered for me. "At the moment you're not sure. You're hurt and confused." She slewed around on her chaise, put her hand on my hand, pressing down hard. "Listen to me, Mildred Burns, listen good. Jay is an attractive man. Not a pretty boy or a sheikh. But with sex appeal. Women go for him; you did, yourself. At first sight. And more than once you've told me how your family raised hell when you announced he was it: our daughter is beautiful; the family's not poor; Millie could marry someone high-class. So she falls for an actor without a job. I can imagine the screams. Yet you married him, you stuck to him. Yes, when the going was rough, you didn't quit: you scrubbed the floors, you ironed the shirts, you borrowed money from your father to pay the rent. You spat in the family's eye—don't say a word against my man! It hasn't been peaches and cream. But you didn't walk out on him. Nor he on you. It strikes me there's been a solid commitment by the two of you. You made your first trip to the Coast—this is a guess on my part—to make sure you still wanted him and he wanted you. You did. He did. He could have left you and Greta in Brooklyn: 'It's all over, kid!' Or you could have gone back north to your folks: 'Excuse it, I made a mistake.' Why didn't you? You know the answer. Jay came to get you. He brought you here—Greta and you. To share his life, his success. For one reason, only one: he wanted you. In spite of all temptation —and he has had plenty of that—James Burns wants you, only you, for his wife. . . . Believe me, honey, if he was up for grabs, there would be a stampede! . . . Stop biting your nails." She slapped my hand away from my mouth. "It's ugly. Infantile."

"Thelma, what shall I do ?"

"Nothing. Do nothing whatever. Say nothing, because if you

245

say A, you'll have to say B. If you say, 'Buster, stop playing around,' you must be prepared for 'or else.' And the 'or else' is, 'I will leave you.' And, Millie, stop, think, consider, he just may say, 'So long, toots.' Because, Millie, there may be something he's missing, something he feels cheated of—a man hates to beg." She hitched her chaise an inch or so nearer to mine. "You know, there are three sides to problems like this—hers, his, and the truth." She offered me a steady, searching look. "And I just wonder, though it's none of my business, whether the truth is upstairs, among your ruffles and chintz."

Heat flooded my throat. She noticed it; she whistled softly.

"So that's where the dog is buried," she said. And when I nodded, too choked up to speak, to tell her, my most intimate friend, about the dread and the revulsion that haunted me, she said quietly, "In *Lady Chatterley's Lover*—I don't know if you've read the book. No? Well, maybe you should—Lady Chatterley's having this affair with the gamekeeper, and for the first time in her life she's enjoying sex, and she asks the man, naïvely, whether everyone enjoys it this much, and he answers, no, they do not. And you can tell it by the *raw look* of them."

Instinctively, I raised my hands to my face. With that quick understanding of hers, Thelma leaned over to grip my wrist. "Not yet," she said. "But you might, you just might. And what a pity." Then she said, "There's a psychoanalyst in L.A., I've heard him well-spoken of—"

"I'm not crazy."

"That's not the point," Thelma said. "You might make good use of professional help. To open your closets. Clear out certain things. That's what analysis is."

"I thought you were my friend," I said.

"I'll get you his telephone number," Thelma said. "Meanwhile, there is tonight. What will you say? What will you do?"

"Nothing," I said. "I don't know," I said.

Jay came late. I had eaten with Greta. He ate alone. After dinner he went to the den, took a book from a shelf, started to read, and fell asleep on a couch. It was just as well, since, had he come up, we might have exchanged brutal words. What you do not say, you do not need to retract.

In the morning, while he was dressing, he chanced to notice my naked arms. He came over and touched the purpled blotch. "I never intended to hurt you," he said. I didn't answer, although I cried after he left.

Thelma brought me the telephone number; I called the psychoanalyst. A secretary answered. "Doctor is in Europe. He's not expected back for another four weeks." . . . Was I a patient? . . . Oh, a new patient! Who had referred me? . . . Oh, a friend, not my physician? . . . Well, she wasn't sure whether Doctor, when he returned, would have the time available. His schedule was crowded. If this was an emergency, she might be able to refer me . . .

I wasn't about to run my car over the rim of the canyon; I was merely unhappy and confused. Is unhappiness an emergency?

"Thank you. I'll try to contact the doctor next month."

She asked for my name. I hung up without telling. In this town, secretaries may have pipelines to the gossip columns.

By the time the doctor was due back from Europe, I had found out that at this particular time I needed an obstetrician more than an analyst.

I was pregnant. And because I had had a dubious obstetrical history—one miscarriage (I could tell this doctor, since he wasn't acquainted with my mother-in-law) and one premature delivery—he recommended vegetation, stay off my feet as much as possible, take leisurely strolls for exercise, nap in the afternoon, cut out the parties, go early to bed.

Jay had to be told. At first, he looked dazed, as if he couldn't recall when he had dropped the seed, and then he grinned. "Still mad at me?" He kissed my forehead, stroked my cheek, gestures that Thelma might have called tenderness. He set up my chaise in the patio, fetched me books and magazines. On weekends he paid some attention to Greta, started to give her swimming lessons in the

247

pool, played the friendly father as well as the penitent husband. But clumsily, since this role had not been scripted for him, and he was more effective in written parts than in improvisations.

Toward what was growing within me, I felt both ambivalence and unreality. It hadn't been asked for, its beginning had not been welcomed, and at times, I thought—even hoped—I would miscarry. Then I feared I might, and I realized I didn't want to miscarry; that would be another rejection of Jay. However harsh the terms were, I had a commitment to him.

During my third month, Mama wrote that my brother, Bram, was engaged. The girl was Judy Eshler—did I remember her? She belonged to a younger crowd; perhaps I hadn't met her. In any case, I certainly knew who her father was—the millionaire Eshler, who lived in a palace on top of Westmount. The girl wasn't beautiful, but she was refined and pleasant. And crazy about Bram. Why shouldn't she be? A handsome young fellow from a respected family. The ceremony would be in the Shaare Hashomayim synagogue, with a reception at the Mount Royal Hotel. The bride had asked for my address: Mama knew we would be invited, and it would be nice if we came; she and Papa would be happy to see us; it had been a long time.

I didn't remember Judy Eshler—it had been at least eight years since I'd lived in Montreal—though the Eshler name was familiar. Everyone knew what *that* family had been mixed up in—bootlegging, rumrunning, during Prohibition in the United States. So that's what my family's acquiring? A bootlegger's daughter. And they raised Cain when I wanted to marry an actor! Ah, but there is a new aristocracy. It's as phony as Hollywood's.

Judy Eshler wrote to me. She was proud we would be related; all her friends were crazy about James Burns; most people refused to believe he was Jewish. She'd love to have me as her matron of honor; her friends would be thrilled to meet me; I was (surprise! surprise!) the local girl who had made good. "I happened to read in a magazine—at the moment I cannot remember which—that the James Burnses were considered Hollywood's ideal young couple," my prospective sister-in-law informed me. All things considered, at this moment, the ideal was not bragging.

I wrote the bride-to-be I was pregnant; my doctor had said not to travel, hence a transcontinental journey was out of the question. Mama had not yet been told about the coming attraction ("Superstitious, you know, not till the fourth or fifth month is it safe to tell; this is just three"). However, she had my permission to bring the news to my folks. But what had occurred to me was, if they hadn't already made honeymoon plans, why not come to California? We would be delighted to have them as our guests.

They were delighted; they came. Judy turned out to be a large girl, plain of face, broad-bottomed, and half a head taller than Bram. However, her traveling costume was stunning, and her engagement diamond like an auto headlight. My brother was handsome—ginger-haired, blue-eyed, rosy-cheeked, with an athlete's build and a punishing handshake.

They emerged from the Super Chief with a load of expensive luggage and an air of high expectations. Olsen and I and the Cadillac were there to greet them. At the hacienda, Jay and the Gruenings were waiting. Thelma and Jay had been drinking; Jay's temper, accordingly, was uncertain.

I had asked the Gruenings for dinner. These best friends of ours were *haimish*; they wouldn't upstage the provincials. However, they were neither glamorous nor celebrated. This was going to be, I realized when I saw polite disappointment on Judy's face, exactly like in Cincinnati.

"But you do know all the big actors, don't you?" my brother asked Jay. "Douglas Fairbanks?"

"And Mary Pickford?" Judy breathed.

Jay looked annoyed. "I know them," he said. "They urinate. Like you and me."

Judy blushed, Bram looked annoyed. The moment was awkward. Thelma drew Judy aside to whisper, "Stars don't like to be quizzed about other stars. They're only human, dear." And, louder, for general conversation, "How was the train trip?"

"Gorgeous!" Judy said.

"Monotonous," Bram said.

"Let me show you the house," I said. "We give guided tours."

"It's so exotic," Judy said. "Just what I dreamed it would be."

"It wouldn't go in Westmount," my brother told me.

"My parents are building a house for us," Judy said. "It's their wedding present."

"Big," Bram said. "We need it, for the wedding presents. Got enough silver to sink a ship."

We sat down in the informal family room, to dine modestly on broiled chicken and rice. Greta joined us, without Josephine.

"Greta, this is Aunt Judy," I said.

"Punchan Judy. Not Annjudy," she corrected me.

"And this is your Uncle Bram," I continued.

Bram, trying to be avuncular, leaned over to give her a squeeze. She squirmed away. "I'm not allowed to let strangers touch me," she said.

"Baby, an aunt and an uncle are special," I said. "They are family."

"And I'm not a stranger," Bram added. "I met you the day you came home from the hospital."

"I never went to a hospital," Greta rebuked him. "A hospital is when people are sick. I never get sick."

"Eat your dinner," Jay growled, "or you *will* get sick."

"I took your picture the day we met." Bram was being persistent.

"I'm not in pictures," Greta told him. "Only my daddy is."

"She's so bright it's a shame she has to wear glasses," Judy said.

Greta began to yank off her glasses. Jay leaned over to grab her hand. He pushed her fork into her fist. "Stop showing off," her father said.

Instead of our glamour, the honeymoon couple was receiving our bickering.

After dinner, when Josephine had collected Greta to put her to bed, Thelma said, "You'll excuse us, won't you? We must run along. Howard has work," and Jay, with a don't-contradict-me air, said he had important phone calls to make. And so I linked my arms into Judy's and Bram's and led them out to the patio, to the chill and the breath-taking beauty of a Southern California evening. A full moon was up, the pool was a silver sheet, the eucalyp-

250

tus trees were grotesque silhouettes, and the air was drenched with perfume.

"Exquisite!" Judy cried. "Your mother ought to see this! She would be thrilled! As it is she brags about you all the time. 'My daughter lives like a queen.' And where is that heavenly smell coming from?"

"Rose garden." I pointed. "They bloom all year round."

She moved off in the direction to which I had pointed. For a few moments, Bram and I were alone.

"Quite a setup," Bram said.

"It is."

"Your husband looks a lot older than when I met him before. At your wedding, that was."

"He is older," I said.

"He hasn't exactly mellowed," Bram said.

"He's tired. He works hard."

"Is acting work?"

"Try it some time," I said. "And what are you planning to do with yourself?"

Bram arched his arms over his head. "Buy a boat and sail far away," my brother said. Neither of us spoke for a moment or two; then Bram asked, "How long are you married, Millie?"

"Seven years."

"The folks were sure it wouldn't last."

"They always knew best," I said. "They must be delighted with the match you made."

"Mama likes Judy." He lowered his voice. "Dad isn't jumping for joy. He's worried I'll go into business with my father-in-law. He needn't worry. I will not."

I changed the subject. "Judy's a nice girl," I said. "You love her, Bram?"

His answer came slowly. "I'll get used to her," Bram said.

Judy strolled back from the rose garden. She linked her arm into Bram's. "You two reminiscing about your childhoods?"

"Not particularly," Bram said. "Millie and I never had much in common. She had her nose in a book and her head in the clouds."

251

"And you had your feet on the ski slopes," I said. "Judy, tell me about your wedding. Who of my family was there?"

She glanced at Bram, questioning. "Let's see," Bram commenced. "Aunt Daisy was there, wasn't she?"

"I can't quite place her, sweetheart, there were so many people. . . . Oh, yes, now I remember, that sweet little lady with the bobbed gray hair. Mrs. Magid. There wasn't a Mr. Magid, was there?"

My brother turned to me. "What happened to the husband, do you know, Sis?"

I shrugged silently.

"Did they have children?" my sister-in-law asked.

I let Bram reply, "Not as far as I know," and add, "Mama goes down to New York now and then to visit with her. She still has the old house."

"Were Uncle Reuben and Aunt Fanny there?" I wanted to know.

My brother scowled. "I don't believe so." And speaking directly into my ear, "They weren't asked. Mama didn't think they'd fit in." Then louder, for his bride's hearing, "They were sick, I believe. She had a gallstone attack. Mama did mention it." He laughed. "You know, I hardly remember that couple. All I remember is voices, loud voices, his, hers, at some kind of party in that Brooklyn house. He was standing up, talking and talking—"

"About his dear once," I said.

Judy gave me a puzzled glance.

"That's a joke," I said. "A family joke." And an accident of accent. But prophetic. "Did the Hitzigs come?" I went on to ask.

"The Hitzigs? . . . Oh, yes, my New York cousins. Karl came to represent his folks. He's a lawyer."

"And very clever," Judy added. "My dad was impressed with him, I believe. It wouldn't surprise me at all if he and Dad—"

My eyebrows shot up. "Really. As I remember, Karl was a Socialist."

"They change," Bram said. "Money does it."

"I'm trying to fix him up with a girl friend of mine," Judy said.

"Work on it," I said. "Bram, did anyone mention Ben Kuper?"

252

"Who's he? Did I ever meet him?"

"You were at his wedding. In a blue sailor suit."

Judy snuggled to him. "I'll bet you looked darling in the sailor suit."

"I remember the sailor suit," Bram said. "There was a war on, I think. I made believe I was in the Royal Navy. Come to think of it, that affair in the Brooklyn house was a wedding, too, wasn't it? Aunt Daisy's wedding. Whatever did become of that groom?"

In the morning, while Bram exercised in the pool, Judy and I had girl talk. "I'll bet you're just thrilled," Judy said, "to be expecting again. How old is your little girl?"

"Greta's five. She was five in January."

"Oh! It's not my business, but why did you wait so long for another? I understand two and a half years is the ideal—the difference in ages, I mean. Of course, we haven't made plans for a family yet. We decided we'd wait till our house was finished. Meanwhile, Bram's being considerate. Which is, I think, very nice in a big, strong he-man like him." She simpered a bit. "I do hope he won't always be. . . . Please don't think me vulgar, but I keep trying to imagine what it would be like to be in ecstasy."

"There ain't no such animal," I said.

"You're so witty," Judy told me.

"I'm so glad we got to know you," Judy said at parting. "We'll tell everyone how sweet and unaffected you are." She said it bravely, though I knew we had given her little to boast about to her friends. My delicate condition and my husband's work had been our excuse. Twice we had taken them out to dinner; the steaks had been good, the celebrities invisible. Jay had arranged a studio tour; they had watched a picture being made; they had seen Jay's footprints in the cement at Grauman's Chinese, and Bram had photographed them. And we had lent them the convertible to drive down the coast. The swallows had not yet returned to Capistrano, and so, in one way, that trip had disappointed them as well, though Judy, sun-and-wind burned (they'd driven with the top down), looked almost pretty, which made me hope that at some overnight stop she had known ecstasy.

253

They swam in our pool, sunned in our patio, picked lemons from our trees, played with Greta, eventually taught her to say "Aunt Judy" and "Uncle Bram" and to accept an occasional squeeze.

"I almost hate to leave," Judy said. "It's a dream world. Unreal. Don't you wonder sometimes what you're doing here? Don't you get homesick?"

"I'll bet you miss the family," Bram said.

"Who do you have in mind?" I replied.

"Of course, you have your own dear little family," Judy said. "And the one who is coming. Which are you hoping for? A boy or a little sister?"

"It's a boy," I said. "His name is William."

Bram quirked his russet eyebrows. "After whom? Someone in Jay's family?"

"In a way," I said. "The last name was Shakespeare."

At the depot, seeing them off, I said, "Bram, you've broken the ice. Now, tell the family we aren't monsters. Tell them to come visit us. We're not sending out engraved invitations; they'd be more than welcome."

"Tell them yourself," Bram retorted. "They have an idea you do not want them, you've cut them off, as if they'd done something wrong."

"Nonsense," I said "They're just being stubborn, because I got married without their permission."

Nevertheless, while I was saying these words, I knew in my heart I did not want my mother to come. Not now. She would sense trouble and say, "I was right, I warned you." And I would never forgive her for being clever.

When I carried Billy home from the hospital, Greta took one look at him, snatched off her glasses, dropped them, and deliberately stamped on them, before she ran off to catch and hug Mac. "*It* can't have you," she cried to her dog. "It can't have anything."

Billy didn't demand anything. A perfect baby, healthy, well formed, he would lie by the hour in his crib or his carriage, sleeping or eyes open—quiet. And because he was undemanding, he was left alone a great deal. Greta ignored him, although she began to treat Mac like an infant, wrapping the dog in a receiving blanket, thrusting a nursing bottle between his jaws. Jay found that more amusing than his son's squirms and grimaces. He tended to walk a wide circle around Billy's crib, glance at him sidewise, before he hurried away. "Daddy doesn't like the baby either," Greta informed me. "We didn't need him at all."

As for Billy himself, he seemed, by his unobtrusiveness, to be aware he had forced his way onto the premises and would need to bide his time until we acknowledged and accepted him.

9 ❧

"Burns residence?" The male voice was young and New York-ish. "Mrs. Burns home?"

"This is Mrs. Burns. Who's calling?"

"The bittlum."

"I beg your pardon."

"Bittlum sitting on a sturbcone." The voice waited for me to catch on. I didn't. "This is W. W. Hitzig of New York City."

"Walt! You lunatic! Where are you?"

"In Los Angeles."

"What for?"

"Los Angeles has many attractions."

I wasn't sure whether he was kidding or being evasive.

"Which attractions? Business or pleasure?"

"Both. I am meeting a friend."

"Who's your friend?"

"When I see you, maybe I'll tell you. If I can see you, that is."

"You're welcome as flowers that bloom in the spring. Have you a car?"

"No. Have you?"

"Wise guy, we have three. The folks must have told you."

"The folks tell me nothing. We aren't speaking."

"Why not?"

"When I see you, I'll tell you. Maybe."

"You sound mysterious. Are you on the lam?"

256

"Mildred, Mildred, you have been watching your husband's moom pitchers."

"Where are you staying? I'll drive down and get you."

"Kind of you, Modom, but I can manage. If it's convenient to you, I could come today. Say around four P.M."

"It's convenient," I said. "Bring swimming trunks. We have a pool."

"I swim by the New York calendar," he said "May I remind you it's December there."

December it was, the middle of that month, and 1936 was the year. All the states except Maine and Vermont had handed President Roosevelt a decisive mandate to dig the country out of Depression, put people to work, as well as give them real beer. In the United States it was a time of hope; elsewhere on the globe, one of dread. For the mad paperhanger who had written *Mein Kampf* was thumbing his nose at the victorious powers who had put together a treaty of peace at Versailles, and he was harrying Germany's Jews; Madrid was under siege by rebels against the lawful government of Spain, and the British throne was rocking because Edward the Eighth had made up his mind to marry the Simpson woman. The radio and the daily press, as I recall, paid more attention to Edward's dilemma than to Hitler and Franco. Or perhaps it was I—a child of the Empire and a romantic female—who doted on the love story and neglected the Nazi-Fascist menace. "Love conquers all. Except Stanley Baldwin and Queen Mother Mary," my friend Thelma said.

At four P.M., when Walt was due, Thelma and I were in the den with the radio on, agog for news bulletins about Edward's final decision. Thelma was still my great friend, though we no longer dissected my intimate problem. I assumed she had assumed that Billy had been the solution, the peace offering, the pledge of our love, as the bromide goes. And I had let her assume, since I had no intention of telling the truth, not to her, not on a psychoanalyst's couch. Because too many guilts were mixed with my truth.

Jay and I shared a room. It was large; our twin beds were walking distance apart; he had become, as Judy, my new sister-in-law, had put it "considerate." The surface was smooth, like our pool on the windless mornings; our encounters were courteous, our manners impeccable. If he chose to dally among birds of passage, I chose to pretend to ignore; if at parties he drank too much, I took the wheel, driving home, and kept my mouth shut. Because when you say, "Cut that out," you must be prepared for "or else." And I, who had seen Ben Kuper and Arnie together, knew the "or else."

The thing to remember—I kept reminding myself—was that I didn't hate Jay. He'd been my choice, personally made; no man I'd met since could hold a candle to him. Yet down deep, there was a nub of anger toward him, for the lies and evasions I'd had to dole out to my parents, which, more than mileage, I knew, had alienated me from people once dear to me. And for this, I was punishing Jay. Yet didn't I share whatever guilt? The girl had come running when he crooked a finger, after he had recited Romeo's lines. And she had brought with her not merely good whiskey but also her baggage of fear. Nevertheless, what was plain was that Jay wished, for his own reasons, to stay married to me. It was plausible—I didn't discount it—that, in his own way, my husband loved me.

Certainly no one could bear a grudge against Billy. Each infant brings its own welcome—that's a cliché of parenthood. Even Greta had accepted him. I had caught sight of her when she'd thought there was no one around, kissing the crown of her brother's head.

Jay played foolish father with Billy, tossing him high, rolling him, giggling, in crib and playpen. And I who had carried him, with resentment, under my heart, could I feel less than grateful for the moment of rage that had given me a lovable child?

The Gruening boys were in our pool. Greta, down at the shallow end, was flailing her arms and thrashing her legs in the mistaken belief she was swimming. Dulcie, our current nursemaid, was supposed to be watching Billy, who had just learned to walk but, not being housebroken, was not taken into the pool. One of the Gruening boys made a shallow dive and grabbed Greta's legs, upsetting her, so that she started to howl. While Dulcie was calming her down, Billy escaped. Reeling like a drunken midget, he was heading toward the gates when Walt came along and scooped him up. Walt banged on the door, singing out, "Hello, anybody! Who owns this kid?"

Mrs. Olsen dashed to the door. "How'd you get in? Who are you?"

"A cousin. Invited," Walt said.

"That's what they all say," Mrs. Olsen told him and called out for me. Walt swept me into his arms, squeezing me and Billy together, so hard the child wailed, and I had to snatch him and mop his tears before I took a good look at Walt.

Met on the street, I wouldn't have recognized him. In the less than ten years since he'd come to a party at my New York flat, he had changed from a stripling into a man, a well-put-together young man. Hannah's third boy; how old could he be? Mid-twenties, no more. He wore a bow tie, rimless eyeglasses, and the air of a rustic, a country storekeeper, perhaps. Nothing about him suggested a mischievous kid from the Bronx. He bowed to me from the waist. "Mildred, what's true can't be denied; you are gorgeous. Why aren't you in the movies? Or are you? And what do you call the *pisher* who peed on my sleeve?"

"William," I said. "Our youngest. Didn't you know we have two?"

"In a roundabout way. Your brother told my brother, I think. Or maybe your mother told mine. One way or another, the news got around."

I felt Billy's bottom, bone dry for a change; my son had been falsely accused. I gave him to Mrs. Olsen to give back to Dulcie and ushered Walt into our house. "*Fancy-shmancy*," he said of our living room, looking nonplused, not impressed. "Who plays the piano?"

"No one," I said. "We bought it to hold picture frames."

"Shame on you. Shame!" He stopped to examine the pictures. "Friends?" His inflection was query rather than statement.

"Business associates," I said.

Thelma came to the door of the den. "Dr. Livingstone, I presume?"

"My cousin, Walt Whitman Hitzig," I said. "From New York. My friend, Thelma Gruening."

"Likewise from New York," Thelma said. She led the way back to the den, clicked the radio off, and coiled her lithe body into a sofa corner. "What news does this messenger bring from the Union Square front?"

Walt's eyebrows rose. "All quiet," he said. "Till the spring thaws. When the counteroffensive begins."

"Quit that," I said. "What will you drink?"

"Two cents plain. Or a squirt of seltzer on strawberry syrup."

Thelma uncoiled, got up to hug him. "You bring back my youth," Thelma said.

Mine too. Walt had whisked me back to an afternoon when Grandpa Springer sat at the head of a table in Aunt Hannah's flat, where a blue seltzer bottle stood on the table and a fat, naked baby squirmed in his mother's arms and yanked at my curls. "Would you take Scotch with your seltzer?" I asked.

Walt made a face. "Iodine. Poison. Yet when a fair lady offers the cup—" Behind the glasses his eyes were twinkling. However serious his mission was here in the West, Walt had remained a clown. He shucked off his jacket, without a "May I?" His shirt was sweat-stained—he must have hiked up the canyon. He might have been short of cab fare. Had he, I wondered, called and come over because he needed money? Come one, come all, the family's invited, I had told Bram to broadcast. And Walt had come, only Walt. Whatever the reason, welcome!

While I mixed the highball, Walt busied himself studying our bookshelves, reading the titles on the book spines. Casing the joint. Is the Burns household literate? We are, Walt Whitman Hitzig. I subscribe to the Book-of-the-Month, buy six selections a year. Our collection of Shakespeare, Ibsen, and Strindberg's complete. We have every Eugene O'Neill play that is in print. My husband has dreams, for after he's through with the films.

I gave Walt his drink. "Tell me about the family. Yours."

He drank half his highball before he replied. "My mother is fine. But obstinate. My father is not quite so fine. And just as stubborn."

"About what?"

"My parents are"—his tone had changed, the persiflage dropped—"Social Democrats. Radicals of an era that's passed."

"I don't get you," I said.

He set down his glass, eying me as if making sure I was not playing dumb. "My parents and I—we do not see eye to eye," he told me. His jaw line, I noticed, had firmed. Thelma was watching and listening with an intensity that made me uneasy.

"Who does see eye to eye with parents?" I hurried to say, and switching the subject, I asked how was his brother, the one we had nicknamed Snooky.

The jaw relaxed. "Snooky is great. I mean that. The kid is sensational. Oh, he can't walk, except like Roosevelt—with braces and someone holding his arm. But he paints like an angel. Water colors. He's beginning to work in oils. Y'know"—his head tilted up, and he smiled—"Lots of big things grow out of small, the acorn and oak, for instance. Millie, do you remember that fake Bar Mitzvah party my parents made him?"

"Do I? I brought him a watch." And Karl gave me a warning, and he and I stopped being friends.

"*You* brought the watch. And our fat-ass uncle brought him a *tallith* he never put on. But the present that mattered, the one that counted in the long run"—he leaned over to tap my knee—"not to disparage the watch, the important present was a cheap painting set from some sissy—I can't remember his name."

"Arnie," I said. "Arnold Kuper."

He nodded. "That's who. Was he a relative? Or a ringer? I cannot place him. . . . No matter, that skimpy paint brush, that tin box of colors, started the kid being an artist. So now, he puts a record on his Victrola, and the music, he says, inspires him—he paints symphonies. And he's great, make no mistake; my brother's an artist, Millie."

"Does he sell?" I had regretted the question before Walt rebuked me.

"Must he? Is selling what matters?"

"No," I admitted. "Yet with that talent, he might insure his future, be independent."

261

Walt waved his hand. "Big brother provides. Your old buddy, Karl. A very successful attorney. Earns a pretty penny keeping *your* brother's in-laws out of the pen. Sharp, very sharp, Karl Hitzig is."

"What happened to his ideals?" I was remembering our walks and our talks and Karl's lectures to me.

"Karl's ideals." Walt set his glass down and smiled sourly. "The only ideal of Karl's I notice these days is a sense of familial duty, keeping the folks off the bread line. You see, my dad's job went to hell in the Depression. He does a spot of Yiddish publicity now and then. That helps his morale, pays for his clothes and re-soling his shoes. But Karl buys the meat and potatoes for them. And he bought them a house—a bungalow in Far Rockaway. No steps for Snooky to climb. The garage is his studio."

"Karl lives with them?"

"Are you nuts? My brother has a suite in a hotel in New York. Friday nights he drives out to have dinner with the family."

"You, too?" I asked.

"Never on Fridays," Walt said.

"Is he married?" I asked.

"Karl? There's a shortage of paragons, haven't you heard?" Walt shrugged while I remembered the winter evening, walking from Night Court to the subway, when my cousin announced, "I intend to keep myself pure for the woman I marry, and I will hope she has kept herself that way for me." Had he kept his intention, and was he the happier for it? Yet how ironic it was that he himself had introduced me to Jay, who had made me unchaste but took me that way, for better or worse.

"Why the silence, Millie?"

"Thinking, Walt, thinking. How your family is drifting apart. Like mine. Going separate ways."

"Gene. Especially Gene. Have you forgotten Eugene? My brother, the doctor. . . . Yes, ma'am, he is, a damn good doctor. And a good guy. Know what he's up to? You haven't heard? . . . Dr. Hitzig took down his shingle and got on a boat to Europe, to Spain, to work with Norman Bethune. You've heard of Bethune, have you not? He's a Canadian, too."

I had never heard of Norman Bethune; Walt's tone implied I should have, and so I said, "Yes, of course . . ."

"Great man, Dr. Bethune. Great human being," Walt went on to say. "Committed—like Gene—to the Loyalist cause."

I caught glances meeting, Thelma's and Walt's; hers sharpening, approaching, his momentarily in retreat, before he said, "Karl is splitting a gut over Gene."

Fleetingly, I considered declaring myself on the Loyalist side, as if to make up for Karl's antipathy—a conditioned reflex of resentment toward a cousin whom I had not seen in several years. However, all I told Walt was "Karl was always cautious."

"Cautious, my eye! Stuffy's the word." Walt grinned. "My brother the doctor, my brother the artist, my brother the stuffed shirt. One out of four. Not bad for the Hitzigs."

"You left one out, Walt. What are you? What do you do?"

His expression changed again, becoming guarded. "I do what needs to be done."

He said it so primly I answered with Papa's word. "Pish! Be explicit, cousin, what brought you out to L.A.?"

He reached for my hands and held them. "To feast my eyes on your beauty. You still have it, kid. Brooklyn's loss was California's gain." He patted the backs of my hands before he released them, hitched up his trousers, settled on the sofa, and said, with deliberate nonchalance, "Since you have twisted my arm, broken my will with your Scotch, I shall confess. I am here to wait for a friend."

"Who is where?"

"On a slow boat. From down there."

"Down there is where?"

"Chile. Antofagasta. Heard of the place?"

I shook my head no.

"The long way around," Walt said. "Slow. But safe." And the way he said that last word gave me an eerie feeling that he had told me too much and I had better stop quizzing lest I learn more than I wanted to know. Thelma's attentiveness was, in its way, as revealing as my cousin's words.

For an instant or two none of us spoke, until Thelma glanced

263

at her wrist. "Whee! It's later than late. I'll go fish my monsters out of your pool." She rose, offering her hand to my cousin. "Delighted to meet you. Hope to see you some more. We live down the canyon. Ask Mildred to bring you down to our place. My husband would be happy to meet you." And reproachfully, to me, "Millie, you never told me you had such a fascinating family."

"It was news to me, too," I told her.

Walt waited until she was gone before he asked, "She's all right, isn't she?"

"Of course she is."

"Her husband, what does he do?"

"He's a screen writer. Jay's friend."

"Jay." Walt repeated my husband's name. "James Burns. He's all right, isn't he?"

"In what way?"

"You married him, he must be," my cousin said.

"That's logic," I said. "Stay to dinner and judge for yourself."

I heard Greta's voice in the kitchen and called for her to come here. She ran, a brown and gold wisp, dragging a toweling robe to the door to the den, stopped when she saw Walt, and looked back for Dulcie, who was trailing, with Billy perched on her hip.

"Greta, shake hands with your cousin Walt."

Her hand groped back for Dulcie. "Say hello, don't be bashful," Dulcie said, giving Greta a push.

This nursemaid was a raw-boned, lantern-jawed girl, the middle one of nine children who'd come to California in a rickety open truck with desperate parents whose Midwestern farm had been parched to dust. We gave Dulcie bed and board and fifty cash dollars each month, and I convinced Mrs. Olsen that it was unfair to search the bundles Dulcie carried out through our gates on her Thursdays off. "But, Mrs. Burns, there was left from dinner a half leg of lamb." "But, Mrs. Burns, I know we had enough eggs. . . . Where went a whole dozen, I can't imagine." I can imagine. And I can't speak for your conscience, Mrs. Olsen, but mine is troubled whenever I think of hungry kids. Why, what goes into our garbage could feed a family. . . .

Walt bent double to kiss Greta's cheek.

"You have glasses, like me," Greta said. "Only mine is upstairs in my room. I don't wear them swimming."

He lifted her, hugged her. She wriggled off, down. "You'll get wet from me." Yet she snuggled to him. After Billy arrived, she had changed phases—from the one in which she'd rejected Bram's hug to this one in which, openly, flagrantly, she courted grown men.

"I had an operation for my eyes," she confided to Walt. "It didn't hurt because I was brave. Only I had to keep the bandage on; I couldn't see one single thing. Mommy brought me a music box; it played a good-night song to me. And I had ice cream every day in the hospital."

Walt stroked her head. "You old ladies with your operations!"

"I'm not an old lady. I am a girl. A sister girl. I got to be a sister when Billy came to this house. He's nice, but he's stupid; he doesn't know how to use the toilet. I had my dog Mac before Billy came. Do you like dogs?"

"I like children better," Walt said.

"I like horses better than dogs. Mommy promised me a horse, didn't you, Mommy? Anyway, dogs are better than babies. They never cry. They only bark; that's how they talk. Do you have a dog?"

"No, Goldilocks, I do not."

"You should. And my name is not Goldilocks. It is Greta Burns. Do you like my name?"

"I'd rather call you Goldilocks."

"I'd druther no. Greta is a very famous leading-lady name, my mommy told me."

"A friend of the family?"

"Oh, no, she never comes to our house. Are you in pictures?"

"No, Greta, I'm not."

"Then what are you doing in Hollywood?"

"Visiting. Visiting my cousin."

"What's a cousin?" She turned to me, and after I'd lamely tried to explain (how do you explain cousins?), she bobbed her head, approving, as though I had made everything plain. "It's people that come and visit you once. Last year I had a uncle and aunt. I am six, going on seven. I am in second grade. I can read sentences."

"Stop jabbering," I said. "Go upstairs and get dressed for supper, sweetheart."

Walt and I had just sat down at the trestle table—the children had eaten earlier with Dulcie and had gone up to bed—when Jay arrived. He was sober, no gin on his breath, though his mood was foul. Fritz Scheller, the German director, the former lover of a certain blonde, had given him a difficult day. "Make no mistake," Jay explained to Walt, "I'm all for the studio bringing these people over, getting them out of Europe, giving them work. But they're hell on wheels to work with. Arrogant. Authoritarian. 'Buhrns, you vill vauk like I show you into duh scene und you vill show no eggspression you ever seen before dat vuman.'" Jay mopped his brow. "Mrs. Olsen, kindly tell your husband to mix a martini. Two martinis. God, I need a drink!" He slid onto the bench beside me. "Hitzig, what's brought you out here?"

Walt waited, glancing over his shoulder, before he replied, "Spain. There is a war."

Jay manufactured a yawn. "So I read in the papers."

Walt hitched up to the table. "Help's needed," he said.

Jay thrust his hand into his pocket, pulled his hand out. "After dinner we'll take care of it. How's your brother doing? The one who was in my class."

"Doing well. Practicing law."

"He giving much?"

"Are you kidding? Karl voted for Landon."

"Somebody had to, I guess," Jay said. "The boobs."

Knowing what I knew about Karl, I'd scarcely have called him a boob—stuffy, prissy, intellectually pretentious, maybe, but by no means an ignorant boob. To change the conversation, I asked, "Walt, whatever became of your friend who wrote a play about the Sacco-Vanzetti case?"

"Nothing much."

"A lousy play," Jay said. "All talk. No guts."

"He was a flash in the pan," Walt said.

"Aren't we all? And that scares the hell out of me." Jay

266

chewed his steak listlessly; it was evident he was too weary to eat. He scraped back his bench. "Let's have coffee outdoors, Millie, do you mind?"

Mrs. Olsen didn't mind, which was more to the point. It made things easier for her when we didn't linger at table; she could get done with the dishes early, take her shoes off, soak her bunions, and play cards with her husband in their sitting room above the garage.

I put the coffee tray on a table between two chairs on the patio and said I'd run up to look in on the children. Billy was already asleep, but Greta was awake and glad to see me, since she had a worry. Dulcie had taught her a prayer, the "Now I lay me down to sleep," but Dulcie's explanation of "If I should die before I wake" seemed to be troubling her.

"Dulcie says die means go to heaven. You fly right up to the sky, Dulcie says. But Mommy, when you buy me a horse for my birthday, he couldn't fly up to the sky with me. Could he?"

"Darling, I'm not sure you're getting a horse for your birthday. I don't think you could look after a horse."

"Oh, I could, Mommy, I could. Only I couldn't die and go up to the sky and leave my dear horse with nobody, nobody in the world, to take care of it."

"Silly Greta, you're not going to die."

"Not before my brithday?"

"Not till you're an old, old lady."

"Old as you, Mommy?"

"No. No. No. Very old. Shut your eyes, honey. Go to sleep."

"If I should die before I wake . . ."

I pushed her head into the pillow, kissed her forehead and cheek. "Enough, sweetheart. Stop praying and sleep."

"Mommy." Her wide-open eyes were startlingly blue. "He can't have my soul. I won't let him have it. I want it for me."

"Good, baby. Good. Keep your soul."

While I was closing her door, she tossed a question at me. "Mommy, what is a soul?"

"If I knew, I would tell you," I said.

Jay and Walt had pulled their chairs, arm against arm; their cigarettes were sending up parallel streams, smoke signals to a bright moon. Walt sprang to his feet to pull a chaise close up for me. Jay remained sprawling and talking. "As I was saying, this friend of mine, Howard Gruening, he read *Mein Kampf*, every word, when it came out in English, and he went around saying, 'This will not happen; this is too stupid.' "

"It happened." Walt tapped cigarette ash into his saucer. "We let it happen. All of us did. But we can stop it. We have a chance. Right now. In Spain."

"Go over there, fight? That what you mean?" Jay flexed his arm, clenched his fist, slapped the bulge of a muscle—a dramatic gesture, an actor slipping into a role. Play revolution, J. B. . . . That's a mean thought, Mrs. B.; it is unworthy of you. Jay's not a boob. Nor a reactionary. He voted for Roosevelt, didn't he? He boycotted Ford cars, didn't he? CCNY taught him to care, didn't it? He's not a Johnny-come-lately in matters of social conscience.

Walt was answering him with quiet earnestness. "Not everyone can, not everyone *should* fight in Spain. There are plenty of other things to be done. For instance, in a place like Hollywood, with its money, its influence . . ."

"We'll talk about that." Jay hauled himself out of the chair. "Come on, I'll get the car, drive you back into L.A."

Amazing, I said to myself, after the car had rolled through our gates, how a man's vigor's restored. Jay came home too weary to eat. My cousin Walt talked politics, Jay came to life.

Walt, the joker, the comical kid. Why, Walt was the little *pisher* who put a hoptoad into my bed when they visited us in the Laurentians! I must remind him of that.

I was in the den, leafing through *Life* magazine while I listened to radio comments on Edward the Eighth's abdication speech. Jay listened with me for a minute or so before he shut the sound off. "A kingdom for a cunt. Big deal!" He kicked his shoes off and sat down beside me. "We stopped at Howie's; that's what took me so long. I figured Walt might want to meet Howie; Howie would like to meet him. They talked—not long—Walt was in a hurry to get back to his hotel; expecting a message, he said." He leaned back on the sofa, licking his lips, savoring a secret before he half whispered, "Guess who's the guy on the boat your cousin is here to meet: a Comintern man. A chap who ran a revolution down in Brazil. It flopped, and he skipped. The local leader was caught—I read that in *Time*. Walt's man hopped a plane to Chile, got on a freighter coming north. Walt's the reception committee, waiting with papers and cash." Jay's eyes had a glitter I'd not seen before, an excitement beyond intoxication or lust, and for the second time in this evening he raised a clenched fist. "I told Walt, when his friend arrives, bring him out here. I'd like to meet the genuine article. Howard would, too. Bet your bottom dollar he would."

His excitement was puzzling; it wasn't in character; he had never mounted the barricades unless it was part of a script. I asked, to restore him to normal, "Shall I fix you a drink?"

"No, had a beer in L.A. with Walt.... Yes, come to think of it, I could use a highball. Make it light, Mill." When I gave him the drink, he swallowed half, set the glass down, and licked his lips, savoring a secret again. "Your cousin's a Commie. A Party member," he said. "From things he said I surmised, and I asked him point-blank. He didn't say yes, but he didn't deny." He watched my face. "And how do you like them apples?"

"I like Walt," I said. "And his politics are his own affair."

"Come on, kid." He chortled. "This is the stuff. The Mc-Coy." He finished his drink. "Walt's staying in a fleabag downtown. I told him, 'For Pete's sake, get out of that dump. Move in with us; we have plenty of room.' 'Not practical,' that's what he said. I gathered he has to live where the comrades can contact him. And maybe he isn't sure about us—where we stand. Can he trust us? That's one reason I wanted him to meet Howie—Howie could be a kind of character reference."

He lolled back, stretching his arms over his head.

"I did ask—and he must have realized I was sincere—was there anything we could do to help? And he said, if we wished, if it wouldn't make problems for me, why, it would be fine if we asked some friends in for cocktails and put the arm on them for money for Spain."

"Shall we?" I asked.

"It needs to be done, so do it," Jay said.

Upstairs, while I was turning down the ruffled bedspreads, I remembered something to tell Jay. "When I was a kid, we had a summer cottage up in the mountains, and my Aunt Hannah's family came to spend a vacation with us. Karl and Eugene—they were both younger than I—plagued me with radical junk; they were precocious pests. But Walt was worse. He put a hoptoad into my bed."

Jay dropped a shoe. He looked up and blinked. "So that's where the trouble began."

"Why, no." I grew flustered. "Why, I was just eight—"

"Don't talk in riddles," he said.

"I forgave Walt," I hurried to say. "Long ago. I don't hold that grudge."

"I don't think your cousin's interested in putting anything into your bed," my husband said crisply. "He has more important projects in mind."

I picked a Sunday afternoon during the social doldrums, after the Christmas–New Year's festivities and after Greta's birthday party. Jay wrote out an invitation list: performers, male and female, of his own rank and salary bracket; a few directors; two second-echelon studio executives; his business-manager; his press agent; and a sprinkling of refugee geniuses, including Fritz Scheller. The Gruenings, being in a lower-income bracket, were not on his list. Nor was the blonde.

"Shall I tell them what the party is for?"

"That's a stupid question." Yet it gave Jay pause. "No," he finally said. "Some pikers might get cold feet." If he was thinking that certain ones might consult the studio brass and be advised not to attend, he did not mention this.

I made the calls. Some acceptances were conditional. "Dahling, we would love to come, we will do our damnedest, but you know how it is. . . ." Normally, I would have taken this to mean, "We'll come if nothing better turns up." However, since this was the season of social slump, I knew we would have a crowd. I ordered liquor and food accordingly and asked Harry, our gardener, to bring a white coat and help Olsen serve drinks. While I toted the bill for the groceries and drinks, it struck me that a straight cash donation might better have served the Loyalist cause. There was, I felt, something crass about shaking down guests.

Thelma, whom I consulted—though she hadn't been asked to be present, her spirit was deeply involved—advised, "Serve one drink when they arrive, maybe two to get them relaxed. With canapés, chopped liver, pigs in blankets, nothing expensive. No caviar, no sturgeon. When they know what it's for, they'll praise you for thrift. . . . You could even . . . no, you couldn't ask them to pay for their drinks; they're not yet warmed up to sacrifices. Who's going to speak, make the pitch?"

"Why, Jay. I guess Jay; it's his show."

She looked dubious. "He never has, has he? I mean for the Cause. Perhaps your cousin could. Yes, your cousin Walt. They like hearing from New York people."

Two days before our party date, Walt phoned Jay at the studio to announce that his friend Nick was in Los Angeles. If convenient, Jay might pick them up after work and drive them both to our hacienda. And if Millie's cook had a few extra chicken wings . . .

I liked Nick at first sight. He reminded me of my father, cheerful and warm. Not tall or short, not plump or gaunt, features regular and unremarkable: a round, smooth-shaven face, a good chin, an inconspicuous nose, eyes gray (I believe but am not positive), light-brown hair, conservatively parted and neatly brushed, the whole of his appearance so agreeably bland that in a crowd you would not notice him. If this was a revolution maker in the flesh, obviously Central Casting had never met the McCoy.

"Guess what Nick does for a living," Jay chortled. "He makes false teeth. A dental mechanic, that is his regular trade; he told me himself."

Mr. Ordinary Man with a dull occupation. Straight off the pages of *Reader's Digest*. Sensible, though, isn't it? When your job is secret as well as dangerous, don't advertise it on sandwich boards.

Nick walked through our pretentious living room, remarking,

271

"You live beautifully," without sarcasm or envy, though with a rueful sigh that implied he'd be pleased if all the world's people lived as graciously. I was charmed. Greta too. From the far doorway, she'd watched him a moment before she dashed in and flung her arms around him. "I am Greta Burns, I am seven years old. Last week I had my birthday party."

"And I never knew. Nobody told me that Greta Burns was having a birthday. I would have brought her a present. Now, wait. Wait one second. I think I have something." He dipped into his pocket, and spread a few coins on his palm. "Here, Greta. This is a peso. It is money from a country called Chile. And this, this is a cruzeiro. From Brazil. If you will put them away in a safe place, someday maybe you will go to those countries and buy yourself something pretty."

"A horse," Greta said. "Mommy didn't buy me a horse for my birthday. She said I was too young for it." She jingled the coins, before she squeezed them in her fist. "Next year, when I am bigger, I'll go to those countries and buy a horse."

"My grandfather used to send me foreign coins," I told her. "From the United States."

Nick flashed me an inquiring glance. "You were born in Europe?"

"In Canada," I said.

A glint, unexpected, appeared in his eyes. "You have family in Canada?" There was an eagerness in the simple question that disquieted me.

Greta tugged at my skirt. "Mommy, where are the coins your grandpa sent?"

"Spent, years ago." For an upper berth to bring Jay to Hollywood.

Greta snuggled to Nick. "Are you a grandpa?"

"No, little one. I am only a comrade."

"What's a comrade?"

"A comrade is a friend," Nick told her.

"My cousin Walt is a comrade," Greta said.

"Out of the mouths of babes," Jay said.

272

"Sit, let's sit down in the den. Relax. Have a drink," I said.

Greta settled herself between our two guests. "What's your name?" she asked Nick.

"Nick."

"Nick what?"

He traded glances with Walt. "Nick Nicholas," he said.

She giggled. "That's silly. Where do you live?"

"In a far faraway country. Its name is Russia. It is a very big country, bigger than the United States. And it is beautiful, too. I love my country."

"I love my country, too," Greta said. "Only not Los Angeles. It's not beautiful. That's what you say, don't you, Mommy?"

I said, "Sweetheart, I think it's time you went to Dulcie, got ready for supper." She shook her head fiercely, clinging to Nick.

"I'll tell you what, Greta, I will tell you a story—a funny story, a joke—and then you will go to get ready for supper. I think maybe your parents will also enjoy my story. Greta, my big faraway country has had many changes, and people have come to see what we have done to make the life better for people. So, Greta, there was this old lady who came from the United States to visit; she had relations in Moscow—that is our biggest big city. And her relations were proud of their city; they wished to show the old lady all of its wonderful things. They took her to the Park of Culture and Rest; they took her to the Kremlin; they took her to the Pushkin Monument; they took her in the beautiful new subway. But nothing pleased the old lady. Whatever she saw she turned her nose up. Nothing was as good as in the United States of America. So at the last they took her to the zoo—what could she find to complain about in a zoo? But she did. That woman did. She took one look at the giraffe and she screamed, 'You terrible, terrible people! What have you done to a horse?' "

Greta looked baffled, as, indeed, she had through most of Nick's story. She looked up to me. "Mommy, how do you make a horse a giraffe?" I took her hand to lead her out—Miss Burns had monopolized the guest long enough. She squirmed from my grasp and wheeled around. "I'll be right back, Nicky-Nicklas. I have to show you my dog." I whacked her behind to speed her along and turned to ask Nick what he would like to drink. A somberness had come over his face.

"The dog," I heard him saying softly to Walt. "I should have shot the dog. The woman, Maria—the woman of the apartment; her husband, I told you, was thrown to the sharks—she said, 'Nick, shoot the dog. The police know the dog. They will watch for the dog. The dog will lead them to him.'" He spread his hands. "I blame myself. I had not the heart to shoot the dog."

Walt said no word, made no sound, though his expression had altered. There was a sternness, mingled, I almost could say, with a fear. But Jay was enchanted. He pushed an ottoman up to Nick's knees and straddled it. "Give, Nicky, give. The real stuff."

Nick shook his head. "You must not try to make a star out of me. It is nothing like that. I am a small gray mouse who is a teacher. I try to teach working people, people who work in the mines, on the docks, on the plantations. I try to help them to be men, not forever be slaves—"

"Nicky-Nick." Here was Greta again. "This is Mac. He is my dog. And that there, with Dulcie, is Billy. He's my baby brother. He can't do much."

"Not bark, not wag a tail," Walt said. It struck me he was relieved that Greta had interrupted. Possibly, probably, my comrade cousin was not entirely sure about Jay. Possibly, probably, he felt as I did, that Jay had found an original drama and was staking out a big part for himself.

Smoke hung like a box lid over the room when Fritz Scheller arose. He wormed his way to the front, a tall man and lean, with a shock of gray hair brushed into a pompadour, a hollow-cheeked face with a narrow, beaked nose—an aristocrat in his looks and bearing and well-tailored clothes. I'd been surprised when he arrived; his acceptance had been so tentative that I'd felt the reluctance had something to do with the stale gossip about his ex-inamorata's flirtation with Jay. I was doubly surprised at his purposeful push to up front. It occurred to me he might be in need of bladder relief, and I nudged Jay and whispered to him to direct Scheller to the downstairs powder room. The man brushed past Jay, to the piano. He struck a loud chord, a second chord, hushing the chatter in the crowded room, before he moved to the bay of our Steinway and began to speak.

"My friends and colleagues. I did not intend when I came here this afternoon to make you a speech. Mrs. Burns, when she called up to invite, did not explain exactly what was the purpose of this gathering." His English had none of the low-comedy gabble of Jay's imitation of it. "I was surprised, like some of you may have been. But I was moved, like some may be, when I heard the young man from New York, Walter Whitman, read to us a letter from his doctor brother, explaining why the doctor gives up his practice in the United States to go to care for the wounded in battles in Spain. And I enjoyed, with you, the songs of the Spanish people that were sung by the beautiful Señora Mintz. She has a fine voice, with much feeling. Also, I was interested to hear our host, Mr. James Burns, explain to you, in an eloquent way, how Spain now is the place, the testing ground, for the struggle between the Fascist Nazis and the democratic peoples. He did well, explaining to you, *aber* I hope he will not be angry with me when I say, to him and to you, he did not do well enough. He could not do more, because he did not experience, he did not look on the face of the enemy. And so he could not know in his bones, in his veins, in his heart, what it is to be afraid of this enemy. I have looked on that face. *Und* so, now, in this elegant house, on this afternoon, I take on myself the duty to make you also afraid."

There was a setting down of glasses, a reaching for ash trays to stamp out cigars, a rustling, a scuffing, a shifting: the audience arranging itself. Then, a silence, expectant and total. Scheller cleared his throat gently; he dabbed at his lips with a monogrammed handkerchief, meticulously put it back into a breast pocket, taking his time, holding his audience in suspense.

"My friends, it is no secret to you I am Jewish. That is a condition to which I was born. And my father was born and my grandfather. Of this I do not boast. Nor apologize. It is what I am. Also, it is no secret to some of you that in Germany I was an important man in the theater. In the cinema, too. This has been my life. But it is no secret that two years past, I came out of Germany. Now, some people have asked me: Why did you stay so long in Germany? Did you not understand what Hitler is? What he plans for all Jews? Did you think you were better than everybody; you are a big man, an artist, he will leave you alone? *Nein*. I did not think so. I stayed in Germany because I was a responsible man. I was a Jew, and I believed I could help other Jews. I could help my Jewish colleagues. Of them, not everyone could go out, you see. A visa is needed, friends in other countries to send affidavits. Not everyone has good friends in other countries. And not everyone has money for tickets to travel. Also not everyone finds it easy to leave his fatherland, his home, his friends, his lifetime's work. So he thinks, Be patient, suffer a little, these times cannot last. So I—Fritz Scheller— stayed there with them. I am given a job. By Goebbels. His name you know? The right hand of Hitler. Fritz Scheller is responsible for the Jewish stage people. Understand, they can no longer perform in the regular theater, in the cabarets. Only in their own places, for their own people. And good boys and good girls they must be, no jokes, no satiric against the regime. And every week, Scheller must come in person to Goebbels and give a report, who is performing in what.

"So every week, I come to the office. I stand in a corner; I stand up straight, looking at him, at his ugly face. And I wait till he gives me permission to speak. And I find myself—this, even now, I find impossible to believe—I, Fritz Scheller, am shivering, like a coward. Because I know if one word I say will be a wrong word— a word that does not please the master—I can be whipped like a dog. And dragged to the jail. Or maybe some word I speak, one single word, will do harm to a friend, a colleague. I must be careful. A breath can destroy a life." His eyes were bulging, his complexion ashen, as if now and here he was reliving the terror. "That, my friends, was how it was to look at the face of evil. To shiver and shake. To be terrible afraid." His voice had dropped to a hoarse whisper, yet it cut through the silence; you felt its edge, carving pain into the sun-tanned faces. "And so, my friends and colleagues, I am happy that we have had this gathering. I did not think in Hollywood it would happen. I hoped, *aber* I did not believe it could happen. You were too far away; you were too comfortable, too rich. So now we have the chance to show we are not too comfortable, we are not too far away. And we can be an army ourselfs, not just to help the Spanish people in their struggle but to help all the peoples of the world in the war against *Faschismus*." He bowed. "I thank you for listening to me."

Someone started to clap. The clapping shocked me. One doesn't applaud statements like this. What does one do? Weep? Pray? Rend garments? Or reach for a drink?

Fritz Scheller turned and twisted in the piano bay, for the moment also unsure. Jay sidled to him, slapped the man's shoulder blade, wrung his right hand, then raised his own, restoring silence within the room.

"This is a new role for me," he began, "and it's a little bit awkward for me. A host shouldn't invite his friends to his house to pick their pockets. Yet what else can I do, what else can we do, after what we have heard? So take out your wallets, take out your checkbooks. . . ."

The rustling began again, the scuffing of chairs. A voice from the back of the room asked, "To whom shall we make out our checks?"

Walt, behind Jay, whispered to him. "Make them out to cash," Jay said. "They'll get into the right hands. You can trust me. . . . Anyone want to borrow a pen?"

It was then I went out to the kitchen to instruct the help to start carrying in coffee and cake and sandwiches. "And if anyone asks for a highball, serve it." Coming back from the kitchen, I noticed a group in the family room: Greta and Billy and Mac, Dulcie and Nick. Billy sat regally upon Nick's lap; Greta leaned against his side; Mac lay across his shoes. Dulcie sat opposite, watching and listening to Greta's chatter.

Nick saw me and waved. "Greta has been telling a funny story about how a horse was changed to a giraffe."

277

"Some bad people did it, Mommy. Honest they did."

Nick kissed the top of her head; she pulled his head down to plant a moist kiss on his cheek.

There was something in Dulcie's expression, a sullen distaste, that made me mildly apprehensive. What report, good or bad, would this girl spread about us and our guests? But why should that worry me?

When the last limousine had wheeled out of our driveway, and the cups, plates, and ash trays had been cleared away, we sat in the den—Walt, Nick, Jay, and I—counting money.

"I stank, didn't I?" Jay said. "Goddammit, I spend my life speaking lines other people have written. On my own, I'm a man of few words."

"You and Scheller and Eugene's letter," Walt said, "got two thousand seven hundred fifty dollars from them." He slapped his palm on the stacks of money and checks. "A decent afternoon's work."

"Let me understand," Jay said. "This goes for medical relief?"

"And whatever else is needed," my cousin told him.

Nick said good-bye instead of good night; he was leaving in the morning. For the East, I assumed. He kissed me good-bye like a dear brother and said, "You and your husband must come soon to us. I myself will meet you in Moscow, at the Pushkin *Denkmahl*."

Walt remained in L.A. He was present when the Gruenings held *their* cocktail party, which raised almost as much as ours did, and from a lower salaried group, not only through Fritz Scheller's first-person appeal but because Gruening, being a wordsmith as well as an activist, was more articulate than Burns. In one way their party was more successful than ours, because a committee was organized in that house to go on raising funds not just for embattled Loyalist Spain but for a propaganda war against Fascism everywhere.

After the Gruening party, Walt came one more time to have dinner with us. As he was departing, I heard him ask, "Well, Jay, how about it?"

278

My husband flushed slightly, and glancing sidewise at me he replied, "I'm flattered, Walt. But nothing doing."

To me, Walt said, "Millie, if by chance mail should come here for Nick—"

"Why should mail come here for Nick?"

He wasn't abashed by my amazement. "Nick told the immigration people he was coming here to be your guest. I'd cabled your name and address to his ship."

"You son of a gun! By what right?"

"Millie, Millie, we do what we must. Something told me, something told Nick—and correctly—we could trust you. And Jay. . . . Your husband's a great guy, Millie, he knows the score. . . . Millie, don't worry, no harm will come. . . . If you do get anything for Nick, mail it to me, at Dave and Hannah's. Here's their address. And what message shall I give your dear ones?"

"What did Walt want you to do?" I asked my husband after my cousin had left.

Jay looked toward the open doorway through which our domestic help might be stretching an ear. He fenced his mouth with his hand. "To join the Party," he said. Then, raising his voice, he let whoever might be listening get an earful. "I am against Franco. I am against Hitler and Mussolini. I am against all they stand for: Fascism, war. However, I am not against private enterprise. I like being rich." His voice dropped again. "We started something good going here. Keep it up, kid."

Day after day, I sat with Thelma, addressing and stuffing envelopes. I made telephone calls; I went to cocktail parties, took tens and twenties out of my purse, continuous donations to further the Cause. Fritz Scheller spoke at two parties after Howard's. Then the studio suggested he curtail his activities; they might jeopardize his immigration status. Through the Gruenings, I learned that certain groups—the Church, in particular—were bringing pressure and threatening reprisals at the box office.

No mail arrived at our place for Nick, though I did get a picture postcard from Paris, saying he had been happy to make our acquaintance and he was on his way home. A ship that passed

279

in the night. Walt, too. From him, not even a card. Ah, well, my kin had never been good correspondents.

Intermittently, I was worried about my cousin Eugene, and I searched for his name in news dispatches from Spain, where considerable dying was going on. Since heroism wasn't usual in my family, I relished the respect that accrued to me whenever I said, "I have a first cousin in Spain, with the Loyalists." Not for one minute did it occur to me that Walt had slipped another toad into my bed.

10 ✳

PAPA AND JUDY, Bram's wife, had been at the depot for hours. "We were sure your train was stuck in a snowbank," Judy cried. Buxom, pink-cheeked, she was smothered in beaver. Papa hugged me and held me, saying over and over, "Pussycat! Pussycat! Pussycat!"

At the moment I didn't feel kittenish. I felt adult and triumphant, having managed a difficult trip.

Papa seemed shorter than I remembered and more roly-poly; the shaggy eyebrows beneath his fur hat were white.

"How's Mama?" I asked.

"Not complaining," he said. "Tomorrow is the big day."

"She has a lovely room," Judy said. "We have special nurses lined up. And that wasn't easy, I can tell you. Lucky my dad is on the hospital board. We're in a war here, you know."

I knew, and I knew my brother was in it, a junior officer in the Royal Navy and out on the violent seas, dodging the enemy's submarines. Canada was in, its Mother Country embattled, while in the States the Congress remained unconvinced that the purging of Hitler was worth the risk of American lives.

"Did you tell Mama I was coming?" I asked.

Papa shook his head. "She would say no, don't bother Millie; she has her family; the trip is too far; it's expensive. A mother finds lots of excuses."

"It might have scared her," Judy added. "She'd have worried if she knew we had asked you to come."

We started toward the exit. Judy glanced apprehensively at my cashmere coat and low shoes. "Good heavens, you'll freeze! It's two below. Stay here, stand inside, I'll have Patrick drive the car to the entrance."

"A good girl," Papa said. "She tries to be a daughter. She tries." His eyes began to marble. "I was hoping you'd bring the children," he said.

"How could I?" I forced a laugh. "They don't have warm winter clothes."

He tried to echo my laugh. "Poor people, heh? We could take up a collection."

Judy's burly chauffeur, muffled up to his eyes, strode into the station, picked me up like a sack of potatoes, and waded with me through the drifts. Papa plodded behind with my valise. The Rolls Royce was deliciously warm. Judy tucked a fur robe up to my chin. Papa reached under the robe to hold my hand.

"How was your trip?" Judy asked.

"The plane was bumpy. I almost threw up."

"You took a plane!" Papa cried.

"To Chicago," I said. "From there a couple of trains. Making connections wasn't a cinch."

"You're tired, Pussycat."

"Don't worry about me. Mama's the one."

"She'll be all right," Judy hurried to say. "I talked to her doctor. He's almost certain the tumors are benign. Of course, they can't be sure until afterward. I told you that on the phone, didn't I?"

She had begun round about in the long-distance call. "You remember me, don't you? Judy, Bram's wife."

"Of course I remember my sister-in-law."

"Well—how are you? How are your darling children? We never did meet your little boy; he was just a bump in your belly when we visited—you hardly showed. I've told everyone how

282

wonderfully hospitable you and your husband were on our honeymoon. Oh, you're so lucky you have your two. Bram and I never did get a family started. First we were waiting for our house to be finished. And then Bram went into the service. . . ."

"He's all right, isn't he?" Was it about him she had phoned?

"As far as we know." A hint of false courage was in her voice. "Mildred, we don't want you to worry; there's really nothing to worry about—and what good would it do anyone to have you worry in California? It's just that your mother has to have surgery—oh, nothing drastic, I assure you—what they call a hysterectomy. You know what that is, don't you? They remove some of the female organs—at her age, they're excess baggage, aren't they? She's been bleeding—and they found tumors. The doctors call them fibroids—" Side-stepping, avoiding the awesome word "cancer." "The doctor is taking no chances."

"She asked for me?"

"Well, she didn't say that in so many words. It was just that one evening when I was over at your parents' house, she said—oh, she said it in the sweetest, sad way—'If the worst should happen to me and none of my children is here, who will cry with Papa?' You see, for his sake. He is a darling, you know."

"I'll come. I'll wire when and how."

"Why, bless you!" A pause. "I don't suppose your husband could join you?"

"He couldn't. He's working."

"It would have been thrilling for my friends to meet him," Judy said.

My household was running smoothly. Lili and Oskar Katz, the Austrian refugee couple who had replaced the Olsens, who had left us for bigger pay from a new female star, were competent, and the children liked them. Oskar had his driving license; he could drive Greta to school, to her ballet and riding lessons, and Billy to kindergarten. We had dispensed with nursemaids. Dulcie, the most recent, had married, was living near San Bernardino, where her husband had a garage—she worked the gas pumps. Ordinarily, I would have asked Thelma Gruening to run up, make sure all was well at our place. However, things had been strained between the Gruenings and us since last summer when Hitler and Stalin agreed on a pact.

Pop-eyed and ghastly, Howard had come in that evening, panting, "Jay, have you heard? . . . What can it mean? One of their damnable lies! . . . Jay, do you have Walter's phone number in New York? . . . But he's Millie's cousin. Doesn't she know his number? . . . Ask information, get him on the phone."

"If I were you, I wouldn't call him," Jay had replied icily. "Not till he's had a chance to receive the line from Moscow. It's an even bet, fifty-fifty, tonight he's as screwed up as you."

Howie had rocked his head in his hands. "The trials," he moaned. "I accepted the trials. Hard to believe. . . . But I accepted the old Bolsheviks. And that man we both knew, the man we liked so much. Nick."

Hearing him, I was grieved. That amiable man who had dandled my son on his knees, on whose cheek my daughter had slobbered wet kisses, had been tried as a traitor—Howie had brought the news item to us—but why? Because he had neglected to shoot a dog in Brazil? Because his revolution had failed? Nick had been sentenced—to what? The quick lethal volley of the firing squad? Or the slow prison-camp death? We never found out. Whatever, it should have brought us a sense of relief; he'd used our name, our address, our status. He had used us. Walt had used us, too. Yet, admit, we had been glad to be used. The using had brought us excitement, relief from the boredom of vapid parties and the illusion of helping to save the world.

"Howard," Jay said with the curled lip of contempt, "tear up your card. You've been screwed. They're sons of bitches; they have sold out."

That pact had divided the sheep from the goats; the meetings and mailings dropped off; friendships grew strained, snapped, broke apart; the very word "peace" took on an ominous sound. Whose peace? Hitler's and Stalin's? Or England's and ours?

Whatever, it was time for me to go home and make my own peace. How long can you pick at old sores?

"Why don't you fly?" Jay suggested. "You've never been in a plane."

"Nor you," I said.

"Call me coward," he said.

"I'm not afraid," I said. "It can't be worse than driving through Pacific fogs."

"I'd hoped you'd stay at our house—my mother's house, I mean," Judy was saying in the car. "I closed our place when Bram left. Mother and I would have been thrilled. But your dad—"

Papa squeezed my hand under the robe. "Millie has a home. She stays in her home." Flat statement, don't contradict.

The chauffeur again carried me over the snow piles up to the porch of the house in Westmount. "I'll be back in a jiffy, with a warm coat," Judy said. "My mother's a shortie, like you. I'll borrow one of her furs. Now about boots—"

"Upstairs in the closet in the bedroom," Papa said. "Millie's snow boots. Mama kept. For when Millie comes home."

I should have been touched, and I was, but in a way Papa hadn't intended—with a pinprick of anger. My mother had hoped, she had expected, my marriage would fail and I, defeated and humbled, would come crawling back to the nest. For a dozen years she had been waiting to say, "You see, Mama knew best."

Papa unlocked the door, held it wide. A blast of furnace heat struck me, the fetid stuffiness of a dwelling calked against subzero weather. I marched through the downstairs rooms, mentally, physically sniffing, like Jay years ago when he'd come to test me. Nothing was changed: the Georgian silver gleamed on the sideboard; the silver compotes, the candlesticks, were mirrored in the high gloss of the dining table; the bone-china saucers and cups sat on their shelves in the array in which I had seen them more than a decade ago. The parlor's Persian rug seemed slightly worn, the brocade on the overstuffed sofa and chairs slightly faded, but the drapery fabric Mama and I had chosen on a summer day had endured. Mama's taste hadn't changed. No imagination, no give. Oh, there were changes—two: they had acquired a console radio, and they had turned a long table into a gallery for gilt-framed family photographs. Judy and Bram's wedding picture and Bram in his uniform were up front; beside them, snapshots I'd taken of Greta and Billy. Yes, here, too, was a faded print of Greta, cocooned in blankets, in Mama's arms, her face half the size of a dime—the one Bram had snapped in Daisy's kitchen the day we brought her from the hospital. Where am I? Uh-huh, Mama framed an old school picture of mine. Such pretty, fat curls! (I never grew up, did I, Ma?) Where's Jay? If you look closely you can see his profile, between his children, the three of them dipping their toes into our pool. (You'd think, wouldn't you? since Jay is famous, Mama would want to show off with one of those glossies the studio mails out for free.) The back row is by far more amusing—the old sepia print of Reuben and Fanny and the rubber plant; Hannah, Dave, and their boys. Only three. Hannah has a prominent belly; that picture must date to the vacation they spent with us before Snooky arrived. The boys are mugging for the camera. Clowns! How they have changed! And here's Daisy with Grandpa in his black mohair suit. She was so pretty, a flower wasting its sweetness in a Brooklyn back yard.

Papa came up behind me. "Mama's dear ones," he said, while he lifted my coat off my shoulders. "I took your valise to your room. You want to go up? The bathroom? No? So sit, rest yourself. Would you, maybe, care for a small glass of sherry before we have lunch?"

A lady's drink, a Montreal lady's drink. "I'd love a sherry, I haven't had sherry in years." And what is more, you never offered me sherry when I lived in this house—it hadn't occurred to you or to Mama that Mildred grew up, a woman, no longer your little girl.

"You don't mind if I take for myself a whiskey?" His tone was deferential, apologetic almost. "I am not a drinker, but on a cold day . . ."

A plump woman with a mustache came in while we were having our drinks. "Marie, this is our daughter, Madame Bernstein. From California. In the United States."

Beady black eyes examined me. "You come to take care for *Maman? Oui?*" And turning to Papa, "*Jolie. Très jolie,*" she said.

"What else should she be?" Papa replied. "She is my pussycat. . . . So set the table, Marie. . . . Pussycat, she made you soup, the good pea soup you loved when you were a little girl."

It was getting under my sensitive skin, the cloying "pussycat," the "little girl." "Dear Papa," I said. "I am no longer a kid." I managed to laugh. "It's really amusing how we look at each other with yesterday's eyes."

He leaned chair-to-chair to stroke my arm. "Good said, yesterday's eyes. But no, Pussycat, with parents and children, yesterday's eyes, today's eyes, tomorrow's eyes are one and the same. It never changes. Because there is love."

In the beginning, I thought, but only then. Afterward, there's the judging, the blame. For what happened. For what never happened. For what was well-intentioned but misunderstood. And in the way a mind plays hopscotch, I remembered Ben Kuper, in a New York Automat, asking—with anguish—"With what eyes will my son look at me?" I remembered the eyes of his son. And I began to wonder with what eyes my own children one day would look at me. How soon would they start judging me? And judging Jay? For something we did. Or neglected to do. For what we were. What we could not change.

Abruptly, I asked, "Is the family coming? Hannah? Daisy?"

Papa's eyebrows twitched. "What is this, a *simcha*, we must invite the family?" He shook his head emphatically. "This is an operation. This is sickness. Worry. Nothing to share with the family. Mama said, when it's all over, and everything, God willing, is okay, we could call Daisy. Maybe she'll come keep Mama company after the hospital."

"How is Daisy?" I asked.

"How should she be? Getting older." He shrugged. "Pussycat, it is a joke: we thank God, we say He is good, kind, wonderful, when He lets us live to be old. We lose the teeth, we can't eat; cataracts grow in the eyes, we can't see; the ears get deaf, we don't hear; we can't catch the breath when we walk up one flight

287

of steps; the rheumatism hurts, the gallstones, the tumors make trouble inside. Some benefits! We thank God!" He laughed. It was his old gurgling laugh. "On one *shnapps* I become a philosopher." And again he reached for my hand. "Anyway, Pussycat, I will thank Him today, He brought you to us." He waited an instant, then carefully, watching my face: "We were figuring, Mama and me, you would be home before now. We were figuring you would get sick and tired of that life."

"It's my life," I said. "Why didn't you come visit me?"

"How could we?" There was a light flush on his cheekbones. "We would be fish out of water, plain people like us."

"We're plain people, too," I told him. "We eat and sleep, we work and we worry. . . ." And again, out of that hopscotching memory: "Just like in Cincinnati."

"Where's Cincinnati?" Taking my hand, he got up. "Marie has the soup on the table. Pea soup like this I bet you can't get in California. Or in Cincinnati."

Before we were finished, Judy arrived, loaded with furs. "The mink is mother's last year's; the seal is new. Try them both." She held the mink open. On the lining, I read "Freda Eshler," embroidered above the furrier's label. I slipped my arms into the sleeves; the sensuous softness of the fur made my fingertips tingle. "Wrap it, fold it over," Judy said. "Mother has more bosom than you."

I eyed myself in the sideboard mirror. The coat made me, I felt, look dumpy, overdressed, vulgar. "I'm not a mink type," I said.

"Don't be foolish," Judy retorted. "Everyone is. Try the seal."

That was too long, it reached almost to my ankles, and the style was matronly.

"Mother isn't sure she likes it either," Judy said. "She was hoping it would fit you, she'd give it to you, a present. . . . Oh, it would be useless in Hollyood, wouldn't it?"

"The mink," Papa said. "You look like a queen."

"I'm promoted," I said. "Jay bought me an ermine cape, so I'd look like a princess."

288

"Only a princess?" Papa said. "Here in this house, you are a queen. Mama will be happy to see you in mink."

I draped Judy's mother's mink coat around and crammed my feet into the snow boots I had worn to high school, and we rode in the Rolls over packed ice, up the side of the mountain, to the hospital.

At the door of Mama's room, Papa halted me. "I will go first, prepare her, she shouldn't get too much excited."

I heard him, hearty-voiced: "Ada, guess what? A visitor came, a wonderful guest, to see how the old folks are getting along."

And Mama, answering: "I betcha Millie."

"Smart like a fox. Come in, Millie. Come."

She was in an armchair near the window, a shawl over her shoulders, an afghan over her knees, and on her face there was an expression so mixed I couldn't be sure whether it was joy or dread.

"I didn't say send for Millie. Why did you send for her, Sam?"

"I wasn't sent for." I put my arms around. "I wanted to come."

Her suspicion ebbed slowly. She ran her fingers down the fur sleeve. "A beautiful coat. You look like a queen."

Papa and Judy had been correct; they had known Mama'd be pleased by the sight of the prodigal daughter, returning in mink. If I had come in my good cashmere coat, she might have said to herself, "A *shlemiel* Millie married; she can't afford a fur coat." Or should I have worn sackcloth and ashes, for the sake of her pride? Come on, Mildred, quit. This war is over, a truce before permanent peace.

"You look wonderful, Mama," I said, using yesterday's eyes. Yet she did. She had kept the porcelain skin of the Springer women, and her hair had remained lustrous and dark. "Who said you were sick?"

She sighed, the profound sigh of Jewish matrons, which is eloquence without words. "I have to be stylish, get an operation. The doctors talked me in."

Papa came behind me to help me out of the coat. He folded it neatly, hiding the lining label, and passed it to Judy to hold.

289

Mama peered at me through her glasses, looked me up, looked me down. "Two children, a young girl's figure."

Papa pushed a chair over for me to sit beside her.

"You look tired," Mama said.

"I am. I should be. The train and the plane."

"You went on a plane!" Mama sucked her breath in. "*He* let you, the husband, go up in the air on a plane!"

There it was, unfailing, unchanging—her critical judgment of him and, through him, of me. Yet she took my hands between hers and stroked their backs. "She doesn't put her hands in cold water," Mama said.

Being travel-exhausted, I slept like a log. Papa probably slept not at all. The morning still belonged to the night when he tapped on my door, rattled the knob, shook my shoulder gently. "The operation is for eight o'clock. She wants to see us before. Come, I made coffee. Marie left cooked oatmeal porridge for you."

Dawn was streaking the sky when we arrived at the hospital. Mama was in her room, in her bed, looking drowsy and vague, having been sedated. Papa leaned over to kiss her forehead. "Remember, Sam," I heard her murmur. "Remember I told you. If anything happens, you should with Daisy . . ."

"Nothing will happen," Papa said. "I'm telling you; take my word."

To me, all Mama said was, "Be a good girl."

We moved aside to let the nurses lift her onto a stretcher. Papa took her hand; he held it while she was wheeled up the corridor. I went to the window and stood looking out, looking down. Beyond the humps of the blanketing snow and the green tips of the pines, beyond the red brick of the old tenements, I could glimpse the St. Lawrence, swollen and bristling with ice. The river. That river on whose banks my whim was conceived: to see an ocean, the Atlantic Ocean. The whim that gave birth to disaster. For Daisy and Ben. For Arnie. And by the long reach of consequence, even for me.

The Pacific is the ocean I see nowadays, chiefly because my

daughter loves it. And is not afraid: of it or of anything. It's I who have fears. A single, irrational terror. That comes with the whine of bead portieres.

Papa tapped my arm. "Pussycat, don't stand looking worried. She has the best doctors; she has the best care. She is a strong, healthy woman, not one day sick in her life." His eyes were brightening with rising tears. "I am glad you are here. I wish—I wish Bram— Walk with me, Pussycat, I cannot stay still. Walk with me. Walk."

We paced the long, sterile corridor. We saw, without seeing, breakfast trays brought into rooms, trays carried out; we heard, without listening, the clang and clatter of basins and bedpans, the rustle of starched uniforms, the muffled murmur of conversations; hurrying figures brushed by, preoccupied. As we also were.

I asked, "Will Judy be here?" I needed her presence, I felt, to share the weight of the worry.

"She will come later; she is a good girl."

I asked, "Don't you need to go to the factory?"

"The factory doesn't miss me."

I asked, "What time is it?"

He glanced at his watch. "She is more than an hour on the table."

An hour and a half, two hours, of marching and silent standing and staring out of the windows at the corridor's end, until a gray-haired doctor emerged from an elevator and came to us. "Mr. Samuelson!"

All color drained out of Papa's face. "Doctor, my wife . . . ?"

"In excellent shape. Took it like a trouper. We removed the uterus, the right ovary. We'll have the laboratory results in twenty-four hours, but we're reasonably certain they'll be negative. She'll be down shortly. . . . No, you won't be able to speak to her, she'll be groggy. And she may complain of some discomfort, some pain. . . . I'll leave an order for something to take care of the pain. If I were you—and the young lady—I would go home, have a good breakfast, nap if you can. You look done in, both of you."

We waited, however, until the stretcher with the small, swaddled form was wheeled into the room, and we stood at a distance, watching the nurses shift her onto the bed, draw the sheet taut, tuck blankets around, place a basin and towels on a stand near the bed. Then, unbidden, we tiptoed to the bedside and saw the gray face, the pallid shut eyelids, the sweat-beaded temples and tousled hair on the pillow; we inhaled the mouse-droppings vinegar stench of ether. We heard a long moan. Tears sprang into my father's eyes. The nurse touched his arm. "She'll be like this for some time. I'd suggest you leave and come back, say, in three or four hours."

Papa bent to drop a light kiss on the damp, gray forehead; he straightened his spine, mopped his eyes with his fist. But I stood staring down at the shell of my mother, rooted, and riven by the bolt of a thought: her womb is gone; the womb that cradled and nourished me is lying somewhere in a garbage bucket. Our bond is destroyed; we are separated; I'm on my own. And I felt an appalling loneliness.

Papa phoned for a taxi; we rode downhill to the house. Papa wanted to talk. "She looks terrible. Anyhow, it is over; the nurse looks like a capable woman." I didn't respond because something important was happening to me: I was forgiving my mother. And at the same time, I kept wondering exactly what it was I had to forgive. That she had mistrusted my choice of a husband? By her standards, her narrow experience, an actor wasn't respectable, not a proper husband for me. What's worse, I had picked him myself, made my decision without asking her, letting her weigh pro and con, argue, arrange. The way her own marriage had been arranged. And Sophie's with Ben. And Daisy's with Ezra Magid. But, Mama, the times were different, the world had changed. I was part of a new generation. Emancipated. Yes, sure, we loved our parents; yes, sure, we respected them. Yes, sure, we obeyed. Up to a point. The point when we thought we held the world in our hands.

Mama, my marriage has not been a bed of roses. But not for the world would I let on to you. There's a gulf between us, the

292

gulf of my guilt. You never knew I was pregnant when I married Jay; you never knew I had been unchaste. I think Daisy knew or she guessed, but she kept my secret. I think—it's a wild guess on my part—she was even jealous of me. I had a lover, I was all a woman should be. But, Mama, there was a fear and a horror in it, that even now I cannot tell you about. Something happened to me in a dark hall in that Brooklyn house, and I think it was then I began to be angry with you. Because you hadn't protected me from what you never knew.

You didn't know, Jay didn't know, of the shame and the fear that was deep within me. Yet you expected, I know you did, for your own reasons, that my marriage would fail. You expected— don't tell me not—I'd made the break when Jay left me to bear our baby alone, when he remained in Hollywood and I stayed in Brooklyn, with Greta, and lived on your charity. I could have come home. My old room, my bed, my snow boots were waiting for me. You would have taken us in, Greta and me, fed us and clothed us, kept us sheltered and warm. Of course, there would have been crowing from you—why didn't you listen to me? And I'd have talked back; we'd have quarreled a lot. But you'd have felt noble and righteous because you'd rescued me.

From what? From a life that is alien to you. From a man who loves me. Yes, say what you will, Jay does love me. And, possibly, more than I love him. There's no reason except wanting to, for him to keep sharing that bedroom with me.

Papa tweaked the mink sleeve. "I'll leave you off at the house; the taxi will drive me downtown. I'll take a look at my mail, maybe some customers are paying their bills. . . . Marie will fix you a lunch. After lunch, we'll go visit Mama. Tonight I will make the telephone calls."

Judy and baskets of fruit and flowers were in the room when we returned to the hospital. Mama was half awake, intermittently groaning and throwing up. The nurse let us toss fingertip kisses before she shooed us out.

"We really can't do much for her by hanging around," Judy

said. "Suppose I drive you to Mother's; we could have tea. Mother would love to meet Millie."

"Millie can go," Papa said. "I will stay. Mama might need something."

"I'll stay," I said. On the day you forgive your mother for being your mother, you do not rush out for tea with strangers.

By the time yellow lights had begun to twinkle in the houses down slope, Mama had sipped iced ginger ale, vomited it, and spoken to us, asking, "I'm all right? I'm hokay?" informing us, "I have terrible pains," and after the nurse had held the basin into which Mama had retched, she had seized the woman's wrist, clinging to it as to a lifeline. "She takes care of me wonderful. You two go home. Call up Daisy, call up Hannah." Her tongue tip moistened her lips. "You could call up Reuben, also." She waited an instant, making a decision. "No, nobody should come, only Daisy, I don't need the family club." The trace of a smile touched her parched lips. "Tell Reuben this week I don't need a place in the family plot."

I sat at Papa's elbow while he made his long-distance calls. His tact was admirable.

"Daisy, this is your brother-in-law. . . . Yeah, Sam Samuelson. . . . Where am I? Where should I be? In Montreal. . . . You can hear me all right? I have a message from Ada. . . . No, she is not home, she is in the hospital. . . . Don't get excited. This morning she had a small operation. . . . No, nothing serious. Women's business. . . . Yeah, that department. Thank God, she is over it; everything is fine. . . . Yeah, I saw her after the operation. . . . How should she be? The ether made her a little sick to the stomach. She has pain; the nurse gives her something for pain. . . . Why didn't she tell you? Why should she tell you? What could you do? Are you a doctor? . . . Yes, she has a good doctor. And nurses. The best. . . . Should you come? Why else am I making a telephone call? Ada said before she went in the hospital, maybe Daisy could arrange to keep me company a couple of days after I come from the hospital. . . . Tell her she should not be afraid for the weather; the house is warm, the furnace works good. . . . Daisy,

294

I have a different proposition. I thought maybe, if it is convenient for you, you could come a little early, maybe this week; we
have a good guest you would want to see. . . . How long will
she stay? . . . I didn't ask her. I'll put her on, you ask her yourself."

I took up the receiver; I said, "Daisy dear!"

She answered, "Darling!" without the Irish lilt, then asked,
"The operation was serious, you came from so far?"

"That was just an excuse. I thought it was time I came
to visit."

"You brought our baby?"

"Both children stayed home; they are in school."

"Our baby's already in school?"

"Greta is ten, a big girl. Why, Billy is five."

"I can't believe how the time flies."

"Daisy, dear, I can't stay here long; I'll have to start back by
the end of this week. I'd love to see you. Could you possibly
come?"

She had to pause while her mind considered arrangements.
"You couldn't come down to New York, visit a day or two, just
you and me? . . . No. Then Sunday, I'll come. I have to find
somebody to see to the furnace, the tenants. Tell your father I'll
take the sleeper Saturday night."

"Now we call Hannah," Papa said. . . . "Hello! This is Sam
Samuelson in Montreal. To who am I speaking? . . . Clarence.
. . . Oh, hello, hello, Snooky! How is the artist? . . . Good, good,
keep up the good work. . . . Your mother is home? . . . Your
father, too. . . . No, just give him my best regards; your mother
I need to speak to—I have a message from her big sister. . . .
Hello, Hannah, how are you? . . . I'm sorry to hear. Yes, sure,
it is winter, everybody catches a cold. Your bungalow is warm?
You have storm windows? Weather stripping? You have enough
coal? . . . Oh, an oil burner, Karl bought an oil burner. A good
son. Maybe he should send you to Miami, you could sit in the sun,
get rid of the cough. . . . Yeah, yeah, you couldn't leave Dave
and Snooky. . . . Hannah, I called because I have a piece of news.
This morning Ada had a small operation. . . . Yes, in the hospi-

295

tal. She is over, thank God! She came through wonderful. . . .
They'll keep her ten days, two weeks. Why should she hurry?
She has babies waiting for her in the house? . . . No, she doesn't
want you to come; you shouldn't bother, you have plenty, enough,
to take care of yourself. . . . No, she didn't want to tell you before; why should you be worried for nothing? After it's over,
she said, you can tell my sisters. . . . Sure, sure, I will give her your
love. . . . Wait, I have here a guest, a good guest, you might enjoy
saying hello."

"Aunt Hannah! Hello!"

"Who is it? Not Millie? . . . Oh, Millie, Millie, you came from
California!"

"All the way. To hold Papa's hand. Mama has special nurses;
Papa needed somebody to hold his hand. . . . Oh, no, he isn't sick.
A little excited, that's all."

"Walt told me you have a beautiful home," Hannah said.

"How is Walt?"

"Running around." She was answering carefully. "And a little
mixed up."

"The pact," I said.

"That lousy Stalin," she said.

"That lousy Hitler," I said.

"Two of a kind," she said. "God help the Jews."

"Amen. And what do you hear from Eugene?"

There was a silence, then: "We don't hear from him. From
Spain he didn't come back. Maybe Walt knows where he is. Maybe
only God knows."

"Gene's doing an important thing," I said.

"Dave and me," my aunt said, "we would be a little more
happy if he was a little less important. We need a son, not a hero.
Some people, if they have a warm heart for the world, have only
a cold stone for the family. . . . Walt, too: a couple of hours spared
for his father would be a good thing. Dave is not young; his
asthma bothers. And the brother needs help. If not for Karl—"

"How is Karl?" I made myself ask.

"Very good. Very successful. A blessing for us," Hannah said.

296

"Now," Papa declared, with patent reluctance, "we call up Reuben and Fanny. You want to speak with them, too?"

"If I must," I said. "Otherwise no."

"Hello. . . . Hello. . . . Who is this? Oh, Fanny, I didn't recognize the voice; you sound like a man. This is Samuelson, your brother-in-law. . . . Yes, Sammy. From Canada. Is Reuben home? . . . Sure, I want to talk to you. . . . Sure, I can ask how you are. How are you? . . . So, if the gallstones hurt, have the operation already. How many years did I hear you complain about gallstones? You're sick, get a doctor. It sounds to me you enjoy to complain about it, not to do something. . . . Listen, Fanny, a long-distance call costs money. . . . Sure, sure, I'm not broke but to spend money to argue about your gallstones! Put Reuben on, please. . . . Reuben, my wife, your sister, asked me to call you. This morning she had an operation. Not serious. Only for her. It is over, thank God. . . . I'll tell her, I'll tell her you'll go to *shul* and pray. . . . She sent you a message; she asked me to tell you this week you don't need to make room for her in the plot. . . . Yes, I got your letter about the fence and the gates. I answered you I would pay my fair share, you should tell me how much. . . . Okay, I'll throw in a couple dollars extra. Maybe I can afford it, maybe not. Here in Canada we are in the war that my son went off to be in the service, and in my factory now we are not spinning gold. . . . Listen, Reuben, listen, don't argue on the long distance. Send for three cents a letter. Or call up Karl Hitzig, tell him to handle the business; cemetery people listen to lawyers. I didn't call to discuss how much to pay for a fence. I called up only to tell you your sister had an operation. . . . No, *no*, NO, she doesn't want Fanny to come. She has special nurses; we have a good char in the house. There is nothing for Fanny to do. . . . Yes, she would be a nuisance. Besides, old people like her shouldn't travel in winter. . . . Your business is rotten, heh? So sell the store. Do you need it? Your wife must have a fortune tied up in her *knippel*. . . . Yes, Daisy told me your great idea—Fanny's idea. It's up to Daisy, not me. . . . Reuben, I can't talk all night. Good-bye, good-bye."

He hung up with a bang and a snap. "Your uncle!" He let out

his breath. "You know what's his big idea right now? He and Fanny should sell their house and their store and move in with Daisy. She should cook for them; she should wait on Fanny. Some nerve! Mama's dear ones!"

We were asleep when the phone rang. We met in the upstairs hall, Papa and I, shivering and scared. "Mama! Something happened!" Papa gasped before he stumbled downstairs to the hall telephone. "Hello . . . hello. Who is it? Yes, this is the Samuelson residence. . . . Mrs. Burns. Yes, yes, she is here. . . . Millie, for you. Person to person from California." He passed the receiver to me. "I hope no bad news."

"Why didn't you call me?" Jay asked.

"Did you expect me to?"

"I certainly did. You were flying. I worried."

"I'm touched."

"You should be. Do you realize this is the first time we've been separated since we moved to California?"

"You missed me?" I was pleased but incredulous.

"Naturally. I've grown accustomed to your face."

"How are the kids?"

"Oh, they're fine, just fine."

"Do they also miss me?"

"Not so you'd notice. They went to the beach this afternoon. Oskar took them."

"I can't imagine anyone swimming today. It's below zero here."

"Are you all right? Warm enough? Please don't get sick." There was an urgency in his voice that I had never previously heard.

"I borrowed a mink. Around here they keep spares for guests."

"Trust you to manage. When do you plan starting back?"

"Is there a reason to hurry?"

"Why, yes. The studio rearranged the shooting schedule. We go on location Monday. Out to the desert."

"Who's going?" A twinge of the old jealousy.

298

"Shall I run down the cast?"

"And run up the phone bill? No, thanks. That means leaving the children."

"It does."

"Oh, dear! Aunt Daisy's coming on Sunday. I want to see her, she wants to see me."

"Who's more important, your aunt or your kids?"

"Don't give me that choice. There must be some way to handle the problem. Could you ask Thelma to sleep at our house till I get back?"

"I wouldn't ask any Gruening to give me the right time of day."

"Bad as that, eh?"

"Bad as that. Shall I spell it?"

"Jay, I can't leave before Sunday night. Don't you realize I haven't been home in a dozen years?"

"And they're slaughtering fatted calves?"

"Hardly. Walking hospital corridors. Mama had her operation this morning."

"Oh!" His tone changed. "She came through okay?"

"She did. And Papa and I have had a hard day. Your call scared us silly. Here it's after midnight, you know. He thought, we thought, when the phone rang . . ."

"I'm sorry, kid. Honest. I forgot the time difference. I apologize. Shall I wire flowers or something?"

"Nothing," I said. "Just try to make some arrangement for the children. Ask Mr. and Mrs. Katz to sleep in the house. Or . . . or maybe the studio could postpone . . . allow you—"

He interrupted, brusque, with irritability. "Not a chance. I am not indispensable."

"That's news. What's up?"

"Nothing, nothing. Forget it."

"Jay, something's wrong!"

"Nuts to you. Do not nag. I'll work something out. Get home as soon as you can. Don't expect a reception committee. So long. *Au revoir.*"

"Feel my heart," Papa said. "Hammering. When the telephone rang, I was sure something with Mama—"

"My husband forgot the time difference," I said. "Jay said to tell you he's sorry. A problem came up. They're making a picture; he has to go to the desert; he was worried about leaving the children alone. I told him I would spend Sunday with Daisy, start back Sunday night."

His face fell apart. "Pussycat, we waited so long. . . . You came, you are leaving so fast."

"Don't make it sound tragic," I said. "We have almost a week."

I spent Wednesday, all day, at the hospital. Mama dozed most of the time, waking to whimper about pain or thirst. Her daughter, relieving the nurse, held a sipper to her mouth for water or bouillon or tea, stepped into the hall while Mama received a bedpan or a doctor's visit, chatted with nurses who wanted to hear about Hollywood life and about James Burns—what was he really like? Difficult, snappish, laconic, I thought. Attractive to women, flirtatious, philandering. Egocentric, ambitious, vain, insecure. "Intelligent, sensitive, charming," I told the nurses. The half-truth was better than truth. My smiles and evasions satisfied them; they declared they were thrilled to meet *me*.

At the bedside I read magazines and waited for Mama to perk and demand. The room was fragrant with carnations and roses, from florists' stocks, and hyacinth and freesia, out of the Eshler greenhouse. It was dull for me, yet ennobling. At last I was being a devoted daughter.

Thursday was equally dull, but with a livening touch of expectancy: Mama had been promised an enema. Opening clogged bowels would clear her head, a medical miracle.

Judy popped in at intervals, bearing tribute: bouquets for Mama, candy and magazines for me. She insisted I go to her mother's for Friday-night dinner. "You must meet my folks; my mother is dying to meet you."

"Go, Pussycat," Papa said. "See how a millionaire lives. . . . No, I would not go with, I already saw. . . . You'll have a fine dinner. They have the best cook in Montreal—a first-class French chef."

On Friday morning Mama was a new woman. She'd had the enema, toast and an egg for her breakfast, and a sponge bath. The coarse hospital gown had been replaced by one of her own, pink and lace-trimmed, like an old-fashioned valentine. And she was so pleased when I told her I'd been invited to meet Judy's family that I confessed the mink I'd been wearing was on loan from Judy's mother.

"From Freda Eshler, I would expect it," Mama said. "She would give you the shirt off her back. He—Harry Eshler—is a *momser*—a bastid—she is a *mensch*." Mama settled back against the cranked-up pillow. "I know Freda Eshler a long time; from her life's history you could make a book. You could make the most interesting moving picture. Rubenstein, the father, the father from Freda, came to Canada a young man. A trade he didn't have, not like your father that was an experienced tailor in the old country. Rubenstein has to have bread, so he has to have work, so he gets a job like a laboring man on the railroad; they are building a railroad up to the north where there is gold in the ground. The railroad gets finished, and there is Rubenstein up in the north; it is wilderness, cold. But a living a man needs to make. For cold weather he isn't afraid. In Russia, in winter, it was no *shwitzbath*. So he opens a store, a general store: groceries, can goods, tools, ropes for the miners. Even nightgowns, underwear for the women, the girls." She blushed and lowered her eyes. "Where there is young men without wives—"

I prompted her. "Prostitutes."

She glared at me. "A girl like you shouldn't know from such things."

"Rubenstein opened a general store," I said.

"I could use a sip water," she said. "Give me, please, if you don't mind."

I held the glass; she settled back on the pillow. "So Rubenstein has a general store," she began again. "He is making a living and saving a couple of dollars. So he goes down to Toronto, and

301

they find for him a wife, a Jewish girl—not beautiful, no money, but a respectable family. The girl is happy to get a husband; she isn't afraid for the cold; she can help tend the store. So they have children together. Only the first one, Freda, has a bad arm, the left arm. (You'll see it, don't make remarks.) The fingers are dried up like sticks. I heard it was the midwife—doctors they didn't have in that wilderness—the midwife, an old woman, an Indian woman, I think, she hurt something in the nerves in the arm; it wouldn't never work normal. So here is a girl, she is growing up, and the parents worry; who will marry a girl with only one hand? Millie"—she paused to shake a forefinger at me—"you think parents don't worry who will marry their daughter? Will she get a respectable man who can make a living for her?"

"Let me straighten your pillow," I said.

"So comes this young man." She continued to talk while I fluffed the pillow. "This *youngatch*, Eshler; he is looking for gold, which for a Jewish young man is exceptional because mostly it is *goyim* that dig in the ground. Money this Eshler doesn't have, not one penny, even to buy what to eat. So Rubenstein, the father, he has a good heart; he invites the young man for a *shabbos* meal in their house. And Freda's father—or maybe her mother —gets the idea, if they help this young man with a—with a—"

"Grubstake," I said.

She beamed. "How do you know so many things? From the college? . . . Well, they decide if they help him, maybe he will help them, their daughter, Freda, shouldn't be an old maid. So that was how it was. Maybe they talked him in, maybe they also gave a *nadan*."

"A dowry," I said.

She nodded. "He was willing."

"And she?" I asked.

Mama frowned. "Did she have better chances? The parents found a husband for her. By herself what could she find? And him, gold he didn't find. But Eshler was smart. He and some feller he took for a partner, they bought the land where they digged their hole in the ground—they owned the property, exact where

—Timmons, Kirkland Lake, Swastika, Noranda—I don't remember. That hole in the ground had in it something, I don't know exactly—"

"Nickel? Copper?"

"Ask Papa," she said. "Papa knows."

A nurse came in, bearing a pill. "Mrs. Samuelson, you shouldn't be talking so much; you should be resting."

"I am telling my daughter a story she could take to Hollywood; it would be a moving picture more interesting than the junk with gangsters." She swallowed her pill. The nurse held her wrist, counting her pulse. "So, Millie, you hear, Freda and Harry are married, they move to Montreal. That's when I got acquainted with her; they lived on the same street with us. In a small flat. She has one baby, a boy; she has the second, a boy. Then Judy, the last. Three babies, no char, all the work she does by herself, even scrubbing the clothes. With the one hand. What he is doing to earn a living, nobody knows. Then after the war, the first big war, it comes out, he is—"

She stopped. "Nurse!" she commanded, "be so kind to leave me and my daughter by ourselfs. Close the door, please. I will ring if I need the bedpan. Millie—" She lowered her voice, not convinced that the nurse was not listening at the keyhole.

"Everybody in Montreal knows the story. Only I don't want the *goyim* to hear. . . . It comes out Eshler was making money selling whiskey in the United States; he was in with some gangsters; they have the trucks, they have the boats, they are coining money. Then somebody tells the RCMP. And Eshler is catched. There is a trial. He goes to prison. And here is Freda with the three little kids and only one hand. What should she do? She asks the father to help. And he is a good father, like your father, Sam Samuelson. The daughter and the daughter's children must have what to eat. But he tells her, him and the mother, the both, 'The man is no good. Leave him. We will arrange a Jewish divorce.' But Freda is stubbren"—Mama looked at me, straight and sharp-eyed, and I began to realize she had been treating me to a parable —"he is her husband; she will not leave him. The children she

303

tells the father is sick, in a sanitarium; when he is well, he will come home. And when he comes home, they should have respect. Not like . . . not like Sophie Kuper." (She had a second comparison on tap.) "Freda Eshler is a *mensch*.

"Harry comes out from prison, he starts right away making money. From that hole in the ground in the north he makes money. A pile. And they move to Westmount, and Freda has plenty help in the house. And the boys go in college. They were smart kids. The first one, Lionel is his name (Leo, he was when he was a kid), he has a big job in Ottawa, by the government. The younger one, Stanley (Solly, we used to call him), is in the business office in New York. And both of them married to refined Jewish girls." She fenced her mouth with her hand for a parenthesis. "That Stanley, I understand, in New York, keeps *shiksas* on the side. And Harry, nobody is supposed to know, he has a French one; he keeps her in an apartment on Côte des Neiges." She removed her hand.

"Judy. That Judy has her eyes on Bram since she was a kid. My son, your brother, is a good-looking feller. To college Judy went only one year; then they send her to Europe she should learn good French. Bram told me himself the whole time Judy was over in Paris, she was writing letters to him. She comes home; they go skiing up in the mountains. She calls him up on the phone: 'Bram, I am driving here, I am driving there, can I give you a lift?' . . . Bram, I am having a couple friends for a party.' . . . Millie, I don't like to criticize Judy, she is a fine girl; from some other girl you could call it fresh, the way she ran after Bram, she wouldn't leave him alone. Everybody, all my friends here, they were saying I should be proud, the Eshler girl is after my son; it is—it is a big compliment. She could, in Europe, with their kind of money, marry a prince. A little bit, I talked your brother in. . . . Sam, your papa, I can tell you, was not so happy. Harry Eshler he does not respect; the money didn't make from him a gentleman. But Judy, I tell Sam, is like the mother, A-one character. . . . Bram is in the service; does she run around, like some wives? . . . No, by the Red Cross she goes every week, rolling the bandages; her own house she closed up to save coal, because there is war. She is plain and simple; from her you would never know the father is a president from organizations and a rich millionaire."

The nurse came in again. "Mrs. Samuelson, I must insist. You have to stop talking. You have to rest."

Mama sighed. "My daughter and me, we are having a wonderful conversation. Such a good conversation we didn't have in I don't know how many years."

I got up to put on the borrowed mink. Mama eyed me from under her drooping lids. "Freda's coat is becoming. Your husband couldn't afford to buy you a mink?"

"For California? Why, we have summer all year! The children went swimming this week."

"Swimming! In winter! Nurse, did you hear? Such crazy people!"

"We'll talk about that tomorrow," I said. In our entire "wonderful conversation," those few were the only words we had spoken about *my* life and *my* family.

Judy picked me up at my parents' house. "You don't mind coming this early do you? Mother likes me to be there when she lights the candles."

While we rode up the hill, Judy said, "We have a surprise for you. . . . No, I won't tell you what, I won't tell you who. I promised."

"If it's someone who says, 'Thrilled to meet you,' I will spit."

"You won't," Judy said. "You'll be thrilled."

The Eshlers had a walled castle at the top of Westmount—no moat, but locked gates like ours in Hollywood. A uniformed maid helped me off with the coat; a uniformed manservant took my snow boots. The entrance hall had Persian carpets so deep they tickled my ankles; there were fragrant fresh flowers in Chinese bowls on the credenzas. The bronze knights in armor were larger than life.

Freda Eshler came down a magnificent staircase to greet me. She was a short woman, tightly girdled, with an unwrinkled pleasant face and blue hair, stylishly coiffed. Her long-sleeved black gown was undubitably Paris; her pearl necklace and earrings were —even to my inexperienced eyes—beyond price. Her left hand dangled, yet she offered the right to me as unself-consciously as though she had two of a kind. "Mrs. Burns! Mildred! This is a pleasure!"

"I appreciate your lending the coat; I'd have frozen without it," I said.

"It was an honor to me that you wore it," she said. "I was thrilled."

"Spit," Judy whispered.

The parlor to which she led us was done with taste: delicate pastel and silver brocade on French furniture, an Aubusson carpet, cream-colored marble framing the fireplace, precious lace curtains, silk draperies. And more fresh flowers in crystal bowls. "My husband has been delayed at his office. He will join us shortly. With"—she caught Judy's eye—"with our other guest. And how is your mother?"

"Doing well, thank you. Better than we expected."

"Having you here did it, I'm sure. She must be very happy."

"Thrilled," I told her.

"That's what daughters are for," Mrs. Eshler said. "To comfort mothers. What's that little rhyme? 'My son's my son till he gets him a wife; my daughter's my daughter all her life.' Judy's a joy—what would I do without her?" She smiled at Judy; Judy smiled back. Not in the Samuelson family, I told myself: it is the daughter who skipped; the son stayed around.

"How long will you be here, Mildred?"

"I leave Sunday night."

"So soon? Judy and I had hoped we could entertain for you."

"Jay has to go on location. Someone has to be with our kids."

A houseman came in to draw the draperies against the fading sunset. Mrs. Eshler rose. "Will you girls join me to light the *shabbos* candles?"

In a baronial dining room, paneled walls gleamed; a mahogany table was set with Spode on lace mats, with sparkling silver and crystal, and a Lalique bowl, filled with orchids. At the near end of a Sheraton sideboard stood a small brass tray, holding a pair of brass candlesticks. "My mother's," Freda Eshler informed me, with a kind of pride. "Out of Poland." She bowed her head and with her right hand raised up her left, making an arch over her head. Judy struck a match; she lighted the candles while her mother said the prayer.

We heard a man's voice, rough-edged, imperious, out in the hall, a younger voice, answering him. The younger voice sounded familiar. "They're here," Judy said, looking at me as if she'd been eating canary.

I saw Harry Eshler first, and it struck me I'd seen him before. Yet I hadn't. I had seen actors he resembled, the burly roughnecks. Eshler was bald as an egg, dark-jowled, barrel-chested. His nose was overwhelming, his tailoring impeccable, his nails manicured. His wife and daughter stepped up, singly; each dropped a kiss on his cheek.

Behind him, Karl Hitzig stood, pale and pudgy, spectacled. "Remember me?" He extended his hand. I took it, the fingers were cold.

"Shall we dance?" I found myself answering and saw a flush rise in his cheeks.

"Not now, for Godsakes," I believe he replied.

"Harry, this is Mildred, Bram's sister. Mrs. James Burns," Freda Eshler said.

"*Gut shabbos.*" The tycoon's stare was disconcerting. I felt undressed.

"We weren't expecting Mr. Hitzig this weekend," Mrs. Eshler was explaining to me. "He telephoned Harry from New York, said he had certain contract details to discuss. Such a coincidence. . . ."

Not at all. No doubt Aunt Hannah had told Karl I was here, and he had decided to come, to see how time and marriage had treated me. "You look wonderful," my cousin told me. I caught surprise in his voice.

"Mildred ought to be in the movies," my sister-in-law said. "She's prettier than most who are."

307

"It's a thrill to see you again," my cousin said.

I found my handkerchief and spat. Daintily.

"Who besides me wants a drink?" Harry Eshler said.

"I don't indulge," Karl said.

"I'd like a martini," I said.

"Me, too," Judy said.

"You will have sherry," her father said.

For himself, he poured whiskey, a double. He drank it neat.

While we sat decorously drinking, Freda Eshler said, "What a pity your husband couldn't come with you. Mr. Hitzig, you have met Mildred's husband, haven't you?"

"I introduced them," Karl said. "At my graduation dance."

"How romantic!" Judy cried.

"He was in my class at City College."

Harry Eshler glanced up. "One of us?"

"Bernstein. Jake." Karl grimaced. Harry Eshler returned the grimace and added a grunt.

"Dinner is served," a butler announced, as in the films. We trooped into the baronial hall.

"Five at table is a little difficult," Mrs. Eshler said. "Mr. Hitzig, suppose you sit next to Mildred. You two must have so much to talk about. Judy, opposite Mildred. Oh, if dear Bram was here ..."

"He could be," Eshler grumbled. "We could have fixed him up in Ottawa. A patriot he had to be."

"Please, Papa!" Judy protested.

"At my table I please myself," Eshler said.

A waitress and butler began to serve. The menu:

> Onion soup, rich and fragrant.
> Crown roast of lamb, sausage stuffing. *Magnifique.*
> Potato balls.
> Fresh peas (from a greenhouse?).
> Miniature rolls, piping hot.
> Roquefort in the salad dressing.
> Marron mousse (does this cook hand out recipes?).
> A chilled wine, a Chablis.

There's a war on, though you'd never guess it at the Eshler table.

The butler carved the crown roast deftly at the host's side. The waitress carried the hostess's plate to the Sheraton sideboard to cut her portions into bite-sized pieces, done unobtrusively, no one but me paying attention to it. Harry Eshler ate head down, shoveling and champing, arrogant in his vulgarity. I must have been staring at him too long and too hard, for Mrs. Eshler coughed the *ahem* cough that calls attention. "Mildred, please tell us about your life in Hollywood."

I laid down my fork. "I keep house, I plan meals, I shop, take care of my children. Sometimes we have friends in for dinner or cocktails; sometimes we're invited out. The only thing that's really different is climate—we do things out of doors all year around. Swimming. Tennis."

Mrs. Eshler looked disappointed. "Don't you belong, aren't you active in organizations? Hadassah, Sisterhood, the Red Cross?"

"Not particularly," I said. "Oh, a few years ago we did some fund raising for Loyalist Spain. That was after my cousin, Karl's brother—"

I felt a kick on my ankle. My, Karl, what long legs you have! We do not mention Spain in this house. Nor the Communist brother. So tactless of me!

"Commies," Eshler was growling. "Had them here too. Gave us trouble. Riots."

"Gone and past," I hurried to say. "Nowadays, all I am is a housewife."

"Nora," Karl said.

"I beg your pardon?" I said.

"Nora Helmer. *A Doll's House*." He went on to explain. "When Millie was in New York, going to college, I used to take her to theater on Saturday nights. We saw *A Doll's House* together."

"I don't think we did," I said.

"You've forgotten." Karl was persistent. "Nora, the doll wife who got fed up and left, slammed the door. I remember we had a serious talk afterward—I pointed out how modern women were doing constructive things with their lives."

"I can't imagine Mildred doing anything except what she does," Judy said. "She enjoys her life. And her husband's devoted to her. Why, when we were there on our honeymoon, he was so thoughtful, considerate. They're an ideal couple, everyone says."

Thank you, dear Judy, you've made my evening. You didn't know, you couldn't guess—we must have put on a good show—that time I was angry as well as pregnant, and Jay wasn't sure how contrite he needed to be. The situation has improved. I see nothing, I hear nothing, and I keep my mouth shut.

Karl said he'd see me to my parents' house; he was staying at the Mount Royal—our house was on his way.

"Patrick will drive you both," Mrs. Eshler said. She said not to wait to say good night to her husband; he was in the library making long-distance calls; it was impossible to know how soon he'd emerge.

In the Rolls, driving down, I asked, "Well, Karl, are you satisfied?"

"About what?"

"Nora did not slam the door."

"He will, if you don't," Karl replied.

"You're never wrong, are you, Karl?"

"I get paid for not being wrong," he said.

Nuts to you, Mr. Hitzig. Change the subject. "You kicked me when I mentioned Walt. What about him?"

"Cuckoo." He tapped his temple. "Not been coherent since Ribbentrop watched the *Swan Lake*. Dithering, babbling about the sellout. I blame him"—he sounded bitter—"for whatever has happened to Gene. I warned Gene, I warned both of them. Believe me, I did."

"You're a great warner," I said.

I slammed the door getting out.

Papa had ledgers and manila folders spread on the dining table. "Catching up. I got behind in my work." His eyes were bloodshot; he rubbed them with his knuckles. "You enjoyed the evening?"

"The dinner was great. The company . . ." I let the sentence end with a shrug.

"Harry Eshler is—I wouldn't say what Eshler is," Papa said.

"Karl, my cousin, was there," I said.

"Why not? Karl makes a good living from Eshler. Eshler buys my nephew; he bought my son. I must be thankful to Hitler —this is a bitter joke, Millie—Hitler saved my son from Eshler. Out from the father-in-law's dirty business to a clean war. For Judy I feel a little sorry; she is in the middle: her husband should do what he wants; her father should have what he wants—the power, the satisfactions out of his money." He thrust his file folder aside. "What for am I sitting here, figuring, wrecking my brain, to keep up a factory, a business? For who? Mama and me are plain, simple people. Rich tastes we don't have. Our daughter has plenty—enough for her family—our son is married, with a rich wife. For who do I plan?" He wiped his brow with the flat of his hand. "For children parents should never plan. You think something for them is right, is good. In their eyes, it is wrong, like a crime." He swept his papers together. "Why do I bother you with my headaches? Let Bram only be safe. Let him and Judy live out their lives in good health. Like you and Jake."

On the upstairs landing, before we separated for bed, he produced his old grin.

"You know, Pussycat, everything is always the same. I also ran from my parents. I wanted a different life from their life."

I was late getting to the hospital Saturday—I had tramped the icy slush of St. Catherine Street hunting for gifts for Greta and Billy. Mama had had her lunch and her nap; she was dressed for company with a dainty bed jacket and a pink bow in her hair.

"You enjoyed?" she began.

"Wonderful food," I said. "And Mrs. Eshler is pleasant."

"If not for the parents, what they arranged, would that cripple woman live like a queen?"

"But he is . . ." I couldn't—I didn't want to express what I had felt about Judy's father.

"He is what he is," Mama said. "Freda and him, they had three children together. He gives her everything the best. She couldn't complain."

"Karl Hitzig was there," I said.

311

"My nephew? He came to Montreal to see me?" She bent forward to peer as if he might be lurking beyond the doorway.

"He came to see me."

She frowned. "Up here he comes to see you?"

"I'm a celebrity, didn't you know?"

She took an instant, absorbing my statement, before she shrugged it away. "So now I am feeling better, thank God, show me your children."

I spread my snapshots on her blanket; she put Billy's pictures aside. "Him I don't know. Him I never held in my arms." And studied Greta's pictures. "A sweet girl. She will have to wear glasses always?"

"She'll find a husband, don't worry. You wear glasses; you found a husband."

"My father found for me," she said. "That's how we did in those times."

And you were so lucky, I thought. That same father also found Daisy a husband.

Perhaps Mama had been reading my mind; perhaps her mind had gone, by itself, on a tangent, for she giggled softly. "It was a funny business. When Sam came for the first time to my father's house, we were three sisters, nobody married. Sam looks at the three—this your Papa told me himself after we were a long time married—he looks at the three, and he decides he likes best the young one, Daisy. But my father, my brother, they decided: Daisy has time, she is only a kid; Ada is the oldest, she must be the first married." Her voice thinned, drifting off into a silence of remembering—or being fatigued. It returned, decisive and strong. "Before the operation, I told Papa, my husband, 'Sam, if something happens to me, I am gone, I want you should marry Daisy. Not be alone by yourself. Daisy will take good care on you. She will have respect. And you will make for her a nice life, an easier life."

"You spoiled the scheme," I said. "You lived."

She looked shocked. "What are you saying, Millie? You wanted me not to live?" Tears filmed her eyes. She groped for my hand. "Millie, Millie, why are you mad at me?"

312

I squeezed her fingers. "I'm not mad at you—honestly no. Not any more."

"You are. You are mad with me, because I said you should not marry a crazy actor. An actor, it was something cheap, not refined, not for people like us. Papa and me, we kept on thinking she will get over the *meshugas;* she will get sensible. When you were struggling with a small infant in Daisy's house and he was in California, looking for what God only knows, and we sent you money, you should have for whatever you need, we thought, we figured . . ."

"Mama," I said, "I made a choice. I took the bad with the good."

"What was the bad?" she asked, too eagerly.

Judy called for me in the late afternoon—she wanted to show me her house—and we drove in the Rolls to a gabled dwelling of gray Scottish stone on the edge of the Eshler estate. "I wanted something modern and simple," Judy said. "But Daddy decided on this. Bram never felt comfortable here." She unlocked a heavy, iron-studded front door.

A closed-up house is a haunted house. It's full of ghost smells, vestiges of flower perfumes, pipe tobacco and charred roasts, mixed with the tar-paper wrappings of rolled-up rugs and the pervasive mustiness. The house was dark—the drapes were drawn —and it was brutally cold.

Judy touched the thermostat. "In a few minutes, we can have heat. I'll make us tea. . . . Oh, I forgot the water's shut off, so the pipes won't freeze."

She walked ahead of me through large, high-ceilinged rooms where everything, sofas and chairs and tables, wore dun linen shrouds. "We bought such beautiful things, Mother and I," she was saying. "I wanted my home to be—oh, as gracious as yours. Oh, Millie, Millie, do you have any idea of how lucky you are? Somehow, your brother and I never got anything started—I think he was glad to get away to the war."

Papa and I met a little old lady, swaddled in wool, at the depot early on Sunday. Papa took her valise; she let me carry her brown-paper bundles. "Coffee cake, strudel, *chalah*," she said. "I baked yesterday. We could bring something to Ada." In the house, with her wrappings removed, I saw a tiny person, thinned to the bones. Her lovely skin had gone into crepe-paper wrinkles; her hair was all gray, and her eyes wore a film of sadness. Not really old—she couldn't be—surely not even sixty. Loneliness, disappointment, and grief, rather than time, had drained youth out of her. Using yesterday's eyes, I told her she looked beautiful.

"*You* do," she said. "*You* haven't changed."

At the bedside, Mama began: "So, Daisy, tell me. Tell me about our dear ones."

"Hannah and Dave," Daisy said, "they worry. Not over money. Karl sees to they have enough. The boys are the worry. Eugene. They heard he got out from Spain; they heard he is in France. But where? He doesn't write. Dave thinks he might be in prison. Dave says some people that got out from Spain were right away put in prison in France. . . . You wouldn't recognize Hannah, she got so old worrying. . . . Walt said he would find out, but he didn't find out. Walt makes them more worries. He comes to see them, and he fights with Dave. . . . Over what? The Russians. The Communists. . . . And they have Snooky. . . ."

"A cripple," my mother said. "Four sons. Not one gave my sister a grandchild. I was lucky." She glanced at me and lifted her chin. "Millie gave me two beautiful children. Look at the pictures, Daisy." These were the first words of praise my mother had ever said to me.

"And what is with Fanny and Reuben?" Mama went on to ask.

"Some other time," Daisy said.

"Tell. You don't tell, I will worry. I'll get a headache. The nurse will be mad."

"Reuben is trying to sell the business. Fanny complains she is sick, she can't help in the store. Reuben complains it gets too

314

much for him to take care of the store, her to take care of the house."

"So what will they do? Where will they go?"

Aunt Daisy moistened her lips, delaying before she could say, "Reuben says they will come live with me."

There was shock on Mama's face, then anger, a hardening jaw, flashing eyes. "No, Daisy, no! Not in one million years!"

My aunt braided her hands on her laps and twisted her fingers. She didn't speak.

"You had enough, you did enough," Mama said. "For Fanny a slave you don't need to be."

When Sunday's twilight had begun to descend and the nurse was giving us hostile glances, I put on the borrowed fur coat for the last time. Mama seized both of my hands, held them, and covered my forearms with kisses, not saying a word, just kissing me. It was an act of humility as much as affection, and startling because I couldn't remember one single time in the past when she had done more than drop a perfunctory kiss on my cheek. "Take care," she said hoarsely. "Be well and be happy, Millie."

While I packed, Daisy sat in the room watching, as she often had watched me preparing to leave her own house. "My sister, your mother, is right," she said quietly. "By myself I wouldn't have the heart to refuse Reuben and Fanny. But in my heart, I would know it was wrong. Before, all my life, nothing was too much, too hard. This would be too hard." Then she said, "But you, Millie, your family, you would always be welcome. That would be pleasure for me."

"Sell the house," I said. "Come to California. I'll take care of you. That would be pleasure for me."

She smiled with the gentle sweetness I had long known.

"I could not move away," she said. "If they came, they would never find me."

I knew whom she meant, I was certain I did, yet I asked.

"Ben and Arnold," she said. "If some day, some reason, they needed me."

"Where are they? Have you heard? Do you know?"

315

She shook her head. "Sophie has moved away. With the boy. They are no more in the telephone book. Not even her brother, the teacher; his family has moved away too."

"Ben?" I was being persistent.

"I tell myself," Daisy said, "he is living, and some day he might come back."

11 ❄

FROM A DISTANCE we saw them climb out of the Ferris wheel's gondola. We watched them starting toward us, Greta ahead, her golden pageboy and her eyeglasses sparkling, her skirt flicking to her body's prance. Jay lagged behind her, dabbing at his jacket with a handkerchief. He was white as chalk. "Daddy's sick!" Billy cried.

"It was scrumptious!" Greta greeted us. "You could see way out yonder. It was unbelievable!"

"It was horrible," her father said. "We could have been killed." I smelled vomit on him.

"Panty-waist!" Greta jeered.

His arm swung out. It missed her cheek and hit her collarbone. He sucked his fist; she rubbed her chest. "You should be arrested, striking a woman," Greta said. Billy looked ready to cry.

Billy had to be reminded—often he reminded himself—that at the age of twelve tears are unmanly. You bottle them, you stopper them, you exchange them for the silent seething of the teens. Girls are different. Emotional fireworks are expected; it has something to do with the menstrual cycle, I am told. Girls weep and storm, threaten and blackmail, until you give in. I should know; I used that technique when I was my daughter's age. Yet in this instance she might have been tolerant, since she knew her father was afraid of heights. Coming east, she and I had taken a plane; Jay and Billy had taken the Chief and the Century.

That being so, why had he given in to her and gone on the Ferris wheel? Because a father should protect a daughter—you can't let her take risks by herself? Or because good sportsmanship is masculine, all-American, and Burns needs, in minor matters like this, to prove he's one of the boys? Or because he is aware of his fear, and its presence embarrasses him?

I had said, "Thank you, no, I don't need the thrill." And Billy felt as I did. He'd bought himself an Eskimo Pie and lapped it contentedly while we watched the gondolas going up, swinging out, as if they planned to dump their passengers, then descend, once more circle and go up. "It's safe, isn't it?" Billy asked anxiously.

"Would they want to kill their customers?"

"Did you ever ride one?"

"I did not. When I came here, years ago, with some relatives, they just let me ride the merry-go-round. I was ten. That was enough excitement."

There were other excitements on that memorable day. What was the use of recounting them? Bill never knew the people involved. Water over the dam, under the bridge.

"Where in hell's a men's room?" Jay was demanding. "Have to wash off this gunk."

"I know where," Billy said. "I used it before." He trotted off with his father to help clean the gunk.

"Dad's a mess," Greta said. "More ways than one."

"That's enough out of Miss Burns," I said.

She sulked. "Well, he is. Believe me, Mother, it wasn't the Ferris wheel made him sick. He was drunk." She pinched her nostrils. "He stank."

Dear Greta, be patient, I thought; dear Greta, be kind. Yet all I said to my daughter was, "We've had enough Luna Park."

Billy was holding his father's arm, leading him, when they returned. Jay's color was normal, his jacket clean though damp. "Let's get the hell out of here," he said. "Had all I can take."

On the subway, riding to Manhattan, he said, "Your fault!" to me and I denied it angrily. Yet, in a way, this *was* my fault. Go back to where all this began: I had a cousin named Walt.

My cousin Walt had a friend named Nick. Ten years ago, eleven, to be precise, I welcomed—we welcomed—both of them into our house; we introduced them to our friends; we shared our food and liquor with them. And our principles. We could not guess—could anyone?—that being an anti-Fascist in 1936 would make you anti-American in 1947.

If Jay had insisted that I take the blame for Walt and Nick I would have dressed in sackcloth and gone down the canyon, beating my breast, crying, "I repent!" He didn't insist. He went mute, looking crushed, pouring himself another and yet another drink. Only after minor disasters like this unfortunate trip did he lash out at me.

But, good Lord! we had to do something, go somewhere; you can't keep the kids cooped up in a flat. Not California kids, brought up alongside a pool, living outdoors more than in, bodies browned, hair bleached by the sun.

The children despised New York. "It stinks," Greta said. "Stink" was her favorite word—she had inherited my keen sense of smell, but never with pleasure, always with repugnance: the apartment building's corridors that reeked of frying onions and camphored rugs; the B.O. in the subway cars; the fetid miasma, drifting from New Jersey factories and swamps, across the river that was a block from our flat.

I might have enjoyed having the river close; since childhood I've had a special feeling about rivers—they keep going straight ahead, shining, smooth, and purposeful. My daughter spoiled this one for me. "I wouldn't go near it if they paid me," Greta said. She was unbearable, impossible. Had I not known, from personal experience, that the teens do not last forever, I would have divorced the girl.

Central Park wasn't far, yet I hesitated to let the children go there alone: taxis, trucks, and trolleys were dangers they never had met; we'd chauffeured them everywhere.

There was a riding stable in Central Park. I promised Greta, after we were settled, I'd rent her a horse. I promised, too, we'd all go rowing on the Central Park lake. I promised Billy he would go to ball games—he had enjoyed the baseball broadcasts. Most of my promises stayed on the "next week, maybe" list. The horse rental was too expensive, and Jay rejected the ball park. "I do not care for those crowds," he had said.

"Your fans might recognize you," I said before I realized I was blurting truth. "They'd wonder what you were doing in New York."

"Exactly. Except they wouldn't wonder. They know Burns is out of work. The whole country knows. And I do not propose to satisfy their curiosity about how a man looks when he's down on his luck."

We did go rowing on the lake one Sunday afternoon, but Jay had insisted on handling the oars. He'd worn a wide-brimmed Panama hat and kept looking down—I don't believe he was recognized. He puffed and panted all the way back to the flat. "Damn near got a heart attack," he said, after he'd cooled off with a bottle of beer.

There were relatives, his and mine, in and close to New York. They were accessible and curious. They telephoned, invited us to them, themselves to us. "Eventually," I had to say. "Right now we're so busy, getting settled, there's such a lot to do."

A lot to do! True, true enough. But how soon do you emerge from shock? We went to the movies often. That was one way of staying in touch with people we knew. And the threaters were dark.

However, mainly through that July in New York we stayed in the flat, nursing wounds. Electric fans whirred in every room; the radio babbled continually. Billy worked up fair imitations of Charlie McCarthy and Mortimer Snerd. He tried them on his father, who was not amused. "One lousy actor per family is all the law permits." Billy and Greta played so much Monopoly that it became, in fact, monotony. Newspapers and magazines were strewn on the floors, on the furniture; we had a half dozen dailies, including *Variety*, delivered every day. Jay skimmed them for leads and tossed them aside. He made telephone calls. On the calls I overheard he was arrogant, head bloody but unbowed.

Restless, he moved from the phone to the refrigerator; nervous nibbling and too much beer made him put on weight. That also worried me. Days he slept, nights he prowled. Never verbal, unless the lines had been written for him, he didn't and he couldn't talk his worries out. Manliness, so the myth runs, requires locking yourself into yourself until you explode. The children, pretending to read, covertly watched Jay and me, alert for the snapping of nerves, for the glancing blows of words that would offer clues to what was happening to us.

We didn't know what was happening to us. It was what we did not know that mortified our nervous systems.

It had come as a shock, yet really it was not that sudden. There had been an encroachment, a creeping up, as relentless as a terminal illness. And a portent, out of Jay's subconscious dread. "I am not indispensable," he had told me in a midnight phone call to my father's house. We made light of the remark. Preposterous. James Burns is a star—competent and popular.

The fear became naked, plain on the day Franklin Roosevelt died. Greta's flippant sentence drove it home.

On the April afternoon when the President died, I was alone in our kitchen—Greta and Bill were at school, Jay at the studio, and Lupe, our Mexican housekeeper-cook, had gone to the dentist with an abscessed tooth; Carlos, her husband, had driven her there in our old Chevrolet. I was seasoning hamburgers for the patio grill; supper al fresco since Lupe did not feel well, the hamburgers to stretch our meat-ration points.

The cold-water faucet had an annoying drip. Carlos was no good at repairs; I hadn't been able to persuade a plumber—these days they behaved like kings—to drive up to replace a washer. The drip was distracting, because I had the kitchen radio on to entertain me while I worked.

I stood alongside the sink, molding meat patties, hearing the metronomic drip of water along with Beethoven's Sixth, until the music broke off with the news flash.

I dropped the meat into the bowl and leaned on the shelf; my knees turned to rubber, my brain to stone, hardening against the acceptance of an incredible fact. I thought—I clearly remember that thought—I'm alone in this house; when there's a death in the family you shouldn't be all by yourself. That man whose voice we had heard, whose face we had seen in newsreels, whose presence we had felt for so many years had become family. The father. The father image.

I heard the telephone ringing. Without wiping my hands, I answered it. I said, "Yes, I've heard," leaving grease prints on the phone. It rang again and again. People were calling, needing to share dismay and bewilderment.

Jay arrived first; they had heard the news on the lot, and the shooting had stopped. Jay took a bottle of Scotch into the family room and poured himself a stiff drink. "Who comforts whom?" he wanted to know. "Me you or you me?" And added, "God, how I loved him! What guts the man had!" He poured and drank a second drink. "This is no time for Roosevelt to die. The war isn't won. We'll be in one hell of a mess."

Billy came next, out of breath. He had pushed his bike up the canyon. "They dismissed us early; the President died." He leaned against my hip. "What's going to happen to us?"

"We'll have a new President," I said.

"Will he know what to do?" Billy asked.

"God knows," Jay said from the family room. He rocked his head in his hands. "We are bereft." His expression was funereal, his intonation dramatic. James Burns, the actor, was playing mourner to the hilt. He signaled for Billy to come to him; he held his son, stroking his hair, the tableau seeming to say, We need to stay close in this hour of extremity.

Lupe came next (Carlos was putting the car into the garage). Lupe held her hand to her swollen cheek. "Bad hurt," Lupe said. "You need me fix supper? Dentist said ice on the face." She spat blood into the sink.

I took out ice cubes, found an ice cap, tied it on her with a dinner napkin. "I'll fix supper," I said. "You go to bed."

Rabbit ears on the top of her head, she peered into the family room at Jay and Billy huddled. "Billy sick?" she asked.

"The President died," I said.

She stared at me blankly. "He was from the *señor's* family?" she wanted to know.

"My family, your family," Jay said.

"I have pain in my face," Lupe said.

Greta came last; she had stopped at a friend's place for tennis; they had driven her home. She came into the kitchen. "What's for supper? I'm famished. . . . Hamburgers again! I wish this darned war could get over. I'd like solid meat for a change." She snatched a gob of raw beef. "How soon do we eat? Have I time for a shower?"

"I don't think so. Dad's home." I pointed to the family room.

She went as far as the doorway, saw Jay and Billy together. She pirouetted on the sill, asking me, "What's the matter with them? Did something happen?" Apparently no one had told her the news.

"The President died," I said.

She reached for another gob of meat. "I was afraid it was something important. Like Dad got fired." A shot in the dark.

"Bite your tongue," I said.

For a while—a small interval, a matter of months—fear kept its distance from us. The war ended; Berlin lay in ruins; Hitler was dead; atom bombs fell on Japan. My brother, Bram, came home without visible scars, and Mama wrote ecstatically, "Now Bram and Judy will live in their house and start a family. . . . Papa says he will retire and give his business to Bram. Eshler is also making an offer to Bram. He and Judy will decide what they want." But Judy had written a poignant note:

"Of coure I am overjoyed to have him home. But, Mildred, it's like we never knew each other at all. I thought he'd jump into bed . . . and whoopee! I'm not getting younger, Mildred. If we're to have kids, we have to start soon. Bram stares at me as if he wonders why I am hanging around. My father says he'll snap out. My dad ought to know; he was away from the family a number of years. Oh, Mildred, I looked foward so. . . . Do you think he's in love with another woman? Or is this what they call combat fatigue? It isn't my fault, is it?"

Eugene Hitzig came home too, all bones and jaundiced flesh, corroded with memories of hunger, degradation, and perfidy. He had been in a prison in Vichy France, Aunt Daisy wrote me. He had opened an office in a slum neighborhood in New York, starting a new practice, lancing boils and giving diphtheria shots to kids. About Walt I had no word at all, and for that I was glad. Because there was a real and present danger to us in acknowledging a relationship to him.

Before the first Christmas of peace, some Congressmen in Washington had made up their minds that those of us who in the 1930s had waged an amateur's war against the Fascist menace had been tools of the Communists. A new war, the "cold" war, had begun. Overnight, a valiant ally was transformed into an enemy, a foe slimy and sly, who had insinuated himself into the blood stream of the United States. Via Hollywood.

Each Sunday night we heard on our radios, "Good evening, Mr. and Mrs. America and all the ships at sea, let's go to press. . . . The Commies, Hollywood Pinkos, the Comsymps . . ."

Laugh if you can, say this is too stupid. (That's what wise guys said when they read *Mein Kampf*.) Look here, both of the Gruening boys were in uniform; the younger one was at Guadalcanal. The scripts Howard wrote rang with patriotism. And Jay, on the screen, wore uniforms of the Army, the Navy, the Air Corps, the Marines. Three times a week Thelma and I rolled bandages and packed comfort kits at the Red Cross. We said goodbye—with tears—to our Japanese gardener when he was ordered to an internment camp; our roses withered, our grass was sere. This is war, my friends! Rationed meat, rationed cigarettes and gasoline. Go bare legged, the Air Corps has to have nylon. No bitching, no black marketing; this war must be won.

But now, with Roosevelt dead and the war won, a strange, sickening fear enveloped us. It began with the dredging up of past words and actions. It was spread by gossip, innocent sometimes, malicious often, out of envy, out of opportunism.

I chose to think that Dulcie, who had been a nursemaid in our house, was an innocent when she remarked to a customer whose gas tank she was filling at her husband's garage in San Bernardino, "Didn't I see you at the Burns place the day the Russian Communist was there?" Her query came back to us—quoted third or fourth hand. On its travels, how many other people had learned that on a certain Sunday ten years back the mysterious Nick had been our guest?

Acquaintances stopped calling on our phone; friends made lame excuses when we invited them.

The uneasy months came to a climax in the spring of 1947 when for the first time in seventeen years James Burns was out of work. A romantic adventure film had been set to start shooting when Jay's agent phoned: "The studio is replacing you. I just got the word." A contract broken, a threat tossed in. "Go ahead and sue. You'll be washed up for good."

Shocked and stunned, Jay sat on the patio, alone through the nights, carpeting the tiles with cigarette stubs. He breakfasted on gin, pulled down the blinds, and slept, sodden, till midafternoon; though now and then, at two or three in the morning, I'd be awakened by the noise of a motor, raced to warm up, and the whoosh of a car down the driveway. Sometimes Jay was gone for an hour or less, other times until late morning. Where he drove, whether he drove alone, whether he called on someone, I never knew, since he didn't say and I didn't ask. His temper was brittle, his rage so close to the surface that—this is a dreadful thing to admit—I was afraid that if I asked the wrong question, chose the wrong moment to pry, he would kill me. Not meaning to, but do you know how hard your hand hits when you slap? Moreover, I knew I bore part of the guilt for whatever was happening to us—if I had not welcomed Walt and Walt's friend—if I had had a grain of practical sense. . . . Yet what I did—what we did—was no crime. It was a right thing, a decent thing, an essential thing, within the framework of its time.

I told the children their father was sick, which was true—sick with outrage, sick with insecurity. They moved in and out of the house like wraiths, avoiding Jay as he avoided them. I envied the children. They were away during the days, off to school, though I wondered whether their classmates were harassing them. I stayed at home, holding my breath.

One evening at dinner, Jay announced he had put the house up for sale.

"But, Daddy"—Greta spoke first—"where will we go?"

"East. To New York," he told her.

"I like it here." She pouted. "This is home."

"Not any more. I belong in New York. I should never have left. I let their money, their fat checks—"

"Money isn't everything," I ventured.

His eyes flashed. "In a pig's eye!" Yet, he hunched forward, elbows propped up on the table. "God, I've missed the stage. Acting for people. To people. Seeing an audience, the audience seeing you. Human beings. Alive. . . . Goddammit, Mildred, do arithmetic; add up how many years it's been since I've heard applause."

It was in the front of my mind, on the tip of my tongue, to ask what stage offers he had. He didn't give me a chance. "I am sick unto death of this company town, of these frightened phonies." He scraped his bench back from the table. "Get rid of this crap, all of it." The sweep of his arm took in the adornments of the family room. "We should get a good price for this junk."

We should have. However, when prospects toured the house, you might have thought we were offering a slum, they found so much wrong with our place: the plumbing was old, some pipes would need to be replaced; there weren't enough bathrooms for this big a house; the kitchen equipment was ancient, that gas refrigerator is on its last legs; some roof tiles are missing, others loose; the house should be painted, inside and out; those bald spots on the lawn—don't your sprinklers work? The complaints were similar and so often repeated that I surmised word had spread: this is a distress sale. Burns, the pinko, needs to leave town; let's take advantage of him. We were lucky to get two thirds of our asking price. "It's a dead branch. Cut it off," Jay said.

Money didn't matter too much. We would not be poor—we had saved, we had war bonds. And if the worst came to the worst, there was my family. What mattered was Jay's morale. He had highs when he wrote letters and made long-distance calls; he had lows when the postman failed to bring replies, when a long-distance phone call yielded nothing more than "Wish you luck."

The children's morale stayed on one level—low. Greta was out-and-out hostile. UCLA had accepted her for the fall; must she give up college as well as her home and friends? And horse? After many tears and much stamping of feet, she accepted my compromise: come with the family to New York for the summer; return in the fall to live on campus. L.A. was near enough to her Hollywood friends. But the horse must be sold. And the house. And the cars. And the Spanish claptrap.

Our books, Victrola records, clothes, good silver, china, crystal, linens, blankets, and Jay's clipping books were packed to ship. To what address?

This time we could not look for temporary shelter in the Brooklyn house; it had been sold. A spate of letters had brought me the news. Mama's first: "I have talked Daisy in. She is not strong; last winter she had again bronchitis. She was too long a slave for tenants. My brother and Fanny, they don't understand; they would like her to be a slave for them. She must take care for herself, have an easier life. If she would only come here to live. . . ."

From Papa next: "You will be interested your cousin Karl found a buyer for the house in Brooklyn. He was smart; he waited till right after the war, when people was looking for homes. He got a good offer. By our old agreement we took a vote; the three sisters voted for, the one brother against to accept the offer. There is a nice few thousand dollars cash above the mortgage. Mama decided; she asked I should tell you—you don't need, Bram don't need, we don't need, all of us, thank God, have plenty—so Mama's one fourth will be in a special bank account in trust for her sister Daisy. Hannah has Karl to provide, Ada has me. Daisy has nobody to provide for her."

From Daisy last: "Your mother thinks she talked me in to sell the house. Millie, I made up my mind by myself. I was waiting, thinking maybe. Why was I waiting? For whom? For Reuben and Fanny to move here, with me? I am too tired, Millie. Karl helped me out; he found me a clean, sunny room with a kitchenette, in a hotel on Brooklyn Heights. What more do I need?"

My father wrote, after *our* house had been sold. "Come to us. If you want, we could rent a place in St. Agathe for the summer, you could enjoy the mountains and get a rest. New York in the summer is a furnace." And with guarded anxiety, he wanted to know why we had suddenly decided to leave California. "I suppose you know what you are doing."

Apparently, he had not learned from the papers or the Winchell broadcasts that James Burns had been dropped by his studio. Why it had happened, how long his nonemployment might last, we could not guess. All I knew was that Jay was in pain and was looking to Broadway to relieve his suffering.

Fritz Scheller, that Berlin director who one afternoon in our house had told us about fear, located shelter for us in New York. Friends of his, refugees, too, were going to Europe for the summer to see what they could salvage of what they had had to abandon when they had fled. They had a large apartment on West End Avenue—immaculate, Scheller guaranteed. If we wished, he would ask his friends to sublet to us. There was, he had heard, an apartment shortage in the city. We rented the place, sight unseen. There was a sorry symbolism, I thought, in living with the household goods of other refugees.

Jay and Billy left on the train; Greta and I spent our last night at the Gruenings. Thelma wept on my shoulder. "You're lucky you can afford to leave—nothing like having money; you can thumb your nose at SOBs. . . . Oh, Millie, Millie, I'll miss you." Howard Gruening said nothing; he looked like a ghost. His ulcer was troublesome, Thelma said.

Flying, Greta and I arrived before our men. A taxi brought us to an ugly building; a sullen janitor gave us keys. We came into summer-stifling rooms where graceless furniture was under shrouds. Greta dropped her valise, sat down on the bare parlor floor, and broke into tears. I flung the windows open. The hot stench of the city swept in. "It stinks, I hate it," Greta wailed. "I want to go home."

There was no home. There was no particular place where we now belonged except this temporary shelter. How long is temporary? It might be months, it might be years, because Jay had assumed a new role. He was The Victim, immersed in the part, playing it up to the hilt, seething with a sense of injustice done, raddled with a need to blame and punish somebody for this, desperately wanting to be cosseted and comforted, even while he rejected the smallest expressions of sympathy. "Confused" is a mild way of describing him.

Things were different for me; I had daily routines and responsibilities: groceries to buy, meals to prepare, clean shirts, fresh underwear and socks to be made available. And arrangements worked out for September: an apartment found and a school for Bill. I had no time to weep, wail, and gnash my teeth.

In sultry August I went apartment hunting. Jay made excuses —he was expecting a telephone call, or he needed to go downtown to meet so-and-so, or there was correspondence to be attended to— all of which stemmed from his reluctance to be recognized on this city's streets.

Greta wouldn't join us either. She said whatever I chose didn't matter to her; she would soon be going home to California. Besides, someone had to be around in case the phone rang and Dad was asleep or hung over. She spent her time writing to her friends and studying *Vogue*, *Glamour*, and *Seventeen*, to learn what the college crowd would be wearing this fall.

Billy went with me, though reluctantly, being divided in his loyalty. Dad needed him; Dad had found a crutch in Billy's sympathetic silence. I also needed him: this boy, so gentle, so compassionate, with no special gift except kindliness—which was more than strange since he had been conceived in violence. Dylan Thomas's wife, in a letter to her husband, once described her small son this way: "Colin is sweet as a bee." Billy, too.

Together we rode up wheezing elevators into decaying tenements, to find dreary rooms that faced dismal courtyards; we saw roaches skittering across cracked kitchen sinks. Billy was sickened by them.

"They aren't worse than the lizards that used to come into our house. You used to play with lizards."

"Our lizards were clean; they were friendly."

"Cockroaches are nuisances, not enemies."

I can bear even this, his slight shrug told me. William Burns, you comfort me with tolerance.

329

Eventually, we found a railroad flat not far from the college I had attended before I met Jay. Its living-room windows faced the Hudson River, the sunsets, and the winds from the west. The floors were parquet; the dining room had oak wainscoting; there was a large kitchen, with ample dish shelves. It had some of the old-shoe quality of the Brooklyn house. Billy said it would be okay, even though his room would be on an air shaft.

Next, I enrolled Billy in a private school, a "progressive" school about which I had read in a magazine. Thelma and I had discussed the article; we had agreed we would have liked this school for our kids.

In the beginning Mr. Niles, the administrator who interviewed us, was negative. William was applying for what they called the Middle School; most of the youngsters in that age group had been together for years; he wasn't sure William could adjust to them. Moreover, he wasn't even certain there would be a place for him this term. Then he took a second look at Billy's transfer sheet. "Burns." He stroked his long jaw. "By any chance related to the motion-picture star?"

"James Burns is my father," Billy said. Red carpets were spread instantly. This school, Mr. Niles hurried to tell us, had several celebrities' children. He tossed out names as if they came twelve for a dime. "I think we might be able to make a place for Bill. He should feel at home here."

We discussed the tuition fee and the cost of extras, like lunches and books. Mr. Niles seemed slightly uneasy, as though he expected me to dicker, to ask for discounts, as if it was my son's right and privilege to demand a cut rate in exchange for the publicity value of his father's name. While I wrote out a check for the first semester, Mr. Niles said, "Now, Bill, let's talk about you. Any special interests?"

"Lizards," Billy said. I stopped writing and stared at my son.

"Aha! Nature study. Biology."

"Just lizards. That's all that interests me."

"Isn't that rather limited, Bill?"

I said, "Pay no atention to him. It's a touch of homesickness."

Mr. Niles brightened. "Aha! He misses California. New York

330

must be quite a change. Was it in the papers—if it was I missed it—that James Burns had moved to New York?"

"He's returning to his first love, the stage," I said.

"And we're privileged to welcome his son." Mr. Niles patted Billy's shoulder. "With or without lizards." He chuckled softly. "One year we had a lad who did nothing except play with a turtle." He eyed Billy apprehensively. "Of course, he was in our nursery school."

"Billy," I asked while we were walking toward a subway kiosk, "why did you say such ridiculous things to Mr. Niles?"

He stared at the pavement. "I wanted him to think I was a screwball. I wanted him not to like me, not let me in his school."

"Why? It's a good school."

"They know who my father is," Billy said. "They'll ask me questions. I'd rather not answer questions about Dad."

In November, after we had moved new furniture into the flat, had emptied our cartons, put our dishes and our books on shelves; after Greta had flown back to California so blithely that her casualness devastated me; after Billy had mastered the subway route for his daily journey to school, Mr. Niles and the boys in Billy's group had no need to ask questions, because everyone, everywhere, knew exactly why James Burns had left Hollywood. A Congressional committee, set up to probe the alleged Communist influence in the films, had subpoenaed Jay to a public hearing in Washington. It was in all the newspapers—front page—and on the radio. Gossip, rumor, and innuendo had become common knowledge.

To my surprise Jay took the subpoena calmly; this was coming to terms with crisis. He even felt a surge of bravado. "I'll make mincemeat of those bastards. We have nothing to fear except fear."

"Won't you need a lawyer?" I asked.

"What for? Have I committed a crime?" Nevertheless, Jay gave it thought. "I don't know any lawyers. . . . Oh, yes, I do know one. Karl Hitzig, your cousin."

"That would be madness," I said.

My vehemence puzzled him. "He'd be a natural. Two of his brothers— Why, if any attorney would be sympathetic . . ."

331

"He is not your man," I said.

He didn't listen to me; he looked Karl's office number up in the Manhattan book and called him while I was out. He looked somewhat sheepish when he told me at dinner that Karl had said, "I don't believe I'm your man. Would you like me to recommend somebody?" He said Karl had sounded sincere when he wished him luck. "If I find I need someone—which I doubt—I'll call him again."

He began to prepare for the Washington hearings as though for a new role on the stage, assembling what seemed to him a proper costume: a pin-striped suit with padded shoulders and sharp lapels, a belted cashmere coat, a snap-brim fedora—a duplicate of what he had worn in *Dooley's Angels,* one of his better-known gangster films. He added a bright red four-in-hand tie, such as he had never worn on or off the screen. And while he preened himself in the mirror, he turned to inquire, "Would my family consider coming along?"

"Me, too?" Billy asked.

"Why not? This could be educational," Jay said.

Our train pulled in after dark. The floodlighted Capitol dome was impressive and serene, a symbol of dignity, strength, and purity. Looking at it, we started to relax. We strolled around the hotel lobby, examining the newsstand and the souvenirs. Billy saw a glass globe that held a miniature White House immersed in a liquid that produced a snowstorm when you turned it upside down. He was entranced.

Just once, when he was four, he had seen snow, on top of a mountain three thousand feet above the town of Claremont. I had driven the children up the mountain and allowed them to make snowballs. However, Billy had gotten a notion that the snow had come out of the ground, had grown like grass, not descended from heaven. There was a lot Bill didn't know.

I said he could buy the snowstorm in the glass if he wanted to. He decided no, let's not waste money; this trip was costing a lot. Jay took out his wallet. "We aren't that broke," he told Bill. Jay's mood was good, a healthy sense of excitement: tomorrow the curtain rises. He decided to step into the bar; you never know whom you might meet; there might be someone in town who will toss you a cue to what to expect. Billy and I could, Jay suggested, go up to our rooms if we wished.

"I've never slept in a hotel," Billy said in the elevator going up.

I began to say I hadn't either before I remembered Bermuda, that honeymoon so long ago, when our marriage began with a miscarriage on rough seas. Trust me, Jay had said. Trust me. Again and again.

In the morning he dressed in the outrageous costume, and before the full-length mirror he practiced the swagger and the strut with which he had played that part. "We'll give 'em a great performance," he said to himself and me. His step was springy while we climbed the Capitol steps.

The rotunda was packed—women and men, bobby-soxers, reporters, cameramen, a noisy, milling mob of celebrity-stalking ghouls. A woman screeched, "Jimmee! Jimmee Burns!" The mob surged toward us. Billy gripped his father's arm. Protecting Jay? Protecting himself? A girl thrust a card at Jay's face. "Sign. Sign, Jimmy. Please!"

All at once, Jay seemed unsure of how this role was to be played. He touched his hat brim, as if greeting an acquaintance on the street; he swept the fedora off, waving it and bowing. The flashbulbs popped. The cameras caught flamboyance.

Someone asked, "You Mrs. Burns? This your son? What's his name?"

"Puddintame," Billy replied. Jay seized my arm. A uniformed guard pushed back the crowd to make a path for us. Billy's face was white, his eyes glazed, as if he was going to be sick.

The hearing room was large, high ceilinged, crowded. Scanning it for vacant seats, I saw familiar faces, out of cocktail and dinner parties, out of the poker games at Gruenings', out of the drugstore at Hollywood and Vine. And I saw Thelma. She saw me. She got up, dropping her handbag on her chair, reserving her seat, and squirmed past knees to get to us. She flung her arms around me. "I've missed you, Millie."

I didn't answer her.

"Hello, Billy," she said. "Shouldn't you be in school?"

"Hello. No," Billy said.

Jay turned away, pretending he hadn't seen her. "Millie," Thelma whispered, "Howie couldn't help it. Honest. Tell Jay, tell him." And raising her voice, "When they break, wait for me. Let's have lunch."

"Maybe," I said, referring to the lunch. The rest of what she said had made no sense to me. What was it Howard had not been able to help? Did Jay know? If he knew, why had he not told me?

Up front, a gavel pounded. The chatter, shufflings, creakings dribbled out. Thelma wriggled back to her place. We sank into chairs in a back row. Across the room's length, I saw a thicket of microphones and, on a dais, a semicircle of men. From my distance they looked ordinary. A butcher, a baker, a candlestick maker. Congressmen. Inquisitors.

A stout man with a suety face twisted a microphone around to his jowls. A squeal, like chalk on a blackboard, rasped taut nerves. Jay inspected the hat on his knees. His lips were moving, as if he was rehearsing lines.

The gavel came down again. "Robert Rawley! Is Robert Rawley in the room?" An aging character actor whom we barely knew moved with a dignified shuffle up the aisle toward the microphones. Jay's nose made a noise—a snort or a violent sniffle. He punched a crease in the crown of his hat.

"Mr. Rawley, are you now or have you ever been a member of the Communist Party of the United States?"

"I am not. Nevah."

"Have you been aware of certain activities, inspired—we may say, directed—by agencies of the Communist Party of the United States?"

"I have most certainly."

"Detail them, if you please."

Whether Jay listened to question and answer, whether he was distressed or dismayed or even remotely concerned by what he heard, I could not guess, since his eyes were shut. Now and again he yawned, without covering his mouth. Once he shifted, as if waking up from a doze, and his hat skidded to the floor. Billy bent for the hat and held it on his own lap, punching the crown crease in with his fist, reshaping it.

"Give me my hat," Jay muttered to him. The mutter was loud. Heads turned in our direction. I heard Jay's name traveling the seats. The gavel rapped. The suet face scowled.

By the watch on my wrist it was half past twelve when Robert Rawley stepped down and the chairman banged his gavel. "The committee will adjourn. We will resume at two P.M."

We edged out slowly, trapped in congestion at the door. I felt Thelma's hand on my arm. "Let's find a nice place for lunch. Some place where we can talk."

"Count me out," Jay said.

"Howie's not here," Thelma told him.

"Nevertheless, count me out," Jay repeated. "I have to see a man"—he stared hard at Thelma—"about a dog."

"But, Millie," Thelma said in the ladies' room at the restaurant, "Howard hadn't a choice. You must understand our position. We're not well-fixed like you—Howie has never been anywhere near Jay's salary bracket. And we don't have relations who can help us out. On the contrary, we're the ones who help out. Howie has an old, sick mother in the Bronx. He supports her, as well as his widowed sister who looks after her. And Howard's ulcer—you know how he's had to coddle it—it's been murder this year. They're talking about surgery. Scares hell out of us—you know what these things can be. Last time I had a physical, my blood pressure was over one-sixty. Me!" She leaned against the washstand, needing support. Her flushed face quivered like a rabbit's. "Millie, Howard *had* to name Jay. But after all, certain details were general knowledge, were they not? . . . Oh, no, he never said Jay was in the Party; Howard would never lie about that. Under no circumstances, Millie, not even these. . . . Why, I can clearly remember how we climbed the walls with Jay when Howie defended the Pact. That proved it to us, didn't it? But, Millie, you cannot deny that Jay brought your cousin and his comrade to our house. Why, both of you were ecstatic about Nick."

"Is Howard working?" I asked.

She had the grace to lower her eyes—"He will be after the first of the year"—though she had to raise them to plead: "Oh, Millie, Millie, it's been hellish for him—for us."

"Let's go in and order," I said. "Be my guest. . . . I insist. I have the rich relatives."

Walking back to the Capitol, she tried to pretend that shreds of friendship remained still. "Billy, do you like your school in New York?"

"It's okay."

"Weren't you lucky they had a place for you?"

"No," Billy said, then hurried to change his monosyllable. "Yes."

"I'll bet you miss your sister?"

"Yes and no," Billy said.

Jay entered after the gavel had pounded, while the brass-haired mother of a female star was testifying; I had put my hand-bag on a chair to hold a place for him. While he lowered himself into the seat, I whispered, "Where were you?"

"Congressional Library."

"What for?"

"To read. Refresher course."

Our whispers must have been loud. "Those who have something to say will get their chance when the committee calls them," the chairman told his microphone. "Please continue," he told his witness. Her tongue tip oiled her scarlet lips. "Well, I have made it my practice to read the script before my daughter accepted a part. Under no circumstances would I allow her to mouth their propaganda. They are sly. Insidious." She'd mangled the final word; it came out "inside-us." It brought strangled laughter.

Jay crossed his legs. The fedora slipped. Billy dived for it; his palms brushed the felt, caressing it while he dusted.

"What did Thelma say?" Jay whispered to me.

"Howie cooperated; she is sorry; let us be friends."

"Now, madam, do you personally know of any individuals, male or female, whom you knew to be members of the Communist Party or sympathizers with it, who appeared in pictures in which your daughter acted?"

336

"Well—" A red fingernail scraped the witness's front teeth. "There were several—most, I would say, were of the Jewish persuasion...."

A loud, long boo came from one corner; an angry murmur raced through the room. Jay ground his teeth. I squeezed his arm; he shook my hand off.

It was after three when the microphone bleated, "Burns. James Burns." There was a rustle, a craning of necks, while Jay marched to the front of the room. His stride was defiant, his spine rigid, as though in a brace. The costume he had on was absurd.

"State your name." The chairman's voice had a peculiar timbre.

"Jacob Bernstein." He flung it out to the room—that name he had discarded decades earlier, a name his son had never heard. Billy's eyes opened wide, questioning. His hand groped for mine as if needing assurance that I had not changed.

"Well, Mr. Bernstein–Burns, since you have been accurate in replying to the first question, the committee trusts you will be equally truthful with your reply to the next. Are you now or have you ever been a member of the Communist Party of the United States?"

"I am not now, and I have never been."

Bill's questioning gaze was on me again. "True," my whisper told him.

"Yet you have demonstrated your sympathy with that party's aims and purposes?"

Jay's chin firmed; his personality appeared to change; his demeanor becoming dignified and grave. "There is an amendment to the Constitution of the United States," he said, loud and clear. "Number Five." Then he clamped his mouth shut.

They hurled questions at him, the chairman and his colleagues. To every question he gave one reply: "I stand on my rights under the Fifth Amendment to the Constitution of the United States."

"Now Mr. Bernstein–Burns." The chairman tried a fresh approach, "You hide behind that Fifth Amendment because you are under oath, and if you decided to answer truthfully, you would be compelled to admit that you have been a participant in activities subversive to our form of government. Is this what you wish the committee to believe, Mr. Bernstein–Burns? . . . Now, is it or is it not true that in the month of December, 1936, you entertained as a guest in your residence at Hollywood, California, one Walter Whitman, an agent of the Communist Party of the United States?"

"I stand on my rights under the Fifth Amendment."

"And is it not true that you also entertained in your residence in Hollywood an agent of international communism, a representative of the organization known as the Comintern?"

"I stand on my rights under the Fifth—"

"Can you deny that in the month of January, 1937, you were the host of a gathering in the aforementioned residence, where both the aforementioned persons were present and where a large sum of money was contributed by your guests for a radical cause, in this instance, a Communist government in Spain?"

With a guileless smile and a gentle tone, Jay answered him: "I was in favor of the legitimate republican government of Spain." He raised his eyes to the chairman. "I was opposed to the Fascists. Weren't you?"

Applause swept the room. The gavel pounded. "I caution the spectators against outbursts like this. If it happens again, the room will be cleared. . . . Mr. Bernstein–Burns," he began again, "is it or is it not true that you voluntarily turned over the sum of money contributed by the guests in your house on that date to one Walter Whitman, an organizer for the Communist Party of the United States?"

"Fifth Amendment," Jay answered him.

Someone stepped up to the chairman, whispering, comparing the watches on wrists. "The committee will adjourn for today. It will reconvene promptly at ten thirty A.M. tomorrow. The witness is to hold himself in readiness for further questioning. We trust that by that time he will have decided to cooperate with this investigation."

People, strangers to me, surrounded Jay. Billy and I waited near the entrance for him to break free. When the crowd had thinned, he made his way to us. "Go back to the hotel. Have your dinner. Don't wait for me."

After we had eaten in the hotel's dining room, I bought an evening paper in the lobby. "Burns Takes The Fifth," a front-page headline announced.

"Does that mean Dad will go to jail?" Billy asked.

"Nothing of the sort," I told him.

"I don't believe those were Congressmen," Billy said. "They sounded so—so un-American."

"Come up to the room," I said. "Let's not talk down here."

He crouched on the edge of my bed, poring over the paper. "They have the name—the other name," he said. "Why didn't I know it?"

"Your father changed it—legally—before you were born. For professional reasons. Actors often changed their names."

"But wasn't Bernstein his parents' name? Didn't they mind?"

"I don't believe he asked them."

"But they're alive, aren't they? Don't they have rights? I mean, how would you and Dad feel if I changed my last name without asking you?"

"Why would you want to?" I thought I knew what answer he was ready to give. He seemed to sense what I was thinking because he said, "I mean I could be William Bernstein, couldn't I?"

"You could. Except your birth certificate says Burns."

"But, Mother, since everyone knows my father's James Burns, why did he have to tell the other name?"

This troubled him, I realized, and I had to try to explain. Making it clear was going to be difficult. "Bill," I said, "I don't believe your father realized until today how much of a Jew—how much Jake Bernstein—he was. You see, Bill, Jews are like chameleons; they take on colorations of wherever they happen to be. They look like Gentiles, they live like Gentiles, they take Gentile names because they think that makes it easier for them to get along. After all, why should they hang on to European names in the United States? But the instant they catch a whiff of danger, a danger not merely to them, but to other Jews—like when that woman made an anti-Semitic remark . . ." I paused. "Bill, do you know what anti-Semitism is?"

"I'm not sure I do." His expression was thoughtful, his

phrases slow. "I read about Hitler and what Hitler and his Germans did to Jews. But that was over in Europe, and that was the Nazi craziness that we had to fight the war against. And what that woman said was only a remark that most of the Communists she met in Hollywood just happened to be Jewish."

"That's it, Bill. That's how it starts. In Germany, in any place. Blame Jews. Accuse all of them of what some individuals may be or may do. Stir up a fear, a hatred. Make what you dislike, what you fear, sound like a Jewish plot. Now, ordinarily your father doesn't go out on the barricades, but there are certain things he does care about—like justice, like the dangers of prejudice. He must have felt this was a moment of danger, so he had to speak up and declare himself, to take a stand, to ally himself with other Jews."

Even while I tried to explain this to Billy, I found myself wondering exactly why Jay had made the gesture. A far as I knew, he had had little Jewish background. My family had been traditional: we'd observed the holidays, we'd tried to keep the moral authority of the Jewish family, we'd even spoken some Yiddish at home. But Jay's middle-class family had seemed to me neither fish nor flesh. Undefined. Yet, after all, how well did I know them? And how well did I know their son? Was this a role Jay was playing, a part he had written himself for himself?

"You think we ought to be proud of Dad?" Billy asked.

"I think we should," I said.

He moved over to a window, pulled up a blind, stood staring at the lights of downtown Washington, thinking, doing his moral arithmetic, I hoped, calculating how much was gained—how much was lost—by his father speaking out. He turned. "Mother, could I be Canadian if I wanted to?"

"Not right off the bat. You'd have to emigrate, be naturalized there. You're American, you know."

"But you're Canadian, aren't you? You could—you could leave the United States if you wanted to. You could walk away from this—this mean, unfair nastiness, couldn't you?"

"Bill," I said, "what makes you think all Canadian politicians are pure and holy? Believe me, they have anti-Semites there, too. In any case, I can't run away. Whatever happens to your father also happens to me. We're married people, Bill. And whatever went on in our house, I was a part of it."

He fiddled with the Venetian-blind cord, twisting it around his forefinger and unwinding it while he decided what next to say. "That was a bum show today," he said finally.

"You have to believe in your father," I said. "You have to trust him."

He picked the newspaper up. "Mind if I take this to my room? I want to read what they say."

Minutes later, before I'd begun to undress, he opened the connecting door. "Another thing, Mother, who was this Walter Whitman?"

This was no time for fresh revelations; the boy was already carrying too much emotional baggage. I dismissed his question with a hand wave. "Dear once," I said.

He frowned. "What does that mean?"

"What does it sound like? That's what it means."

"You're as hard to understand as my father is," Billy said.

I filled the bathtub and soaked to get kinks out of my nerves; they had been twisted hard by what went on in the hearing room, by Thelma's admission that Howard had played Judas and by the need to try to explain to my son what was hard to explain. "With what eyes will my son look at me?" Ben Kuper, if I live one hundred years, I shall not forget how *you* looked when you asked that question. Nor forget how you and your son looked at one another. No more awful thing can happen between a father and a son. . . .

Where is Jay? With whom? Is he getting drunk? I hope not. Sober, he has damaged himself sufficiently. By what? By revealing his name? Is that criminal? By admitting he was an anti-Fascist ten years ago? (And exactly when—exactly why—did that become criminal?) No. By defying. By taking the Fifth.

To protect himself? Or to protect me?

I climbed into bed, thinking I would read. Billy had the news-

341

paper. I found a Gideon Bible in the night-table drawer. One book I always intended to read when I could spare the time. . . . "In the beginning God created the heaven and earth." . . . Out of chaos, into chaos. My eyelids were heavy. I closed the book and slept.

I woke to the noise of retching. The bedroom lights were on full, and in the bathroom Jay crouched over the toilet bowl, pale as death, heaving, with no stench of alcohol. I swabbed his face with a cold, wet towel before I led him out. I helped him to undress, turned back his spread, prepared his bed. Apparently, he had been in the room quite a while; the desk was strewn with scribbled sheets, the wastebasket full of crumpled paper. "Statement," he managed to mumble. "Read it to the bastards tomorrow."

"Tomorrow," I echoed. "Tonight, get some sleep."

I pulled up his blanket and sheet, tucked them around, started to gather up the scribbled paper.

"Read it, why don't you?" he said from the bed.

"Tomorrow," I said. I snapped off the desk lamp.

"Come here," he said.

He seized my hand, both hands. "Millie, what do I do about Gruening? How do I fix that SOB?"

"Tomorrow. Think about it tomorrow," I said.

"Now." His eyes were desperate.

"You were wonderful today," I said. "Bill and I were proud."

"I was crazy. Cooked my goose. Sent my career to hell. I should have cooperated." He was clinging to my hands. "Like Howie. Son of a bitch."

"Don't talk. Don't think. Not now." I drew my hands out of his. I put out all the lights. In the total darkness I climbed into his bed. Surprised but pleased, I believe, he shifted to leave room for me. I put my arms around his body and held him tightly. It seemed to me his tautness lessened just a bit. I stroked his cheeks, his throat, his chest. He clutched my wrists, guided my hands down to his groin. "Here, Millie, here. Try, Millie. Please! . . . Keep trying, Millie!" His mouth was on mine, his teeth bruising my lips; his loins on mine, pushing, rubbing, panting. His penis remained limp and unresponsive. At last he flung himself away. "Even this!" he sobbed in the darkness.

When we let ourselves into the flat, the telephone was ringing. I picked it up. "Will you accept a collect call from Miss Burns in Los Angeles?" the operator asked.

"Put her on," I said.

"Mother, where have you been?" Greta demanded. "I have been calling and calling."

"I've been in Washington. With Dad."

"Then it's true—what he said, what he did, what the papers reported. . . ."

"I've not read your papers, I don't know what they said. . . ."

"But is it true he consorted with Communists?"

"You, too," I said. "With love and kisses."

12 ❋

"UNEMPLOYMENT, JAKE, you should know, I should not have to tell you, is and has always been an occupational hazard of your profession." Quotation from Karl Marx Hitzig, Esq., spoken in the living room of the Burns apartment in New York on a March evening in 1949.

The speaker sat in our comfortable armchair, facing the sofa where Jay and I awaited The Word. Between us, in an ash tray on the coffee table, a Corona-Corona smoldered.

Jay had bought the cigar, had, in fact, bought half a dozen, a wanton extravagance in our circumstances. He had also purchased a bottle of Courvoisier, to demonstrate to my cousin that we were not candidates for Home Relief. Not yet, though it was close. Since November, 1947, James Burns, motion picture star and one-time Broadway actor, had had three weeks of paid employment, no more, in a Chekhov play produced on a shoestring by a high-minded Greenwich Village group. Salary eighty-five a week. No rehearsal pay. One reviewer had mentioned Burns: "Others in the cast included . . ." Consider this an act of mercy. Malice might have written that Burns had had trouble with his lines. Drunk? Demoralized? No, gentlemen of the press and ladies of the gossip columns, it's merely that Burns is not in good health. He doesn't eat; he rarely sleeps—not in his own bed anyway. His nerves are shot. I've begged him to see a doctor. He won't. I've never had much influence over my husband's personal habits. A willful man. Stubborn. Moreover—this I keep in mind and perhaps he also does but will not admit—his theatrical experience is limited. In that long-run hit that boosted him to Hollywood, he wisecracked, he sang and danced (with a girl named Bonnie Granger). He has aged beyond male ingenu yet isn't mature enough for Uncle Vanya. With his background, he should have been a natural for television. There has not been a nibble from the agencies.

How do we pay our rent and buy our groceries? Well, in the fat years on the Coast, we did put money into the bank; the sale of the hacienda gave us another nest egg. However, savings melt; they turn to water when each day is rainy. But there's a great gentleman who made a special trip from Montreal. To get acquainted with his only grandson was the excuse he gave.

Diffidently, unnaturally formal, he extended his hand to Jay. "Sam Samuelson. I bet you couldn't recognize me. I don't blame you, a long time since we met. You, I wouldn't have one bit of trouble recognizing; you look just like in the moving pictures." He bit his tongue, fearing he'd been tactless. "Mrs. Samuelson, my wife, Millie's mother, she nagged me, I should run down to New York, see how the children are getting along, if they need something. Mrs. Samuelson gave me the privilege to extend an invitation: come, all of you, to us. We have a big house, we rattle around in so many rooms. It would be a pleasure—*our* pleasure. Especially to introduce your fine young son—our grandson—to our friends. You would have no expenses, no overhead, no worry, a good char so Millie wouldn't put her hands in cold water.

"And Judy, Bram's wife, my son's wife—Millie knows what a fine girl she is, goodhearted as the day is long—she sent a special message to you, Mr. Burns: I should remind you in Canada we also have theaters. And we make some moving pictures. A little television, also. A man with your experience, Burns—they would welcome you with opened arms. And for such *momsers* like your big-mouth Congressmen, we have very little respect. A clean country, Burns. Not scared of a—of a—" He faltered, for the moment finding it impossible to pinpoint Jay's iniquity.

"I'll think about it," my husband said, but desultorily. Citizens of the United States do not lightly abandon their country. There's an ingrained birthright of national superiority. And a dread of change of climate. It *is* cold up there.

"While you're thinking over," Papa went on to say, "Mrs. Samuelson and me, we don't want our daughter's family to worry over money. We have plenty and enough for our own selves—how much do two older people need? And everything that is left when we pass on will be for Millie and Bram, anyway. But why should Millie wait till we pass on? I will send—every month. Please, Millie don't give me arguments; let your father have his little pleasure. Only stay healthy. That's all Mama asks."

Stay healthy when rejections and humiliations gnaw your gut. When the fear that was all we had to fear has moved in with us.

Jay and I talked little because there was little to say; how often can you ask your husband, "Did you find a job?" He was trying—this I had to believe—seeing people, telephoning, making contacts. I dared not let myself suspect he had given up. Yet—what's true is true—his stage experience had been limited and long ago. In normal times, producers might have considered the publicity value of a Hollywood name. Today, the word was out: Don't touch Burns with a ten-foot pole, unless and until he clears himself.

Moreover, Jay and I talked little these days because previously we seldom had. From the beginning of our knowledge of one another, we had failed to build a base of verbal exchange. A spontaneous, mutual attraction was what we'd started with before we'd built a loyalty out of our respective guilts. There had been a time when his philandering had troubled me, and I had thought of leaving him. Yet when I found myself wondering why I had stayed, I realized this was because he had never mentioned wanting to leave me. He wanted me and needed me, more than he wanted and needed any other women he had met. Though in this prolonged period of stress, we rarely found the words to help one another, nevertheless I sensed that the very fact that I was at his side gave him courage to continue, to fight to get back.

The days, of course, were easier for me than him. I had the household duties, the shopping and the cooking, the making beds, the tidying up. And Billy to care for. Jay had spurts of interest in him. Some evenings, he'd sit in Billy's room, watching him do his homework, looking over his written papers, mildly offering criticism. Sometimes he read Shakespeare to Bill. *Hamlet*. Never *Romeo and Juliet*.

We had been lucky in our choice of Billy's school. To its liberal-leaning faculty and parents, the reasons for Jay's present plight were admirable. When, for instance, I mentioned that I might not be able to pay a term's tuition promptly, Mr. Niles wrote, offering Bill a scholarship. His letter brought tears to my eyes. So did the "round robin" testimonial from a group of the parents, though Jay was furious at it. "This and a dime gets me a cup of coffee in the Automat!" he jeered. "I don't want to be their hero. I don't want to be a martyr. All I want is to get back to work."

But Bill was sheltered, Bill was safe within that school. He had his daily subway trip, his place to go to, his nine-to-four sanctuary.

And Greta at UCLA also was safe, cocooned in the selfishness of youth, accepting her allowance checks with ill grace, hinting that, really, we should buy her a car—it was impossible to get around Los Angeles without a car; didn't we want her to have a social life? Judging and misjudging her parents, the way young adults do, knowing and stating emphatically what they should have done and what they ought to do but making a world of her own, as I had made mine at her age. And keeping a *cordon sanitaire* between herself and our insecurities.

The problem was Jay. He had become desperate. Desperate men do foolish things. He telephoned to Karl; he made a date for Karl to come to our flat. I would not have sent for Karl. I had no stomach for the moment when he'd say, "I was right about Jake, wasn't I?"

The resentments I had harbored all these years had been bolstered when I read the letter he had written to Uncle Reuben.

"Go, Millie," Mama had begged me during a long-distance call. "Take a couple of hours some afternoon, pay Reuben a visit. You go sometimes to see Daisy in her hotel; she appreciates the visit. Reuben will appreciate even more. He is terrible lonesome in that Home. Hokay, crazy about your Uncle Reuben you never

347

were, even when you were a kid. He was bossy; she was more bossy than him. But when he was an active man, he tried the best for the family. Now he got old, and he is alone; she is passed away. And his sisters can't do nothing for him. I could maybe take him for two weeks, give him a vacation from the Home. But Papa says if I had him in the house two days he himself would get a stroke. . . . I know, I know, Reuben is a *nudnick*. You listen to him he tells you he knows more and better than everybody. But, Millie, Reuben is a human being. Be a good girl, do a *mitzvah*, give him a visit. What will it cost you?"

The price of a box of Schrafft's chocolates and subway fare to the northern reaches of the Bronx, to the Goldmark Home and Hospital for Aged Hebrews, a monument in yellow brick to that legendary Herschel whom Grandpa Springer had tutored for Bar Mitzvah. And to Herschel's warmhearted wife who had furnished bed and board to greenhorns back in the last century. Aunt and uncle to my Aunt Fanny. And to her brother, Ben.

At first, I didn't recognize my uncle among the ancients in the lobby: the old, old men in baggy pants and open-at-the-collar shirts; the old, old men with blue-veined, rust-splotched hands and rheumy eyes, sitting, staring at nothing, lost in the haze of memories. Reuben had been nodding, dozing with an open newspaper on his lap. The sound of my voice, asking where the information office was, woke him up. "Millie!" He braced himself on the chair arms, rising. The Kaiser Wilhelm mustache was gone; his sunken cheeks were gray with stubble; his once-ostentatious paunch was a pendulous sac.

"Millie, you came to see the uncle!" His eyes began to tear. Arms extended, he shuffled toward me; his carpet slippers were too large. I side-stepped his embrace and shook his hand. He nudged the old man who'd been sitting beside him. "Itzkowitz, here is my niece, Mrs. Burns. From Hollywood . . . Yeh, she came from Hollywood to visit me. You sometimes saw her husband's moving pictures, Itzkowitz? . . . Yeh, yeh, James Burns, the gangster."

Itzkowitz offered me a flabby hand. Other old men, jolted out of daydreams, eyed us. Jealously, I thought.

"Come upstairs, Millie. Come up to the room." Uncle Reuben held my hand, propelling me toward the elevator bank, imperiously commanding an attendant to take us up. In a corridor that reeked of disinfectant, he hoarse-whispered, "Downstairs, they shouldn't hear my private business. The *alte kockers*. Buttinskis." He opened a door. "My home. Mr. Reuben Springer lives here."

It was eight by five; it held a dresser, an armchair, a single bed, covered by a faded light-blue crinkled cotton spread. The narrow window, half-curtained, offered a glimpse of sky and motor traffic. The walls were drab, needing paint. On the dresser stood a radio and a framed, familiar photograph. He saw me eye the picture; he carried it to me. "My bride. My life's partner," he said. His eyes started to tear. I hurried to offer him chocolates.

"Candy?" He shook his head. "They don't let me eat sweet stuff. They watch every bite I put in my mouth, Millie." He leaned to my ear. "The food is for a dog. And baby portions they give. You remember what a wonderful cook my Fanneh was? You ate in our house when you was a kid."

I remembered the quantity too well.

"You remember, Millie, our beautiful home? With the front porch and the yard? Now, this, like a closet, is Mr. Springer's home." A sigh came from deep in his chest. "A private room. They do me a favor. If not for my Fanneh, she should rest in peace, she had an uncle, Herschel Goldmark, he also should rest in peace, he left a big sum money to build the building, so for the family of Herschel Goldmark they give a private room." He examined the candy-box lid, reading aloud the Schrafft name, nodding as if approving my selection. He put the box on the dresser, alongside the picture frame. "To the head nurse I will give this. She looks all the time for presents. Graft." He managed a wink. "Sit down, Millie. Sit."

"You take the chair," I said. "I'll sit on the bed."

He pursed his mouth, forbidding. "Not allowed. It dirties the spread." He sounded like Fanny, warning young Millie.

Nevertheless, I made him take the chair while I perched on its arm. He seized and held my hand, kissing the back of it. "You came to see the uncle, you had pity on him. . . . You heard my

Fanneh passed away? . . . I thought maybe nobody told you; you didn't come to the funeral. Since you married with the actor, you became a stranger to your dear once. . . . Hannah's children didn't come neither, not one single one. . . . My Fanneh is in the plot that I arranged for our family. When God calls for me, my place is waiting; we will be again together, me and her. . . . She was a long time sick, my Fanneh, how much that woman suffered, nobody knew, only me. The worst, I tell you, Millie, the pain that killed Fanneh, was the aggravation, the worry from what happened to her brother, Ben. . . ."

Knowing much, yet knowing nothing, I asked, "What became of Ben? What happened to him?"

Reuben shook his head. "What happened—I tell you the honest truth—nobody knows, like in the ocean he fell." I doubt he realized what he was saying; his subconscious, possibly, had evolved the parallel. "Fanneh thought maybe they took him to the war, he was shot dead by the Nazis. I told her he was too old for the war. Fanneh was going crazy, worrying. Millie, from the day he walked out from the house in Brooklyn, not one word from him.

"Fanneh loved him like a son," he went on. "From a little child she raised him after the parents died in Europe. With her own money, she bought the ticket to bring him to America. And she found for him a good wife." He paused, his forehead furrowed, trying to pull threads together. "There was a son, a smart kid. Fanneh had a little sum money saved up in the bank. 'We have no children,' she used to tell me. 'This will be for Benny's son.' How many times she called up Sophie on the telephone. Every time Sophie gave her only insults. The last time Sophie said, 'We are moving away, me and Arnold, with my brother's family.' To Florida. Not Miami Beach, some other place. 'I am sick and tired of the crazy calls from his rotten family.' Yes, Millie, to Fanneh she said 'rotten family.' What could Fanneh say? A dirty business is a dirty business. A married man, the father from a son, makes monkey business with a *nafke*." He slewed around in the chair, fixing me with a defiant stare. "Millie, Fanneh was sick ashamed from that kind monkey business. . . ." He straightened himself in the chair, as if forcing, bracing, his dignity. "Millie, I tell you something I never told to anybody. Like a brother and sister, me and Fanneh lived out our lives. She said a doctor told her she could never born a child. So, if not to have a child . . ."

I drew away, repelled. Fanny had cheated this man; she had made him a eunuch. Why, he had been a romantic youth. Those treasured volumes in the bookcase in his house, *Hid from the World*. But am I different from Fanny? Yes, I've not denied my husband. Nor have I welcomed him.

Reuben tugged my sleeve, drawing attention back to himself. "She was a sister to me, a better sister than the three I brought from the old country, that I gave the start in their lives. For your mother, Ada, I found a husband, a first-class husband. No? . . . Hannah grabbed for herself. What did she grab? A Socialist. He made a poor living always. And from her sons what does she have? Two Communists. One cripple. One snob. The big cheese. The fixer." He pulled himself up, out of the chair. "Wait, Millie, I got something to show you." He shuffled to the dresser and rummaged in its cluttered top drawer. He handed me an envelope that bore the name and address of a Manhattan law firm.

"Read the letter, Millie. Read what he wrote to an uncle. Read!"

I read:

Dear Uncle Reuben:

It is a long time since you and I have had a visit and a chance to talk together. I would have liked to sit down and have a good *shmoos* with you, but as you may have heard, my profession keeps me hopping. In addition, I have responsibilities toward my parents and my youngest brother. Whatever time I have to spare, I spend with them. So you see, I do not have much opportunity to visit with other members of the family.

I am writing this letter to inform you that I have finally arranged for the sale of the Brooklyn house. I believe I have gotten a good price, considering the condition of the property—the building is run-down and needs extensive repairs, including a new roof.

According to an agreement signed by you and your

351

sisters, as heirs of the late Yankel Springer, all cash above the mortgage is to be divided equally among the four of you. As soon as we receive the payment, I shall mail you a check for your one-fourth share. Since I am acting as a favor to my Aunt Daisy, and also at the urging of my mother, who joined her sisters, Daisy and Ada, in approving this sale (according to the existing agreement which required the approval of three parties), I am charging no fee for my services.

You had written to Daisy, stating that as soon as you could sell your business, you planned to retire, and you and Fanny proposed to move into the house in Brooklyn, which you used to call the "family shrine." Aunt Daisy was troubled when she received your letter, because, as you well know and I do not need to remind you, she is devoted to her family. However, she felt she was no longer in a physical condition to maintain the house and provide for the comfort and care of you and your wife. And so she urged me to put the building on the market and requested me to inform you that you and Aunt Fanny must work out another solution for your retirement.

With best wishes for your health and happiness,

Your loving nephew,

Karl Hitzig

P.S. Regarding the condition of the family plot, I have been in touch with the cemetery people. They have assured me the fence will be repaired as soon as they can obtain the necessary materials. I shall keep after them.

I thrust the letter back into the envelope and offered it to him. He refused to take it.

"Keep it, Millie. I saved it for you. You were secretary of our Family League. Show it to anybody, everybody, whoever you want. Intelligent people should understand what can happen in a lifetime to a family." His eyes and throat were filling; he could barely speak. "It stabbed my Fanneh to the heart," he faltered. "I called up Daisy on the telephone, I asked her what got into her? She forgot Fanneh has rights? Fanneh found the house before the sisters came off Ellis Island. Her uncle, Herschel Goldmark, helped out to buy the property. Daisy started crying on the telephone. They talked her in, she said. Who talked her in? Who is they? Him! The big cheese, the fixer, Hannah's boy. Who needs to listen to that *shneck?* Does he know from family feelings? Daisy keeps on crying she is tired. So who is not tired? Fanneh and me are not tired? Like dogs we worked our whole lives. It has to be like this, Daisy said to me."

"Has to be." This cruelty that grew from the earlier cruelty. Fanny and Reuben had earned this, hadn't they? You play God; you manipulate other lives; a day of reckoning arrives.

Reuben snuffled. "Daisy comes sometimes to visit me. I cry. She cries. We have a good cry together, thinking how with nothing we come to our old age. In little, small rooms by ourselfs. Without family."

I got up, saying it was late, I was expected at home. He pulled out a handkerchief, mopped his eyes, blew his nose, and again gripped my hands. "Millie, maybe in your apartment you could find a place for Uncle Reuben?"

In the subway, riding home, it occurred to me that Reuben hadn't asked, not one word, about my husband or children or indicated that he had learned I also had difficulties. And so I tried to harden my heart against this wretched man who dripped tears for a wife who had wrought much misery. Yet I found I pitied him, and it was Karl whom I despised. Karl had delivered the last crushing blow. With smugness, with hypocrisy. "Your loving nephew, Karl Hitzig."

"Tell me, Jake," Karl was saying in our living room, "on whose advice did you decide to take the Fifth?"

"My own," Jay replied.

Karl took the Corona-Corona up, shook off ash, puffed, blew smoke toward the ceiling, all in slow motion, deliberating. "From my standpoint," he said finally, "the decision was praiseworthy."

"Thanks, pal," Jay said. "Thank you very much."

"The thanks belong on the other foot," Karl said. "I am gratified you did not volunteer to identify the man the committee referred to as Walter Whitman." His fingers drummed the chair arm. There was a nervous glance over his shoulder, a lowering of voice. "We're alone, aren't we?"

"My son's spending the evening with a friend," I said. "And we don't have a maid."

He looked relieved. "My brother, my two brothers. I walk a chalk line myself."

My heart bleeds for you, I thought. "Where is Walt?" I asked.

"Must you know?" He renewed the nervous drumming. "I suppose it doesn't matter, I don't think you're apt to go running to the FBI. Walt is in the country, this country, U.S.A. In New England. Farming. Don't laugh. Back to nature. Raising chickens. White leghorns. Not Rhode Island Reds, which might be appropriate. He bought a couple of acres with a run-down house. Kerosene lamps. An outhouse. Lives there with a woman, a Hungarian or Czech. A refugee. Gentile. They have a cow, a couple of goats. Olga milks the animals. She makes the cheese. Sells eggs and cheese to summer people. Walt drives down to visit the folks a few times a year. He tells them he's enjoying life." He paused, eying me. "If you have a yen to see him, forget it. Keep your distance. You can't afford that friendship."

"I like Walt. I always did," I said.

Jay gave me a peculiar look, half anger, half agreement. "Mind the big brother," Jay said.

"Where's Eugene?" I went on to ask.

"Here. In New York. He has an office. A practice of sorts. Without hospital connections. I've tried; I talked to men I know on several boards." Karl spread his hands. "Gene is not acceptable. His past."

"It's strange," I said. "There's no forgiveness for the Americans who helped the Loyalists."

"The Communists," Karl corrected me. "I don't believe you've grasped what's going on. The swing to the right. Mind, I don't say it should be that way. Remember, Jake, I was City College, like you. Social consciousness, social justice. We learned it along with our math. Better yet, my parents have been lifelong

Socialists. My name . . ." He forced a laugh. "If you have seen my office letterhead, you may have noticed there's no middle initial to my name. Ask no questions, I will tell no lies. However—you may appreciate this, it is irony—my Socialist parents are more anti-Russian, more anti-Communist, than I am myself. The debacle of the Weimar Republic, the trials of the old Bolsheviks—"

"Can the lecture, Hitzig; we can do without." Jay had risen. He was pacing behind Karl's chair. "What I need, what I want from you, is help to get off that goddam black list."

Karl picked up the Corona-Corona. "If there is a black list—" he began.

Jay wheeled. "Who are you kidding? You know damn well—"

"Possibly, Jake, you are out of work," Karl went on smoothly, "because of certain personal habits." He glanced at me, momentarily unsure of how candid to be. "Word has gotten around —I've heard it a number of places—James Burns is unreliable."

A short, dirty word was on Jay's lips. He checked it. The effort to strangle the epithet showed. He was purple.

"Keep your shirt on, Jake. Control your temper, you'll live longer. From where I sit—mind, I'm a lawyer, not an M.D.—I'd suspect high blood pressure. Why don't you call Gene, have him check you over?"

"Brandy," Jay told me. "Pour it for me."

I rose and poured Courvoisier for him, glancing at my cousin to see whether he also wanted brandy. He nodded. He did. I carried over a snifter. "Hebe," he said with a smile like a smirk. "Handmaiden to the gods."

"Not Hebe," I said. "Or Nora. The name is Mildred Burns."

"You still have your sense of humor." Karl swirled his brandy and inhaled its bouquet. "Jake, consider yourself lucky they didn't cite you for contempt. Several of your former pals will be serving time." He inched his chair nearer the sofa. "Let's talk *tachles*, practical sense. I gather you asked me here—a unique invitation, I might add, and as far as I am aware, not extended to the rest of Millie's kinfolk—to get my advice and counsel on the situation in which you find yourself. Now, my considered opinion, given free for nothing and possibly"—he forced that dubious smile—"worth just what it costs, is that you issue a statement to the press, the radio, and TV (I'll be glad, if you wish, to go over it with you), naming no names, involving no one. Denying subversion. And claiming stupidity. . . ."

"Get out," Jay growled. "Get the hell out of here."

Karl didn't stir. He went on, saying blandly, "There's a fairly widespread opinion that actors are not especially bright—keep your shirt on—they're children, politically. They earn their livings speaking words other people have written, projecting ideas that have been hatched in better brains. You know this as well as I do. Let's not kid each other. So the only sensible course for you now is to beat your breast, confess your mistakes. You loaned your house for a party years ago; you served highballs to the crowd; you collected money for a cause that was popular before we got into the war. Everybody—all kinds of people—were in it then. Some smart cookies used you—your name, your fame, your generous instincts. They fattened your ego, told you you were making history. How could you know what else was involved? How much did you understand? You know now they took you for a ride. Made a sucker out of you. From here on in, you'll mind your own business—"

"Get out!" Jay yelled.

Karl tamped out the cigar. "I've given you my best advice. It may work, it may not. There's not one other damn thing you can do."

"Except tell the committee whose brother Walter Whitman is."

"Which you would not do." Karl's voice was smooth as oleo. "Millie would not permit it. As little interest as she shows in her relatives, nevertheless, I am certain she would not wish to take the bread and butter from Aunt Hannah's and Uncle Davy's mouths. Or deprive a crippled Snooky of—"

I began to cry.

"There's your answer, Jake," Karl said. "Calm down, Millie," he began again. "Dry those tears. They do not become you. And the disaster is not imminent. Or even probable. My practice is solid. Thank God for Harry Eshler and the Eshler business interests. And, Millie, I will be frank to acknowledge your family's connections made this possible. If your brother hadn't married Judy Eshler, if I had not gone up to the wedding, I might still be an ambulance chaser." He allowed himself the smirk-smile. "The Eshler connections. As they say, it's who you know." He buttoned his vest, readying to leave. "Sleep on my suggestion, Jake. I know a good public relations man. He can help you work out the statement, give it the slant, the tone, the emphasis. . . . Let me know. Give me a buzz at the office tomorrow. . . . I'll expect your call."

Jay said not a word. Nor did he stir from the sofa. I walked Karl to the foyer, handed him his hat and topcoat. "Millie," he said, hand on doorknob, "if you're short of cash, I can . . ."

"No," I said.

"Okay, don't get huffy. Just bear in mind, pride never paid the butcher. I hear your boy attends a private school. Sorry the kid wasn't home; I'd have liked to meet him, maybe tell him a few facts of life. You, too, Millie. Realism never was your strong suit. It wouldn't occur to you, I suppose, that a private school is not a necessity. We went to public schools, all of the Hitzig boys. Your kid's father did, too. What was good enough for us . . ."

"I'll think about it," I said, reaching behind him to turn the doorknob.

"Your daughter," he persisted. "Granted she's in a state university where the tuition is minimal. Yet living in a dorm, that's an expensive proposition. Advise her—insist on it, Millie—make her study shorthand, get a secretarial job, full-time, part-time. Or wait on tables. Anything to help to pay her way."

"No," I said again, though a more rational woman might have admitted he was making sense.

"And if things are really grim," he went on, ignoring my noes, "you might consider going to work yourself. Jake is not employable—not at the present time. Not even as a salesman in a department store. His face is too familiar, his manner too arrogant. In the real world, a touch of humility is helpful. But you, you're moderately intelligent—as I recall, you spent a year at college and you did well—and you're still a pretty woman. True, you've had no training, you have no skills, but offhand, I know a few offices that might be pleased to hire you for a receptionist. . . ."

"Good night," I said. "Thanks for nothing."

"Have Jake call me in the morning," he said.

When I returned to the living room, Jay asked me a single question: "Do you believe I am stupid, Millie?"

"Of course not," I said. "Forget it," I said.

"It was right then. It still is right," Jay said.

"Don't listen to Karl," I said. "I never did."

Jay didn't call Karl in the morning. He was asleep; he didn't wake until midafternoon, because he had gone out last night and stayed out very late. Where he went I did not know, since as usual he didn't tell and I had learned not to ask. He didn't phone Karl in the afternoon or any day after that.

However, for a few weeks, he toyed with a new idea—which Karl, by mentioning the Eshlers and their extensive connections, might have triggered. Jay decided to find a play script, with a great part for himself, get financing, hire a cast, and return to Broadway as an actor-producer. He made the rounds of agents, brought home blue-bound manuscripts, soiled and dog-eared from their months of wanderings, dusty from hibernations atop filing cabinets. We read the scripts together. They were dreadful. That hope faded; the nothingness began again, and his nocturnal prowlings from bar to bar, from acquaintance to acquaintance. From here to where? He slept through the days and asked when he woke, "Any mail? Any calls?" as if this day might be the day of the miracle: the studio sending for him.

When the doorbell rang at half past ten in the morning, I was still in my robe and nightgown, in the living room, having a second cup of coffee, watching the river and wondering whether I ought to telephone to someone and, if so, to whom? Because, for the first time since we had moved to New York, Jay had not come home. All the other mornings, when I woke to fix Billy's breakfast and see him off to school, I would hear Jay snoring in the other twin bed. Wherever he had been and with whom, he had come home. This room he shared with me was his anchor, his permanence.

358

Full of dread, I could not allow myself to think of what was possible: accident. Worse: suicide. A man whose pride is gone is vulnerable.

He had tried to make a feeble joke of that loss of pride last night before he left the apartment. "Millie, would you happen to have some loose change around? For the moment, I find myself short." He turned a pants pocket inside out to prove it. I fetched my wallet, as he had known I would—we'd played this scene so often before. I took out a ten dollar bill. "Double it, if possible. Who knows when a man will meet a bargain? Thanks, kid. Put it on my charge account."

A uniformed policeman, young, rosy-cheeked, stood at my door. Beyond him in the hall, I saw the building superintendent, hovering. "Mrs. Burns?" The policeman glanced into a notebook. "Mrs. James Burns?"

"I'm Mrs. Burns." My heart started to thump.

"Patrolman Loughran." He mumbled his precinct number before he crossed the sill.

"Has something happened?" I had trouble breathing. "My husband?"

Patrolman Loughran closed the door. "Are you alone?"

"My son is at school. My husband—"

"Is there some friend in the house you could call?" Whatever this might be about, it had made him uneasy; possibly my negligee bothered him.

"What is it? What happened?"

"Suppose you sit down, Mrs. Burns."

I led him into the living room. He motioned to me to sit down, while he stood facing, towering over. Self-conscious, I buttoned the top of my robe.

"I'm sorry, Mrs. Burns. We police have to be bearers of bad news. Believe me, we hate to be. Your husband—James Burns is your husband, isn't he? Now take it easy, please try to stay calm —he passed away. During last night. Or the early hours of this morning. Natural causes. The Assistant Medical Examiner examined the—the—him. Said heart attack, probably. Won't know for sure till they do the autopsy. . . ."

I must have gone white, because he said, "Put your head down, down to your knees. . . . That's a good girl. . . . Let me get you a glass of water."

I raised my head. "Where did it happen?"

He blushed—he was young enough to do that—and glanced into his notebook to read off an address. "That's down in Greenwich Village, ma'am. The apartment of a Miss or Mrs. Bonnie Granger."

Anger surged in me. And choking shame. Yet from somewhere I drew the strength to salvage my dignity. "*Miss* Granger," I said. "An old friend. A friend of the family."

He exhaled—with relief, I believe—then, deadpan, went on to tell me the rest. "Granger reported she and Burns went out for dinner, to a restaurant on MacDougal Street. They walked back to her place; they drank a couple of brandies. Burns said he didn't feel well; he thought maybe the mussels he had for dinner didn't agree with him. She mixed him a Bromo. He drank it, but he still complained of the indigestion. He asked could he lie down awhile. He went into the bedroom. By himself, she said. He took off his shoes and lay down on the bed. She said she watched television for an hour or so in the living room. Then she got sleepy, she said, and she decided to go to bed. He was sleeping so sound, she said, she didn't have the heart to wake him up, so she—" He was studying the carpet, not looking at me. My mind completed the sentence he did not speak. Bonnie Granger lay alongside my husband; he died in her arms; he died on her body. I knew this with a certainty that neither I nor Patrolman Loughran needed to put into words.

He resumed his narration, using a toneless precision of phrasing—he was reading from notes. "Granger stated she woke up around seven A.M. Burns was sleeping. She stated she went into the kitchen to put on the coffee. She made the coffee, poured a cup, and carried it into the bedroom. Burns was asleep. She shook his shoulder; she couldn't wake him. His body, she stated, felt cold. Granger stated she went immediately to the telephone and called a doctor—Dr. Maxwell Rosenstein who resides in the neighborhood. (I'll leave you Dr. Rosenstein's phone number, Mrs. Burns, in case you want to contact him.) Dr. Rosenstein arrived at eight thirty A.M. He pronounced Burns dead on arrival and notified the Medical Examiner's office." He closed his notebook and sat down beside me. He took my hand. His hand felt warm and soothing around my icy fingers. "Natural causes, Mrs. Burns," he said, and, after a moment, lamely, "Miss Granger is quite upset."

"Miss Granger is an old friend," I said.

"Maybe you would like to talk to her. Maybe you'd feel better if—I have her number."

"No," I said, "I don't want to talk to Miss Granger."

The telephone, out in the foyer, was ringing. "Shall I answer it for you?" Patrolman Loughran asked.

I rose. The fact that I could stand, that I could walk, surprised me. It was as if I had expected this and had stored up strength to receive it.

"This is Janet Bernstein," the voice on the phone announced. "James Burns's sister. Who is this?"

"His wife," I said.

"Mildred? Oh! We've just heard something on the radio. Mother's terribly upset. Is it true?"

"It's true," I said.

"How do you know?"

"A policeman came to tell me."

"What happened? Did he say?"

"A heart attack."

"At his age! Why weren't we told he was sick? We're his family, you know. We do care about him a little bit, even though he—"

"He wasn't sick," I said. "Not that way, as far as we knew. He took an old friend out to dinner. He died in her house."

There was a prolonged silence before she answered, "There's more to it than this." I hung up before she did.

Patrolman Loughran said gently, "Hadn't you ought to get some clothes on? People might be dropping in. If you'd like, I'll answer your phone while you're getting dressed." And added, "Is there anyone you'd like me to call? You shouldn't be here all alone, by yourself."

"Please call my son. He's at school." I gave him a telephone

361

number. "Please ask the school to send him home. Not tell him why. Just say there's an emergency."

I left the policeman at the phone and went into the bedroom, but could not begin to dress because my arms and legs were numb. And so I sat on my bed's edge, shivering, and stared at the bed Jay had not used. I need someone, I thought. I can't take this alone. Mama. Mama, why aren't you with me? . . . No, no, no, I can't have you here. I can't have any of my family. Because there's a shame I cannot tell you. Jay died in another woman's bed. There is a shame that's greater than the sorrow; there is a sorrow that's greater than the shame.

Our children will feel the sorrow, and they'll feel the shame. My mind's eye—that inner eye that has photographed all I have ever seen—was showing me a seedy man in a white-tiled Automat, asking desperately, "With what eyes will my son one day look at me?" God, give me wisdom for what I must do for Jay's children.

I rose, washed my face, and rinsed my mouth of its taste of gall. I combed my hair and put a dark dress on. Beyond the closed door, I could hear the ringing phone and was grateful that the young policeman was there to answer it, for I knew if I had to listen to questions or to condolence I would fall apart.

"Two calls, Mrs. Burns," the policeman said. "One, Associated Press. I took the liberty of saying you were not at home. Right? I figured you weren't ready to be interviewed. The other was a Mr.—Mr."— he glanced down at the phone note pad— "Mr. Karl Hitzig. He'd heard it on the radio."

"Oh, no!" I said.

"He asked was anybody here with you. I said you were alone. He said he'd be right over."

"Oh, no!" I said.

The policeman scratched his temple, looking worried. "Did I goof? He said he was a member of your family. Ma'am, if he's a faker, some kind of crackpot, don't you let him in. Call us, we'll send someone over if you have trouble. It's more than likely you'll get cranks, people calling out of morbid curiosity. On account of who James Burns . . ."

362

"Karl Hitzig *is* a relative," I said.

"Then no harm done. He said he'd cancel his appointments. Hop into a taxi."

"I want my son," I said.

"On his way. The person that answered at the school said they already knew; the secretary had heard it on the office radio. . . . No, they hadn't told the boy; they were waiting for some word from you. They're sending a teacher with him. In a cab. . . ."

"Thank you," I said.

He turned to go but hesitated, still looking concerned. "You're sure there isn't a woman neighbor you'd like to have step in and stay with you?"

"I'll be all right," I said. "Thank you for being kind."

He stroked my shoulder. "I hate this part of my job," he said. "Bringing bad news to nice people."

While I shut the door after him, I caught a glimpse of a crowd in the hall: women home from marketing with bags of groceries; women home from airing their babies, with strollers and diaper bags; and the janitor, like a major-domo, aligning, organizing this massing of ghouls. They surged toward my door before I slammed it shut.

I went into the kitchen to heat coffee up. The phone rang and kept ringing. I didn't answer. This is on the radio; it will be in the press; Mr. and Mrs. America and all the ships at sea will know before the sun sets that James Burns died in Bonnie Granger's bed.

While I was pouring my coffee, I heard Bill's key in the door and his voice, hoarse with anguish, crying, "Mother! Where are you?" I rushed out to him.

It struck me, all at once, that he had grown young-man tall, this gangly youth in the corduroy pants, the tweed jacket with the leather elbow patches. And his pale face was like his father's, unhandsome yet piquant, provocative. I was seeing Jay in him, and for this I felt a surge of gratitude. I spread my arms and drew Billy in.

"Mother, you're all right?"

"It's Dad," I said. "Your father died."

363

A shudder ran through his long frame. His glance veered toward our sleeping room, where a man might be when he dies in his bed.

"He isn't there," I said. "He died in"—my throat was tight, I had to force my words—"in a friend's house."

He stumbled toward the sofa and pulled me down to sit beside him. His face was buried in his hands, his sloughing sobs were uncontrollable. Someone pushed a sheet of Kleenex toward him. I looked up and saw a pleasant-faced young woman who said quietly, "I'm Ellen Maynard. I'm the secretary at Bill's school. We decided not to tell him; it was best that you . . ."

"Thank you," I said.

"Is there anything I can do?"

"There's nothing anyone can do."

"I'd like to help. Can I fix a cup of tea or coffee?"

"Tea and coffee won't help us. Please go." I heard my own voice, sounding harsh and peremptory, yet I knew I had to make this stranger leave, since what I had to say to Bill and he to me had to be said before Karl arrived.

"Bill," I said, as soon as she had left us. "Dying is a part of living. We have to face up to it."

Through his splayed fingers Billy said, "I loved my dad."

"He loved you, too," I said.

"I used to have fun with him before—before our trouble. He took me places; he taught me to swim."

"He loved you very much," I said. And you were his proof of himself, I thought, his blind, violent assertion of his masculinity.

"I wanted to help him," Bill said. "He was hard to help."

"He was hurt," I said. "Badly hurt. By injustice. By the way his friends . . ."

Billy's hands came away from his face. "I knew he was. That's when he needed us. He wouldn't let me show him I sympathized. He barked, he snarled . . ."

The way he said that, childishly petulant, was faintly comical, and I must have smiled because he drew away as though I had belittled his feelings. "Bill, darling, understand this: your father was a gifted actor. He was talented; he worked hard; he liked to work. And success came early to him. Without a struggle. But this he took in his stride—no swelled head, not puffed up. His profession, his craft, was his life. Failure was what he couldn't take. And until you learn to live with failure, you are not mature."

He stared. "But he didn't fail. They destroyed him. With their lies."

I didn't answer. I could not.

Bill clenched his fists. "I'll make them pay for this," he said. "Those Congressmen. That President."

I edged away. I said, "You can't blame them, you can't blame any one person. Things grow out of other things. One thing leads to another. Why, I was as much to blame. . . ."

"You!" His stare, his tone was hostile. "You're not a Communist, are you?"

"No," I said. "No more than he was."

"Then what?"

We were thinking quite different things, I realized; we were seeing entirely different places. He was seing a crowded hearing room in Washington, I a damp sea-smelling room in Provincetown. I grasped his slender shoulders and turned him around, to face me. "Bill, you're going to see this in the papers; someone is going to mention it to you before today is out. It may help for you to hear it first from me. Your father's death is sad enough. But there's a circumstance about it we need to face because we shall have to live with that one for the rest of our lives." My voice was thinning, running down. I tried to breathe in, to firm it. "Bill, your father died in a woman's apartment. He had gone to dinner with her; he said he didn't feel well; he went to sleep on her bed. He never woke up. People are going to say—people are going to make rotten jokes—"

He was managing to control his face, but his hands were betraying him, clenching, unclenching, writhing on his lap.

"The woman was a friend of his, an old friend, an actress. They had been together in a Broadway play, oh, years and years ago. He may have been lonely; he looked her up. He went to her,

365

I believe, for what I couldn't give him, what I didn't know how to give him. Not sympathy, not understanding, a special sort of closeness, an acceptance of his—his—"

Bill's flush, the lowering of his eyelids, told me that he'd understood without the final word. His jaw line hardened with an ugly anger that I found unbearable.

"Don't hate him, Bill," I cried.

"Don't you?" he answered.

"No," I said. "Do you?"

He waited, thinking hard, before he said, "I'm not sure yes or no."

And I waited, also, thinking, before I could say, "Bill, I loved your father when I married him. I've always loved him. I still do. I think he loved me, even more than I loved him."

"I don't believe you," he said. "You don't believe that yourself."

"I have to." I reached for his hands and held them in mine. "Bill, don't judge your parents," I begged. "You don't know, you just can't know, what the real reasons are for the things that happen. It's complicated. Everything is."

The telephone was ringing, ringing, ringing. Bill looked at me. "Aren't you going to answer?"

"Take it off the hook," I said. "I don't want to talk to anyone but you."

He left me to go to the foyer to silence the phone. I heard his footsteps going beyond, to the kitchen. Then I heard a crash and, in panic, ran to where he was: at the sink, glaring with wild fury at the shards of a milk bottle. An accident? Or his deliberate venting of anger? With the spontaneous unreeling of memory, I saw myself in a flat on Fifty-seventh Street, standing over a broken glass bowl. Aunt Fanny's wedding present. Aunt Fanny. If not for her—

I put my arms around Bill's shoulders. "Billy, please! Please don't be mad. Not at him. Or at me. We couldn't help ourselves, neither of us. We did our best. With what we were. Don't be hard on him, Bill. Don't spoil your memory of him. Remember the good things, the sweet things. . . ."

366

He pulled away from me. "Have you called Greta? Does she know?"

"It's on the radio. She'll know."

"Don't you think we ought to call her? Or send a telegram?" He was changing, turning brisk, taking charge.

"We'll wire," I said. "She might not be home; a call would be a waste of money."

"And we can't waste our money, can we?" Bill said. "We've got none to spare." He stepped out to get a pad and pencil. "What do you want to say?"

I leaned against the kitchen sink, deciding what to say. "Tell Greta, just tell Greta, 'Dad died suddenly today. Remember him with love.'"

He glanced up from his scribbling. "She won't," he said. "They were not *simpatico*."

He was at the phone, calling in the telegram, when the doorbell rang insistently. I opened the door a crack. Karl stood close-pressed against the door. The horde of curious strangers was at his back. I opened the door wide enough to let him slip in. His hands were full: a briefcase and a big, brown paper bag. "I tried and tried to call you. Got a busy signal. Has the kid been monopolizing the phone?"

Billy dropped the instrument into its cradle.

"Bill," I said, "This is my cousin, Karl Hitzig."

"*His* cousin, too," Karl corrected me. "Sorry, son, our first acquaintance is under these unhappy circumstances." He extended the paper bag to Bill. "Take this to the kitchen, son. . . . I stopped at Tip-Toe on my way. Tried to get you on the phone to find out if you wanted anything special. Your line was busy. I didn't want to waste more time, so I had them pack a couple of pounds of cold cuts, a loaf of rye. Rolls. And one of their cheesecakes."

My jaw went slack, this was so incongruous.

"Use your head, Millie. People will be dropping in: the family, friends. The living get hungry, you know; life goes on." He glanced at Bill, coming back, reached out, patted Bill's head, as if my tall son were a little kid. "Where can we go, Millie, for a quiet chat, some privacy?"

"Nowhere. Whatever we have to say my son can hear."

He glanced from one of us to the other before he took the armchair. He drew his breath in before he began. "I called a couple of guys I know on the evening papers. I spoke as a member of the family, asked them to go easy, play down a certain bit of information."

"Bonnie Granger was an old friend, a family friend," I said. "Jay had every right to visit her."

He nodded, as though approving my broad-mindedness. "I'll pass that word along," he said.

"'Don't pass anything along," I said. "Just leave it be." And I added, "It's no picnic for Miss Granger, I am sure. Most inconsiderate of Jay to die on her premises."

"Are you being cynical?"

"Realistic. Don't I have to be?"

He shook his head, gravely. "I was afraid something like this might happen. Afraid for you, I mean. I always was, you know. But I thought, I honestly believed, he'd changed."

"Billy, please take that receiver off the hook," I said. "The noise is giving me a headache."

"Young man, while you're up," Karl said, "make yourself useful. Fix a sandwich for your mother. Make a couple while you're at it—one for you, one for me."

"Don't bother, Bill," I said. "This is not a family picnic."

Karl shrugged, his exasperation visible. "Millie, I am trying to help you. I came here to help you, cancelled my appointments for the day—by Jesus, that might be my office calling."

"This number isn't answering," I said.

He sighed, resigning himself to my irrationality. "Who do you want me to notify? I have the family list—oh, I rang your parents from my office. They know. I told them to await word from me about the funeral arrangements."

"Funeral." My throat closed and locked like the fingers on my lap.

"Up to you. Decide what you want. My advice, if you will take it, is keep it private. Dignified. Have some rabbi—not one of the liberals, please—say the Hebrew prayers. And a short eul-

368

ogy: mention his talent, a high light or two of his career, his devotion to his wife and children. No radical stuff, nothing controversial. What's your reaction, Millie?"

"I'll think about it," I said.

Suddenly, Bill spoke. "I don't think Dad would go for it," he said. "I think Dad—I saw him at that committee hearing in Washington—I think he was proud of what he did for the Loyalists. And the way he stood up to those Congressmen—"

"I'm thinking of the family," Karl interrupted. "Your mother and *his*—his mother is living, isn't she?—how they would feel about raking up the—" He glanced at his wrist. "Holy gee! I told the Medical Examiner's office I'd be right down. Make the identification, get the remains released. . . ."

"I'll go with you," Bill said. "I'm the one to identify him. I've known him all my life."

"You will not," I said. "I want you to remember him living, not—not dead."

Karl was studying his notebook, ignoring us. "Then I have to notify the Riverside—that's the funeral chapel. Would you care to meet me there, Millie, select a casket?"

"I would not," I said. This part of the death, the public part, I wished to reject. The other part, the personal part, was the only one I'd face. Because in that, and only there, lay a consequence. How James Burns would be buried, in what sort of casket, with whose eulogies, was of little moment. What mattered, all that mattered, was that his children—my children—would have no heritage of shame or hate.

"Millie, I am trying to relieve you, to help you, every way I know," Karl said. "Blood, after all, is thicker than water."

"Tar's thicker than both," I said.

"You're acting strangely, Millie. I wonder do you happen to have—look in the medicine chest, young man. What do they call you, Billy or Bill?"

"William," my son said. "William Burns."

"Well, William Burns, look in the medicine chest in your bathroom, see whether there's some phenobarbital. If not, plain aspirin might do. . . ."

369

"Stay here, Bill," I said. "I don't need pills."

"You should have a woman with you, Millie, till your mother comes. Shall I call Aunt Daisy, have her come over? . . . No, she's rather feeble; it might be asking too much."

"I'll call her," I said. "I'd like to have her. Only her." We belong together, I thought, we have lived together; we've both been scarred by the same cruel circumstance.

"You never cared for my advice," my cousin was saying. "Now and then"—he produced a small, sarcastic smile—"I happen to know what I'm talking about."

A clot of remembered angers rolled into my chest, lay like a stone against my heart. "My relatives," I said, "have always acted with good intentions. Those loving people Uncle Reuben called dear once."

"Uncle Reuben." Karl blushed slightly. "I forgot. I didn't put him on my list." He scribbled in his memo book. "I'll have my office give the Home a ring. Unless you'd like to call him yourself."

"I think you'd better go," I said. "Identify your old friend, have him moved to the Riverside. When I've talked things over with Greta, after she arrives . . ."

Bill stared at me, surprised. "Your wire didn't say for her to come."

"Send another. Tell her to take the first flight she can get." Before the gossip, pitiless but true, can reach her. Saying to myself that it was Greta's hurt I wanted to lessen, denying to myself how much I needed her.

Bill kept eying me. "Can we afford it?"

"We can afford it," I told him.

"I hope Jake kept up his insurance," Karl said. "If you will let me have the policies . . ."

"Eventually," I said.

"Millie, if you're short of cash, I'll be glad to—Millie, believe me, I want to help."

"I'll bet you do," I said. You're happy, so very happy, I thought, to help to bury Jay.

Karl dropped his notebook into his jacket pocket. "I'd better get going. That business at the Mor—the Medical Examiner—is likely to take time. I'll contact you as soon as we have transferred him."

At the door, he turned around.

"Oh, one thing more. Do you want him buried in the family plot?"

A shudder raced through me. "Certainly not!" I'll have to find a green lawn on a ridge, I told myself, the sort of place he was accustomed to.

The door closed behind Karl. I drew Bill to my side, laid my head on his shoulder, and for the first time on this dreadful day, I cried. For Jay whose years had ended too soon, whose time had run out. Then for myself, for whom time remained, the blank wall of time that surrounds the arid core of widowhood.

An end. And a beginning.

I heard the knob carefully turned, the bedroom door inched open. A night light in the hall cut a pale stripe across the room. I watched the slender figure in pajamas tiptoe out of the lane of light into the blackness around the twin beds, reach to the taut spread on Jay's bed, edge away, fumble in the blankets on my bed. And gasp.

"Greta! Over here!" In the armchair at the window where I'd watched the lights going out, room by room, in the apartment house across the way and the traffic diminishing in the street below. The winding down, the tapering off, the dark hush before a new day. Around midnight it had begun to rain. The swishing, slithering noise the tires made reminded me of hissing palms above a pastel-colored bungalow. That remembering brought another one: Jay's hair, wet and glistening, when he ran to me, out of the rain. Tonight, the rain is falling where he is. He won't get soaked; we've sheltered him.

Greta came to my side. "You all right, Mother? I thought you'd be asleep."

"Eventually," I said.

"He asked me to look in on you, make sure you were okay."

"Who asked you?"

"The doctor. The thin, gray man. A cousin, isn't he?"

"Eugene," I said. "Aunt Hannah's second boy."

"He said he'd left you sleeping pills. He said you needed the help to relax."

I hadn't taken Eugene's pills. All I had accepted was the warm pressure of his hands, clasping mine, and the wordless sympathy, flowing from him into me. For between us there was a special bond: we both had been victims of a small war in a distant country years ago.

"He suggested I take a pill, too," Greta went on to say. "I didn't. I couldn't. I wanted to stay up. To look after you."

"Come here! Sit here!" I heard my voice, brusque and harsh, out of a throatful of tears. I squeezed my thighs together, to leave an empty corner in the chair, for the sharp hipbone of a skinny girl, the soft, smooth arm flesh of a child, and the woman scent of perfume, lingering in her hair. She had her arm around me before I could put mine around her. "You were wonderful today," Greta said. "Everybody said you were. Bill and I were proud of you. Your poise. Your dignity. With all those people watching you. Like hawks. Like ghouls."

"I wasn't aware of them." Not true. I'd been aware of everything and everyone. All of me had become a giant eye, seeing the furtive glances and the bold stares, the avoidance and the impudence, the pity, true or false. If there is compassion here today, let me find it and hoard it. I will need it, eventually.

Before the mourners and the mockers had begun to straggle in, I looked at Jay for the last time. The bright spark of personality had vanished utterly. The vacant, hollow face within the oblong box belonged to someone I no longer knew. Perhaps had never known. The blanket of roses on the wood was Greta's thought: "Let's order it, Mother—if we can afford it. To make it less stark."

My Uncle Reuben sidled over, bleating, "No *tallith*. Why didn't you put a *tallith* on him?" My father, angered, gripped Reuben's arm to lead him away, but I found myself trying to explain, clearly and precisely, as I might to a child. "Jay never wore a *tallith*. He wasn't an observant Jew." Though while I

372

spoke, it occurred to me Jay might have wished to wear a *tallith*. That's appropriate for the role of a dead Jew. An actor's costume must be correct for each part he plays. "An actor is parts, only parts." The subway, rumbling, muffling the warnings from my cousin Karl.

We sat in a stuffy, dimly lighted parlor receiving awkward spurts of sympathy from people whom I barely knew. "Time will heal" . . . "God will comfort you" . . . "You have these fine children to live for." . . .

"These fine children." One each side of me on a narrow, hard settee, with my family flanking us on folding chairs. Opposite, Jay's parents and his sister were on *their* settee, with their uncles, aunts, and cousins flanking *them*. Jay's mother wore a black mantilla over blue-tinted hair. She didn't speak to me or I to her. Our memories were separate, like our angers and guilts. Jay's father, stooped and waxen pale, did cross the room to try to speak to me but choked on tears before he said a word. Jay's mother's features were hidden by a black-bordered handkerchief; mine were naked to the world. ("Judy, you were kind to bring that veil for me. I don't wish to wear it. Let everybody see—not guess—how his wife is taking this.")

Fritz Scheller bent over my hand, saying gravely, "A gifted man. Sensitive. Such a tragic end!" I thanked him for flying in from the Coast. "I could not do otherwise," he said. "I was greatly touched when I received your telegram, asking me to come." I blushed, distressed, because for the moment I had forgotten we had telegraphed to him. In these last few days so many wires had been sent, received; so many letters, opened, glanced at, stacked; so many phone calls made, answered; so many individuals coming, going, milling in my flat.

It was Bill who persuaded me to send for Fritz. My son had insisted someone must be there to speak about the interlude of anti-Fascism that had wrecked Jay's career. Bill had prodded me until I remembered Fritz: a distinguished man, brave enough and famous enough to take this risk of praising the black-listed and dishonored Burns.

How twisted are the paths that lead to a convergence in our

lives. A crazy tyrant in Berlin sent Scheller to my living room in Hollywood. And Scheller's erstwhile mistress sent Jay into my bed. And Bill is here because of her. And Fritz is here because of Bill.

Because of Walt. Where's Walt? Was he afraid to show himself? "Welcome as flowers that bloom in the spring." If, on a December day in Hollywood, I had sung a different tune . . .

And where is *she?* "My Bonnie lies over the ocean." She hasn't come to me. To pay respects? To offer sympathy? Should she? Should she not? He belonged to her. Not so. He belonged to me. "Put it on my charge account." The last words, the very last, Jay said to me. Who owed what to whom?

How twisted those paths, and how obscure—a ten-year-old who talked too much, a frightened girl in a dark corridor. . . .

"Darling," Aunt Daisy was whispering to me, "are you looking for somebody? Tell me who. Maybe the person is outside; I'll ask Karl to see."

Karl, the manager, black Homburg on his head, black notebook in his hand, checking lists of who would ride with whom in a decorous procession to a green lawn on a hill. "I'm not looking for anyone," I told my aunt. "Everyone is here." My mother and my father, Bram and Judy, Daisy, Hannah, Dave, Eugene, Clarence on his crutches, Uncle Reuben, hectoring, complaining. The whole family. Missing Walt. And Fanny. Missing Grandpa Springer. Missing Ben.

Take a small chapel, Karl had said; keep it intimate and personal. For once he had been right. The families, Jay's and mine, and a scattering of professional associates, heard Fritz speak of him: "One who felt in his heart the travail of these times. A man. A decent man." I hung on Scheller's words, to treasure them, to string them in my mind like pearls, as with those first reviews of Jay's. A rabbi chanted a Hebrew prayer; a funeral attendant touched my arm. We rose, Greta, Bill, and I, to follow the closed oblong box, up the aisle, moving slowly to the cadence of the psalm—"Yea, though I walk through the valley of the shadow" —out of the Old Testament, whence came the Song of Songs.

Outside, on the pavement, horror greeted us. A horde, a mob, surged toward us, as on that morning in the Capitol rotunda in Washington. I saw men with cameras, and uniformed police, struggling to push back the crowds. My family surrounded us, a phalanx, protecting us from *them*. My brother, Bram, swung out ahead; his broad shoulders divided the crowd and made a path for us. Bram helped me into the hired limousine before he wheeled and plunged his fist into the fat belly of a cameraman. Greta screamed. Bill turned white as a sheet. As our car moved off, I saw Karl, too, arguing with the photographer—a pummeling, a pushing, and Karl's black Homburg rolling in the gutter's filth. Bill leaned across me to pull down the car shades.

Back in my flat, Judy had set out a traditional after-funeral feast: the hard-boiled eggs and bagels, those round symbols of life's continuity; the herrings and the lox, whose tang might cut the sullen edge of grief; and the cakes and cookies to sweeten the aftermath. The family began to take seats around the dining table, as in the Brooklyn days.

"Millie, darling, sit down, have a cup of coffee."

"Not now, Daisy, please!"

"I'm brewing tea, real English tea, if you'd prefer."

"No, thank you, Judy, I don't want a thing."

"A bite something you should take. I bet you didn't even have a cup of coffee for breakfast."

"When I'm hungry, Mama, I will eat."

Papa held a little glass to me. "A *shnapps*, Pussycat, to give you strength."

"Please! Everybody! Let me be!"

Their solicitude was angering me. It was an excess, a jockeying for position—which of us will be the kindest, most considerate, most big-hearted, broad-minded? An act of repossession, making me their child again. "I'm very tired. I'll go to my room and rest."

At the door, I turned around. What I saw made me return to them. Uncle Reuben was settling himself into the chair at the head of my table, the place that had been Jay's when Jay was home with Bill and me.

I tweaked my uncle's sleeve. "That place is mine." His jaw

dropped; his eyes looked hurt. Hannah rose and took his arm to lead him down the table to a chair next to her. My father smiled; my mother scowled. An embarrassed silence settled over them. Judy filled a plate and passed it up to me. I pretended to pick at food, aware of their studied inattention and their covert vigilance. They were watching me and waiting, hoping I would offer cues —what to say, how to behave, what to conclude. For this had been no ordinary death and burial. It was a complex, burdened thing, and none of us, not even I, had as yet discovered how to live with it.

"You were lucky, Mother, you could close your door," Greta was saying in the darkness at my side. "They stayed and stayed. I thought they'd never leave. That weird old man, he kept lecturing and making speeches. . . ."

"He always did," I said.

"Telling Bill and me what we ought to do and what we shouldn't do, bragging about all he did and tried to do for his . . ."

"Dear once," I said.

"Exactly," Greta said. "It sounded Freudian to me. The slip. I got the idea the family's fed up with him. A pain in the ass." She tried to squirm in her small wedge of my chair.

"There's a footstool around," I said. "Pull it over."

"I'll sit on the floor. I can lean against your knees. If you don't mind."

"I don't mind," I said. And thank you for wanting to, I thought, and stroked her hair.

"It was sort of overwhelming," she went on, "meeting them en masse. How come I never met them before?"

Because I orphaned you, I thought. I took you far away from them. "You met Bram and Judy," I told her. "They came to visit us."

"They reminded me they did. I didn't remember them. It was before Bill was born. They said I was a fresh kid."

"No change," I said.

She stroked my shin. "Oh, come now, come, I'm a responsible young woman, you know that."

376

"I'd like to believe it," I said.

"Time will tell," she said. "My grandparents—your parents—are all right. Except they nag. They kept insisting we ought to go and live with them."

"Do you want to?" I asked.

"Not particularly. Do you?"

"Not particularly," I said.

"I asked them why they never came to visit us in California. Your mother said it was too far to travel. She said it in such a peculiar way, I got the feeling she felt she and your father weren't welcome there."

"By whom?"

She rootched on the carpet. "Dad, I guess. I got the impression—don't get angry, Mother, please!—that none of them cared too much for Dad."

I didn't answer her. She took my silence for assent.

"Takes all kinds to make a world," she said.

"Does the university give a course in clichés?" I asked.

She ignored my jibe. "That wispy, spinsterish little woman, the one they call Daisy—is that her real name?—she seemed rather nice."

"Rather nice? Daisy is an angel, a true saint. She was your first friend. You lived in her house; she fed you, bathed you, changed your diapers, oiled your little bottom—"

"Didn't I have a mother?"

"You had three: Daisy, my mother, me."

"They must have thought you were an idiot, didn't know how to raise a child."

"True. Quite true," I said. She stroked my shin again, affectionately. We were doing well, the two of us, keeping the conversation light, skittering around the deep, dark places where the dangers lurked.

"My cousin Karl is pompous, a stuffed shirt," she said. "But I gather the family has respect for him. Knows what to do, does all the right things."

"Want to bet?" I said.

"Do I hear bitterness?" my daughter said.

"I'm too tired," I said, "to tell you all that's wrong with him."

"Shall I leave you, let you go to bed?"

"Up to you," I said.

She settled back against my legs and sighed into our silence. I am lucky, I thought; I have a daughter who wants to be with me.

"Dad's parents," she began again. "They didn't even try to talk to us. Hostile. As if it was our fault."

"Everything was," I said. "From the start."

"You mean they objected to Dad marrying you?"

"They'd hoped for Mary Pickford," I told her.

"Who's Mary Pickford?" Greta asked.

I nudged her with my knee. "Shame on you! A Hollywood brat!"

"I'm kidding," Greta said. "You're prettier today than she ever was." And paused. "That's why I'll never understand—" And paused again, waiting a moment before she asked, "You wouldn't have a cigarette around, would you?"

"I don't smoke, never did—" I began to say before I interrupted myself. "Your father did. There might be a pack in one of his pockets. In his closet, if you want to look. . . ."

She began to rise, stretching her legs, but squatted down again. "I'd have to put on lights to look. I prefer this."

I saw through her excuse: she wasn't ready, nor was I, to open Jay's clothes closet, to evoke the smell and feel of him. We must keep this impersonal—if we can, as long as we can—as though what we'd left in that green hillside was not half of our lives.

She settled back against my legs. "Mother, Bill and I had a long talk after the relatives left—he's a grand kid, Mother; he has a lot of sense, a lot of sincere feeling—he wanted to stay up and talk, but his eyes were closing, he was pooped. I sent him off to bed. I said we'd have all week to decide."

"Decide what?"

"About my going back."

"Of course you're going back to college! You want to, don't you?"

She didn't answer directly. Instead: "Bill brought up the question of money, whether we could afford—"

"We aren't poor," I said. "We've never been, have we?"

"Yes, but with Dad gone . . ."

"Your father didn't get a pay check for two years."

"Then how'd we get along?"

"Thrift," I said. "And Santa Claus. A roly-poly man who lives up north."

"Oh," Greta said, just "Oh," her inflection saying as much as a paragraph. We let silence close around us for a moment.

"Just one thing has changed for us," I began again. "That single one. You can go back if you wish. Do you?"

She slid back against me, her hands clasped around her knees. She was thinking hard. "Well, the university's a drag. I'm not the greatest student in the world, you know. I'd rather swim and ride than crack a book. And California's difficult without a car. . . ."

"You'd rather call it quits?"

"Yes and no," she said, and paused to wait till she had formulated what else she had to say. "Bill thought—Bill said—his feeling was that right now I ought to stay with you, you needed me. . . ."

I do, I do, I thought. Yet a mixture of confusions was welling up in me. I need myself more than I need Greta, more than I need any other individual. I need to know who I am and why I lived the way I did. I need a quiet time, alone, to get to know myself.

"Bill said," my daughter was continuing, "he couldn't imagine what you'd do with yourself, now that—"

I interrupted her. "I haven't lost my job. I have a daughter and a son to look after. You're still my kids, you know. . . ."

"But we won't be around forever. Mother, do you realize how old I am? Mother, do you realize I'm not a kid?"

I began to tremble. The trembling was inside: I hoped she could not notice it.

379

"Mother, I don't know how you're going to take this." She was speaking tentatively and very softly. "I realize it's a peculiar time to break the news, but there may not be a better time for you and me—I'd been hoping that this summer, you and Dad . . ."

"There's a man," I said. Short, simple, declarative sentence, saying all of it.

She tried to face me. Sitting on the floor, she made a turn, halfway. I saw her profile, tilted up. "We're in love," she said. "Oh, Mother, you're shaking, you're shivering, your hands are ice! If I'd thought for a minute you'd be so upset . . ."

She's sleeping with this man, I was thinking; my daughter no longer is a virgin. Centuries of moral strictures, pruderies, and fears were surging in me: my daughter may get pregnant; my daughter may be hurt; she'll commit herself to him before she's ready for the consequence. How ironic that I, of all people, am shocked. "What's his name?" I managed to ask.

"Manuel," Greta said.

"Spanish?"

"Mexican. Half. His father was Irish. Manuel O'Connor."

"Does he know you're Jewish?"

I felt her headshake. "He never asked, I never mentioned it. . . . Oh, he knew about Dad, the political mess; it was in the papers. It didn't bother him. He's not in any way political."

"What does he do?" I asked.

"He owns a riding stable," Greta said. "Where I used to go to rent a horse."

I was my mother, I was my father, at a supper table in Montreal. Is *this* my daughter's choice? Why, she's too young, too inexperienced to make a choice. She surely can do better than this, if she waits. It simply is not suitable.

They chose a "suitable" for my mother. An excellent marriage it turned out to be. Blind luck. *They* chose a "suitable" for Daisy; it brought tragedy. But Daisy lacked the courage to take love where it was—in a shoddy man. Yet Ben might have turned out differently if she had married him. Hannah chose for herself. She's lived with struggle, toil, and sacrifice. And bachelor sons.

Has the example of that marriage frightened them? I made my own choice. And now I am afraid to let my daughter do what I did. What can I tell her, how much do I know? I know—and all I know—is that the experience of living is a mixture of things.

"Mother, Mother, you seem so upset." Greta was pleading with me. "Wait until you've met Manuel. He's a gorgeous man. You should see him on a horse. Like a Persian prince."

"Has he asked you to marry him?"

"Oh, Mother, don't be quaint! We know we're in love. Sufficient unto the day."

Oh, daughter, daughter, I said to myself, I *have* neglected you. I've let you be free as a bird while you were growing up. And you've come to the time of choosing, of telling me you are in love, without knowing what love is.

She had turned away from me; she was facing front, hands gripped in her lap, chin tilted up, immobile, as though holding her breath, waiting for me to talk. It was a long minute before I could. And when, finally, I did, I said, "Greta, falling in love and loving are separate and different things. One is the fantasy, the other is fact. It's the acceptance, all and absolute, of what the other person is—the weaknesses as well as the strengths, the hopes, the failures, the success. The scars, the guilts."

I heard her sigh. It had the sound of impatience. "You loved Dad, I suppose." I caught a hint of sarcasm, even of contempt.

"He loved me," I said.

"And that's why he—"

"*She* didn't count," I said. "*She* was an incident. An accident. No more."

"Mother, you really are remarkable. Such nobility. How you can, after—after—?"

"Greta, I loved him. I always did. And I do now." What had puzzled and confused me, in this darkness was coming clear. Love *is* the total acceptance; love is loyalty and trust.

From the beginning, Jay had made a big thing of trust: "Trust me, trust me, kid" . . . "I do, I do" . . . "You're loyal, I feel safe with you." In spite of my fears and my failures, *safe*.

381

"Greta," I said. "Go find a cigarette. Open your father's closet, don't be afraid. Put on a light."

She groped toward the table between the twin beds and switched on a lamp. Finally, we could see each other. Despite her California tan, she looked ashen, drawn. This talk in the dark had been difficult for her.

"Relax," I said. "We'll talk more about your Manuel. Eventually." She had opened the closet; her back was to me while I added, "Don't think for one single minute that your mother is your enemy. Trust me," I told her.